PRINCESS
OF BLOOD

TOM LLOYD

This edition first published in Great Britain in 2018 by Gollancz

First published in Great Britain in 2017 by Gollancz
an imprint of the Orion Publishing Group Ltd
Carmelite House, 50 Victoria Embankment
London EC4Y 0DZ

An Hachette UK Company

1 3 5 7 9 10 8 6 4 2

A CIP catalogue record for this book is
available from the British Library.

ISBN 978 1 473 21321 0

Printed in Great Britain by
CPI Group (UK) Ltd, Croydon, CR0 4YY

www.tomlloyd.co.uk
www.gollancz.co.uk

'From the very first page, this first book in Tom Lloyd's new Twilight Fragments hurls you head-first into the action . . . the world that Lloyd wraps you in is just as gripping as his storytelling'   *SFX*

'[. . .] a fantasy adventure in the modern style, comfortably mixing gritty realism with swords and sorcery. Imagine Steven Erikson's Malazan marines teaming up with Lara Croft for a mad dash across Joe Abercrombie's Red Country with an unplanned detour through the forgotten deeps of Moria and you'll be most of the way there'

Forbidden Planet International

'A fun and fast-paced romp in which a mercenary company's latest job goes horrendously wrong and they have to evade pursuit. A great cast and some very good action set pieces'

Aliette de Bodard, author of *The House of Shattered Wings*

'[. . .] tightly written heroic fantasy with deftly drawn characters in an intriguing, action-filled world'

Adrian Tchaikovsky, Arthur C. Clarke
award-winning author of *Children of Time*

'[. . .] an outstanding and refreshingly original work of fantasy fiction; and even in a genre crowded with incredible talent and content, it will undoubtedly stand out and, I hope, propel Tom centre-stage where he clearly now belongs'

James Barclay, author of *Heart of Granite*

'Grips you from the beginning and doesn't let go until the end. This is Tom Lloyd at his best, and my money is on *Stranger* being a standout fantasy for 2016. And just look at that cover!'

Ed Cox, author of The Relic Guild trilogy

'Thrilling, heart racing, fast and furious fantasy fiction'

ook Bag

The B

For Pippa Livia Wright

Soldiers of Anatin's Mercenary Deck

	SUN	STARS	BLOOD	SNOW	TEMPEST
PRINCE	ANATIN		TOIL		
17	Foren				
16	Sonnersyn				
KNIGHT	PAYL	~~OLUT~~	REFT	SAFIR	TESHEN
14	Karra	Dortrinas	Silm	Layir	Finc
13	Fashail	Arut	Brellis	Aspegrin	
DIVINER		ESTAL	HIMBEL		LLAITH
11	Haphori	Rubesh	Crast		Flinth
10					
STRANGER	VARAIN		ULAX		LYNX
8	Darm		Toam	Sandath	
7	Brols		Sethail	Ylor	
MADMAN	CRAIS	KAS		BURNEL	
5	Fael	Hald		Shoal	
4				Ismont	
JESTER	SITAIN	~~ASHIS~~	DEERN	~~TYN~~	BRAQE
2			Hule		Tunnest
1					

What Has Gone Before

Stranger of Tempest –
Book 1 of the God Fragments

Once, Lynx was a soldier – an idealistic young man in the warrior state of So Han. As a commando lieutenant he was at the spearhead of So Han's war of conquest, but refused to engage in the atrocities being committed. After killing his commanding officer in a duel he was sent to the brutal To Lort prison and forced to labour in the mines there.

Eventually the Hanese conquest imploded and To Lort prison was taken over by a foreign governor called Lorfen, who saw something of himself in Lynx. He taught the damaged young man the philosophy of the Vagrim brotherhood – a nebulous group of war veterans who had found renewed purpose in helping and protecting others – and released him.

Years later, an older, wiser and slightly more rotund Lynx arrives in the town of Jangarai. Hoping to find more work as a bodyguard, he meets Kas, a woman of Anatin's Mercenary Deck, and with his welcome in town fast running out Lynx agrees to join her company for a rescue mission.

On the way the company encounters a group of Knights-Charnel of the Long Dusk – one of the most powerful of the militant religious orders on the continent. They are escorting a young half-Hanese woman who appeals to Lynx for help and when he confronts them, Lynx learns she is a mage. The power of the Militant Orders stems from their control of mages and fragments of the five shattered gods, which they use to create magical cartridges that every gun across the known world uses.

When the smoke clears, the Knights-Charnel lie dead and Lynx has a new ward, Sitain. Matters become further complicated when the rescue mission turns out to be covering the escape of an assassin called Toil from the city of Grasiel. Their flight turns into a street battle after Lynx and Sitain are betrayed to the Knights-Charnel by one of the Cards, Deern, and they are pursued from the city by the Knights-Charnel's elite Torquen regiment.

Toil persuades Anatin to leave the road and head across the wilds surrounding Shadows Deep, an ancient Duegar city-ruin where elementals and monsters reign. Forced underground, the outnumbered Cards are beaten to the only bridges that cross a miles-deep canyon blocking their path. To even up the odds Toil awakens a huge dragon-like creature and in the ensuing chaos Lynx ends up luring the monster out on to the main bridge where he and his comrades manage to bring it down. Leaving any surviving Charnelers lost in the darkness, the Cards escape to the surface and don't look back.

Honour Under Moonlight – a novella of the God Fragments

Midwinter in Su Dregir brings a festival of costumed revelry and Lynx arrives at Toil's apartments to escort her to the Archelect's ball. There he discovers two corpses in strange costumes instead of one living Toil. Before he can work out what's going on, a watchman appears and an assassin attacks. The watchman dies and Lynx flees.

Following a clue left by Toil, Lynx goes in search of her. More costumed assassins ambush him and despite the efforts of his comrades, he is captured by Toil's enemies. Toil meanwhile has discovered a plot to upturn the balance of power in the criminal gangs of Su Dregir. After preventing a massacre she goes to rescue Lynx and, with the assistance of her employer's bodyguard, turns the tables on the remaining assassins before killing the traitor.

Interlude 1
(Now)

'So a pederast, an assassin and a convict walk into a palace.'

'Shut up.'

Lynx sighed. 'What? I'm bored.'

'I don't care.'

'No one's listening.'

Toil's voice lowered to the whisper of a razor being sharpened. 'What part of "I don't care" confuses you?'

'What's the harm in passing the time with a joke?'

'Because if you don't shut up I'll rip your kneecaps off and use them for earmuffs to block out your bloody whining. You're not standing here for your health, we've got a job to do, remember?'

Lynx shut up and looked around at the grand hall of Jarrazir's Bridge Palace once more. It was magnificent, he had to admit. Jewelled light shone through a long bank of stained glass windows running almost the entire length of the hall. Dancing motes of emerald, blazing orange and glittering sapphire washed over the assembled crowd of Jarrazir's nobility. A spray of red carpet surrounded the pair of thrones at one end, all canopied by pristine white cloth bearing the symbols of the city and prayers stitched in red. Flanking them was a battered pair of stone urns that bore only fragments of faded glazing. They looked strangely out of place there until Lynx realised they were Duegar artefacts.

After an hour of the sight Lynx felt it was all very pretty, but lunch was fast intruding on his thoughts as the scents of spices and roasted meats hung thick in the air. As a portly and tattooed ex-soldier of a nation everyone hated, he was very aware how noticeable he was at the best of times and right then the great and the good were out in their finery to notice and be noticed. Unobtrusively sidling over to the buffet probably wasn't an option.

Swan-necked maidens with bare shoulders stood like serene statues, or perhaps well-behaved cattle, while watchful matrons in silk headscarves fussed at their side. Prowling around the girls displayed like goods were knots of young noblemen, searching out both marriageable flesh and offence. Several had more than one glove tucked into their belt that did not match their clothes, proof of a duel to come.

Official delegations studded the throng, obvious by their matching clothing and uniforms, while members of the priesthood stood out even more clearly. Just ahead of Lynx were the starkly austere priests of Insar, in plain white robes with heads cleanly shaved, while red and grey figures displaying the intricate braiding and geometric patterns of Catrac's cult loitered near the far wall. Lynx looked down at his own clothes. Fortunately the grey and green of Su Dregir's Lighthouse Guard was as understated as he could have reasonably hoped for. The fact he was in any form of uniform was a detail he remained unhappy about, but now wasn't the time for *that* discussion so he contented himself with not looking like an utter tit. This was Toil's business and he was just window-dressing for the hour.

Lynx felt a nudge from the man beside him.

'Tell me the joke instead,' Teshen said. 'Distract me from the urge to fire a burner into the roof.'

Lynx glanced up at the huge pale beams, so high the grain of the wood was invisible. Flags of every colour fluttered in the slight breeze, representing each of the city-state's several hundred noble families, while the beast emblems of Jarrazir hung over the empty thrones.

'It'd stop the boredom,' he conceded. 'Maybe even cook a dove or two if one is lurking up in the rafters.'

'You're not still bloody hungry are you?'

'I could eat.'

Toil turned around, eyes flashing with anger. Ahead of her stood the Su Dregir Envoy himself, chatting to a doughy old lady wrapped in purple silk like a child's sweet. The captain of his personal guard stood just behind them, but if either man had heard the conversation over the general hubbub they chose to ignore it. Lynx doubted it, given the pederast comment was aimed at one of them.

'Both of you, shut your traps right now,' she hissed. 'At least try to look like real guards.'

'Sounds like *someone's* a little on edge,' Teshen whispered primly once Toil had turned back. The tone didn't exactly match the man's dead-eyed killer look, but joining a mercenary company had forced Teshen to develop a light-hearted side, even if he remained firmly in the alarmingly lethal category.

'It's the dress,' Lynx said. 'Maybe the heels. They don't look comfy.'

'Oh, I like the heels,' joined in Payl from the other side of Teshen. 'The poor bugger who had to buff her feet to make them presentable, however – now *they* have cause for complaint.'

Lynx smirked over at Payl. The woman was usually calm and professional – as second-in-command to a lazy, roguish drunk she had to be. That she'd joined in was a testament to the sheer boredom of standing amid that crowd and waiting for the city's ruler to finish whatever was taking so long.

'Was it you, Lynx?' Teshen asked. He was a burly man with long pale hair and under normal circumstances wore the Knight

6

of Tempest as his badge – Lynx's direct superior – but today he was just another Su Dregir guardsman.

'Well, I don't like to brag,' Lynx said. 'But I reckon I've a certain deftness with a pumice stone.'

It was just possible he could see the tips of Toil's ears turning scarlet with fury, but he knew she wouldn't give them the satisfaction of turning around again. Toil – ruin-raider, assassin, agent of Su Dregir, plus half a dozen other unsavoury things – had scrubbed up remarkably well, he had to admit. A layered silk dress of the Archelect's green and grey ran from calf to neck, following the Jarraziran form of leaving arms and feet on show, with her dark red hair in a complex triple braid down her back.

'Almost fell over with shock when I saw her,' Teshen said. 'Who'd have thought under those hobnailed boots was a pair of feet like that? Probably best Anatin didn't come with us; man's got a thing for a well-turned ankle. I know I'm new to this, but I'm guessing elite guardsmen shouldn't have a hard-on.'

Lynx had to agree, the feet really had been a surprise. Toil wore thin sandals – straps of grey silk exposing neat, uncallused heels and pristinely groomed, painted toenails.

'Are all you fighting women like this?' he whispered to Payl. 'All with your little beauty secrets?'

Payl snorted. 'My feet look like they got chewed on by feral dogs. Just as well I'm tall. No man ever bothers to look that far down.'

'I'll tell Fashail to report back next time he's hard at work down there,' Teshen said.

'The boy knows he'll get his nuts cut off,' Payl said confidently. 'As scary as you are, Teshen, he ain't that stupid.'

'It's the arms that get me, I reckon,' Lynx said after a moment's reflection. 'So she's secretly a delicate little princess when it comes to her feet, now we all know, but it takes real skill to pull off the arms.'

'Not so much,' Teshen said dismissively. 'I've seen Reft do it easy enough.'

'I meant, pull off that concealment.'

'Ah.'

While almost every woman not in fighting dress had bare arms, none sported the number of scars Toil did. A lifetime of fighting and clambering about the pitch-black caverns of Duegar city-ruins had done little to support today's role of bookish secretary to Su Dregir's official Envoy.

It had required a complex variety of ribbons, torcs, bracelets, painted charms and rings to distract from the battering Toil's arms had received over the years. Close scrutiny would catch her out still, but with luck few would be getting that close. Toil was a distractingly beautiful woman for those who would be distracted and physically imposing for those who wouldn't.

'How about you, Aben?' Teshen asked the last of the group serving as guards to the Envoy. 'Anything you'd like to add?'

Aben was new to their number, a bigger man even than Lynx, with tanned skin, an easy smile and neat black curls spilling out from under his official cap. Currently his face was scarlet and he seemed to be having some sort of silent shaking episode, possibly a coronary.

'You okay there, friend?' Lynx said with a nudge. 'Looks like something in your head just burst. Was it the feet? Does a well-turned ankle do it for you too?'

Aben's eyes swivelled in their sockets as though seeking an escape. He'd worked for Toil for several years now. She was *the boss* to him, a ruthless and remorseless figure within the Su Dregir underworld. She *wasn't* a person to be joked about in her earshot and *was* someone with a long and enthusiastically vengeful memory.

'Hey, look, more people come to join the vigil,' Payl commented. 'And of fucking course it's the last bastards we want to see here, there or anywhere else.'

8

Lynx turned as Teshen voiced the words they were all thinking.

'Bastard shitting Charnelers.'

'Least all those who chased us will be dead by now,' Payl added quietly. 'Don't fancy getting recognised by anyone after Grasiel.'

'So – an assassin, a convict and a whole boatload of pederast shites walk into a palace,' Lynx muttered.

Toil spun right round, cheeks now spotted pink with anger. 'If they're here, you lot keep your mouths shut, understand? No jokes, no witty asides, no . . .' Her eyes narrowed as she focused on the Charnelers and Lynx saw anger turn to murder in her eyes. 'Godspit and the shitting deepest black!'

Without warning she started off, shoving Payl out of her way. In his surprise Lynx barely noticed her slip a dagger from Payl's belt as she stalked forward.

'What? So it's all right for her to swear?' Teshen commented in a mock-hurt voice.

'I'm going to fucking gut you like a fish!' Toil roared across the great hall.

Lynx and Teshen exchanged looks while Payl and Aben started off after the spirit of vengeance. Ahead of Toil the crowd erupted into chaos.

'Well, that's the boredom part sorted out,' Lynx said.

'Should we . . . ?' Teshen nodded after the others.

'If you like, but they can handle it I'm sure. And I'm damn sure Toil can handle herself. Not like I'm keen for her to win friends here anyway, given what she wants to volunteer us for. More importantly I've just spotted a roast pheasant that no one's watching. Reckon it's near enough lunchtime.'

'Is there beer?'

'Round here? Fat chance.'

Teshen shrugged as shouts filled the air. 'The sacrifices we must make . . . Lead on, my friend.'

Chapter 1
(Three Weeks Earlier)

A dusting of snow lay on the ancient city of Jarrazir as five figures hurried through the still hours of night. Every stone and tile sparkled in the silver glow of the Skyriver, every curl and twist of the bay's waters was limned in white moonlight. Statues of heroes and rulers watched from the great arc of the Senate wall, beneath which the Deep Market nestled. The market itself was a sweeping warren of walkways and arches, arcades and canopies, spread over three storeys in parts and bewildering in the detail and intricacy of its design.

The five figures kept silent as they wound their way towards the market's heart, the three who led moving with the confidence of familiarity. Jarrazir was a city of old names and older customs, one of which was a prohibition on alcohol so the night-time streets were empty and silent. The Deep Market in particular was deserted – the cold of winter and its unsettling, unearthly design of both Duegar and human magery meaning even vagrants kept clear at night.

Had she been alone, Lastani would have been apprehensive at best. She had lived her whole life in Jarrazir; a childhood of tales and superstitions not so long left behind for more academic pursuits. Only the reassuring purpose of Mistress Ishienne ahead kept her focused on the task in hand.

No, not quite. Not just that. She suppressed a nervous giggle. There was something more bringing her here, to the oldest part

of an ancient city where even the light of the Skyriver struggled to reach. *There is the possibility of something quite wonderful
too – a place in history perhaps, should we be successful.*

Lastani bit her lip and kept on walking. She would not be
the one to draw Ishienne Matarin's ire this night, not at the
culmination of all her teacher's work.

*Let Castiere do that. He's incapable of keeping his mouth shut.
Let him be the fool who sullies this night with some idiocy, I will be
the perfect pupil at least this once.*

As they rounded a corner and entered a small square cut
through with jagged shadows, she glanced once at Castiere as
the slender young man drew level in his haste to get to the
market's heart. He saw her looking and flashed Lastani a grin,
his excitement bubbling close to the surface.

'Almost there,' whispered Mistress Ishienne, her voice
carrying clearly in the hush despite the scarf across her face.

The words were unnecessary, perhaps an indication of
Ishienne's own anticipation. This might prove a breakthrough
in her work, the fruits of years of translating and deciphering
a script thousands of years old. Lastani could not fault this
one crack in the detached calm that had been a constant of
Lastani's four years tutelage.

She looked around as they neared the Fountain, as it was
called, though in truth it was the entrance to a labyrinth built
before human civilisation. A mystery lurking beneath the city
streets that had never been opened in recorded history, but
was mentioned in texts from across the continent. Lastani had
spent so many days here amid the bustle of humanity as wares
were sold and all manner of services offered from dawn until
dusk. Day after day of transcribing and sketching, measuring
and dreaming – losing her purse twice, her heart once and her
maidenhood along with it. But now it was alien and frightening
here, scoured of life and the things of men. The stone mages

who had built the Deep Market, hundreds of years before, had chosen the fountain itself as inspiration for their otherworldly craft and, by custom, only stone remained here at night.

There, where the stall of kind Uslien normally stood, only bare and empty stone. Here, dear Lefaqe's tent of silks would be strung each morning – to see the space empty was to feel a curious hole in her heart though their affair had ended months ago. But no one would leave their belongings here, certainly not so close to the Fountain that was at the heart of it all. The Fountain which was no fountain and no crafting of a stone mage – at least, no human one.

They turned the corner and stopped, Lastani almost running into Mistress Ishienne as the Fountain itself came into view. It was a forbidding, squat lump of stone almost invisible in the darkness of shadow, but somehow all the more chilling for it. In the light of day she found it fascinating – the intricacy and otherworldly beauty of the ancient artefact breathtaking to behold – but now it was profoundly disquieting.

A nine-sided stone block the height of a man was set within a trio of fat, sinuous serpents of some unknown metal. The Fountain was Duegar-made and the finest example of that race's artistry within a hundred miles. Every flat surface was covered with wind-scoured carvings of remarkable intricacy and complexity – a puzzle of knots and patterns that incorporated every face and facet of the Fountain into one vast mathematical pattern. A domed stone canopy stood over it, perhaps twelve feet above, and it was this that restored Lastani's courage.

The Duegar script that covered the inner face of the dome was just as intricate as the decoration below, worked into a three-branched spiral that wound into the centre. And now, amid the blackness of night, the curling metal script was faintly glowing.

Lastani had always half-believed that to be nothing more than embellishment – a lie told in the assumption that no sensible person would visit at night to refute it. But there it was; the star-script of the Duegar now shining bright, almost as perfect and complete as the day that long-dead race had set it there. Two small pieces were missing. She had read the accounts of the enterprising thieves a dozen times or more, and the gruesome deaths that had found them before they could escape the market. Lastani was still staring when a figure stepped out from behind the Fountain and gave her such a fright that she squeaked in terror, breaking the reverential hush.

Mistresss Ishienne turned and fixed her with a stern look, unperturbed by the stranger's sudden appearance. Lastani covered her mouth and ducked her head, cheeks flushed with embarrassment. They were there on an errand of momentous and grave scholarly import, not to jump at ghosts. Lastani felt Castiere's patronising hand on her shoulder, the youth suppressing a laugh before he followed their mistress's lead and bowed to the newcomer.

'Master Atienolentra,' Ishienne called through the still night, 'you are well met again.'

'Let's hope so,' the man replied in a deep, rumbling voice. 'You, Mistress, continue to be a delight on the eyes.' He paused. 'Your pronunciation less so, however. Perhaps best just call me Atieno.'

'My apologies,' Ishienne said, inclining her head. 'It seems I have spent too much time favouring dead languages over existing ones.'

With a start, Lastani realised she had seen this man before, or glimpsed him at any rate. At a meeting Ishienne had taken, just a week before. Lastani had been returning to the house when she saw Master Atieno leaving. Hidden from the faint shine of the Skyriver by his hood, she had only glimpsed the white threads of his neat, pointed beard, but it was enough.

13

With piercing light brown eyes against a dark face of crow's feet and prominent cheekbones, Atieno would have been a handsome man but for the glowering severity he wore. His greying black hair was long and tied back, his worn clothes kept clean and neat. In his fifth decade at least, he remained tall and strong-looking – a marked improvement on the handful of suitors who had attempted to woo Mistress Ishienne during the time Lastani had lived in her house. Judging by Atieno's words, the idea had crossed his mind too.

The last two figures of Ishienne's group stepped out from behind Castiere and eyed the man suspiciously.

'Who's he?' Bokrel demanded.

The mercenary fingered the rounded butt of his holstered mage-pistol as he stared at Master Atieno. Bokrel was a monkey-faced wretch with grubby cheeks, a scrappy beard and wandering hands. Right now there was a livid pink frost-burn down the back of his left hand, a testament to how slow the mercenary was to take a hint, but he was the brains of the operation compared to his rotund comrade, Ybryl.

'He, Master Bokrel, is a key component of what we attempt tonight,' Ishienne said sharply. 'Try not to shoot him please. I doubt it would end well for you.'

Atieno pushed back his hood and gave the two mercenaries a stern look then seemed to mentally dismiss them. He carried a large walking staff that looked like a weapon in his hands, but like the mercenaries he also had a mage-pistol in his belt. With stiff movements that spoke of a lame leg, he walked around to the face of the Fountain that was, by common agreement, the front.

'You believe you can do this?' Master Atieno called.

Ishienne gestured to the swirls of script glowing above them. 'I have seen it in the stars,' she said with a small smile.

'That, I have heard before. Rarely has it inspired confidence.'

'The difference, I suspect, is that I've had to understand enough to teach my pupils.'

Lastani took a step forward. 'Mistress Ishienne translated the Duegar script, but the riddle within has been something we have all devoted our lives to unpicking.'

'The young say such things so easily,' Atieno said with gentle mocking. 'They've had less to devote thus far.'

'I have given it enough years for all three of us,' Ishienne declared, 'and my assistants contributed several of their own on top. The sacrifice has been shared, and now we must see if it was in vain or not.'

'Where do you want us?' Bokrel asked abruptly.

'At the edge of the dome,' she replied, pointing to the arched gaps between the dome's stone supports.

'And then what?'

'Keep guard,' Ishienne said simply. 'We must not be disturbed. Most likely you need do nothing to earn your pay, gods grant. I require you only to be awake and ready in case anything . . . unexpected occurs.'

'Like what?'

'If I knew that, it would hardly be unexpected. Come now, Master Bokrel, you led me to believe you were an experienced soldier and had explored Duegar city-ruins.'

Ybryl snorted at Bokrel's side, causing the man to glare at her. 'We ain't explored the damn things.' Ybryl chuckled, not noticing the look Bokrel gave her. 'We ain't that stupid.'

'What then?'

'Guard duty, escort,' Bokrel explained reluctantly. 'Let the other damn fools go underground an' play with monsters.'

Ishienne hissed in irritation. 'You have combat experience at least?'

'Yeah, we've been in a few fights.'

'Good – in that case keep your eyes open and your guns loaded, your mouths shut and your wits primed.'

Before Bokrel had a chance to object, Ishienne turned away and gestured to her two charges. 'Come, take your places.'

Lastani and Castiere ducked their heads in acknowledgement and went to stand beneath the nearest two snake mouths, peering up into the dark, toothless maws that looked down on them.

'And I?'

'Just as you are, Master Atieno,' Ishienne said, making her way around to the last of the snake mouths. 'Yours is the most complicated of tasks I'm afraid.'

'It always is,' he said. 'Firstly, your powers, though. What are they?'

'Does it matter?'

'It does.'

Ishienne frowned. 'Very well, but I will be doing the sculpting of magic – you need but be the key around which I will fit the lock. I am a stone mage, Lastani an ice mage, and Castiere fire. Does that meet with your approval?'

'It does,' Atieno said with a nod. 'There are powers that my kind will not work with. The risk is too great.'

'And those are?'

'Not stone, fire or ice.'

After a moment it was clear he would say no more on the subject so Ishienne gave a cluck of the tongue and went back about her task.

'For the first stage, you are not required, Master Atieno,' she informed him. 'The job is ours alone.'

At her nod, Lastani stretched up to the mouth of the metal serpent above her and opened herself to her magic. A faint white haze appeared around her hand then she felt the bite of cold on her skin – not painful to her, just different, for all that it would freeze the skin off any other human in a matter of seconds.

A soft crackle from the far side told her that Castiere was doing the same, sending magic up into the mouth of the serpent with all the control he could muster. Ishienne was silent, but Lastani could just see her out of the corner of her eye and the woman was reaching up also. She concentrated on the task at hand, allowing the magic inside her to flow out through her fingers and coil up into the snake.

All this they had expected. The months of deciphering and research meant she could quote the words above by rote, but still Lastani felt a thrill at it working. The Fountain was drawing her magic, not greedily leeching off her but gathering all that she released to flow down the bodies of the serpents. Mistress Ishienne had described it as a votive offering, something that had made poor pious Castiere wince, but Lastani saw now how right she was. They were giving the Fountain something of themselves, a trace of their power, to prepare the way for what would come next – what they would ask of it.

The flow of magic steadily grew and Lastani began to be able to sense the others, the heat of Castiere's magic and the cool weight of Ishienne's. There was a balance in what they were offering and Lastani knew not to overtax herself in this initial stage, but still she freed a little more of the clean, cold bite in her bones to more closely match Castiere.

Their powers were to be most obviously in balance, as they often had been in Ishienne's library while debating the grand puzzle of the Fountain, the labyrinth beneath and whatever was hidden at the heart of that. Whether by chance or consequence of their magic, the two thought in entirely different ways. Sometimes Castiere's dancing focus would alight on the path, sometimes Lastani's careful method would instead.

'Enough,' Ishienne called and the trio cut the flow of their magic.

Lastani stepped back so she could see her teacher's face. Though the woman's expression was hidden in the shadows, years in her company told Lastani that Ishienne was satisfied with the first step.

'Now we wait,' Ishienne added for the benefit of Atieno. 'There is a precise order to this ritual that must be followed.'

'You are confident in your interpretation?' Atieno replied in a voice that betrayed neither scepticism nor belief. 'Many have attempted to best this puzzle over the centuries.'

'And many have got this far,' Ishienne said. 'This pause is the first test, your presence another, the details of the crafting a third. A plain translation of the text above your head will get you no further than this.'

'And a mistranslation would see Lastani dead,' Castiere added drily.

'Now it is your confidence that concerns me,' Atieno declared. The man leaned heavily on his staff as he spoke, but made no effort to move away from the Fountain.

'Our confidence is well founded,' Lastani found herself saying. 'Otherwise I would not be so willing! The work is a puzzle, understanding that is the crux of Mistress Ishienne's breakthrough. By mirroring the decoration on the Fountain—'

'I'm sure Master Atieno isn't interested in the details of our research,' Ishienne broke in. Lastani couldn't tell whether that was through a desire to preserve her secrets or impatience to be getting on, but she shut her mouth with a snap and tried not to picture Castiere's smirk.

'Research is not where I excel,' Atieno agreed sombrely, 'so I will take your word as though it were scripture.'

'Would that the Book of the First Sun could stand up to such rigour,' Castiere muttered.

'This is not the time, Castiere,' Ishienne reminded him. 'Now, are you both ready for the second phase?'

Lastani nodded and stepped forward, opening herself again as Castiere did the same. This time they let their magic only gently bleed out and Ishienne, controlling something within the Fountain itself, regulated the magic in a precise pattern before both assistants threw one long, sustained burst of raw power in. When Lastani stepped back again, she was light-headed and suddenly weary, but there had been no apparent effect on the Fountain.

'Now you, Master Atieno,' Ishienne said, stepping to the side until she could see the man. 'Palm against the middle panel, please. Let the stone draw your hand in and take your magic. I will guide you, a core of tempest magic that will ensure the stone is responsive to me.'

'Have a care,' Atieno warned her as he stepped forward and placed a hand against the stone. 'Tempest is unlike your magic. There is cost and wildness other mages do not know.'

Despite everything, Lastani felt a shiver down her spine as he said the word. The mages of tempest were so rare most considered them a myth, their magic not of elements but of change. The Militant Orders had no use for them and struggled to control them, so they demonised Atieno's kind and killed them when they could. It had taken Ishienne's extensive contacts and several bribes before she had found Atieno and convinced him to come.

'I understand,' Ishienne said calmly. 'A trace of tempest is required, nothing more. It is the key, not the shoulder to the door, and I know you pay for every drawing.'

'Not only me,' he said. 'It would twist every strand of magic it touched, if you tried to draw much, and turn your power against you. It cannot be controlled – refusing to accept that has killed more of my brethren than the Militant Orders ever managed.'

'Your warning is appreciated, then,' she replied. 'Should anything more than the tiniest amount prove inadequate, we will break off and reassess.'

A grunt was all Atieno replied with, but he set to work without hesitation. Lastani resumed her place, hand stretched up to offer a steady, modest flow of power. The mingling she had sensed within the Fountain remained, but she could not feel any of the tempest magic within that blend. Only by the sound could she tell the carved surface under Atieno's hand had opened under Ishienne's stone magery and closed again around it.

At first there was nothing, no indication that the magic was affecting the Fountain at all, but eventually she began to feel the ground faintly tremble. Carefully regulating herself to match Castiere, she touched one finger to the metal snake. It was doing the same, a tiny shudder running through the entire Fountain and deep underground.

Off to her right there was a slight gasp from Ishienne, then a sound of satisfaction. Lastani could not tell that anything had changed until she heard a telltale grind and the whisper of stone on stone – Ishienne forming and shaping the very structure of the Fountain. It was a Duegar construction, designed with magic in mind and made to respond, but still Ishienne moved slowly.

Lastani saw the brief flourish of surprise on Atieno's reserved face as the stone abruptly split and opened like a double door, freeing his arm and allowing the man to take a laboured step back. That face of the Fountain continued to open, petals of stone peeling organically back under Ishienne's deft touch until the stone had folded right back to the metal snake-shapes on either side.

'There,' Ishienne declared, releasing her magic and stepping back. 'It is done.'

Lastani smiled and moved to do the same when with a jolt she realised she couldn't cut the flow of magic.

'Ah, mistress?' called Castiere from the other side. 'I've got a—'

Either he didn't get any further or Lastani didn't hear him. The mouth of the snake snapped shut on her fingertips and for a moment there was only the white-hot pain of crushing. From the howl that broke through it, Castiere had experienced the same. Lastani had time for one brief flash of fear before the snake began to feed savagely on her magic and all rational thought vanished from her mind.

She wailed and hauled at her trapped fingers but her muscles had turned to jelly, her mind a cold void as the trickle of magic was turned to a raging torrent. The air whitened before her eyes as her ice magic turned the chill night freezing. Within moments she couldn't feel her body except the unremitting pressure on her fingers, everything else subordinate to the wild plunder of magic.

Her eyes blurred and a veil of darkness started to descend. Lastani barely noticed hands on her body, the shouting voices. Even when the hands began to pull then frantically haul at her, it was distant and unreal. The pain receded, the world around her darkened and contracted to a single, diminishing point of light before everything snapped back with terrible force.

Lastani took one ragged breath then screamed with all her might as something popped in her fingers and she was dragged away. Shrieking, she curled over her injury but strong hands unpeeled her fingers and roughly stretched them out.

'The other one! Go!' roared a man above her, just a dark blur through her tumbling tears.

She fought him but could do nothing against the man's strength and with perfunctory jerks he yanked one finger then the next straight. Each movement sparked another shriek from Lastani, but afterwards the pain dampened and her wits returned. Her vision cleared a fraction to see Atieno and Mistress Ishienne staring down at her bleeding, pinched but no longer dislocated fingers.

'He's on fire!' Bokrel yelled, prompting Atieno to turn with a snarl on his face.

'Cut the hand!' he bellowed, rising. 'Get him away or he'll die!'

An orange corona lit the inscribed canopy above and haloed the Fountain. Lastani couldn't see Castiere from where she lay, but she knew how the fire mage would be looking if he was trapped as she had been – surrounded by the unchecked ferocity of his magic.

There was a grunt and a wet crunch. The light vanished and she heard a weight fall to the ground, but not the screams of a man whose limb had just been severed.

'Castiere!' Ishienne yelled, running past the open face of the fountain towards her pupil, but never reaching him.

A flash of pale grey light darted out towards her, as fast as a striking snake, and snatched the woman up like she was a toy. Lastani screamed in terror, Ishienne's cry cut off in the same instant it began. Impaled on blades of shining mist, she hung helpless – her mouth open in a silent scream – as an indistinct nightmare hauled itself out of the darkness inside the Fountain.

Long, slender limbs unfolded, two, six, eight – the ghostly creature seemed all limbs and no body, just a knot where the joints met, but it moved with fearsome purpose and speed.

A great detonation crashed against Lastani's ears. She reeled, eyes watering and barely registering the taste of ice magic in the air. Atieno had fired his mage-pistol, but though the horror flinched there was no damage Lastani could see.

Wailing in terror, the two mercenaries backed away. Bokrel had his gun out, wavering uncertainly in the apparition's direction, but when he fired the white trail went high and out into the night beyond. Ybryl hadn't even got her gun out, the woman just quivered and wailed quietly as the horror turned their way. It dropped Ishienne and she fell limp, a dead thing on the floor. That was enough to make the mercenaries turn tail, but before they could get a step or two it slashed forward and tore furrows down their backs.

The mercenaries fell, their cries cut short as the horror stabbed forward to dispatch them with perfunctory savagery. Lastani was paralysed with fear as she watched them die, unable to run while she had the chance. When it turned towards them she still couldn't move, a leaden chill filling her body.

Atieno growled a curse and pulled something from his waist – small, just the size of a hazelnut. Lastani barely saw anything of the dark object as Atieno hurled it towards the ghostly spider-thing. The small shape landed at its feet. The ground seemed to shudder and twist, the horror somehow tangled as Atieno dragged Lastani upright and started hauling her away.

'Come on!' he roared in her ear, slapping her face to jerk her back to her senses. Lastani gasped at the impact, her head rocking back, but then some trace of her strength returned and she found her feet again.

'Move!' Atieno roared again, leaning heavily on his staff with one hand and the other gripping Lastani's arm so tight it hurt. His bad leg dragged heavily underneath him, but still Lastani would have fallen behind without his hold on her.

Together they fled as fast as they could, not daring to look behind in case the creature was right there. Only at the edge of the Deep Market where they were surrounded by dark empty silence did they pause and check behind. There was nothing there – all was still and silent. No screams of the dying, no darting movements of whatever had attacked them.

'Ishienne,' Lastani gasped. 'Castiere?'

'They're dead,' Atieno said gruffly, 'and we're not out of danger yet.'

'What? How do you know?'

'I don't,' he snapped. 'But I ain't a man to gamble on his own safety. I don't know what we just unleashed, but I for one won't hang around to see how far the danger goes.'

'But . . . what do I . . . ?'

His face softened. 'Come, girl, we need to keep moving.'

'Where?'

'Your teacher's house. Your home. You need to pack your belongings.'

Lastani stared up at him with incomprehension. 'But . . .'

'Come on,' he urged, pulling her along with him as they headed for the coiling ramp that led up to the inhabited part of the city. 'Folk will have heard the gunshots, they'll fetch the watch.'

'I should stay.'

'Not a good idea. At best they'll find some brutally murdered people, at worst . . . Well, you don't want to be anywhere near the fallout and I need to get paid.'

She gaped at him. 'Paid?'

'Aye.' His face hardened again. 'My fee. I ain't so rich I can afford to go without that. I did as your mistress asked and I need to pay for food somehow. Compassion doesn't help there. And you – you don't want to be at her house when some angry watchmen come looking for answers. Asking why some monstrous ghost just got set loose in the city. Take what you can without it looking like you've killed and robbed her.'

They started up the slope, Atieno's face taut with apprehension. Lastani followed without willing it, her body just obeying even if her mind couldn't comprehend his instructions.

'What then?'

'That is anyone's guess.' He paused and frowned at her for a moment before seeming to make up his mind. 'Come with me if you want, lie low a few days and let the worst pass. After that . . .' He shrugged and started walking again, labouring up the slope until they were at the top and he could peer suspiciously around. There was no one in sight so he waved Lastani onward and pressed on to the cover of the nearest side street.

'After that, let's just hope what we did doesn't come back to haunt us.'

Chapter 2

Wrapped in the snug embrace of his blankets, tucked into the corner of his bed with his back pressed against the wall, Lynx fought the wakefulness stealing over him. The bed shuddered faintly underneath as the stamp of boots on a bare wooden floor reverberated through the building. He winced as a fist pounded on the door just a few yards from his head and a voice roared out to echo through the building.

'Company muster!'

Lynx growled and rolled his generous frame over. Distantly he heard a creak as another of the room's occupants did the same, but the pounding didn't stop. The stamp of boots grew heavier and the voice took on the unmistakably gleeful tone of their commander, Anatin.

'Up, you bastards! I told you not to drink so much, reckon some of you lot have a bloody problem with the sauce!'

Anatin started hitting doors along the corridor with his one remaining hand so hard the walls shook. Lynx heard one crash open under his efforts and that only increased the man's mirth.

'Morning sunshi— Wisps and shadows, Reft, put him down! Shit, that's more o' Deern than most gun-addled veterans could stand to see this early. Clothes, you bastards – put some on! There are women and children hereabouts!'

Blearily, Lynx scratched his belly and sat up. In the bed

opposite another man emerged from his blankets – Safir, the Knight of Snow.

'Do you think it counts as mutiny,' Safir wondered idly, 'if we shoot Anatin for being maliciously cheerful?'

The easterner stretched, his lean body hidden by a long shapeless robe that the more foolish members of the company said looked like a girl's smock.

Lynx rubbed the sleep from his face and nodded. 'I'll back you up. We'll call it the morning coup. Folk will be singing your praises for years to come.'

In the corridor, Anatin continued, no doubt well aware half his company were idly considering murder of one fashion or another. Another door was battered open as he yelled out his good mornings.

'Speaking o' women and children, get yourselves – shitting gods, Sitain! What're you doing to the poor girl? That can't be hygienic!'

From elsewhere there was laughter, thin and mocking, that told Lynx the rat-faced wretch Deern, naked or not, was enjoying the embarrassment of others.

'Sitain?' Lynx asked muzzily.

He recoiled as a face hoved unexpectedly into view from the bunk above. 'Oh yes!' Llaith grinned. 'Some merchant's clerk with blue eyes, pretty little thing. I could stand to be hearing that through the wall, let me tell you.'

'Gods, man, don't sneak up on me like that,' Lynx groaned.

'Sneak up on you?' Llaith cackled, plague-scarred cheeks crinkling in his mirth. 'We've shared this room for bloody weeks now, where did you think I was going to appear from?'

'First time I saw Lynx,' Safir said with a sniff of disdain, 'I knew he'd be an ungrateful wretch. We go out of our way to save that ample backside of his at the Skyriver Festival – risked our lives in the face of mad killers no less – and does he show any appreciation?'

'Mad killers?' Lynx shook his head. 'Bunch of costumed goat-fuckers more like. And you didn't save me for long, did you? About one minute in total, half of which was taken up by Llaith trying to get his sword-stick to work properly. Toil did most of the work.'

He rubbed his arm absent-mindedly, the livid red of a newly forming scar. The Skyriver Festival was meant to be a night of wild abandon in Su Dregir as the city descended into one extended, hugely drunken, costumed ball. With his usual talent for attracting trouble magnified by Toil's own, Lynx hadn't had quite as much fun that night. The bruises had mostly faded, the sliced flesh mostly knitted, but it was another scar on the surface of a soul that was now just a patchwork of repairs.

'Aye, she did.' Llaith gave him a sly smile. 'Question is, did you get to thank her properly? It's only polite you know. I could pass on a message if you needed some help?'

Lynx shoved the man's face away. 'Rein it in, you filthy old man. You want to thank her for doing what you couldn't, the risk's all yours.'

'He doesn't even give us our due recognition,' Llaith sighed dramatically, swinging his bare feet over the edge of the bed and dropping down to the ground. 'Filthy foreigners, eh, Safir?'

'Bastards,' agreed Safir, pulling his not-a-smock off to reveal a smooth, lean nut-brown figure in complete contrast to Llaith's puckered white flesh. 'Coming over here, killing *our* torture-loving assassins . . .'

Even after a hard night of drinking, the former nobleman looked neat and composed, his dark beard never less than perfectly trimmed. With characteristic grace Safir slipped into his cotton leggings and kilt almost in one deft movement, while Llaith scratched his backside distinctly too close to Lynx's face for comfort and bent over to work out which boot was which.

'One hour!' yelled Anatin as a parting message, sounding like he'd finally tired of his game and was halfway back downstairs. 'Muster in one hour! Breakfast, shit, shine and shave – anyone not ready gets left behind after Reft's had his way with 'em and if you'd just seen what I have, you'd all be fucking running by now!'

Lynx jumped to it. One to the gut – assuming Anatin was joking about what he'd just walked in on between Reft and Deern – was standard punishment for being late to muster. Given the pale, hairless Reft appeared more ice-giant than soldier, he could punch a man into next week's hangover. Still, it was more the suggestion of breakfast that got Lynx going. Pain might have been an old friend of his, but breakfast would always be a delicious new friend.

'Aye, boy, you go get the coffee brewing,' Llaith said approvingly as Lynx hauled his clothes on. 'Bat yer eyelids at that cook's maid and have the grub waiting for us.' He eased open the window shutter and a thin shaft of sunlight spilled across the room. 'Looks like a fine morning. We'll be on the morning tide I reckon.'

Lynx nodded. After a quiet winter in Su Dregir under retainer, Anatin's Mercenary Deck had orders to move out again. Their employer hadn't changed, the Archelect's agent, Toil, having apparently adopted the company as her own. But other than knowing she'd hired a ship, they had no idea where she would be taking them next.

Sure it'll be a fun surprise, Lynx thought bleakly, *Toil's full of those.*

He finished dressing and left his small pile of belongings on his bed. It still felt strange to do so, but the Cards had occupied this whole inn all winter and there wouldn't be strangers wandering around the place. The few speculative thieves had been enthusiastically thrown out on their ears and word had got around – the words in question being 'second storey'.

The inn remained chilly in the morning despite the late winter sun, so he pulled his jacket on. He realised distantly that he'd finally grown used to the sight of the playing card badge stitched on the breast – the Stranger of Tempest, a hooded figure with a staff in one hand, a burning torch in the other. While half the company weren't averse to a little light theft, it made him a bad prospect to steal from. Perhaps more importantly, he shared a room with Safir, the Knight of Snow. The senior officers of the Cards took a grave opinion of theft unless they were the ones doing it.

Out in the corridor, Lynx nodded to a few faces there. Deern lounged on the bed in a room almost opposite his, the worst thief of the lot in Lynx's opinion. Half-naked and smirking, the man looked wiry and scarred – far smaller than Lynx, but a killer to the bone who wore the Jester of Blood on his jacket.

'Morning, fat boy,' Deern called. 'That's gotta be a kick in the fork, eh?'

'What is?' Lynx said wearily.

He had no time for Deern, but they were both quick-tempered and it was too early for a fight. On top of that, Lynx caught a glimpse of deathly white flesh behind Deern before Reft pulled on a shirt. Any fight broken up by that huge man stayed broken up and people tangling with Deern tended to come off worse.

Deern nodded to another doorway down the corridor. 'Your girl there, gettin' more action than you.'

Lynx shrugged as Sitain appeared at the doorway, hair rumpled and scowl deeper than usual. 'I ain't his fucking girl,' Sitain snapped, 'so shut your mouth, Deern.'

'Watch your tongue, girly.'

'Get burned, you don't outrank me, remember?' As though to make the point Sitain slung her jacket over her shoulder, the Jester of Sun just about visible. She wasn't an experienced soldier at all, just a half-Hanese young woman who'd fallen in with a bad crowd, but she was a night mage and that meant she had a skill none of the others could match.

And technically, Lynx reflected, *she'd have the best chance of putting Reft down in a fight. Might wet herself if I suggested it o' course, but that's life for you.*

'Just 'cos Anatin's got a weird sense of humour and you've cuddled up to some murdering convict, that don't make you a real soldier, Sitain. Keep that mouth in check till you've seen a real fight. Running away from bugs underground don't count.'

'I've seen proper soldiers, Deern,' Lynx broke in, 'and you ain't one. You're the sort who leaves the field with every dead man's purse, but never got around to firing a shot.'

'Try me, fat boy.'

Before Lynx could reply a head poked around the corner of the end room. Payl, Knight of Sun and Anatin's second in command.

'Enough of that crap, the three of you. Make like Reft and keep quiet until I've had some coffee or someone's getting their papers before we leave. I ain't going to be cooped up on a boat with you lot bitching again, hear me?'

The woman didn't bother waiting to see the reaction to her words, just stepped back into her room to allow her young lover, Fashail, to leave. The youth was another untested recruit and still faintly blushed as though he had been caught sneaking out of her room in the middle of the night, but they were old news and no one else cared.

Lynx turned his back on Deern and went to Sitain's room. He clapped a comradely hand on her shoulder as he peered round the door and was unsurprised to have it shaken immediately off.

'Get your nose out,' she said, but without the venom of a few moments earlier. 'Don't pretend you're not rushing to be first in the breakfast queue.'

Lynx ignored her and smiled broadly at the other women in the room – the company seer, white-haired Estal; the more beautiful of the two scouts, Kas; and a woman he didn't recognise. A few years older than Sitain, she was indeed pretty, with deep blue eyes, but not apparently intimidated by the harsh company of mercenaries.

'Morning, miss. I'm Lynx.'

'That much I guessed,' she replied, a challenging tilt to her nose.

Lynx forced himself to grin only wider. 'Heard I was the most beautiful man in the company, eh? Sitain is prone to singing my praises of a morning.'

Just as obvious as the tattoo on his cheek was the fact he was from So Han and therefore unpopular across half the continent, but Sitain was half Hanese too. If the woman had a problem with his homeland of bastards she'd likely not be in Sitain's bed.

'I think I said the most *something*, anyway,' Sitain replied, prodding his belly.

'Insatiable in my appetites?'

'Yeah, let's go with that.'

By then Kas had finished getting ready and she drifted forward, jacket draped over one brown shoulder and fixing Lynx with a dazzling smile.

'Come on, Lynx, don't make me blush by getting her to repeat all the things I said about you. You know what us women are like when we get together, it's just talking about boys all night long.'

'Now if I believed that, I'd be sorely disappointed in these two young things.'

'Oh the stories I could tell there . . .' She winked. 'Now leave these two to their goodbyes and take a girl to breakfast before Llaith starts asking for details, okay?'

Without waiting for a reply Kas took Lynx's arm and swept the helpless man on down the corridor. In their wake came Estal, scowling as usual at her friend's cheerfulness in the morning as she tied her hair back and scratched the large scar at her hairline.

'Any idea where we're going?' Kas asked breezily as they filed down the narrow stair to the common room below.

'None. Anatin likes you more'n me, why would I know?'

'Ah, but I've not caught the eye of our employer,' Kas said with an exaggerated wink. 'Least, not in *that* way. I get the impression she don't like me playing with her toys. Toil's not mentioned anything to you?'

'Not her toy and I've barely seen her,' Lynx replied gruffly. 'That fun at the festival left her with a few broken bones; she's been resting when she's not been about her business.'

'Which is?'

'Don't think I really want to know, to be honest. Reckon she's got her fingers in more pies than we'll ever find out – some sanctioned, others not so much. Mebbe it's a good sign she's telling us nothing. Believing what we were told the first time round was hardly worthwhile now, was it?'

'Maybe you could press her for some details in future,' Kas purred. The woman's voice was like honey when she wanted it to be, thick and rich even though Lynx couldn't quite shake the hint of a sting too. 'We got lucky in Shadows Deep; let's not see how far we can stretch that, okay? Toil pays well and Anatin usually has his reasons for not sharing, but I'm a scout and I like to see what's ahead o' me.'

'Like I said, I ain't seen her much and she's not one for straight answers anyway.'

Kas pursed her lips and glanced away. 'You find a way to get some,' she said in a softer voice, 'or that girl's gonna chew you up and spit you out.'

'Yeah, I know.'

'Aye, that's the sad thing about it.'

'Eh?'

'Never mind.'

They said no more until they reached the bottom and turned the corner out into the almost deserted common room – bar one person, but the sight of her was enough to make Lynx stop dead.

'Ah, the very woman,' Kas declared in a slightly forced way, rounding Lynx and giving him a hefty slap on the backside as she passed. 'I've warmed him up for you. Enjoy!'

For good measure Estal gave Lynx a slap as she passed too, then headed for the kitchen, whistling loudly. Momentarily alone and subjected to Toil's sharp scrutiny, Lynx found himself feeling unaccountably nervous as the seconds ticked silently past.

'Ah, morning,' he said at last, unable to stand the quiet.

'It is,' Toil acknowledged.

For a moment he thought she was going to say more but the woman fell into silence again. The yellowed stains of bruising were still visible on her face, along with a trace of weariness she'd not had even after days of running from maspid packs through a Duegar city-ruin.

'Still need the stick?' Lynx asked, nodding to the walking stick in her hand. It was made of some white wood with no decoration and Lynx couldn't help but assume there'd be a blade concealed somewhere in it.

'Means my leg heals faster.'

Toil was dressed in a plain tunic and trousers, high boots and a heavy sheepskin coat – not too different to most of the mercenaries she was employing, just a better cut. True to form she wore no jewellery or decorations, just her distinctive dark red hair tied back with a strip of red ribbon. She was a noticeably muscular woman, but it was the glittering, arresting smile that most people saw first.

'You, ah, you know Kas was joking, right?'

'Not my business what you get up to.'

Lynx hesitated. 'Oh. Okay, right then.'

Toil shook her head and a smile appeared on her face. 'I know she was joking,' she admitted, 'but I never get tired of watching you squirm. How is it you've seen so much of this world and still can't work women out?'

Lynx felt a flush of relief. 'Hardly think I'm the only one like that round here,' he muttered.

'True – most don't tie themselves up in knots over it, though.' She cocked her head to one side. 'Don't worry, it's an attractive quality.'

'Experience tells you might be in a minority there.'

The glittering smile returned like the sun breaking through clouds. 'Oh, I didn't mean attractive to me.'

'Ah. Good.'

'Toil!' yelled a voice from the private room behind the bar, where Anatin took most of his meals with his officers. 'Stop playing with your food, the tide doesn't wait.'

'It'll do so if I bloody tell it to,' Toil yelled back. 'See you on the boat, Lynx.'

He raised his eyebrows. 'Boat to where?'

'Oh, I wouldn't want to ruin the surprise.'

'Haven't you learned I don't like surprises?'

She laughed and headed back into the dining room. 'But *I* like them. This one's for all of you anyway. I wouldn't want to spoil the fun of seeing your little faces.'

*

Given the improving weather, Lynx and Llaith didn't have their sunny corner to themselves for long. With a plate of sweet buttery pastries inside them and good headway made through a large jug of coffee, they smoked in relative silence as the rest of the company stirred to life around them.

Safir had been called in to eat with Anatin and Toil – along with the other Knights of the company, Payl, Reft and Teshen. There were five suits in the Mercenary Deck, but the Knight of Stars, Olut, was one of those who hadn't made it through Shadows Deep.

It wasn't long before Himbel, the company doctor, and Sitain joined Lynx and Llaith. None of them were a ray of sunshine in the morning, so they often started the day together, Sitain ignoring the clouds of smoke in favour of the relative quiet around the table.

'Said your goodbyes then, Sitain?' Llaith asked after a while, stretching contentedly.

'Yup.'

'Fancy telling us about it in painstaking and lurid detail?'

'Not even a little.'

Llaith smiled. 'Fair enough. Anyone got word on where we're heading to next? Lynx?'

'Fuck's sake, you too? No, I don't know.'

'Hmm. Anatin just laughed when I asked, which is never good, but Foren was looking pleased which normally means he's seen what we're gonna get paid.'

'Deern's offering the best odds on Militant Order-controlled cities,' Himbel said.

'Which means he don't know shit and is just trying to scam folk,' Llaith snorted. 'Anatin knows his crew and he likes what's left of his body – he'd not try that. So if no one knows, let's talk about Lynx's promotion instead.'

'What?' Sitain and Lynx demanded in the same breath.

He shrugged. 'We're a Knight down. Anatin won't want to keep it like that.'

Lynx scowled, not at the idea of promotion, but at the memory of seeing the last Knight of Stars die. He glanced at

36

Sitain and saw a similar expression on her face. Olut had been a big bear-like woman, fierce and fearless, but she'd hardly seen her death coming when a monster in the depths of Shadows Deep had gutted her.

'I'm not taking Olut's badge,' he said slowly. 'Or any Knight's. Had my fill of command in the war.'

'Well you sure as shit can't *take* orders, might be you're better suited to giving them instead.'

'Still not going to happen.' Lynx shook his head. 'Why'd you even think so? I'm new to the company.'

'Lot's o' reasons.' Llaith grinned. 'One – most everyone hates you anyway, what with you being a Hanese bastard commando, so being jumped up above them won't change things on that front. But it also means you've seen enough action. Even Braqe couldn't claim you weren't fit for the job.'

Lynx looked over to where a woman with dark skin sat on the far side of the courtyard, the Jester of Tempest badge on her jacket. 'Want to put money on that?'

'Hah, mebbe not *Braqe* then, but the rest. Anyway, way I see it Estal's too broken in the head to lead a suit and I'm too old. Next in the order of cards is Varain, Ulax and you—'

'There's me!' protested Himbel. 'I'm a Diviner too, remember? We're the same rank!'

Llaith waved his hand dismissively. 'Yeah, but you're, well, *you*.'

'Fuck's that supposed to mean?'

'It means you're a crap soldier and a miserable sod most of the time,' Llaith laughed. 'A worse leader I can hardly imagine. You stick to sewing the rest of us up and keeping Deern in his place, my friend. Where was I? Ah yeah, Ulax ain't cut out for command and Varain – now, Varain's got a lovely singing voice and the man can fight, but he ain't much with the thinky stuff.'

'Reft's the Knight of Blood and he can't bloody talk!' Himbel pointed out.

Llaith raised an eyebrow. 'Sure, but – well in the same way that you're *you*, he's fucking *Reft*. Look at the man. You don't hide a monster like that where no one can see it, let alone not pay him as well as any other merc in the company. Deern does enough talking for the two of them, Reft manages fine.'

'So that leaves me?' Lynx scoffed. 'Anatin's favourite recruit? Ulfer's horn, he'd be better off promoting Kas.'

'But he won't 'less she asks him to. He likes keeping her out of command. She already does a damn good job holding this collection of fools together. Bet you she gets paid more'n the other Madmen – or you'n Varain too for that matter – but she's worth it at twice the price to Anatin.'

Even the more recent recruits, Lynx and Sitain, nodded at that. They'd only been part of the Cards for a few months, but Kas's effect on the rest was plain to see – not least because she had a warm heart and no sharp edges, unlike most mercenaries. She had befriended almost every man and woman there and put this to good use heading off trouble; sometimes smoothing over ruffled feathers, sometimes having a quiet word. Like most mercenary groups, the Cards were only ever a few drinks away from shooting each other, but mostly they didn't and Kas was a big reason for it.

'Who does that leave?'

'Not many, none worth giving the Knight of Stars card to.'

'Well I ain't taking it,' Lynx repeated. 'It's not for me.'

If Llaith had anything more to say on the subject he was beaten to the punch by Payl exiting the inn. The woman had her pack and mage-gun slung over her shoulder, while the company quartermaster, Foren, followed close behind her.

'Finish up, boys and girls,' she announced. 'Fetch your kit and muster outside in five. I don't expect you to be able to march like real soldiers, but anyone not at the Dawn Dock when we're ready to leave loses any pay owed to them, get me?'

The mercenaries scrambled to obey and Payl stepped aside to let them pour through the door. She gave Llaith a small smile and a nod.

'You too, old man,' Payl called over the clatter of feet. 'You don't want to miss Toil's surprises.'

'Surprises? More than one?'

Her smile widened. 'Oh, she's got a couple up her sleeve. Thought you knew that by now?'

Chapter 3

The city of Su Dregir sat on both sides of a hill overlooking a flattened horseshoe bay on the eastern shore of Parthain, one of the continent's great inland seas. The stepped districts of the shore-side saw none of the morning sun this early so the rooftops and gutters remained edged in frost as Anatin's Mercenary Deck shambled down the street.

The Dawn Dock was the further corner of Su Dregir bay, a longer walk than anyone wanted but it was the deepest water so there the largest ships docked. A high sea wall extended the line of the bay almost up to the small fortress island that guarded the bay's inlet and it was clear their path was leading them along the wall's inner face to a single tall ship. They continued on their winding way down through the dock district and across a humped stone bridge. A long wind-swept avenue ran around the southern edge of the bay, skirted by a shallow pebble beach that tailed away as they reached the sea wall.

The grey flag of Su Dregir flying from the ship's mast, a lighthouse rising from a crown of green glass, was plain for all to see in the sparkle of morning sun. It told enough of a story to set the mercenaries chattering like excited schoolchildren. Lynx tried to peer over heads to see what was going on at the front, where Anatin and Toil led the company. Everyone carried their own kit so he guessed they weren't taking their wagons on board to use on the other side.

'We're going somewhere on Parthain?' he said out loud to those near him, the suit of Tempest as usual bringing up the rear in their column.

'Looks like it,' Llaith said through a puff of cigarette smoke. 'More interesting question is, are those flags anything to do with us or are we just making up the space on someone else's voyage?'

'Both,' Teshen, sergeant of the suit, confirmed. 'You'll see soon enough.'

Llaith scowled. 'Are we going to like the answer?'

The Knight looked back, his smile half-hidden by a veil of sandy hair. 'Put it this way, you won't hate it as much as some.'

'Oh great.'

A painted white plaque on the tall ship's stern proclaimed it *Veraimin's Beacon*. No great surprise there, Lynx realised, given the city's lighthouse emblem and throwing in the Sun God for good measure. Walking down the dock towards the ship, the Cards passed a small procession of robed figures coming the other way – a deputation from the temple of Ulfer, lord of earth and sea.

The priestess led the way; a straight-backed elderly woman in green and white, behind whom trailed half a dozen novices in green. Each novice carried one aspect required for the blessing ceremony that many journeys began with – rushes, a prayer mat, jars of honey and consecrated water, a now-extinguished torch and a thurible still leaking a thin trail of pungent, earthy smoke.

As they reached the ship, Lynx could see that supplies were still being loaded by a dozen shiphands. More interestingly, there was also a carriage to one side of the gangway. Four soldiers in the grey and green uniform of the Archelect's own Lighthouse Guard waited beside it on horseback. They were a strange mix, Lynx realised, as they came closer – all natives of the city, but not quite so neatly ceremonial as the handsome black horses and maroon carriage, freshly painted and sporting shining hammered brass.

The company shuffled to a halt at Payl's command and Anatin called out to the nearest of the soldiers, a tall officer with a hawk nose and weak chin. 'Captain Onerist?'

The captain seemed to puff out his chest as he stepped forward. 'That I am,' he replied stiffly. 'You are Commander Anatin?'

'At your service.'

'The Envoy is aboard,' Onerist announced, 'speaking to the ship's captain. I will conduct you to him later. These are . . .' The man gestured back at the other soldiers and seemed to hesitate as though needing to remind himself. 'These are my men. We will be in sole charge of the Envoy's security unless I direct you otherwise. The rest of the Envoy's staff and servants are already aboard, have your men keep clear of them. Your company is to accompany us to, ah, to our destination and remain on standby should I require your services.'

The three he seemed unsure about dismounted too, one ambling over with little military precision, while the other two hung back. The bolder man was a big, barrel-chested soldier with thick black curls and an easy smile. Behind him came a thin, awkward and bespectacled man in an ill-fitting uniform, and a small blonde woman who didn't look much more like a soldier but moved with considerably more grace. The big one was perhaps a little younger than Lynx, the other two almost a decade shy.

'Very good, sir,' Anatin replied in a drily obsequious tone which the captain appeared oblivious to.

'I will fetch the first mate to direct you and inform the Envoy of your arrival. Have your men on board and squared away as fast as you can, captain.'

'That I will, sir.'

As Captain Onerist headed stiffly up the gangway, Anatin gave a snort and turned his back.

'Right, you lazy murdering sods,' he yelled to his assembled troops. 'First things first, we're going on a trip and you're all going to behave. We've been hired as escort for one Senator Ammen of this fair city, who's off to be an official Envoy of Su Dregir. It's the usual sort of escort duty, most of you have done it before and it's easy money so no dicking around, understand? That means no throwing sailors in the sea, Reft, no hanging men by their ankles off the sail, Brols, and no gelding of *anyone*, Braqe, okay?'

Lynx nodded to himself as a few sniggers and low comments came from the troops. Few cities had significant standing armies and, especially when sending delegations to other city-states, it was not deemed politic to assign them a troop of professional soldiers given the havoc a small number could wreak. Keeping a contingent of mercenaries in the vicinity and on retainer was actually considered less hostile, given few people trusted secret plans to mercs.

'Second – we're a Knight short. For the time being Estal's in charge of Stars, but this is escort duty so we should be all keeping together anyway. Lastly, we've a new recruit and any kiddie in the class who don't make her feel welcome is a damn fool.'

He nodded his head towards Toil who looked briefly around at the company as though daring anyone to comment. Lynx caught a glimpse of a badge pinned to her jacket, but he couldn't see the details – only that it was a red card, either the suit of Sun or Blood.

Up ahead, though, the mercenaries had a better look and a mutter of surprise soon raced around the company. Several turned towards the hairless white head of Reft, the Knight of Blood, towering over the troops, but the silent mercenary didn't deign to notice.

Anatin looked over to the ship to see a bald man starting down the gangway, presumably the first mate, so he continued quickly.

'Nothing changes as far as any of you are concerned so keep your gossipy traps shut, keep out the way of the sailor people, and try not to shoot holes in the bottom of the boat. And don't win all their money at cards until our destination is close enough to swim to. Any questions, keep 'em to your fucking selves.'

Teshen turned back to his small suit of mercenaries and gave them a cold grin, lingering on Lynx for reasons he didn't like.

'Want to know her card? Read as much as you like into it, or none at all so long as you act like it's fine and normal, okay?'

'Let me guess,' Lynx said with mounting trepidation. 'She's the Princess of Blood, isn't she?'

'Got it in one.' The grey-eyed man's smile widened, shark-like. 'You won't be the only one doing what she wants now, we all got that pleasure.'

As the first mate reached Anatin and they started to talk, Lynx cast his eye over the ship. He knew little about them, having sailed only a handful of times in his life. The continent of Urden had several inland seas like Parthain, but the ocean surrounding it was a barrier few attempted. With wind mages it was possible to brave the storms, but the distances were vast and the rewards few, while even the largest of the arrow-straight Duegar canals that spanned the continent required only barges.

Shuttered window ports ran all the way down the steel-plate-clad flank of the ship and there were pairs of fixed guns fore and aft, bolted down to withstand the force of firing earth-bolts. A sling-thrower sat behind the fore pair for hurling grenades. Icers were the only mage-cartridge with a useful range and they couldn't stop a boat, but a grenade could be hurled far beyond the range of sparkers or burners since the magic only activated on impact. Whether as a statement to the other city-states on Parthain or a response to piracy on the sea, in his limited experience Lynx had never seen a more overtly armed ship.

Soon the Cards were being herded on to the deck, past the watchful eyes of the ship's crew, and into one of two large rooms strung with hammocks. A flight of steps led to the lower deck where they stowed their bags and secured their guns and ammunition in the armoury. Few mercenaries liked seeing their weapons locked away, but they all knew that any loose cartridge could end up sinking the ship.

'You'll be assigned to watch teams,' the first mate called to the company at large, 'stationed on deck at the guns. If you're caught with a gun or cartridge at any other time, you go over the side. No exceptions.' He pointed at Lynx. 'You, that sword gets locked away too, and any others like it. Nothing bigger'n an eating knife or you get a flogging. I've had mercs on board before and I know what you people are like when it comes to blades. I don't want any o' my crew getting stuck over nothing.'

Lynx looked down at the falchion hanging at his hip and shrugged as he unbuckled it. The heavy chopping blade wouldn't be so useful on a rolling deck anyway so he didn't bother to argue. Soon the variety of bayonets, hatchets and short-swords the mercenaries carried were all stowed away and locked up by the mate after he'd checked each cartridge box was secure.

Lynx went back up to the deck just in time to hear the order to cast off. Most of the mercenaries filed up with him to watch the ship slip beneath the huge arch of Su Dregir's harbour bay. Before it a shoal of fishing boats scattered and, once they were clear, the main sails were unfurled and began to haul the ship forward. Lynx looked around, surprised at the strength of the breeze, only to find Toil had slipped up beside him.

'Looking forward to a bit of adventure?' she asked.

'Mostly just wondering how we caught the wind so fast.'

She nodded back to the aftcastle where Captain Onerist and the rest of his command stood behind a knot of finely dressed figures. Two were dressed like ship's officers, three others like rich passengers, with Anatin on the fringes but clearly part of the conversation. Lynx guessed the fatter of the two men he didn't know was the Envoy – a large man with a pale, fleshy face and a cloth cap.

'Our ship's captain is an impatient woman,' she said. 'See the tall, dark woman?'

'That's the captain?' Lynx asked, confused. The woman wore a sleeveless pale blue coat, tied with a red sash and edged with fur, a mass of hair fluttering in the wind held back by a band that kept it from her eyes.

'No, the one in the stupid hat's the captain, next to her. The other one's more valuable.'

Lynx gasped. 'A wind mage?'

'Yup – this ship's too big and expensive to risk a drop in the wind. They've got a mage on permanent crew.'

'Damn, all this for one man?'

Toil laughed at that. 'Why waste the opportunity for a little showing off to the neighbours? The Envoy has to get there somehow.'

'And where's that? For that matter, why're you on board? You're not the Envoy's bodyguard, so what's your angle here?'

'Oh, Lynx, haven't you learned yet? I've no fewer than six or seven angles at any given time.'

'Care to share any of them?'

'But what if you don't approve?' Toil said, feigning coyness.

'When's that ever stopped you?'

She cocked her head to one side. 'Best you don't know, in case *you* tried to stop me. But here's a titbit for you – this isn't really escort duty. You're under my command, whatever Captain Inbred thinks. Where we're going, if I'm right, life's about to get pretty nasty and I aim to offer your services.'

'How nasty?'

'Like you'll wish you were back underground.' She saw him stiffen at the reminder. 'Yeah, I reckon even *you*.'

'Oh blackest hells.'

Just then Anatin strode down from the aftcastle and walked the length of the main deck.

'Boys and girls,' he called, with a wide grin on his face. 'I bring good news.'

No one replied, they all knew his humour well enough for trepidation to still their tongues.

'Our destination, my feeble and sickly cadre, will cleanse your souls and purge your bodies of the demons that, as I noted this very morning, you all seem to be plagued with.'

Lynx heard a few angry mutters from behind him, clearly one or two of the company hazarding a guess at what he was about to say. Anatin pointed past him to where Varain stood, the veteran's reddened cheeks deepening in colour.

'Indeed, I see the Stranger of Sun has caught on. No need to thank me for this boon to your health, my friend!'

'Are you fucking serious?' Varain growled.

'I am! We sail to the Jewel of Parthain, Shrine of the Inner Seas and grand old lady of the Ongir Canal.'

Lynx had to suppress a laugh as he finally cottoned on. *Grand old lady* was a term he knew and it didn't just refer to the city's age. It also meant the pious attitude of its rulers and the restrictions they placed upon the population. He'd heard some call the place 'nagging old crone of Parthain'.

'Yes, my friends, we sail to Jarrazir – City of a Thousand Shrines, two bloody big statues, one possibly mythical labyrinth—'

'But not even one fucking pub!' Varain snapped.

Anatin laughed. 'But not even one fucking pub,' he agreed. 'Now you see why I didn't tell you until you'd been disarmed.'

*

Tucked into a nook on the forecastle and facing back down the boat, Sitain put one arm out over the side and let the breeze drift through her fingers. This was now her second voyage on a ship and still it bewildered and unsettled her even as it fascinated. The constant pitch and movement, the lurch in her stomach and the treachery of the shifting deck – it all left her on edge, never quite able to rest.

She'd fallen into a fitful sleep the first night, swaying alarmingly in a hammock and for most of the morning had been glassy-eyed and monosyllabic. And yet . . . Her gaze drifted out over the water again as the sun emerged from behind a cloud.

Every crest of wave glinted gold then faded in the next instant to be replaced by a thousand others, darting elusively away as her eyes followed each wink of light. The water itself was a deep and rich blue, a shifting, shining sapphire that stretched as far as the eye could see.

They travelled within sight of land at all times, their journey taking them up the coast rather than across Parthain. She had already seen huge wheeling flocks of white seabirds, some mere specks in the sky, while others punched like icers down into the water in search of the fish below. Pebble beaches with brown basking seals lying below slanting lines of blue-black slate cliffs. Tiny shelves of pink wild flowers perched above hammering waves that cast columns of spray twenty yards straight up – she drank in the sights and left the world behind her.

Except she found she couldn't. Time and again her mind brought her back. Time and again her eyes turned towards the aftcastle where the first mate stood with a hand on the ship's wheel. Behind him stood one of the junior officers, a young lad apparently taking measurements of some sort, one of the Envoy's personal guards – and the wind mage.

Sitain sensed movement at her back and leaned into the side to give them space to pass, but felt the person stop directly behind instead. Whoever it was, they stood over Sitain a few moments, looking down at the water below.

'Are those elementals?' Toil asked, pointing down.

Sitain heaved herself up to look over, but knew instinctively they weren't. Water elementals were a more common sight than most, but she would have sensed their presence if any had been so close to the ship. No more than ten yards off the port side a half-dozen dark shapes slipped through the water, not breaking the surface and keeping up with the ship with no apparent effort.

'Just fish,' she sighed, sinking back down.

'Big bloody fish,' Toil commented.

'Yup.'

Sitain felt a strong hand close on her shoulder and squeeze it. 'What's up your arse today, Sitain?'

'Nothing. Just didn't sleep well.' She scowled. 'Why do you care? Not like I've got any duties right now.'

''Cos you're staring, girl.'

'What?'

Toil snorted. 'Not very subtly either. Someone on the rear deck owe you money?'

Sitain looked away, a guilty flush pinking her cheeks. 'I, ah, no. It's nothing.'

'If it was nothing, you wouldn't be staring. Come now, tell Auntie Toil.'

Despite her mood, that made Sitain laugh. She turned round and squinted up at the woman from Su Dregir. 'Auntie of Blood, eh?'

'You ain't met my aunt, it's not so far off as you might like.'

Sitain hesitated and took a proper look at Toil. She didn't know the woman well, most likely few did, but the days they'd spent in the Duegar city-ruin and the weeks that followed meant there was a familiarity there at least. *And now we're comrades-in-arms, apparently.*

'You're a well-travelled woman,' she began hesitantly, 'I mean, you've been all over, right?'

'I suppose so. No more than most of this lot.' Toil gestured at the mercenaries on the deck behind them, at the ship's guns. 'But I think you mean that I've done more than kill, drink and screw in all the places I've been to, done more than just look to the next bottle.' Her eyes twinkled. 'I've also done a lot of those three, mind.'

'Yeah, I know,' Sitain sighed, 'you're as much a man as the rest of these swinging dicks.'

At that, Toil laughed. 'Hey, it doesn't pay to advertise a brain,' she said. 'Dumbshit mercenaries and the like aren't in favour of women being smarter than them; especially one who's as strong as them too. Best they think I'm a mad killer with the same limitations as them – gives them something to understand, so they don't look for any more.'

'But you know the way of the world.'

'From what Anatin's been telling everyone, you're way past *that* talk.'

Sitain made a disgusted sound. 'Ah, fine, forget I asked.'

Toil raised her hand in apology and sat down on the deck beside Sitain, slipping her feet under the rail that ran down the inside edge of the forecastle. 'Sorry, force of habit. What do you want to ask?'

Sitain was quiet for a long while, but eventually she found her attention drifting to the aftcastle again. 'Wind mages, know much about them?'

Toil tucked an errant curl of brown hair behind her ear. 'Some. One of the free trades, so you get more of them around. I've met a few over the years. They're not chatty as a rule, but if you live on Parthain and travel a lot, you come across them.'

'They're not tied to the Charnelers?'

'Ah, I think I see what you're getting at. Charnelers? I doubt it. On the other hand, as for some Order dedicated to Ulfer, Knight of the Fist and the like, there's a good chance. Their magic might not have so much military use given wind-cartridges aren't likely to kill, but if you've got a policy of enslaving useful folk, why be overly picky?'

'But they're free to travel?'

'Aye, but have you ever met a young one? Those water and wind mages who ply the seas and canals, they've got to grow up somewhere. There are a few guild-houses and the like, but they're rare. Only the stone mages have one of any significant size. The Orders gather every mage they can on general principle, as you yourself know. Some will never leave the ammunition factories – sorry, Sanctuaries of the Divinely Blessed – but the ones with "trade magics" come out with a good education and, likely, a deep-rooted loyalty to the Order. I've no idea how many of those I've met are Order trained, but I wouldn't trust one with my secrets.'

'Right.'

'Not what you wanted to hear?'

'Not really. I . . .' Sitain tailed off and looked out to sea again.

'Looking for someone to teach you?'

'Or just someone to ask a few questions, someone who'd know what it felt like.'

'Sorry, not an easy hand you've been dealt. My advice, for what it's worth, is to keep it all close to your chest. Bad enough the rest of the company knows if you ask me.'

'That's a cheery thought.'

'Cheery doesn't keep a woman alive, so keep your eyes open and mind working. Collect your pay and be ready to drop the company at a moment's notice.' Toil smiled. 'You and Lynx are more alike than you might think.'

'Now you really are depressing me.'

'Just don't eat so much as him and you'll be fine. He owns only what he can carry, never stays in one place too long. Live your life ready to walk away, plan for it, and you'll never be caught out.'

'And that's how you live?' Sitain asked, faintly horrified by the casual way Toil had said it.

'Of a fashion. I've got a few ties that complicate it.'

'Family? Guess I don't have that. I'll never see mine again.'

'You think?' Toil gave her a fierce smile. 'I'm not so sure. You prove yourself to Anatin, make him value you. In a year or two you'll likely be passing by that way. Might be you could wander into your village with a rich coat, a gun on your shoulder and a few of the Cards at your side. No company badges, of course, or distinctive faces like Lynx's, but descriptions of a few bastards like Varain aren't going to help the Charnelers. By then I'm sure everyone in the village'll know who informed on you. Could be you have a little chat with the treacherous shite as you look in on your folks; make anyone think twice about causing 'em trouble.'

Sitain felt the breath catch in her throat.

'That, I think I might enjoy,' she said, nodding slowly.

'Good. In the meantime, mouth shut, eyes open. Don't get noticed, don't get caught. And for Banesh's sake, learn to bloody shoot straight.'

Chapter 4

Lynx looked down at his cards, trying to ignore Anatin's slyly smug expression and the cloud of cigar-smoke being puffed in his direction. He'd learned the mercenary commander had a thousand faces when playing Tashot and all of them were irritating. It was his company after all, his word that commanded forty-odd guns, so driving his opponents to distraction was a long-standing practice.

'I don't like his chances, my princess,' Anatin commented as he watched Lynx. 'Think there's something of a tempest in our Stranger's thoughts.'

Tonight he'd decided to narrate the game to Toil, who sat beside him. The woman wasn't playing, electing to repair a shirt – of all things – and relying on her fearsome reputation to dissuade any jokes. More Cards stood behind and watched, but Toil was the only one of seven at the low table not playing. Again that had gone unquestioned, which to Lynx's mind proved even rats had a sense of preservation.

Next she produced the cloth badge bearing her Princess of Blood card, one made with more artistry than most worn by the company, and began to stitch that on to her jacket. It bore a rather more refined image than the one on the cards they were playing with – a crowned woman all in red, her hair hanging down over her right side. A cuirass with red teardrop shapes replaced the bared breasts that mercenaries preferred, but the usual mage-pistol and stiletto combination remained in her hands.

Teshen was dealer as usual; the burly man hunched low over the deck with his hair half-obscuring his face. Four cards lay face up, a fifth face down and off to one side to appease the god Banesh. Of what there was on view – 16 of Stars, 11 of Snow, 7 of Blood, Jester of Snow – none of them did Lynx much good after a promising start. He held two Madmen in his hand.

Chances are, no one's got much with that lot. 'Okay, I'll raise.'

'Oho, man doesn't like to hang around,' Anatin said. 'Anyone would think he's on watch soon.'

Damn, I forgot about that.

'How about you, Safir?'

'Gambling is a profanity in the eyes of the gods,' Safir intoned, 'and sinners shall be cast into the uncertain depths between worlds.'

'That means he's got a shit hand,' Anatin whispered to Toil theatrically, 'he'll fold.'

'I raise.'

Anatin winked. 'Also means he can be talked into playing a bad hand.'

'The gods hate me already,' Safir announced as though replying to Anatin. 'Might as well rub salt into the wound and profit from the failings of others.'

'So now we've got a game,' Anain said. 'Lynx is hurrying us up, Safir's feeling maudlin and reckless, Himbel's miserable which means he's got a decent pair at least, Reft's out, and Varain's constipated and keeps forgetting his cards. Lastly, there is our scholarly soldier – who's either marking cards and about to get his face shot off, or wondering what order the noble cards run in again.'

'These cards are all marked,' the last player said in a distracted voice, twitching in surprise at the growl he got from the other side of the table.

'Now that's a dangerous accusation.'

The man blinked at Anatin through his round spectacles as though only now registering who he was talking to. He was one of the Envoy's personal guard, the awkward one who looked as intimidating as a drunk toddler.

'Is it? Why?'

Toil leaned forward, pausing in her sewing to fix the man with a hard look. 'I think Corporal Paranil is making an observation rather than an acccusation, correct?'

The man blinked at her. 'Certainly, correct, ah – Princess Toil.'

'Just Toil.'

'Right, of course. But yes, all I meant was that regular use and a certain lack of hygiene has left a distinctive pattern on certain cards, albeit a faint one.'

'Calling us dirty now?' Anatin asked.

The corporal looked down at his own hands, which were certainly cleaner than those of the mercenaries he sat with. 'Ah, simply that the daily requirements of your profession impose certain—'

'You don't sound like any corp I ever met,' Anatin interrupted.

'I don't?'

'Nope.'

The man paused. 'Well I am, I assure you. I have the little marks on my coat to prove it. If you dispute the fact, please take it up with Captain . . . ah, my commanding officer.' He blinked at the mercenaries, who all looked like cats watching a mouse lecture them. 'In fact, it's not your place to question my rank at all. I am not under your command at all so what opinion—'

'Relax.' This time it was Toil interrupting. 'He's just messing with you.'

'I was?' Anatin asked.

'Yeah, you were. Now back to the game, kids.'

'What about the cards?' Teshen interjected. 'They're not far off new.'

'Still there is certain marking, general wear and tear. That one, for example,' Paranil said, pointing at one on the table in front of Anatin. 'There's a slight curl to the edge and a finger-stain. I had the card in the first hand, it's the Jester of Tempest.'

Anatin's lip curled slightly and Himbel let out a long, loud groan of irritation. With a baleful look Teshen swept all the cards back in from under the hands of the players and gathered them up together. Without saying a word he rose and went to the gunwale and tossed the whole pack over the side.

'You owe me a new deck,' he informed Paranil.

'Why, none of the rest of you saw the patterns?'

Teshen grabbed the man by the shirt and hauled him up close. 'Not until you pointed it out, but no bloody point using the cards after that, is there?'

'Ah.'

'You know, I've met a few educated corporals in my time,' Anatin mused, 'and a few with eyes as sharp as yours, but none so gods-howling clueless.'

Paranil opened his mouth to reply but before he could say anything a bell rang out over the deck.

'Watch change!' barked the second mate from the rear of the deck. 'Shift yourselves!'

As Lynx reached for the pot where their stakes had been put he raised an eyebrow at Anatin. The commander made no comment so Lynx took his game stake back and left the table.

The afternoon was well advanced by the time he reached his station, the sun slipping behind looming herds of cloud drawing in from further out to sea. A haze lay over the water ahead, rendering the horizon an uncertain shapeless grey. Already it reached its tendrils over the water towards them as though readying for an embrace.

Sitain was already positioned beside one gun placement with Braqe, Lynx's least-favourite member of Tempest, at another. Since they had returned from Shadows Deep, Braqe hadn't got in his face much, which was a relief. From their first few meetings, Lynx had assumed one of them would end up killing the other because of Lynx's past, but she'd been careful to avoid him ever since they'd escaped the caverns.

He guessed Teshen had had a serious word in her ear. The dark woman glowered every time Lynx was forced to speak to her, just in case he'd been foolish enough to think anything had changed, but the imminent prospect of violence had lifted, at least.

'Mist coming in?' he asked Layir, who'd been in charge of the last watch.

'Fast too,' the young man confirmed. 'You won't have much to look at for the next few hours.'

Layir wore the 14 of Snow and was, to all intents and purposes, Safir's son. Lynx hadn't got the full story there, but Safir had travelled west with the infant Layir for reasons best not asked about and had lived as his father ever since. Now Layir was seventeen years old and fast catching his adoptive father in both size and skill with the rapier, but it was the box hung around Layir's neck that Lynx was focused on.

'The watch is yours,' Layir said ceremoniously, lifting the rope strap over his head and handing the box to Lynx. 'All guns loaded.'

Lynx nodded and accepted it. The box was heavy, with steel sheets riveted to the wooden structure, but he didn't object to that when it contained half a dozen grenades and thirty-odd cartridges in padded compartments.

'The watch is mine,' he confirmed.

Lynx looked around at the fellow Tempests who were on watch under his command – Braqe, Flinth and Tunnest – and manned the guns with Sitain. She was a member of Sun but was making up the numbers. Lynx had a suspicion it was also a reminder from Anatin that she was still his responsibility, rank or no rank. Flinth was a quiet woman with a steady manner, Tunnest a brash olive-skinned youth a few years older than Layir but lacking any of the other's maturity.

The afternoon progressed slowly and continued dull and overcast. The only thing worth looking at was a passing merchantman that kept a respectful distance as it hugged the coast, the stink of salt and seaweed thick on the breeze. As he settled on the gunner's bench at the very front of the foredeck Lynx realised there was little to see now as the faint outline of the coast had faded to nothing in the distance.

Their ship turned slightly further out to sea as he stood his watch, to ensure a clear run through the mist, but from what he'd heard from the crew the captain knew the route and her charts well enough that the precaution was barely necessary. The haze continued to thicken, however, and as he stared into the uncertain bank of grey the ship's bell rang again, five swift clangs.

'What's that?' Sitain asked as they all looked back down the deck to the aftcastle. Sailors scurried about with sudden urgency and the second mate began barking orders down through a hatch. More busied themselves under the sails, trimming them to slow the ship.

'Gunner?' Lynx asked as a man in black scampered up the steps to the forecastle.

'Five strikes of the bell means beat to quarters!' the man snapped. 'Keep clear and be ready with ammunition.'

'Eyes on the water,' Lynx said to his command. 'What's going on?'

'Fog's come on fast,' the gunner said as he unshipped the ties around the grenade thrower and started winding the mechanism that powered it. 'Too fast – might be natural but we don't take chances.'

'Pirates?'

'Some have ice mages,' he said with a curt nod. 'Can't face us at range unless we're outnumbered, but they can close under cover of fog once we cut speed. First mate'll be pulling your guns out now.'

Lynx nodded, watching the man work as a second sailor appeared and joined in. The grenade thrower was a sort of small catapult with a sling fitting on the end. The whole contraption was bolted to a platform that could be turned to face in most directions except back towards the sails.

'We can't push on through? Go fast and blind to get past it?'

'Not in these waters, even as good as the captain is with her charts.'

The mist tightened like a spider's web around the ship, a gauze shroud creeping closer until Lynx could see just a few dozen yards. Without warning the ship turned, a sharp move that made him stumble and clutch at the rail.

'There'll be more,' the gunner warned him.

Lynx nodded and dropped to one knee, his free arm wrapped protectively around the ammunition box. As predicted, another turn came half a minute later, then a third to correct and put them roughly back on course. At the aftcastle the junior officers were working frantically and barking figures at each other, keeping a track of their speed and direction. It could be pirates, he knew, or wreckers hoping to drive them on to rocks. Sitting dead in the water wasn't an enticing prospect; better they trusted to seamanship and kept moving.

In contrast to the captain and her officers, one figure appeared serene – the wind mage. Lynx watched her stand apart from the others. She was watching the sky as though searching for a scent.

'Our mage don't seem to be doing a lot about it,' Lynx commented.

'She's waiting,' the gunner said. 'Won't use her strength 'less she has to.'

'Why? She could sweep all this away.'

The man shrugged and nodded off towards the water. 'You reckon I know more about magic'n you? This is how she works. If you don't like it there's the side, get off any time you like.'

The hammer of boots on the main deck interrupted them, two dozen Cards racing out into the open with mage-guns in their hands. Under the first mate's instructions the Knights led their units to their designated areas of the ship while a detachment of crew carrying small barrels escorted a man with an ammunition case like Lynx's to the stern.

'Barrels?'

'Bomb-barrels,' the gunner said. 'Tricky li'l things, but we can't throw grenades behind us. Ship's deck ain't a good place to use a hand-held thrower.'

'You shoot at the barrels?'

'The other buggers have to do that! Gives 'em something to worry about if they're following us. The barrel bangs into something too hard and the grenade pin gets slammed against the side – they don't work too well, but they're real nasty when they do.' He gave Lynx a nasty grin. 'One ship I served on had a water mage and the bugger could zig-zag their bomb-barrels all the way into the side of an enemy boat.'

Lynx watched the men and women of Sun take up shooting positions down the starboard side of the main deck, Safir's Snow troops filing down the port side. Teshen led Stars and the rest of Tempest up to fill the forecastle, everyone kneeling at the rail before they loaded their guns. Toil and Reft went to the aftcastle with the mercenaries of Blood, while the sailors took to the rigging or stood ready on the main deck to await orders.

All the while the noose of mist contracted around them; it was now beyond all likelihood that this could be natural. Lynx felt a tap on his elbow and realised Teshen was passing him his weapons. He nodded his thanks then looked to the rear of the ship, hoping to get a sense of what was going to happen next.

Some sort of exchange went on between captain and mage, the words lost to Lynx, but he could tell they were waiting. The mercenaries and crew followed their lead, each one watching the curtain of mist in the hope – or fear – of seeing something through it.

'Heave to or be sunk!' came a distant shout that made more than a few of Tempest flinch. Lynx turned to face forward, thinking the call had come from that direction, but the mist made it difficult to gauge.

'Heave to or be sunk!' added another deeper voice from somewhere off the port side.

'How the shit can they see us?' someone behind Lynx muttered.

'They can't,' the gunner replied in a whisper loud enough for them all to hear, 'they just know their waters and know their mage.'

'What now, then?'

'Now we see what our mage can do. It's a waiting game, can't fire blind without giving our position away.'

'WHO CALLS?' roared a man's voice from the rear of the ship. Lynx turned and realised it was the Envoy of Su Dregir.

Standing beside the captain he looked a tall and imposing figure, with a barrel body and not much older than Lynx, so likely there was some real strength in that frame.

Under the captain's hand, the ship began to turn, not much but enough to edge to starboard, away from the second voice.

'Heave to!' the second voice yelled again, the splash of oars briefly reaching Lynx's ears as they sought to keep up with the ship.

'I AM SENATOR ELTRIS AMMEN, BARON AND HIGH ENVOY OF SU DREGIR!' came the reply. 'SINK US AND THE ARCHELECT WILL SCOUR THIS SEA OF PIRATES!'

'Someone's got a high opinion of himself,' Braqe muttered, away on Lynx's right.

'No law on Parthain!' the voice yelled, slightly fainter than before. It sounded a well-used line to Lynx's ears, no doubt the mantra of pirates. They had a point too, he realised. No city was strong enough to impose its law on the water, or the wilds beyond their boundaries, and these pirates wouldn't be sailing easily identified galleons, but boats that spent most of the year as a fishing fleet.

'Get ready,' hissed the gunner, checking back at the aftcastle.

Almost as soon as he spoke the ship began to turn harder, swinging away from the voice. As it did the breeze stiffened, surging up from the rear of the ship to whip across the tips of the waves and drive at the curtain of mist surrounding it.

Lynx watched in fascination as a corridor started to open in the mist, the chill air fading as the wind mage cast her hand towards it and growling gusts tore forth. Above her the sails danced and stretched at the fitful bursts of wind, but steadily the mist was parted and the ship turned into their avenue of escape.

Before they had gone far the chill in the air started to deepen, the cold magic of the pirate mage seeking to renew the cage around them. It wasn't enough, though, and the first of several boats emerged from the gloom, at first insubstantial but swiftly resolving into the real. A second appeared almost immediately after the first, a third as they started to try and flee.

'Range?'

'Two hundred.'

The gunner sucked at his teeth and wound the tension of the grenade thrower, muttering the number of turns under his breath. 'Grenades.'

Lynx stepped forward and carefully withdrew three red-striped grenades from his box, handing them over to the gunner to place each in the special sling lying below the thrower's arm. Once he was satisfied each was correctly in place he took the pins and quickly primed each.

'Stand clear.'

They all stepped back, a few of the mercenaries watching the sling with a faint look of horror on their faces as the deck rose and fell. The rest were watching the boats as the pirate crews pulled around and tried to flee.

'Firing,' the gunner announced, pulling the lever a moment later.

Lynx flinched as the catapult arm slammed forward and whipped the sling end up and over. The grenades all flew high and vanished into the mist as the thrower bucked and heaved like an enraged animal. They all held their breath as they waited for the grenades to fall, knowing there was always a chance they would land in a way that the pin wasn't forced into the magic-charged core, sinking instead of exploding.

Without warning there was a flash of light, followed almost immediately by the crack of an explosion that boomed out across the waves. A smear of fire spread across the water's surface, then a second burst some way to the right of it. The second caught the nearest boat and smashed into its flank with a hammer-blow. The side of the boat caved in and fire washed over the handful of pirates inside. If there were screams Lynx didn't hear them, but he caught the flash of movement as people dived overboard.

'There's one,' called Tunnest, his face coming alive as he half-stood and pointed out through the mist.

Lynx turned but couldn't make much out through the gloom, even as Teshen grunted his agreement.

'Where?'

Even as he asked Lynx caught a glimpse of a grey line of shadow lifting on the water and the outline of a small sail.

'Can we fire?'

'You won't hit at that range,' the gunner scoffed. 'Three hundred yards off a ship's deck?'

'Try me,' Teshen said, his usual cold assurance making the gunner hesitate. In that moment there came whistles from the rigging where the lookouts were stationed, mage-guns strapped to them.

In reply the ship's bell rang twice.

'Hold your fire,' the gunner relayed.

They all kept silent now, Teshen and two others keeping the boat in their sights while the rest scanned the flanks, hoping to spot any more pirate ships before they could close the distance enough to punch a hole in the ship's flank. Both earthers and burners had a short range, but could be devastating. Any fool with a gun could kill them all if they got close enough.

Above their heads the wind grew steadily stronger, lifting the mist as it drove it back. The mage didn't seem to be overly taxed by the work, but as Lynx watched the hundred-yard curtain driven back he realised it was unlikely anyone could keep it up for long.

As the mist receded further the full sails were unfurled again and the ship began to pick up speed. More boats were glimpsed off the bows, but even with three peals of the ship's bell signalling they were allowed to fire, the targets weren't worth the shot at that range through fog.

Just then Lynx felt a chill on his face and sensed the clouds loom once more around them, drawing in from their port side.

'Mage,' the gunner announced, readying his catapult to fire again. 'Must be ahead of us, trying to escape.'

In response the ship's mage gave a shout of effort and the steady wind rose to a tumult that whipped up the peaks of the waves and tore curling strips from the mist. Lynx kept his eyes to the front, waiting for something to shoot as the air grew wintery. He realised the gunner was right – the pirate mage was desperate now, throwing all their magic into a last bid to escape. That much he didn't care about, but the heaving sea was not where he wanted to die. A tightness appeared in his chest for a moment as he imagined the chill, dark depths closing around him. Fighting the feeling he pulled the stock of his gun harder against his shoulder and kept scanning.

At last they saw the boat, a sleek-lined craft with a pair of oars heaving away at each side and a straining sail above. The gunner fired long, over their heads and only serving to disrupt their rhythm, but by that point the Cards had decided it was time to get involved.

Given free rein, the report of icers began to crack out across the water. Lynx measured his shots as best he could, but it was a tough task to shoot a shifting target while standing atop another. Teshen had the best luck, his second shot punching high into the side of the boat. Again the mage tried to envelop them in a concealing mist, but the wind mage redoubled her efforts. The captain didn't turn the ship for a broadside from the remaining Cards yet, still cutting the distance between the vessels, while several more shots from Tempest's forward guns punctured the boat ahead.

As Lynx aimed another shot he felt a curl of wind on his cheek, warmer now with the taste of salt returning to the breeze. With a jolt he realised the cold emanating across the water had gone – either one of them had hit the mage or they'd just broken off, exhausted by their efforts.

'Eyes open on the flanks!' he yelled. 'Mist's clearing!'

Before anyone could ask why, there was a roar of effort from the wind mage and the air lashed down at the mist beyond them. In seconds it started to clear from all around, ribboned by the breeze and more boats appeared on their flanks. Lynx wasn't sure who was more surprised, pirates or prey, but it was the Cards who reacted.

The men and women of Snow fired first, so close together it sounded like one great detonation. Lynx glanced back and saw a boat only fifty yards away, just a crew of four all at their oars. One or two died in the volley, he guessed, and the rest would soon be gone as icers punched holes in the side of their boat. For good measure someone put an earther into them too – it caught the boat high in the prow, but with enough force to snap the beam and soon they were going down.

Moments later there were gunshots ringing out in all directions, the sailors running to Anatin's side of the deck to add their guns to the ragged volley at the other boats now visible, but all three were running and too far to pose much threat anyway. One or two shots came back the other way, but the white streaks troubled no one.

Further behind them there was still a bank of mist, though the fixed guns and Toil's troops were firing at something within it. More shots came out of the mist, but had little effect and before long the cloud of mist was left behind. Only a trio of what Lynx guessed were bomb-barrels remained in the ship's wake, falling further behind but still a good distance from the mist.

'Two mages?' Lynx wondered aloud.

'Aye,' the gunner agreed between puffs of breath as he cranked the grenade thrower back.

'Explains how they wrapped us up so neatly.'

Under the mage's efforts the ship surged forward and Lynx watched the wreckage of one boat drift past with no survivors visible.

'Enjoy the swim,' the gunner growled, spitting a gobbet of phlegm over the side of the boat. 'Good riddance to pirate scum.'

'S'pose so,' Teshen said enigmatically, looking out to sea a while longer before he stood. 'Right, fun's over, Cards. Clear your breaches, stow your cartridges, toss any spent ones.'

The Tempest mercenaries did as ordered, checking their ammunition was secure and raising their guns to see daylight down the barrels.

'Looks like the watch is yours again, Lynx,' Teshen continued once he was satisfied. He collected Lynx's gun and started back down to the main deck. 'Don't know about the rest of you, but all that killing's just fired me up. How about grappling practice?'

There was a collective groan.

'Hey, it's either that or one o' you lovely ladies takes me somewhere private to have your way with me.'

When there were no volunteers Teshen laughed. 'Right, grappling it is. Main deck in five, let's show the rest how it's done.'

*

Below decks, once the weapons had been safely accounted for and locked away, the cabins emptied rapidly. Few of the mercenaries spent any more time down there than they had to, the fug of unwashed bodies in the cramped, poorly lit rooms ensuring most kept to the decks. Deern had the narrow passages of the cargo hold to himself, so he thought, as he made his way from the briefly unattended galley with a sliver of salted bacon in his hand. Just as he passed the stacked water casks, though, a low whistle brought him up short.

Her face and newly stitched badge almost the only things visible in the gloom of the hold, Toil sat on a makeshift throne of boxes, a thin bottle in her hand.

'Want a drink?' she said.

'Celebrating?' Deern asked cautiously. The two weren't friends – he barely knew Toil – but he could sense she was a dangerous one. They had that much in common at least.

'Bored,' Toil replied. 'Don't know about you, but that fight was a bit too much foreplay for my liking. Didn't come good on its promise.'

'You wanted to go hand to hand on the deck?'

She shrugged. 'Like to get up close and personal myself, not take potshots from a distance then break off like a tease.' She took a swig from the bottle and offered it again. 'Reckon we're more of one mind there, eh?'

Deern raised an eyebrow. 'Give over, woman,' he scoffed, ignoring the bottle. 'Go play with your Hanese toy if you've got all worked up. I ain't playing your games.'

'Bah, Lynx doesn't see it quite the same way. Anyway, I just offered you a drink, nothing more.'

'Go tell your eyes that, 'cos they're making you look a fucking liar. And I doubt your jacket was unbuttoned so far earlier.'

'It's warmer down here than on deck. Still, more for me.'

Deern felt his mouth go dry as Toil deliberately raised the bottle above her head. She poured another shot of the clear spirit down into her mouth, a small amount trickling down her chin. She ran one finger down her neck to catch the errant trail then purposefully licked it clean. Deern found himself suddenly thirsty and very aware of the sweet scent of rum in the air.

'Okay, gimme some.'

She cocked her head at him for a moment then laughed and offered it over. 'Help yourself to a box,' Toil added, nodded at the pile beside her.

Deern eased himself down, fingers tight around the bottle in case this was some sort of ruse. He and Lynx weren't the best of friends, less so than the Hanese imagined even, and a lifetime of being a skinny, shorter-than-average mercenary meant he was always on his guard.

He couldn't help but sniff the rum gingerly before drinking, prompting another laugh from Toil, but then took a big swallow. As the fiery liquid slipped down his throat Deern sighed and half-closed his eyes, free hand resting by his knife just in case, but nothing happened and he relaxed a touch more.

Mebbe she does just want a quick screw. Doesn't sound like Lynx is giving her the goods, for some reason.

Deern looked Toil up and down. Her beauty didn't have the same effect on him as it did others in the company, but she was a muscular woman who walked with her head high – arrogance to some, but Deern couldn't stand meekness. Her reputation for danger only added to her allure. Word had it she'd been masquerading as a courtesan in Grasiel, but he couldn't square that image with the perfumed flowers Llaith was forever chasing. Toil was a blood-red rose perhaps, but her thorns were always on show.

I always liked a bit o' power under my hands, though it Deern thought as he considered her unbuttoned jacket and the glimpse of cleavage it revealed. *Just look at Reft, after all.*

'So what about you and Reft then?' Toil asked.

'What about us?'

She shrugged the question off and took another swig of rum. 'Nothing, not my business.'

'Reft an' I understand each other,' Deern said simply. 'Anything more is between us, and if you think I'm so dumb I'd mess with that understanding . . . well, then you ain't seen my boy angry.'

She gave a small laugh and nod. 'True enough. You're a man not afraid to take a chance, but that'd be pushing things.'

'Damn right. Mercs don't last long playin' the honourable fool. Might want to remind your boy Lynx that.' Deern almost reached out towards the bottle, resting suggestively between Toil's legs, before his own words brought him up short.

Nah – too fucking easy.

He eased his way up, letting his gaze drift from the bottle up to Toil's cleavage, then whipped his knives from his belt-sheaths.

'While you're at it, remind yourself I'm no damn fool,' Deern growled, glancing around in case anyone was creeping up on him. 'Sucker the rest o' this lot with that whole bottle-between-yer-legs routine, I ain't fuckin' buyin'.'

Toil tensed, hand moving to her own knife but not drawing yet. 'What are you on about?'

'You heard me.' He couldn't hear or see anyone, but every instinct screamed at Deern that he'd walked into something. Only indecision between fleeing and stabbing Toil kept him still. 'What is this? What do you want?'

'Oh sit down, you're just embarrassing yourself.'

'Reckon you're the one who's just been made ta look dumb. If you want a slice off that pretty face o' yours, keep at it.'

Quick as a flash Toil tossed the bottle forward, using the movement to buy enough time to get herself up and clear as she drew her knife. Deern batted the bottle away and moved left, not wanting to present a stationary target.

'There's the girl's true colours, behind the tits and smiles.'

'Funny, I was going to say the same about you,' Toil spat.

'Fuck you on about?'

'You and your little secret.'

'Eh?'

She edged back, comfortably out of knife range but with her blade still raised, and Deern relaxed a touch. Maybe she had something to say, maybe she was just fishing, but he was admitting to nothing, that was for damn sure.

'Best thing my dad ever taught me? To plan – to think long and hard, look at a problem from every direction. Mercs like you think I flounce around relying on tits and smiles and that's damn useful, but I'm a woman who likes a good plan.'

'Fuck's that got to do with me?'

''Cos you messed with my plan.' Toil straightened and lowered her knife. 'You didn't mean to, so you ain't dead already, but you fucked me over and that doesn't bring out my good side.' She held up a hand. 'Don't speak, don't say a thing. You deny it and I might run out of patience, so just listen.'

Deern felt a cold sensation down his spine.

Did Braqe talk? Shitting gods, why? She's in it up to her neck just like me and we got away with it. Okay so Ashis an' Olut died 'cos of us, but she weren't great friends with either and there's no guarantee things would've gone better anyway.

Toil nodded. 'The look on your face tells me you know what I'm on about. You were the only one who didn't come back when the company was cut loose in Grasiel, and after that, the Charnelers were on our backs all the way. Anatin didn't tell his sergeants the plan so he wouldn't have told you either, but like I said, I like to think long and hard about anything I do. It's how I stay alive. There's no way the Charnelers would've been so tight on us from the start unless someone meddled, no chance a gods-burned Exalted of the Torquen regiment just happened to be in the area. Elite troops like the Torquen don't exactly get lumbered with routine night patrols.'

'Starting ta sound paranoid here, Toil,' Deern broke in. 'You're chasing ghosts round and round in your head.'

She gave him a nasty grin as he spoke and his heart sank. 'Nope, sorry. Your Charneler friend sold you out, right at the end. I don't think the others noticed, but she said she didn't care about the Hanese and the girl by then, she only wanted me.' She pointed her knife at him, emphasising her point. 'She didn't *know* about me when she started out after us,' Toil hissed. 'She was after Lynx and Sitain! Someone sold 'em out

71

to the Charnelers before the operation went down – and that someone was you.'

'You call that proof?' Deern asked.

She shook her head. 'Nope, but I'm not going for a trial here so I don't need written proof. I know, understand me? I know you sold us out. By mistake, maybe, but all the same you almost killed us. And before you get any silly ideas, I don't work alone – I've told one or two folks who can be trusted not to overreact, in case of accidents at sea.'

'Not to overreact?' *Shit, not Lynx then.*

'I'm not here to kill you,' Toil said firmly. 'You'd not have seen me coming if that was the case.'

'Big words, especially with Reft on board.'

'Like I said, I'm a planner – all it takes is a little thought and preparation. But Reft's a consideration, yes, and so are you. You're a rat who sold out his new comrades. I just hope you got a good price for them, 'cos I now own you.'

'Eh?'

'You're a survivor, you said it yourself, and a man like that is useful. There's little room for honour in this game, and sometimes I need nasty and devious.'

'What do you want from me?'

She shook her head. 'Nothing yet. Nothing but you keeping your nose clean from now on. Anyone with their own agenda messes with my plans and I can't have that. You do so, or anything unfortunate happens to me, the best you can hope for is explaining to Anatin why he's missing one friend and one hand.'

Deern allowed himself a moment to curse the memory of Exalted Uvrel, a woman not so different to Toil herself. Braqe had her own share of the gold they'd been paid, so she wasn't likely to confess any time soon and it didn't look like Toil knew about his co-conspirator so Deern was keeping that card close to his chest. The Knights-Charnel would be hunting a fictitious mercenary company, and the Exalted – along with any of her command who'd seen his face – was dead in the darkness of Shadows Deep. That should have been the end of it. Except clearly it wasn't.

'So what now? You say you'll gut me if I deny it, you say you don't want me to do anything about it. What the fuck do you want?'

'To make it clear who's in charge here.'

'Oh that's obvious enough, Princess,' he sneered. 'Anatin's the only Prince we ever had. Your card tells its own story to those of us who know him.'

'Glad to hear it. You just keep that in mind.' She nodded down at the bottle on the floor and made to walk away. 'You keep the rum. Call it your signing-on bonus. You work for me now, Deern, and don't you forget it.'

Interlude 2
(Now)

Toil prowled the room. The others watched her in silence, as they would a snarling mountain lion. It was a strange setting for such anger – a starkly elegant room with murals on the wall and an ornate square table in the centre, polished to a mirror shine. Her hair had fallen loose in the struggle, a bruise was forming on her cheek, but her silk dress remained pristine despite the fact it had taken three people to wrestle the knife from her hand.

They had been thrown in here without ceremony. The Envoy spitting blood in his fury, the Monarch's bodyguards just as enraged, while the Charneler delegation roared and huffed in the background. Yet it was Toil's manner that worried Lynx the most. The Envoy was a puffed-up fool and the Charnelers looked predictably delighted behind their outrage, but this was a new side to Toil.

Under fire or running from monsters through the pitch black, he'd never seen her lose control like that. Never seen her so distracted and overwrought, never so vulnerable and human. And the rage burned hard inside her still, a roiling mass of white-hot anger that drove her to movement even as she cursed herself and the Charneler she'd tried to kill under her breath. A woman with a mission, that was Toil, and now she'd jeopardised everything.

What the Envoy was doing right now, Lynx could only imagine. Throwing Toil to the wolves most likely. There were guards outside their door, he knew that much. It hadn't needed to be said that they were more than happy to shoot someone, but they'd said it anyway.

Lynx felt a nudge on his elbow and turned. Payl raised her eyebrows and nodded at Toil. Once he realised what she wanted, he shook his head and looked at Aben, given the man was the one who'd known Toil longer than the rest. The big man shook his head vehemently, black curls flying and easy smile absent.

Ah shit, no time like the present. Lynx cleared his throat. *Not like she's calming down any time soon.*

'Um, Toil?'

'What?' she snapped.

'Who, ah, who was that?'

'None of your damn business!'

Gods-in-shards, how did anyone get under her skin like that? 'Kinda feels like it is,' he ventured. 'We're in here together.'

'And you fidgeting children aren't helping me think about what to do next.'

'Ain't that in the hands of Envoy Ammen?'

'Fuck the shitting Envoy,' Toil roared. 'He doesn't matter, he knows nothing. You think a man like that'd be trusted with my mission?'

'What, then?' Lynx glanced back at the others. Payl and Teshen seemed mystified, but Aben didn't appear at all surprised.

'The Envoy's just the figurehead to get us in the door. Other than that, the only useful role he plays here is being miles away from Su Dregir.'

Lynx paused. 'Is this the whole pederast thing?'

'City senators don't get publicly tried for raping little boys,' Toil growled. 'That's not in the interests of the city, to have the office tainted by the actions of a man. Men like Ammen

75

are discreet enough not to cause a scandal that would force the Archelect to have them arrested.'

'So he gets you instead?'

She gave him a savage smile. 'Men like Ammen are also so gods-damned stupid that they think their position protects them entirely from the Archelect's laws. They avoid the lash, sure, but they get me instead. I needed a name and title to put me near the Monarch just when she'll need someone of my skills so that won him a stay of execution. But once the main mission is done his usefulness will be at an end and accidents happen on long journeys.'

'So what happened back there? You forgot all of that?'

'That . . .' For a moment the red mist of rage returned, but Toil mastered it somehow. 'I knew that Charneler a long time ago. And I swore to kill him.'

'What for?'

'He was the guide on my first relic hunt,' she said in a tight voice. 'He led us underground and betrayed us. Grabbed what he wanted and left me for maspid bait. Left me to die a mile underground.'

'But you survived,' Lynx pressed, 'you conquered the dark, you told me that yourself.'

'Yeah, I survived,' she spat. 'You of anyone should understand, though. No light, none at all. I crawled for days up out of that hole – four fucking days and nights so far as I can tell, half dead and out of my mind with terror. Arms and legs all torn up, couple of bones broken along the way and licking water off the walls to stay alive. You want to know why I'm not scared of the dark? It's because as far as I'm concerned the dark's already killed me once, claimed me as its own and spat me out on sufferance. One day it'll take me back for good, but until then I'll never stop fighting.'

Toil paused, breath ragged as her rage loomed closer to the surface, before continuing in a more controlled voice.

'And now the man who left me to that blackest hell without a moment's pause is here, sniffing around one of the greatest Duegar mysteries ever known, with the Knights-Charnel to back him up. He's a coward and a danger to anyone around him, but the man knows ruins as well as anyone and doesn't care what chaos he leaves in his wake. *He* is as big a threat to this city as any army and I might have just handed him the keys to the labyrinth.'

Lynx was quiet for a long moment, as much unsure what to say as waiting for Toil's blood to cool. 'So what do we do about it?' he finally asked, quietly.

Toil straightened. 'You all follow me; I'm going to need some muscle to back me up here. Muscle and a lot of luck.'

'Muscle? Toil, we're under guard. They'll likely shoot us if we put a foot out of line.'

'Then we better get it done before they can. Come on.'

From somewhere she produced a small knife and sliced her dress open at the bottom to allow her to walk better, then opened the cleavage up for good measure. She pulled a slim pouch from her waist and jerked the door open to speak through it.

'Guard, it's urgent I speak to the Monarch.'

'Back inside,' the man growled, eyes drawn to her chest even in his anger.

Instead Toil flung both doors back and tossed her hair in upper-class outrage.

'It is vital to the interests of your city,' she declared, waving the pouch in his face as though it was a written order from the Monarch.

'I don't—'

Toil hit him full in the face and in the next moment swung around to backhand the other guard. Both staggered but before they could react Lynx and Teshen were there to slam their heads into the wall and toss their guns away. In the next moment Toil was off down the corridor, striding with an exaggerated sway to distract the next soldier she met. The Cards shoved the unconscious guards into the room and closed the door behind before hurrying to catch her up.

'I need to speak to the Monarch,' Toil repeated as she rounded the corner. 'It's urgent!'

They were not far from the throne room, Lynx knew. He'd had a decent view as he was marched away at gunpoint. Following Toil round the corner he saw her brandish the silk pouch at a soldier so vehemently she managed to slap away his hastily drawn pistol at the same time.

'I have a letter for the Monarch, I must deliver it at once.'

Payl raced forward to barge the soldier with her shoulder as he turned to follow Toil. The soldier stumbled and Lynx grabbed him before he fell, babbling apologies to distract him while Teshen slipped the gun from his hand. Toil stormed onward, growing in her role and letting the clouding rage fall away behind her. Lynx realised that Toil's greatest protection was not the three mercenaries following her, but rather the incongruous image of her striding towards the throne room making as much of a show of herself as possible.

She hadn't been the epitome of ladylike refinement earlier when they'd dragged her away, swearing like a thirsty sailor. This time, however, she was bewilderingly determined, unarmed and compellingly magnificent to Lynx's eye. Judging by the nobles and courtiers Toil strode past, he wasn't the only one to think so.

Another guard appeared from a side-room and levelled his gun, but dithered over shooting an unarmed madwoman. Preferring confusion over violence, Payl deliberately stumbled into Teshen and sent him flailing into the guard, knocking both to the ground.

Leaving Teshen behind, they rounded one more corner and headed down the side of the great hall, towards the inner door that led to the throne room. More curious and startled faces turned their way, Toil ignoring them while Lynx did his best to look apologetic and helpless. Toil made it all the way into the great hall before a guard sought to forcibly bar her progress, whereupon she deftly wrong-footed the man and was around and past him in the next instant.

Lynx put himself between the two of them and then it was only the pair of personal bodyguards at the great door to the throne room she had to negotiate. With the Monarch inside, however, they were less open to Toil's act, but again surprise came to her aid. The first guard didn't take the threat of an unarmed woman as seriously as he might and just grabbed her by the arm to arrest her progress.

Toil headbutted him. As he staggered she stepped inside the reach of the other's gun and slammed him bodily into the jamb of the closed door. A swift knee and a punch felled him while Lynx put the first guard down, then she was through the door.

Inside there were squawks of alarm and the rush of bodies – a roar of surprise from Envoy Ammen, a shout for the guards from someone else. Lynx followed close behind and saw Toil punch some richly dressed nobleman full in the face and put him flat on his back. The Envoy charged towards her, waving his arms as he bellowed furiously, but Toil simply grabbed him and manoeuvred the big man around as a shield while one final guard levelled his gun.

From the throne there was a shout as the Monarch called for the guard to hold his fire, while the Crown-Prince leaped from his seat to put himself between Toil and his wife. The Crown-Prince drew his sword and mage-pistol in the same movement so Toil barely avoided impaling herself on the tip of his sword as she abruptly yanked the Envoy aside. She dropped to her knees, now bellowing her request to the Monarch.

'Crown-Princess Stilanna!' she called above the clamour. 'I come to beg your forgiveness—'

Toil broke off as the Crown-Prince's rapier touched her throat, a thin line of blood welling up where the razor-sharp edge kissed her skin. Lynx had ground to a halt just a few steps inside the room, not wanting to appear any more of a threat, and didn't see the blow from behind that knocked him down.

'I beg your forgiveness, Monarch,' Toil continued in a more subdued voice, 'both for the incident with your guest and this intrusion, but I have a letter I must deliver upon forfeit of my life. Such actions as I took earlier, I swear it was in the interests of your city – let your husband's blade take my life if I am mad or a liar.'

She looked up straight into the Monarch's eyes as she said that last before slowly raising the pouch she carried.

'Envoy Ammen has already begged my forgiveness,' Crown-Princess Stilanna said coldly. 'Your master is already engaged in his job and attempting to undo all that you have done.'

'I understand, Monarch,' Toil said, lowering her eyes, 'but my mission is not only in his service. The letter, I implore you.'

'What letter is this?' Ammen demanded from behind her. 'There was no further letter in the official correspondence.'

'Your Envoy disagrees with you,' the Monarch said to Toil.

'The Envoy does not know of it,' Toil said. 'The Envoy's function here is already fulfilled. The letter, Monarch, is for royal eyes only.'

Stilanna glanced up at her husband and gave the tiniest of nods. Without a pause the man struck down at Toil's head with his mage-pistol. She was thrown to the ground under the blow and went limp. Lynx shouted and tried to scrabble forward but was pounced upon by black-uniformed soldiers. He stopped struggling, realising they would kill him if he fought, and watched the Crown-Prince retrieve the pouch, ignoring Ammen's protests. The man slipped a letter free, then Lynx's vision was full of mosaic tile floor and little else as he was dragged away.

Chapter 5
(Two weeks earlier)

The lamplight seems to barely touch the walls. Rough, undecorated stone surrounded them – as much a cave as ancient crypt.

'There's nothing here!' whispered Staul, turning with his lamp raised. The yellow light trembled as he moved and his gun was no more steady.

Asolist snorted, the sound echoing loud enough to make the others jump. Two of them anyway, Staul and Lirish. His Hanese manservant, Yel Dan, was unmoved and appeared unimpressed with the underground room. Asolist hadn't intended to make that much noise but his blood was still fizzing with a combination of Wisp Dust and firedrake leaf. The mixture of drugs, excitement and childhood terror meant he couldn't keep still.

'What were you expecting? Piles of gold and God Fragments? The bodies of Duegar kings?' Asolist shook his head. 'That'll be far below the surface, this is just a back door.'

The youngest of the group, Staul had gone white when Asolist announced they were off to explore the labyrinth after a spirited evening in a local alchemist parlour. He'd not argued, though, he never did. His family were minor vassals of Asolist's father, the Lessar-Prince, and knew when suggestions were really orders.

'Still not safe,' Lirish said in a breathless voice. He was a skinny, unlovely third son of a count, but a loyal friend to Asolist. 'Weren't just that academic got killed, she had guards.

Then the brown-jackets that never came back up, folk say they screamed for hours.'

'Fucking mercenaries and watchmen with cudgels?' Asolist spat. 'Useless scum the lot of them.' He brandished his mage-pistol, one of a pair with beautiful polished brass inlay. 'Now keep your eyes open.'

The stone room was an uneven, kidney-shaped space about twenty yards long. At the foot of the stair they'd descended was the only flat wall. One stretch at waist height had been polished smooth, but no amount of prodding or inspection had yielded the reason for it. Round behind that, at the far end of the room, was a tunnel mouth leading further down, but the sobering effect of stepping into the labyrinth had tempered Asolist's usual bravado.

'What was that?' Staul hissed, whirling around.

They all turned their guns that way, but Asolist could see nothing. He kept quiet, though, he'd heard some sort of scratching noise too.

'There!' Lirish gasped.

The blond youth fired on instinct and the deafening report of an icer crashed against Asolist's ears. Despite everything he winced at the noise, magnified by the enclosed space. In the dim light Asolist could see nothing but the trail of the icer and shards of stone bursting out from the wall.

'Godspit and curses!' Asolist yelled. 'Don't do that!'

'I saw something!'

'You jumped at bloody—'

Yel Dan cut him off with a gesture, stepping across Asolist towards the nearer wall. Before Asolist could summon words he saw a thin wisp of white dart out from the grey stone. It flickered forward then pulled back and vanished, but they had all seen it.

'We go,' Yel Dan commanded.

With his free hand the Hanese urged Asolist back towards the stair but he barely had time to move before the room exploded into movement. More wisps of white flashed out from the wall – long spider-legs probing delicately at the ground. Staul fired at one and the icer passed straight through the ghostly limb without effect. He cried out and stumbled as the legs reached towards him, falling on his backside and spilling a cartridge as he tried to reload.

More legs darted out with shocking speed, then a monstrous blurring body obscured the entire wall. Yel Dan fired in the same moment as Asolist, but the Hanese had loaded an earther. A dark mass seemed to smash into the ghostly creature and hammer it back against the wall behind. Stone exploded behind it and shards lashed Asolist's face. The creature reeled and its long legs thrashed madly for a few moments, but before any of them could load another cartridge it struck.

One leg caught Staul in the back of the calf and dragged him off his feet. Another slapped across Lirish's belly and he collapsed with a shriek. Asolist watched, frozen in horror, as Staul was hauled towards the huge spider-like ghost. The youth had time for one scream of terror then the legs rose and fell, three stabbing down as one and tearing his chest open.

'Run!' Yel Dan roared, shoving Asolist back.

He dropped the pistol he was loading and pulled his second. The icer had no effect, seemingly passing through its misty body without touching it.

Yel Dan thumped Asolist in the shoulder with the butt of his mage-gun and sent him stumbling towards the entrance. There was a crazed wordless roar from the Hanese then a blinding flash of light.

Asolist turned tail and ran, one arm across his eyes to shield them from the light of the burner. Behind him Yel Dan continued to shout and Lirish's screams took on a new, awful intensity. Asolist didn't look back – even when Yel Dan's yells turned to pain. He scrambled up the steps and out into the cool dark of night, running as fast as he could to the open. Only then did he even glance behind. The voices behind had fallen silent and a ghostly shape reached up out of the ground. A jolt of terror ran through his body and turned Asolist's muscles to jelly. He tripped and fell.

*

In the cold light of morning, there was no avoiding the silent scream on the corpse's face. He lay on his back in the street, arms splayed wide and green velvet coat spread beneath like wings. The ruin of his chest was displayed for the world to see, as though he had been left purposely on display, but Crown-Princess Stilanna, Monarch of Jarrazir, thought not.

There was no trail of blood leading here, only the blood that had spread evenly underneath him. The young man had run and tripped, rolled over on to his back and then . . . Well, she doubted his heart had actually been taken, but things were such a mess in there it was difficult to tell.

She looked up toward her husband as the Crown-Prince conversed quietly with Colonel Pilter, commander of the city regiment. The men could hardly have been less alike; one tall, dark of hair and complexion, handsome to boot, the other portly and bald with sandy mutton-chop whiskers and some sort of stain down the sleeve of his grey uniform.

'My love?'

Tylom glanced up and nodded, breaking off his conversation to join her. His face was grim as he passed the corpse. For all his skill with rapier and pistol, the man had never been comfortable around the sight of blood.

Just as well he's not the one who's going to give birth, she told herself, one hand rubbing her swollen belly in what had almost become an unconscious action to her these days.

A ring of soldiers in the austere black and silver of her personal Bridge Watch kept onlookers back both from her and the fat stub of a pillar a few yards away. For all her life it had stood there, the height of a child and unremarkable in every way except for a single glyph inscribed on its flat top. Until the night some foolish scholar had gone into the Deep Market, a mile west of here, and performed a feat of magic everyone had always assumed was impossible.

Stilanna was still coming to terms with the shock of that. She'd paid the legends of the labyrinth no great regard in her life, but it was literally the bedrock of her city – an enduring fact that predated Jarrazir itself, unchanging and unknowable. Except now it had changed and now it had killed people. The bedrock shifted beneath them all and the prospect of what might come next worried her.

'I know him, don't I?' she said, almost in a whisper. 'I'm sure I recognise his face.'

Tylom nodded. 'Lesser-Prince Besh's second son, Deuxain Asolist. We've met him a few times, a foolish boy who could never stay still, if memory serves.'

Stilanna nodded slowly. 'Of course. Merciful Insar, he was little more than a child.'

'I suppose we must count ourselves lucky,' Tylom said. 'Besh never seemed to like the Deuxain. If the Primain was lying there, we'd have an armed expedition about to charge down into the labyrinth.'

'A scant mercy that. This brings the total to what? Nine dead in three days? Probably more, some of the casualties must have been part of groups who went inside and were just the only ones to actually get out again. Killed by gods-cursed spectres rising from underground as though all the silly stories we were told as children were true. And if it wasn't for those stories, how many more might have attempted it?'

The Crown-Prince scowled. 'Eleven dead,' he corrected. 'Veraimin embrace them all. It turns out there were two people in the house in East Armoury Street when it collapsed.'

She grimaced. 'And still we've no idea how to stop it. Colonel, join us.'

As Pilter approached he beckoned forward a young woman she didn't know wearing the uniform of a lieutenant, albeit one of a far better cut to most.

'Monarch,' Pilter and the lieutenant said together, bowing low before the woman did so again to Tylom, muttering, 'Crown-Prince,' in an aristocratic accent.

'This is Lieutenant Gerail,' Pilter said, 'she has specific command over the Fountain investigation.'

'What is your progress?'

'We are looking for a pupil of Matarin's, Monarch, one Lastani Ufre. Her body was not found at the Fountain so we believe she escaped and is in hiding. She was a mage and would have been part of the ritual that opened the entrance.'

'*The* entrance?' Tylom corrected. 'Try all of the bloody entrances.'

'My apologies, yes. *All* of the entrances. She must bear some blame for this situation given she's fled, but most importantly she may know how to close them again.'

'We've gone beyond that point!' he snapped. 'Word's out already, in a few days half of Parthain will know of this.'

'And half the continent by next week,' Stilanna agreed. 'Colonel, I want a detatchment of guards at every entrance – admit no one without my personal warrant, understand?'

'Yes, Monarch.'

'Good. The city's already nervous and these deaths will only worsen that, but I know our noble youth. They'll bribe or browbeat their way inside, seeking fortune and glory. It appears these spirits only attack once someone goes inside, but who knows how far they will roam once disturbed?'

'How many entrances have we found?' Tylom asked Gerail.

'Six others thus far, Crown-Prince. Most like this, stairways opening up around blocks that have done nothing in centuries. It's lucky more people hadn't used them as foundation stones for their houses really.'

'What do the glyphs say?'

Lieutenant Gerail fumbled for a piece of paper in her jacket. She wore grey like the colonel, but better tailored and subtly picked out in red and white. A noble daughter clearly trying to make a name for herself in the city guard. Such things hadn't been so fashionable when Stilanna had been her age, but apparently the young men of the city all went mad over a girl in uniform now.

'They incorporate numbers and a complex form I'm told could be a name. We've found entrances numbered one, two, four and six; if they follow the pattern suggested, three will be in the north of the city and five near the university so I'm arranging a search of streets and cellars.'

'And the others?'

'No numbers, but other engravings from what can be seen. The Fountain of course, what appeared to be a doorway that's opened behind a stone wall in the North Keep—'

'The North Keep?' Tylom and Stilanna gasped together. That wasn't just news of ghostly monsters walking the city streets, but a threat to the whole of Jarrazir. The bombardment spheres stored there were mage-built weapons of such power, each could obliterate a half-dozen streets.

'Yes, Monarch – we've just been informed. I'm sorry, I assumed word had reached you by now.'

'Shattered gods,' Stilanna said in a stunned voice. 'This changes everything.' She shook her head then glared around at the others. 'Who knows? Is it common knowledge?'

'I, ah, I don't know, Monarch,' Colonel Pilter broke in. 'I received word from the armoury commander not an hour ago. There is no damage to the keep, but I cannot say how many know of it.'

'Well damn well find out, man!' the Crown-Prince snapped. 'Go now – secure it and contain the news for as long as possible!'

'Wait,' Stilanna said. 'First, I want a search party sent down. We cannot continue in ignorance if our defences might be vulnerable.'

'I will order an expedition party,' Gerail replied hesitantly.

'Do so,' Stilanna snapped. 'Armed troops – burn out these spirits if you have to, but we must know what lies down there. All it would take was one fanatic from the Militant Orders to destroy half the city if they got into the armoury!'

'Yes, Monarch, I will lead the party myself.'

'Why so many entrances?' wondered Tylom. 'If it really is a damn labyrinth protecting a tomb, why not just one?'

'If I may, Crown-Prince?' Lieutenant Gerail said. 'According to the writings in Ishienne Matarin's house, it was not always believed to be a tomb. She was *the* authority on the labyrinth I'm told, obsessed with the Fountain but a scholar held in the highest esteem rather than some crazed eccentric. She seemed to think it may have had a different function.'

'A vault for God Fragments like in the stories we used to tell as children?'

'There is mention of a cache or a treasure within, but Matarin seemed to have her doubts as to whether its intended purpose was to house God Fragments. She thinks mistranslation or fabrication by a writer during the Revival age was just as likely, believing the labyrinth older than the Fall, though some great cache is the most common belief. She knew there were multiple entrances and suggested it might have served as some sort of contest ground or a temple complex.'

'Marvellous,' Tylom growled. 'We're risking siege by the Militant Orders over something a bloody scholar might have made up hundreds of years ago?'

'Right now, that's not my concern,' Stilanna said. 'Colonel Pilter, our priority is the security of the deep armouries. Seal the entrance that's opened up in the North Keep. Move most of the bomb-spheres to the other armouries, just make damn sure those are fully checked over first. Gerail, I want more information about what's down each stairway, markings, anything. We need to know what tunnels there are and where they go – before we even get to the question of what is really at the heart of the labyrinth. We've always known that the Militant Orders will have a better idea than us, but until now that's been a mere academic detail. Now it could be the city's downfall. Take a squad in – shoot anything that moves and have scribes on hand to detail it all. "It's dark and there are ghosts that can kill" isn't enough information, understand? I also want every text and translation that mentions the labyrinth, every scholar in the city scouring their libraries. Find the pupil too; I want her standing before me when I start handing out blame for this mess.'

'And once we send a full expedition all the way inside, she'll be part of it,' Tylom added. 'We can't trust bloody relic hunters to read and write their own names, let alone the ancient Duegar script. Whatever blame there is to apportion, her expertise may take precedence.'

'Oh Blessed Catrac and all his workings!' Stilanna sighed. 'You're right – relic hunters. We'll have an army of those unwashed madmen flocking to the city. Pilter, that'll be another problem for you. Anyone who wants to get in needs to go to you first; weed out the obviously stupid or insane and let us know if there's anyone likely to be useful. I don't like it but we may need their expertise.'

'Keeping fools away is paramount,' Tylom agreed. 'We need to know what's down there, but the rest of the city must be kept away.'

Stilanna looked over at the body once more, taking note of the distance between it and the stairway that led down into the labyrinth. Not far, but far enough to be a concern.

'If these ghosts aren't confined to the labyrinth itself, how long before entire neighbouring households are killed too? How long before the city is in chaos? The relic hunters and Orders are welcome to compete among themselves so long as they don't go down without my authorisation. Pray gods we find answers soon.'

*

The afternoon found Lastani in the Deep Market against her better instincts and watching the Fountain with a growing sense of trepidation. The soldiers of the Monarch had set up a cordon that took up a third of the market, but despite the current of fear in Jarrazir some traders were still doing wary business beyond that. The Fountain – or stairway, or entrance or whatever it was now – stood on the low ground. Two walkways overlooked it and a curved shelf of stone, normally covered with carts selling glassware and cheap jewellery, ran down the eastern side. That was where Lastani stood, wrapped tight against the morning chill in a dark woollen cloak.

She hadn't wanted to come, for all that she refused to flee the city. In a city of ancient names and dynastic wealth, she wasn't so foolish as to think her account of events would hold any more water than the Monarch or her ministers wanted it to. She had been present and was of no consequence to the city. If a quick execution calmed the simmering panic that might be exactly what she got. But at the same time she felt a duty to be present – a twofold obligation. This was Mistress Ishienne's legacy and this was Lastani's city. She would not flee while the former was ruined, nor did she want to abandon her home when her knowledge might help.

And that brought her back to the Fountain this cold afternoon, despite Atieno hearing a survivor was being sought.

Part of her just wanted to run home to her family, to scream and wail at the deaths of her friends from behind familiar walls. Nothing in their research had suggested other entrances would open by what they'd done, nor that others would die as a result. Still – people she'd loved had died, and strangers too. As she lay in bed at night, praying for a dreamless sleep, she felt the weight of those deaths while the nightmares stalked her.

Flashes of movement, shining inhuman shapes and blood in the light of the Skyriver. None of the writings had warned them of this, but perhaps they should have known. The guilt gnawed at her in her fitful sleep, their world of books and transcribed tablets now forever marked by the blood of innocent lives.

A knot of brown-jackets loitered uneasily near the Fountain. With collars turned up high, cudgels hanging from their belts and wearing battered brown hats, they looked a criminal lot. Half were nervously smoking as they watched the briskly efficient soldiers arrive with a laden mule.

Oh gods, they're really going inside.

Lastani felt a shudder run through her as the soldiers began to unload pitch-soaked torches and oil lamps that could be hung off long poles. They carried guns too of course, no matter that it wouldn't help and might only serve to damage whatever vital writings were inside.

Her instincts screaming for her to run, Lastani took a deep breath and pushed her way through the small crowd, back down to the floor of the Deep Market. As she approached the

Fountain a soldier spotted her and moved to block her path, mage-gun not quite dropping to point at her but being shifted in readiness nonetheless.

'That's as far as you can go, miss,' the man declared, walking right up to Lastani and forcing her to stop. He was a thin young man with a wispy beard and a long grey coat over his uniform, a cartridge box and bayonet visible on his belt.

'You're not going inside, are you?' she found herself asking in a nervous squeak.

He cocked his head. 'Who's asking?'

The words caught in her throat for a moment. 'I – no one. I mean, I just saw what happened. At one of the other entrances. I work a stall in the market normally.'

'Your name?'

'It doesn't matter. I'm sorry, I'll go.'

'Just wait right there,' he said sharply. 'You saw what happened where?'

'At one of the other entrances.'

'Which one?'

Lastani blinked at him, too flustered to think for a moment. 'Why does it matter?'

His response was to slide his mage-gun off his shoulder and hold it levelled. 'We've got orders to be looking for a woman, a pupil of the one who did this. Tell me your name now.'

'My name? You don't . . . Catrac's mercy! I've done nothing wrong! My name is Seniel. I told you, I work a stall here, or I did until this happened. I work for a textiles merchant, we'd normally set up over there.'

She pointed and the young soldier turned in that direction on instinct. It only took him a moment to realise his mistake but by then Lastani's magic filled the air. The sharp snap of cold flew from her fingers, cast widely and without focus so that the soldier vanished from sight behind a cloud of white mist.

Lastani turned without a second thought, knowing the mist would soon disperse. Her heart pounded as she sprinted away through the ragged crowd and gave a sudden, violent jolt as a great crash rang out behind her. The gunshot echoed around off the stone formations of the Deep Market, soon joined by screams. She didn't see the icer's trail flash past, but she heard the panic erupt like a volcano.

Soon she was being barged as people ran blindly then more soldiers began to fire in their alarm – the flash of icers darting left and right. Screams and shouts rang out from across the Deep Market as Lastani fought to keep upright. Someone fell nearby, blood spraying from an icer wound, but she didn't stop – couldn't stop running now the tide of Jarrazir's fear had swept her up. The screams echoed in her head, her own mingling with those of people around her, and still she ran, tears of shame and terror streaming down her cheeks.

Chapter 6

Lieutenant Gerail took a long breath and looked over her small command. The day's dull grey light seemed to barely reach down to the Deep Market floor, while the chill breeze had made the place its own. Distantly she heard the sounds of life continue in the furthest parts of the market. The stampede of earlier had left three dead, all because of some jumpy idiot. This whole side of the market was now deserted but for the debris left behind by those fleeing and spots of blood. A jangle of fears rang in her head and in that quiet corner of the city she could find no peace. Those deaths were on her head, the failure hers as senior officer, and they added to the weight on her shoulders.

The remaining stallholders on the far fringes were barely audible, the distilled panic of that stampede still flowing through their veins. The usual babble of background sound was absent, a pall hanging over the entire market and the city beyond it. The longer she stood there, the more Gerail experienced a sense of the world contracting around her, the air of uncertainty and fear in the city condensing to this bare patch of stone. Time seemed to have slowed, her soul feeling untethered in the breeze as even the gods themselves held their breath and waited for what was to come.

Twelve soldiers from the City Regiment stood ready in front of her, faces almost as grey as their uniforms and clutching their mage-guns tightly. Six brown-jackets from the civilian watch loitered beside them, carrying cudgels and oil lamps hung from the end of short poles. She shook her head to try and dispel her mood. A pair of young scribes stood with them, hugging sheaves of paper to their chests.

Nineteen armed men and women, nineteen! All to walk down one bloody staircase and still I'm frightened.

The sweat was icy cold against her skin as she glanced back at the bare stone steps just a few yards away. There was no sign of life down there, no movement or anything else, but she'd grown up in Jarrazir, as had the rest of them. The labyrinth was the dark heart of the city and the tales told in it – stories handed down generation to generation. The children whispered them to each other at night, the elders folded warnings and morals into their more austere retellings.

Gerail's fingers went to the charm around her neck, tucked out of sight behind the high, rounded collar of her uniform. A simple sun device, the emblem of Veraimin.

Embrace me with your light, Lord, she said in the privacy of her mind, knowing most of her soldiers would be doing the same. *Walk with me in the deepest heathen dark. Cast your radiance over all those around me and scourge these profane creatures from the land.*

Had they been going into battle a priest would be there, speaking similar words over them while they knelt, but this was just a staircase. Just a few plain steps down into some sort of room, most likely. She would have looked foolish if she'd requested a priest, though, despite her desperate desire for a blessing, and no doubt word of it would get back to her family soon enough.

'Move out. Veraimin be with us.'

It sounded like a stranger speaking in her own voice. Gerail waved forward the oldest of the brown-jackets, a tall white-haired man who looked like the bravest of the lot. He nodded and twisted a knob on the side of his lamp to increase the flame before pulling his cudgel from his belt. Gerail unbuttoned her coat and slipped her mage-pistol from its holster, checking first it was loaded and then that she had spare cartridges on her belt.

The two of them led the way to the stair and paused at the top. Only a few yards away, the darkness down there was profound. Gerail forced herself not to look at her company and took the first step down.

There was a collective exhalation as nothing happened. The lieutenant herself gasped with relief, only then realising fear had looped tight bands around her chest. She raised her gun and continued down, waving forward the brown-jacket. He kept a step behind her, lamp lowered like a lance to light the way. The stairs were plain and smoothly cut, awkwardly shallow by human standards, but she went slowly and placed each foot with great care as she watched the darkness reluctantly recede.

It didn't take Gerail long to cover the two dozen steps visible from the ground above. The walls were plain too, cut stone quickly giving way to bare, mage-worked rock. There were faint veins and colours in the rock, barely visible in the weak light. A few grooves had been cut into it – one long undulating line with shorter ones branching off from it at random. She could make no sense of it so she kept her eyes ahead – copying it down would be the job of the scribes.

Another dozen steps and the floor levelled out into a small, almost disappointingly bare chamber even if the lack of ghosts was a profound relief. A wall stood just a few yards in front of the foot of the stair, curving away in both directions as though it was a broad pillar. Looking right, Gerail could see the roof sloped down to meet the ground not far behind, while off to the left the chamber opened up. It extended about twenty yards and contained a six-sided pillar standing slightly off-centre and a wide tunnel leading away at the rear.

'Spread out,' Gerail whispered, her voice carrying easily through the empty stone room.

Her troops filed down, keeping to their assigned trios – two soldiers and a brown-jacket moving in tight knots until they were spread around the room and the walls were fully illuminated.

There was nothing there. The ceiling rose to a slight peak where the pillar stood, but beyond that there was nothing more than a musty, faintly unpleasant smell that Gerail couldn't help but imagine as that of a tomb.

'What now?' one of the scribes said, scuttling up to Gerail's side as the other finished sketching the groove down the side of the steps.

'Look around,' Gerail snapped, her anger only amplified by the apparent foolishness of the statement.

It was bare and empty – nothing she could see, at any rate, and very little room for anything to be hidden. The rock was typical mage-working; nearly flat with an almost organic flow to the mineral. Unfortunately that also meant a lack of decoration, detailing or anything else the Monarch was looking for.

'There's nothing here, should we go down the tunnel?'

'Check the walls more closely, look at the pillar, do something!'

The scribe, through fear or natural obedience, didn't question her command and went first to the pillar, his nose almost touching the stone as he ran his fingers over its surface.

'Wait, what's that?'

Gerail's head whipped around. It wasn't a scribe who'd spoken, it was one of the brown-jackets. He raised his lantern and peered forward, then touched something on the wall with his finger before Gerail could stop him. She saw nothing but heard him yelp an instant later and jerk his hand away.

'What is it?'

'Cut misself!' he whined, inspecting his finger then sucking at the tip.

'What did you see?' she insisted.

'Thought I saw a, ah . . .'

He tailed off as it suddenly became obvious – a wavering thread of light that drifted forward from the rock like some sort of plant on a sea current. The brown-jacket backed off, finger still in his mouth, then made a strange choking sound. He dropped his lantern and clutched at his throat, wheezing frantically, but no one moved to help him as more fronds emerged from the wall. There was a judder of light as the lantern struck the ground and almost went out before the spilled oil caught light and flared yellow.

Gerail felt her guts turn cold as some sort of shape was illuminated on the bare blank rock. A whimper behind told her she wasn't the only one to see it – the shape was a creature, unlike anything she'd ever come across, with long, angular limbs and legs detailed in a blink of shadow.

Without warning, the fronds twisted and jerked forward. An indistinct mass of glowing mist pulled itself free of the wall and ran the nearest soldier through. The impact was real enough; a gout of blood and a shriek erupted across the room. Gerail raised her mage-pistol and fired. The icer's crisp shaft of white slammed dead-centre into the apparition, briefly arresting its movement but doing no obvious damage even as a chunk of stone burst from the wall behind it.

The apparition scuttled forward, as bulky as a lion in the low room but with long bladed limbs. Two soldiers died in the next instant, another a few seconds later. Then those who remained were all firing. Staccato flashes of light and booms assailed Gerail as the demon was thrown jerkily back. But still it would not stop; still it was not hurt; still it threw itself across

the room. Through the chaos of noise and movement it eviscer-
ated a scribe in one deft stroke before killing again and again.
Gerail's head filled with the hammer blow of gunshots and the
screams of her troops, running feet and the wet chop of flesh.

She never even saw her death, just a blur of white amid
the whirl of lantern-light and shadows that danced around
the chamber. Then the noise and clutter and light receded
and there was only the cool deepest black as it enveloped her.

Chapter 7

It took ten days to travel the length of Parthain and reach the narrow bay where Jarrazir lay. Perched on the foredeck, Lynx watched the city unfold from the morning mist. This wasn't his first visit to Jarrazir. In the years since he turned his back on his homeland, Lynx had been many things – mostly a mercenary in the messy little skirmishes that passed for war in the little republics and principalities that dotted the five inland seas. He'd travelled south too, all the way to the ocean coast there, but found the heat and scouring winds too much for him.

There was little work for him there anyway. The raging ocean tossed away human lives like a feckless, careless god and was treated as such by the locals, their efforts focused more on survival than war. While few there knew of So Han and its violent efforts at conquest, and even fewer cared, he had stayed only a few months. Enough time to turn nut-brown in the sun, contract an illness that had lingered for a year in one form or another, and find employment on a slow spice barge that traded with the tribes inhabiting the scorched deltas.

Trade on Urden kept to the interior, centred on the calmer inland seas and huge Duegar canals that crossed the continent. Lynx had been a canal-barge guard several times in the last decade. It was a good job for rootless, drifting men of violence such as himself, their sedate travels taking them across the continent, and few raiders were so bold as to try and raid the barge-trains that plied the canals.

While he'd never managed to keep to any job for long, there had been some remarkable sights that had stayed with him long after he'd moved on. Arriving in Jarrazir on the Ongir Canal was one of those, most particularly when it reached the Bridge Palace.

In his mind he recalled the surging whisper that seemed to draw the barge into the vast echoing tunnel beneath the walls of the palace. A susurrus of breath as the barge was swallowed into the red-glazed maw and dark gullet that ran for almost two hundred yards before finally opening out on to the lagoon beyond.

In his dreams that journey had evolved into the shrouded veil between this life and the next. The red tiled walls and forbidding black pillars; the centuries-old mosaic that covered the arched belly of the palace and flocks of white-winged bats that roosted there.

The scent of night jasmine brought him out of his reverie. Lynx didn't need to turn to realise Toil was standing behind him. The faint scent she wore was an affectation perhaps, but one he'd found himself craving since the day they met. It seemed incongruous for this fearless, muscular relic hunter and assassin that she might wear a delicate scent even when covered with the grime of travel, but Lynx was starting to understand it.

We've all got our own ways of handling this strange life we lead, he realised, *and hers is to cover the stink of travel, of animals and dirt and fear.* A small smile crossed his face. He'd just remembered something else about Jarrazir – smoked eels stuffed with garlic, fished from the canal and the supposedly bottomless lagoon that served to connect canal and bay in the centre of the city.

Yeah, we've all got our ways, Lynx reminded himself.

He looked up at Toil, the woman scrutinising the city as though trying to pick out a single figure on the docks beyond.

'Going to tell us any more about what we're doing here?'

'Might be there's nothing for you to do,' she replied.

'Not much of an answer.'

Toil shrugged. 'I'm no seer, I can't say what's going to happen. Ask Estal if you want a reading.'

'I'm not asking that,' he said, swallowing his irritation, 'but there's a plan. There's stuff you know and aren't sharing.'

'It's too early for sharing anything.' She shook her head. 'Want me to tell you a few things that may end up not having any significance at all? How would that make me look then?'

'Human?'

'Hah.'

'Tell me the lot then.'

'You're not my boss, remember? To him you're the hired help, one of the guns I might need to call on and not even a very senior one of those.'

'To him,' Lynx repeated. 'And to you?'

Toil sighed. 'Really? You want to have that conversation now?'

'Nope.'

'What, then?'

'If things go to shit, chances are I'll be one of those standing right beside you. Prefer not to be in the dark when I do that.'

She smiled at that. 'You handled it pretty well last time things went to shit down in the dark.'

That brought Lynx up short. 'There going to be more of that?'

'Maybe.' She looked back up at the city ahead. 'That much I'll tell you. There might be some light petting with the deepest black, sure. Best you decide ahead of time if you want to hang back in that case. Of course, hanging back may not be the easier option if it really does go to shit.'

'Aren't you little Miss Sunshine today?' Lynx sighed.

She grinned unexpectedly. 'Ah, Lynx, this is the fun bit! That first step into the dark, the jolt of excitement and fear because you don't know what's coming next. Isn't this what you're really here for?'

'No, that'd be the smoked, stuffed eel they eat here.'

'Eel?' She screwed up her face. 'You're a madman, my Hanese friend.'

*

The bulk of Jarrazir city occupied the eastern shore of the bay. To reach that they had to pass through an inlet less than a hundred yards wide and defended by a pair of huge mage-carved towers. The outer faces of the towers were rounded and had arched openings all the way up for ballistae – while huge trebuchets stood at the very top within a perimeter wall.

Lynx was more interested in the carved inner faces of the towers, however, which depicted the ancient pagan gods that had been the patron deities of Jarrazir until the five gods had been recognised. Now they were beloved emblems of the city. Despite centuries of fierce piety the Monarchs of Jarrazir kept those heads prominent on the city's flag that hung from each statue before him, each halved red and white with a beast on each side. On his left, looking down at the ship as it passed between the towers, roared the face of the Urlain, a mythical bear-like creature with stone scales for skin, while on the right the great serpent Holoh watched, fangs half-unveiled.

The former signified unwavering power and fortitude, Lynx recalled reading once, while the latter represented elegance and intellect. It was the serpent that filled him with faint trepidation – reminding Lynx far too much of the golantha they had faced while trying to cross the great rift in Shadows Deep.

Three miles in length and half a mile at its widest, the narrow shelf of land on Lynx's left nestled in the lee of three steep-sided hills and boasted the mansions of the oldest and richest families of Jarrazir. The sprawl of great houses was overlooked by the three palaces of the Lesser-Royals on the waterfront, while a squat fort atop the largest hill behind surveyed them all.

Ahead of him was the mouth of the lagoon and the peaked towers of the Bridge Palace straddling the Ongir Canal, but their ship veered right, towards the merchant districts instead. There was no challenge as they crossed the bay, just fishing coracles fleeing ahead of them. The ship had been scrutinised as they passed the towers and Lynx guessed it had done this route many times before, for all that it would rarely fly the state flag of Su Dregir.

The city's deepest docks stood to the right of the lagoon, naturally leading to the merchant's district of Sentrell behind. Eateries and teahouses studded a dockfront of limewashed merchant offices, cobbled alleys leading to goods yards behind. Smoke rose from every house, the scents of baking mingling with mud and refuse on the air. The people were little different to any dock on Parthain, mostly tanned white faces and hair ranging from blazing orange to black. The tribes of the inland sea had intermingled for more centuries than anyone could count, but trade was such that the black faces of some of the Cards wouldn't be noteworthy anywhere.

They were received with all courtesy, the dockmaster coming to greet the captain himself and bowing to the Envoy when introduced. On the dock behind waited six soldiers in grey, likely from the dock armoury. While ships were permitted to keep their weaponry on board, after a careful inspection, armed mercenary companies were rarely allowed to keep theirs. Normally their weapons would be impounded and stored there until the company chose to leave, but Envoy Ammen apparently had other ideas.

'I require a Crown dispensation and bonding, for my personal troops and their equipment,' the man called out as the ship was being tied up and the gangplank secured.

'In which case you will have to remain on board, Envoy,' the dockmaster replied. 'I will send word to the palace and make the request for you.'

'My escort will remain,' he countered. 'I'll be over there having a cup of something warm and spiced with the captain of my guard, awaiting the Monarch's pleasure.'

Once a messenger had been sent, the Envoy and Captain Onerist headed to the teahouse he'd indicated, while the rest settled in for a wait. As the armoury soldiers catalogued the weapon stores, the mercenaries sat around playing cards and by the time a writ had been brought from the Bridge Palace, most of the cartridges were ready for transport to a fortified building down the street.

Anatin lingered for a short while then beckoned Toil over before bellowing across the deck. 'Payl, Teshen, Reft, Lynx, Varain, Safir – get down here.'

Lynx hurried forward with the others, realising that the Envoy's dispensation must have included him for some reason. He knew he was one of the more experienced fighters in the company, but still it was a small surprise until Anatin explained.

'The Envoy is permitted a small personal guard beyond the handful he's got. Given the rest of the company is to go unarmed, best you're the ones holding on to your guns.' He smirked at Varain and Lynx. 'O' course, in case there's any actual guarding to be done, seniority counts.'

Ah, that's why. Great.

As the weapons were distributed Captain Onerist marched over with a greying man in a tall hat and severe frock coat.

'Commander, this is Master Tipore – he serves as a factor for several prominent Su Dregir interests and has secured accommodation for the Envoy and your company.'

Tipore bowed to Anatin, all the while casting nervous glances at the giant, Reft.

'Commander Anatin,' he said hesitantly. 'The, ah, the blessing of the gods be upon you all. As instructed I've secured an inn close to the Envoy's residence for your company. I will conduct the Envoy to his house and then return for you once the ship is unloaded.'

'Instructed, eh?' Anatin said, glancing at Toil.

'An Envoy doesn't arrive unannounced, or without somewhere to stay,' she said. 'No point having the Cards too far away, either. Do try to keep your pets off the furniture,' she added with a smile. 'Some of them aren't housetrained and it'll be a better area of the city than your usual lodgings.'

'Hear that, Reft?' Anatin cackled. 'No letting Deern sleep on your bed, it's his basket or he's out in the yard.'

Reft had nothing to say to that of course, but Anatin had spoken loudly enough that there came a muffled string of curses from the ship behind them.

'We've taken an inn?' Varain said in a hopeful voice.

'Bed and board,' Tipore said gravely. 'No alcohol.'

'I hate this place already.'

Interlude 3
(Now)

Toil opened her eyes and had to blink twice to make sure she'd really done so. It wasn't just dark. She found herself surrounded by the palpable, utter darkness of underground – blacker than night and twice as terrifying.

She groaned and tried to move; rolling on to her side and almost falling off the narrow wooden frame she'd been dumped on. Her right arm was numb to the point of being immobile. She lay back and looked up at the blackness above while a cold tingle started to spread through her fingers as the blood returned. There was a blanket underneath her, old but clean with a rough, scratchy quality to it.

Touching her fingers to her face Toil winced and the memory of being struck by the butt of a gun loomed large. The journey here was mostly a blur, movement and pain. The whisper of carpet under her heels, then wood, then rough stone and steps.

I'm alive, she acknowledged, reaching out to find the wall with shaky fingers in an attempt to get her bearings, *so that pretty much went according to plan.*

By feeling around she could tell there was a wall just inches to her left, another up past her head and a third near her feet. A small stone box with rough-hewn walls then, but lacking the stink of waste, bodies or much else at all. Not even the scent of water, the air was dry and chill for all that the blackness felt like a living thing. Somewhere outside the cell she heard a sound break the profound quiet, the clink of metal in a lock. *And that's the only sound there is – I'm alone down here. This isn't a regular gaol, but is that a good sign or really, really bad?*

Footsteps echoed in the corridor beyond, several pairs of feet – some in soft soles, some in heavy boots. She guessed at two of each approaching the cell door. Toil resisted the urge to roll over and face it as a key was turned and bolts drawn back. Light spilled into the room, but no one entered.

'Good afternoon, Monarch.'

There was a pause behind her. 'Good guess.'

'Not really,' Toil said. 'Easy enough even before I smelled your perfume. This ain't a regular cell and the city's ruler doesn't need to dump me somewhere out of the way if she wants to have me killed. But if she wants to talk away from prying eyes and ears, some hole underneath the Palace Armoury is as good as any.'

Again there was a pause.

'Nap's over,' said a man eventually, an aristocrat by his accent and one more overtly hostile than the Monarch was. 'On your feet when you address the Monarch.'

'Well now,' Toil croaked, rolling over so she could squint at them in the weak lamplight, 'that all depends, doesn't it?'

'No,' he said in a cold tone. 'Whatever her opinion on your letter, you stand in her presence or you'll get another enforced nap.'

Toil groaned and heaved her feet on to the floor, but as she did so her head spun so she remained sitting on the side of the bed. Nearest to her was a grey-haired guard carrying a lamp and a cudgel, smelling of sweat and nervousness. He stood slightly to one side to afford the Monarch a better view of the prisoner. Behind Crown-Princess Stilanna were two figures too dark to properly make out, but guessing their identities wasn't hard.

'I might need to take that bit slowly, Crown-Prince,' she said. 'Seems like someone caught me a small blow on the head earlier.'

'Be glad that is all you got.'

'Oh I am,' she admitted. 'Could have gone a whole lot worse, I'm aware.'

'And yet you took the risk,' the Monarch said before her husband could say anything more. 'That interests me.'

'Aye well, as your friend at the back can testify, I've been known to be a mite impulsive in the past. It was a risk I needed to take to get the letter to you, given I wasn't getting inside the palace again.'

She saw the ruling couple of Jarrazir turn at her words to where the fourth of their party stood, carefully back from the expensively dressed nobles. He was a large man, broad and bearded, wearing a dark frock coat and a red scarf around his neck. The light only hinted at the lines in his face, but they hadn't changed much since she last saw him.

'Impulsive is one way to put it,' said the man at last.

'Is she the one who hired you?'

'No, but she's good for the money.'

The Monarch turned back to Toil. 'So how did your employer know about the labyrinth opening? You couldn't have heard in time to get here this quickly.'

Toil forced a grin. 'I told him it was going to happen.'

'And how did you know?'

'Academics talk to each other.' She shrugged. 'I know a few who're aware the Duegar are of interest to me, they told me what Ishienne Matarin was trying to do. More importantly, they said she was making real progress. More than I'd realised; I was going to offer my services to her originally, I just had that letter for you as contingency.'

'Yet what am I to make of such an offer?' the Monarch mused. 'Given your employer is a foreign state, one that is no ally to Jarrazir and rarely generous. Or should I simply trust I have your skills and experience at my disposal with no question of reward – all based on the innate, unblemished nobility of that renowned brotherhood, the relic hunters?'

'Firm assurances are rather tricky to offer,' Toil admitted. 'All I've got is that we predicted you'd need help and that helping you serves our own purposes. Su Dregir is no friend of Jarrazir it's true, but you've always been fiercely independent and the Archelect prefers that to continue. Whatever sympathies there may be for the Militant Orders here, Jarrazir's noble families would never accept Order rule unless there was no other option. Better for the Archelect if he helps you find another option.'

'And you think sending mercenaries into my city will help that? How can I trust them?'

'Ask the Red Scarves to leave and they'll do so,' Toil said. 'They've been paid a retainer to come and offer their services, obey your instructions, make themselves available to you until summer. We could only plan for possibilities – namely that if the labyrinth gets opened, you'd likely need an experienced relic hunter to investigate it and reliable troops available to bolster your armies. It's your choice what to do with them.'

Again the Crown-Princess and Prince turned back to the large man behind them. He just grunted and inclined his head.

'And your own relic hunter company?'

'Too small to be a threat,' she said with a dismissive wave, 'just large enough to be useful for my modest purposes.'

'One might be sceptical that the woman who wants to lead our expedition into the labyrinth disrupted the announcement of said expedition.'

'There's lots to be sceptical about. Blackest rift – if you're feeling suspicious that whole confrontation could've been a way to establish my credentials!'

'Indeed.'

'If it helps,' Toil added, 'bring Sotorian Bade here to me. Picking a fake fight is one thing, ripping the man's windpipe out with my bare hands another.'

'Bade?' the mercenary at the back rumbled.

'In the flesh,' Toil confirmed. 'The one and only.'

'That explains that, then.'

The Monarch turned slightly, expecting a further comment, but the mercenary commander behind her merely looked impassive.

'The Knights-Charnel have already withdrawn to the general's barge amid protests and threats,' Crown-Prince Tylom said. 'I think the damage you've done there is enough for everyone's liking. As it is, you've given them ample reason to lay siege to the city rather than negotiate with us over entry to the labyrinth.'

'I gave them the excuse, I'll admit, but they'd have found another if I'd not been the fool to hand it to them. Or they'd have given up looking and tried some other way. With those fuckers it's always the same. "Give us what we want or we'll burn the whole world until we get it."'

'That may well be true, but still you made matters all the easier in a city that is not your own,' the Monarch pointed out. 'Robbing me of even the chance to negotiate a more peaceful outcome for my home. Would you have been so reckless in Su Dregir?'

'I do what needs to be done,' Toil growled. 'I might've made a mistake, but a Jarraziran life's worth the same as any other – whatever our indignant Charneler friends might claim.'

'Not enough reason to trust you, however.'

She shrugged. 'Got anyone else who can lead this expedition into the labyrinth?'

'Three noted crews of relic hunters have petitioned the court thus far, in addition to whatever the Knights-Charnel might have offered.'

Toil cocked her head at the Monarch, a crooked smile on her face. 'Yet you're still talking to me.'

'You claim to be a representative of Su Dregir – certainly you are in the employ of the city's official envoy, though he says you are nothing more than an educated mercenary.'

'You doubt the Archelect's seal on my letter?'

'I remain suspicious on a whole variety of levels.'

'Who're the captains of the crews?'

'Their names are Gorotadin, Fini and, ah, Rubil.'

Toil snorted. 'Rubil can't read Duegar – or even the language she speaks, for that matter. As for Hales Fini, he's just a bounty hunter and not even a very good one at that, a chancer who thinks blowing the crap out of a ruin is the way to explore it. I'm amazed either is still alive, frankly, and neither of them would make it past the guardian spirits most likely.'

'But you can?'

'Any decent relic hunter could – all you need is experience and a Duegar lamp.'

'What about Gorotadin?'

'Don't know him,' Toil admitted, 'but I've heard he's no fool.'

The Monarch looked at her husband. 'It seems we share an assessment of all three,' she said. 'We also asked who the best relic hunter they knew was. Rubil, ahem, doesn't like you very much – *really* doesn't like you – but didn't say you were bad at your job. Fini just looked frightened and started to make excuses—'

'To be fair, I did say that next time I saw him I was going to tear his ribs out of his chest and choke him with them,' Toil broke in.

'Quite. Gorotadin didn't know you, but said somewhat gnomically that your reputation spoke volumes. He did, however, name Sotorian Bade as the best – presumably the

113

Knights-Charnel would have offered us Bade's services had you not attempted to gut him like a fish first.'

Despite her best efforts, Toil knew the Monarch spotted her tense and she took a moment to phrase her reply rather than let her animosity win out again.

'Bade's good at his job,' she said slowly, 'but his job is doing what the Knights-Charnel want. Bounty hunter, saboteur, tomb raider, bandit, it's all the same to him and leaving witnesses isn't his style. You hire him and he'll forget that little disagreement soon enough, but you won't get anything out of the labyrinth either.'

There wasn't a twitch on the faces of either the Crown-Princess or her husband. Toil realised they'd come to the same conclusion too even before the Monarch said, 'Hence why I'm here.'

A sharp pair then, to assess all four correctly straight off. 'I've got at least one advantage over Bade, though.'

'And that is?'

'The mage – Matarin's pupil. I've got her.'

The Monarch indicated the doorway. 'That's a good start. Get up; you can continue to persuade me somewhere a little more civilised.'

Toil did as she was told, moving slowly to keep her head from pounding too hard, past the Monarch and the tunnel. She paused as she reached the mercenary, however, his stony expression not even twitching as their eyes met. Hard grey eyes and scars half concealed by his thick beard, the man could stare down a rabid dog but Toil merely sighed and kissed the man on one cheek.

'Hello, Vigilance. Miss me?'

At first there only came an indeterminate rumble from deep in his chest, but eventually Vigilance spoke. 'Always. Even mother says life is dull when our little hellcat isn't around.'

'We all have our roles in this life.' Toil smiled and headed off down the corridor with the silent guard carrying the torch right behind her. 'She wishes you'd write more, by the way.'

'I'm sure she does.'

As Toil shuffled through the dark tunnel, a face continued to intrude on her thoughts. It dragged her back to a place five hundred miles and fifteen years distant – an unnamed animal track to the south-east where, whenever she recalled her life before all *this*, it had all began. Not when she first met Master Oper nor got on his cart in the grey gloom of dawn. Not when she took her first step underground, nor even when she almost died, but sitting in the back of a cart looking at a cave in the distance.

*

'Some folk call 'emselves seafaring men,' the bearded man driving the cart had declared, throwing an arm out wide. 'Married to the waves so they are, ever drawn to the sparkle of water and cry of the gull.'

He cocked his head and gave them a small, dangerous smile. 'We're no different, not really. We just heed a different call. The deepest black, that's our mistress and oh by the shattered gods is she a hard one to please. Sailors like to curse their love for being a fickle bitch and I'm sure the sea is, but our black queen is all that and more.'

'It's just a damned cave,' the largest recruit muttered, a square-jawed lump called Hoyst.

Toil thought for a moment the bearded man would explode at that, but he did no such thing. There was murder in his green eyes, that much she could see – that much she'd learned to see in her short span of years – but no weapon was drawn.

'Just a cave,' the bearded man whispered. 'Well now, that's a thing to say.'

Sotorian Bade, Toil reminded herself. *That was his name.*

She looked around the crew Master Oper had assembled – three old hands, Bade the oldest of the three, and four wide-eyed recruits, herself included.

'That's no simple cave,' Bade continued, sidling towards Hoyst. 'You'll see my boy, you'll see.'

Toil had to admit it looked like a cave, and not much of one at that, but she wasn't such a fool as to speak up. An attractive young woman in the company of men couldn't afford to look stupid or thoughtless – and this was her first adventure away from home. She knew there'd be more than enough opportunity to look naive without bringing it on herself.

'There's a scent in the air,' Bade continued, affecting a wistful air. 'A lover's perfume, for those of you who take the black queen as your mistress.'

'Probably just Toil,' Hoyst said, prompting a barking laugh from the man beside them, a spotty youth of Toil's age called Fittil.

Toil leaned forward in the wagon and took hold of the big man's earlobe, giving it a sharp tug. Hoyst growled and drew his fist back, intending to cow her into an apology, but Toil just raised an eyebrow.

'Put it away,' she advised him, 'or you'll get more'n an ear-twist.'

'Touch me again and I'll break those pretty lips, little girl.'

Toil gave him her best smile and lazily reached for his ear again. Hoyst made to grab her hand but she snatched forward like a striking snake with the other. She pinched his top lip between strong fingers and twisted hard. Hoyst yelped and swatted her hand away with a stinging swipe, but howled as he did so – Toil not giving up her prize easily.

A sheltered upbringing had its advantages, Toil reflected as Hoyst clamped his hands around his mouth, a trickle of blood

116

running down his teeth, *if when you're stuck in the one place, some o' the dirtiest fighters on the continent are welcomed in like family.*

'Ladies and gentlemen,' called their employer in a deep baritone from the cart behind them, 'I don't recall paying any of you to brawl among yourselves. Master Bade, please shoot the next person to step out of line.'

'With pleasure, Master Oper,' Bade said with an evil glint and a pat of his holster. 'Now then, where was I?'

'Something about me taking a mistress,' Toil said before she could stop herself. *Dammit, what happened to keeping quiet? Anyone'd think I was my father's child.*

'Ah, yes, so I was.' Bade beckoned them forward as though they were walking rather than riding in a cart loaded with supplies. 'There's no arguing with love, Toil – but we're not sailors, are we, girl?'

She made a show of looking around at the tall grasses skirting the track and long bank of willows on their left, then the cart they rode in.

'Nope, doesn't look like we are.'

'Very good, girl, you'll go far with observation like that. No we ain't, boys and girls – a sailor falls in love with the sea or he doesn't. But the deepest dark, it don't care for your love – it's a hungry mistress and it ain't one to take no. It falls in love with *you*, my boys and girls, it sinks its shadow teeth into you and either chews you up or leaves its mark for ever. Fickle she ain't, but a monster she is.

'The sailor may read the wind, see the rise and fall of waves, and know his time has come. He may know his fickle love affair is over and his sea-wife has cast him aside, but our black queen don't play that way. There's no warning with our mistress, no sign nor whisper. One moment she loves you and the next she don't.'

'And what happens then?' Fittil asked.

Toil eyed him. The youth was lapping Bade's bluster up. Sheltered she might be, but she'd seen his sort – every colour and cast.

Shattered gods, my own da spins a tale this way. I've heard it since before I could walk – turns out there was a lesson in it for me too.

'Then?' Bade asked slowly, as though only now hearing the question. 'Oh, my boy, then . . .' He let out a deep sigh. 'Then if you're lucky, there's just a click and a snap.'

As though to demonstrate, Bade slapped his palms together and Fittil jumped at the sharp sound.

They rode on in silence, but after that Toil noticed Bade paid no attention to the youth, not even to look at him or give instructions. As the carts crested the rise and the cave mouth unveiled – as the recruits gasped, the veterans chuckled and Oper let out a rumble of approval and opened the next flask of wine – Fittil had ceased to exist in the eyes of Sotorian Bade.

They set up camp well short of the cave mouth – the entrance, Toil realised. A great, hooded arch of stone rose up from the ground to invite them down, but Master Oper ignored it as he set his camp and waited for morning. In the distance behind there was a tower, slender and vast – ten times higher than any tree Toil had seen, but the riches were to be found deep underground, Bade told them around a campfire that night. The tower had been scaled in generations past; there would be no wonders to be found there now.

Toil still wanted to climb it, still wanted to feel the mage-worked stone beneath her hands and look out on the world from the place of birds, but the adventure she craved was underground. Deep down, where the darkness was a living thing according to Bade, and horrors stalked the unwary.

'Fortunes are made there, in the black,' Bade said, eyes glittering darkly in the firelight. 'A tavern of your own perhaps, Toil, an army commission for you, Hoyst?'

Hoyst grinned at the prospect. 'I'd go east,' he said in a hungry voice, 'sign with the Knight-Artificers, Knights-Charnel mebbe – fight the heathens of Ikir or Ei Det.'

'Might be I could give you a nod in that direction,' Bade commented, pulling at a pipe as he spoke. 'If you show the right stuff.'

He looked from Hoyst to Toil but she said nothing. She had no grand plan for her life. Her brother had joined her father's company and acquitted himself well, by all accounts. There would be a place for her at the Red Banner for sure – that grand sprawling way-station on the road to Su Dregir which the Red Scarves called home – but right now she wanted adventure. A life away from her great-hearted tyrant of a father and implacable, imperturbable mother. A life where she was child of neither, but Toil Deshar herself.

'Me, I'll be a barge-master,' Fittil piped up, 'see every corner of Sinabel.'

'Sure, sure,' Bade murmured, never taking his eyes from Toil.

She glanced at Fittil. The youth's gaze was distant, lost in dreams of his future. A future that Toil knew he'd never have, as though Sotorian Bade had looked into the young man's soul and seen some crack or flaw that his mistress, his black queen, would reject.

He's dead already, Toil realised, unable to find the words to tell Fittil and warn him off, but ever more certain with every passing moment that Bade was correct.

The deepest black will take him. He's dead already.

Chapter 8
(One week earlier)

'Fancy taking a walk? I want to see one for myself.'

Lynx paused and looked up at Toil. The newly appointed Princess of Blood stood in the doorway, wearing a long leather coat and hat. She had a gun-belt in her hand, freshly oiled by the smell, and another around her waist. Toil wore it so the buckle sat on her hip, the holster behind her back – hardly practical for fighting, but better than being stopped by every passing watchman.

'One what? Oh, the entrances. Aren't we supposed to be on guard duty?'

Toil shrugged and handed the gun-belt to Lynx. He looked it over briefly before nodding. There were eight unobtrusive pouches with icers cradled inside steel tubes.

'The Monarch's busy, what with entrances to the underworld opened up. She's presented her compliments to Envoy Ammen and offered an audience tomorrow.'

'So we're free to wander the city?'

'Best we take the opportunity while we can.' She brandished a rolled slip of paper. 'The Monarch's writ – permission to be armed in the city so long as we behave ourselves.'

Lynx nodded and stood. 'You believe the rumours about this labyrinth then?' he asked, putting on the gun-belt before hauling his coat over his shoulders.

'Depends which rumours you're talking about,' Toil said. 'Mostly they'll be so much shit, but there's certainly something down there. I've read translations that speak of a treasure or a cache – of a funeral for the Duegar race itself and the interment of their last great leader here. Take your pick which one you believe.'

'And no enterprising soul has ever raided it?'

'It's been tried, but these texts aren't exactly in your average library. The translations are pretty poor for a start – during the Revival period it was mostly being written by the predecessors of the Militant Orders to fit with their religious doctrine.'

Lynx nodded. The Revival was the period when the five gods had been 'rediscovered' by humanity and their followers had crusaded against the many pagan gods that held sway. More than twenty years of bloody conflict had raged before the five prophets had been handed a new weapon by their mage servants – the first ice-bolt. Once guns and cartridges were being mass-produced the result was inevitable and the equanimity of victorious, armed religious fanatics was unsurprising. Anything relating to the Duegar was hoarded, all knowledge restricted and filtered through doctrine.

'How did you know?' he said after a moment's thought.

'Know?'

Lynx gestured to the world at large. 'About all this? What was going to happen here – don't tell me it's a coincidence that we've arrived days after this happened.'

'Someone in my line of work needs to keep an ear open for news,' she said with a small smile. 'Not to mention have contacts with scholars. You can go one of two ways – break into tombs and blow up everything in your path or learn to read Duegar, do your research and have an idea what you're looking for. Most of what can make your fortune isn't in tombs or under a labyrinth. There are other dangers involved in getting to them, but something that was an everyday tool to the Duegar could be worth a fortune now.'

'Even after all these years?'

Toil nodded. 'It's been so many centuries, there's only the mage-made stuff left. Everything else has degraded and turned to dust, but the mechanisms, the buildings and the like; they'll outlast us all.'

'And that's why you're here? To take a crack at this prize?'

'Who could resist the biggest prize in a generation – perhaps ever?' Her grin widened as she said it, a flush of excitement appearing on her cheeks.

Lynx jammed his tricorn on his head. 'When you put it like that, I almost believe you.'

'You wound me,' she laughed, 'always thinking I've got an ulterior motive.'

'Aye well, I've known you more'n a week.'

She shrugged. 'You know who I work for, you know who I think are a danger to all the cities of Parthain. Even if it doesn't turn out to be a whole lot of fun that guarantees my legend among relic hunters, getting to whatever's down there before the Orders do might prove the difference when war comes a-calling. That enough of a reason for you, sunshine?'

'Yeah, guess so. Almost sounds simple when you put it like that.'

'I'll remind you of you saying that in a few weeks, shall I?'

'Please don't.'

'Let's get moving then.'

*

The company's lodgings led out on to a broad square with a hive-shrine to Ulfer in the centre, flanked by narrow hedges and troughs of medicinal herbs. A spattering of rain greeted them to the city, as warm and welcoming as the looks the mercenaries received from the middle classes passing by.

Colourful cloth and tall boots were the style here in the rich parts of the city. While Toil's brown coat was tailored and new, it remained a functional item designed to last the years rather than impress the neighbours, and everything about Lynx was somewhat battered.

The square was not far from where they'd disembarked. A busy area of upmarket shops and townhouses, it was too expensive a place for their kind normally, but Toil had come to some sort of agreement with Anatin. The Envoy had taken a townhouse just one street away and she wanted to keep close. To the west they could see the towers of the Bridge Palace over the steep rooftops, while the pinnacles of a temple could be seen on the high ground to the east. There the four enormous temples to Veraimin, Insar, Catrac and Ulfer marked the religious district, a shrine to Banesh serving as border post between that and the alchemist district.

While there was no alcohol permitted in Jarrazir, there was a bustling trade in drugs of all sorts so the grumbling among the Cards had been tempered for the meantime. What alchemy was actually done there, Lynx didn't know, but given the smell when the wind turned he was prepared to believe at least half of the rumours he'd heard.

'The Deep Market's this way,' Toil said, pointing left. 'Might as well start at the beginning.'

They headed down through the narrow residential streets that proliferated behind the main commercial district, towards the oldest part of the city. There were shrines at almost every corner and more than once Lynx saw statues he would have sworn were of the last kings. When the kingdom collapsed centuries ago, most vestiges of the royal house that had dominated the great lakes had faded away. That this grand old city kept hold of so much told a clear story of the way things were here.

Away from the religious district there were still temples studding the city streets – always slightly apart from the tangle of narrow alleys and tall houses. A small park of aspen surrounded one to Ulfer, their branches bare in late winter, but Lynx could easily picture their blazing colours at the god's autumn festivals. Within that stood great stone pillars surrounding the temple itself, beautifully carved to look like trees, while the metal roof was embossed with a beech-leaf design. Despite a chill in the air the temple was busy, several dozen worshippers on their knees or burning offerings.

Off to the south-west he caught glimpses of square-topped towers and peaked copper roofs all worked with intricate devices and emblems. Those were the palatial guild-houses that served a variety of trades from metalworkers to mages, while huddled somewhere within them was the glowering bulk of Jarrazir's famed university. What dominated the view, though, looming bright in the dull light, was the white fortress wall of the Senate, where the city administration was housed around a great oval forum chamber where the commoners could speak as equals to the nobility.

They reached the Deep Market when trade should have been at its height, but instead it was half-abandoned by a fearful population. The market itself was an arresting sight, mage-worked stone of piecemeal levels and irregular patterns. Dozens of sweeping stone walkways connected the various levels and sections, half of which were normally packed with stalls. It was far quieter than Lynx remembered from his last trip to Jarrazir; the noise and even the stink from the few remaining livestock stalls more subdued. The crowds had been replaced by mere handfuls of people moving quickly and furtively rather than a great press of humanity – all afraid, all keeping to the fringes of the market.

'There we are,' Toil commented, stopping at last. 'Sod.'

Lynx pulled his coat tighter around himself, the cool of day becoming cold down there and the view chilling him further. Ahead of them was a small militia camp, cordoned off by a rough rope line, a hundred-yard stretch of the market that was patrolled by grey-uniformed soldiers. A makeshift camp of five tents stood halfway between Fountain and cordon, debris and bloodstains scattered liberally between.

The dome of the Fountain was pitted in several places, chunks of broken stone lying on the floor and the distinctive scarring of sparkers showing a violent gun battle had raged there recently.

'Hey, who're you? Get lost!'

They turned to see a scowling soldier advancing towards them. His uniform was rumpled and his eyes bloodshot, his mood clear before he'd even pulled the gun from his shoulder. There was a pink rookie burn on his cheek, the livid mark of a man whose own comrade had almost shot his face off with an icer.

'Just looking,' Toil said, raising her hands submissively.

'Well fuck off.'

The look on his face was one more of shock than rage. Lynx had seen it often after a battle and clearly Toil had too. The relic hunter backed carefully away from the cordon before asking what had happened.

'What does it look like?' the soldier snapped. 'Some damn horror crawled up out of the labyrinth and tore half my squad apart. I barely got out alive.'

Toil gasped. Lynx couldn't tell whether it was real or feigned. 'You got sent down there?'

'Yeah. Left the lieutenant and eight others down there.'

'By some sort o' ghost? Is it true what they're saying?'

'What's it to you?'

'Nothing, I just . . .' She paused. 'Well, I know a man, a relic hunter.'

The scorn was plain on his face. 'Oh right, you're one of those. Well you tell him to go jump in the lagoon, he ain't getting in. Damn thing followed us out halfway to the cordon. An entire icer volley didn't stop it.'

'So there wasn't a relic hunter leading your unit?'

'Just the lieutenant.'

'Shattered gods,' she breathed.

'Yeah well, icers slowed it up some, bought us time to run clear. Just glad it didn't follow us, there were hundreds in the market beyond. Only the desperate came back this morning.'

'What was it?'

'Damned if I know. Some shining ghost of a monster – who knows what curses those Duegar used?'

'You only saw one? How big?'

He gave her a suspicious look. 'This you asking or your friend?' The look he gave Lynx was more unfriendly until the big Hanese shook his head.

'Not me,' Lynx said with feeling, 'you wouldn't catch me wanting to go down there.'

'Not him,' Toil agreed, 'but my other friend would be interested. He's led hunting crews before, told me something about it. He'd ah, he'd be willing to pay for any details – anything you've not been told to keep back of course.'

The soldier glanced at his comrades. One was watching them, the others still patrolling. 'Pay?'

'When he hears about this, he'll come as fast as he can,' Toil said with a nod. 'My guess is he'll petition the Monarch to be allowed to try and get in. The more he knows about what happened, the more he gets direct and not from rumour, the more he knows what he might be dealing with.'

The combination of Toil's looks, her earnest interest and the prospect of money seemed to suitably soften the soldier's resolve. 'There are a few families mourning today,' he acknowledged.

'Death pay ain't great in a city regiment, I'm guessing,' Lynx contributed. 'Those families might be in arrears by summer.'

'I'm not asking for anything to get you in trouble,' Toil added hurriedly, 'but a first-hand account is valuable currency to my friend.'

'Don't reckon your friend's getting in, though, we've orders to shoot anyone who tries it.'

Toil gestured towards the bloodstains. 'After this, the Monarch's going to need experts to explore the labyrinth – her only other choice is blowing the entrances. If she's hiring experts, the more my friend knows, the better a job he can do to stop this happening again.'

The soldier looked unhappy with the idea, but he didn't contradict her. 'We're relieved in a few hours. Come back then – and bring your friend's money.'

Toil nodded. 'A few hours it is. Thanks, friend.'

'It's your funeral if you go down there,' he said, turning away again, 'money won't be much good to you then.'

*

Two hours later, the soldier turned out to be as good as his word and so did Toil's purse. Over a few pipes of spearleaf root the soldier's nerves were soothed and he told them all he knew about the scholar, Ishienne Matarin, and her opening of the labyrinth, little though it was. He couldn't say where all the entrances were, but confirmed they'd all opened at the same time so far as anyone could tell, and anyone descending was attacked by nightmarish ghosts with great spear-like limbs. Mage-guns warded them off, maybe even hurt them a little, but several volleys had barely bought the surviving soldiers enough time to flee.

Armed with a third-hand description and the name of the mage's surviving pupil, along with the street where Mistress

127

Ishienne's house stood, Toil and Lynx retraced their steps back to their lodgings. Toil continued straight past, however, and Lynx realised their actual destination was Envoy Ammen's rented house, just a street away.

It turned out to be a tall five-storey townhouse nestled at one corner of a narrow garden square. The garden in the middle was carefully cultivated with box hedges and three circular stone ponds filled with water lilies. White wooden pavilions stood in each corner and children played as uniformed nannies looked on. It certainly wasn't the sort of place one of the Mercenary Deck would be welcome and as they neared the house, it appeared Payl was endeavouring to demonstrate exactly why.

'. . . you chinless shit-grubbing cockroach!' they heard Payl yell as they came close enough to hear.

As one, Toil and Lynx broke into a trot.

'Stand down, soldier!' snapped Captain Onerist, waving his finger in Payl's face. 'Corporal, take this woman into custody.'

The man in question was the runt of the Lighthouse Guard. Onerist's order made him squeak in surprise and almost drop his mage-gun. To his credit, before he did anything completely stupid he glanced at the man beside him.

Reft smiled back – that wide grin of his that had all the warmth of a shark getting ready to bite. Unnaturally pale with neat white teeth and gold canines on one side, even the hardened veterans of the Cards were unnerved by Reft's smile. This bespectacled weakling who Lynx could hardly believe was a real soldier almost pissed himself.

'Corporal!' Onerist rounded on the man, but also faltered at the sight of the white giant.

Reft slowly shook his head. Onerist took a pace back then recovered himself and returned to the less daunting prospect of Payl.

'If you have an objection about your betters,' he growled, 'I suggest you inform your commander and *he* can be the one to bring it up with me.' Onerist jabbed a finger against her chest and Lynx winced at his foolishness. 'And *he* will get the same response from me. It is no more his place to question the actions of the Envoy than it is yours. Any more insubordination and I'll have you up on a charge.'

'You can take your shitstick of a charge and shove it where your Envoy friend likes to—'

'What's the problem?' Toil demanded, stepping between them. Lynx blinked at the Knight of Sun, shocked by her animation. Payl was the most in-control and calm member of the company. For her to be so enraged it had to be something serious.

'These mercenaries are the problem,' Onerist said, voice thick with contempt. 'They seem to possess delusions—'

'Ain't fucking delusions,' Payl broke in. 'I saw where we—'

'Enough!' Onerist roared. 'You're dismissed. The Envoy has no need of your service, pack your filthy belongings and leave your company. Just be glad we are not in Su Dregir or I'd have your legs broken before you were thrown into the street.'

'Now both of you need to calm yourselves,' Toil said firmly. 'No one's getting fired; no one's getting their legs broken in the street.' She raised a hand as Payl opened her mouth to shout once more. 'Wait! Both of you, inside and tell me what's going on.'

'I don't answer to you, woman!' Onerist snapped. 'Get this one out of my sight or I'll have you dismissed too.'

Toil cocked her head and gave him an irritated look. Lynx sighed, this man really was determined to get his bits cut off. He stepped to one side to obscure the view of anyone watching the exchange.

'Let me just say one thing, as the highest-ranking member of the company present?' Toil said in an apologetic voice.

'Well?'

She kneed him hard in the balls. The captain was almost lifted off his feet by the force of the blow, a strangled gasp of pain escaping his lips as his knees buckled. Toil grabbed his shoulder before he fell and Reft took his other arm. Together they guided the shuddering man through the main door of the townhouse and into a dim hallway and the others followed.

A young girl was inside, polishing a sideboard furiously as they came through – no doubt listening in. At a look from Reft she fled while Payl pulled the door closed. Toil let Onerist drop to his knees and the man doubled over, retching in pain.

'Now then,' Toil said brightly, 'isn't that a little quieter and more civilised? Captain, do you have a point to make to me?'

A thin keening was the only sound he made in response so she turned to Payl instead. 'How about you?'

'Your Envoy is a gods-damned pederast! You know where he's been? Where we had to escort him to? Some bloody whorehouse where they gave him a child. I only saw his face on the way out, but the boy can't have been more than ten years old. Ammen struts out with a fat grin on his face and a swagger in his stride.'

'I know,' Toil said in a small voice.

'You do?'

'Yup. Sorry to say it's not illegal here, though.'

'Still ain't right.' Payl shook her head. 'I ain't standing by and letting that happen again. Next time he wants to go visiting I'll geld him on the doorstep – right in front of all the other sick fucks to make 'em think twice.'

Lynx cleared his throat. 'Am I the only one thinking we should just shoot him right now?'

'Nope.' Payl's expression was savage and Reft gave a curt nod.

'It won't happen again,' Toil said firmly.

'Why? Can you control him?'

'He'll be too busy. There's work to be done in the next few days and pervert that he is, Ammen's a good diplomat who's got the right sort of family name to be of use in a city like this, to be of use to Su Dregir. A titled senator doesn't get his name dragged through the dirt, both the nobility and Senate raise objections in half a dozen ways when that happens.'

'So, what then?'

'So the good captain here,' Toil said, giving Onerist a kick, 'will be delighted to assist us in ensuring the Envoy is steered clear of all such places.'

'Damned if I will,' mumbled Onerist from the floor. 'Consider your company's contract cancelled, anyone wearing your badges will be imprisoned if they ever set foot in Su Dregir again.'

Toil properly put her weight into a second kick and Onerist howled. 'I don't think you really understand me, captain. It wasn't a request, it was an instruction. If you want to raise an objection, please do be brief – if nothing else but because while you're talking I'll ram a signed warrant from the Archelect down your throat.'

It took the man a while to stop moaning, but at last he squinted up at her again, face contorted and panting.

'What?'

She gave him a pitying look and bent down to speak to him as she would a child. 'I'm not just some mercenary, Onerist, and I have a job to do so be a good boy and don't get in my way.' She straightened up. 'As for you lot, you'll help the captain divert Ammen's attention for a few days, I'm sure you can be creative on that front.'

'And him?' Payl asked, nodding towards the terrified Lighthouse Guard.

'Oh, don't worry about Paranil,' she said, smiling sweetly at the man. 'He's not much of a soldier, I admit, but he has his own particular skills. Captain Onerist's family standing got

131

him this position, but he's not picky about who he commands so I chose for him.'

'You?'

'Suitable for special assignment,' she confirmed.

'Ah right,' Lynx said. '*That* sort. Guess he's an improvement on the last one I met at least.'

He scowled as he spoke. Toil was a woman of many parts, one of which was a presence within the Su Dregir underworld. Both Lynx and Toil were still carrying the injuries they sustained during the Skyriver Festival, when one of her associates had attempted a coup.

'I assure you,' Paranil stammered, 'I had no part in what was done to you.'

'Doubt you'd still be breathing if you did.' Lynx felt his glower deepen as he remembered the torture, but the writings of Vagrim loomed large in his mind. *Hate is a poison, drink it and you sicken. Anger is a drug, indulge in it and you will lose yourself.*

Lynx took a deep breath. 'No one left for me to hold a grudge against anyway,' he said with a certain effort, 'the rest is Toil's business. Only question is whether she's going to tell us what this is all about yet?'

'Hadn't planned on it, no.'

He bit back his irritation. 'So what then?'

'For the time being, we let the Envoy do his work. There are serious trade negotiations to take place and I don't want to get in the way of that. Relations between Su Dregir and Jarrazir have never been particularly good and he's not got long to improve that position.'

'And it needs to be improved?'

Toil shot him a sharp look. 'Yes, as much as possible. Until everything goes to shit here, he's important, understand me?' she added, speaking directly to Payl.

'You seem pretty confident it *will* all go to shit.'

'I've read the same books about this labyrinth the Militant Orders will have,' she said. 'Damn right I'm confident. It's been what, a week, since Matarin opened it? Two?'

She started listing on her fingers.

'There's a toll-fortress just a hundred miles up the canal full of Knight-Artificers who'll claim anything like this labyrinth falls under purview of the god Catrac and those Orders devoted to him. A monastery of Knights of the Fist even closer in the Kitrabil Hills and might sniff an opportunity. But Salorine Bas is our biggest problem; the city's a staging point for Knights-Charnel campaigns in the east so we could have a full army marching south right now. Even if they act all polite at first, if there's any chance of God Fragments they'll come in numbers and they won't leave without the full cache – it's just a case of what they bother to offer in return. They're armed fanatics the lot of them, so one misstep by the Monarch in negotiations and they'll turn like rabid dogs.'

'So what do you want us to do about it?'

'Before anything else, find Lastani Ufre.'

'The fugitive mage?' Lynx said as the others looked blank. 'Isn't the whole city looking for her, though?'

'But they've not found her,' Toil replied. 'Nor has she turned herself in. It might be she fled the city, it might be she's just keeping her head down. She's a local girl and a scholar, not a criminal. Staying on the run won't be easy and leaving poses its own problems. If an outsider is looking for her she might take a risk and come to me instead.'

'Why?'

She gave Lynx a brief smile. 'Don't you trust my charms?'

'If you were looking for a horny teenage boy, sure.'

'Your lack of faith is wounding, but I have a plan.'

'What about the rest of us?' Payl asked.

'The Cards? Who're the tactical brains in the company?'

'You're looking at her.' She paused. 'I guess in a booze-free city you could say Anatin too.'

'I need a map of the city. If it does come to a fight I want to know where everything is – mark the defensive points and entrances to the labyrinth.'

'Sounds like spying,' Payl pointed out, 'the locals might not like that.'

'Try not to look like spies then.'

'Oh right, when you put it like that, sure.'

'And me?' Lynx asked.

Toil nodded. 'I've got a special job for you, one men have killed for in the past. I need you to watch my arse while I trawl the city.'

Lynx snorted.

Her eyes twinkled. 'Oh, and bring a friend, would you?'

'What for?'

'Chaperone.' Toil grinned. 'I wouldn't want to get a reputation now, would I? Sitain will do. I'll meet you both at the lodgings, first I need to make friendly with the Envoy.'

Payl's face went stony. 'Why?'

'Groundwork. Flair and a certain devastating charm may get me . . . well, almost everywhere come to think of it, but sometimes laying a few foundations doesn't hurt.'

Chapter 9

Toil paused outside the Envoy's study door and straightened her tunic. She took a deep breath and worked her mouth into an obsequious smile before knocking on the door.

'Come.'

She opened the door and stepped through. The Envoy lounged in a wing-backed chair at the window, looking out through diamond panes at the gardens beyond. He was a big man, comfortably taller than Toil and broad-shouldered. Middle age had softened the lines and rounded every corner, but one look at those dark brown eyes was enough to convince her that he was no soft son of wealth.

'Senator Ammen,' Toil ventured after she'd closed the door behind her and bowed.

He glanced over, looking her up and down like a side of beef.

'Yes?'

'My name is Toil, I'm second in command of the Mercenary Deck, as I'm sure you'll remember,' she said, adopting a more refined accent than usual.

'And?'

She gave a small bob of the head. 'I merely came to apologise for the disruption outside, I'm not sure if you heard it.'

'Hard to not notice a commotion, even from this side of the house. That woman, was it? The one with a hatchet face?'

'She had a disagreement with Captain Onerist, yes, sir.' She hesitated. 'I'm afraid my colleagues are a mixed bunch, some rather more of the "vile brethren" than others.'

Ammen's eyebrow raised, as she'd expected. 'Vile brethren? You've studied the works of Subest Rer?'

Toil bobbed again. 'I was not born a mercenary, senator.'

'Yet you are one now, and comrade to some uncouth fools who do not know their place.'

'It grieves me to admit that is so, but they have their uses and their place has been explained to them once more. I'm afraid they're a little out of their usual haunts in the better parts of town – it's caused them to act up in the way children do.'

'At least they are commanded by someone who knows how to be civilised.' He turned slightly to give her his full attention, a twitch of his fingers. 'Tell me, how is it you came to be part of them?'

'My brother inherited some of my father's boorish ways,' she admitted, choosing a variant of the truth. 'He joined a mercenary company when I was young. Not long after, the family suffered a setback and we were left destitute and shamed. My education could not overcome certain barriers so I joined my brother to serve as his assistant. He had risen to quartermaster by then, an educated man always being in demand, and I quickly discovered the more violent aspects of the life didn't bother me as much as I'd anticipated.'

'And your family name?'

She gave a small bow at that. 'My apologies, senator, but as we say in the company, "no card's past continues to the new hand". We all bear only one name and do not allow our past to count against us. I would not want my father's failings to affect me any more than they already have.'

'I understand,' he said as he leaned forward and steepled his fingers. His lips tightened as though he'd just sucked on

136

something sour. 'I've seen some of your men, however. Their past is clear to most. That Hanese thug, that Olostir fop in the skirt – not the usual sort I'd want guarding my door.'

'The Olostir wars are remembered by few these days, I would venture, senator, and Safir is a man of considerable culture and refinement. In addition to that, he had the finest weapons tutors in his youth; you will rarely find a finer man with blade or gun. I realise the shade of his skin counts against him in some parts, but he is a valuable sergeant of the company.'

'And the Hanese with that tattoo on his face? Don't tell me he's a cultured and honest soul!'

Toil smiled. 'Merciful gods no, he's a thug and a killer when he's not stuffing his face with any food within reach. But So Han did not value morality or intellect among their soldiery, preferring skill and obedience instead.'

Ammen nodded approvingly. 'And the one who quarrelled with Captain Onerist?'

'She will be disciplined by the company. The captain was, ah, a little undignified in reminding her of her place, Senator Ammen. If you could see your way to ignoring the entire incident I believe we would all be grateful for your magnanimity.'

'Undignified?' the senator sniffed. 'He's a man of good family, how he chooses to deal with his inferiors is not yours to judge.'

'Of course not, sir, but the gentlefolk of Jarrazir were somewhat taken aback. They are a deeply pious folk after all and the captain was less than politic in his choice of words – however appropriate they might have been in Su Dregir. I believe he would choose differently had he the opportunity again.'

The Envoy's face darkened. Any gross profanity publicly spoken by one of his own bodyguards could be reported back to the Monarch to colour her view of Su Dregir. As loyal as he was to his class, Toil suspected that Ammen's own success would take precedence.

'I see. Very well – see to it no such altercation happens again and I'll look away. Just ensure that woman's presence doesn't darken this place again.'

'Very good, sir.' Toil bowed again. 'If that will be all, sir?'

'Yes.'

He had already turned away by the time she retreated to the door and shut it behind herself. Toil was careful to be down the corridor by the time she let her fixed expression fail.

'Smug inbred prick,' she muttered darkly. 'He'll be no great loss.'

*

'I'm starting to see the flaw in this plan,' Sitain muttered two days later, hugging herself and stamping her feet to restore some warmth.

Lynx chuckled bitterly and blew into his cupped hands. 'Flaw? What flaw? I love the cold.'

'Well that makes one of us. Gods-in-shards, how many more places is she going to try today?'

A few tiny flakes of snow drifted past their faces in the fading light of day. The last few days had seen the cold steadily deepen, one last unexpected gasp of winter that had coincided with the pair being outside for hours on end.

'Your guess is as good as mine,' Lynx said, 'but the more miserable you look, the more likely Toil is to call it a day.'

'You reckon?'

'Not a bloody chance. She's the one who's spending half her time inside, remember?'

Sitain growled and hunkered down in her coat even more. She had a scarf wrapped over her head and across her face, looking more like a vagrant than a mercenary. She didn't have a gun either, only a dagger she could barely use, but as a mage she was never entirely helpless.

'This is a long bloody shot,' she said after a less than a minute.

'Yeah, you said that before,' Lynx replied. 'And yesterday too.'

'So why're we still out here?'

'You're the damn fool who wanted to be a mercenary,' he said with a slightly forced grin. 'That Jester o' Sun card not keeping you warm? I'm afraid this is the soldier's life, long periods of getting bored, hungry and cold, followed by very short periods of getting killed.'

'Piss on you. Why're you still here if that's the case? Can't be just for her, can it?' Sitain said, nodding towards the coffee-house Toil had gone into ten minutes earlier.

Lynx shrugged. 'All I'm good for, really. It's not for her.'

'Sure about that? Could've fooled me.'

Lynx didn't reply. He didn't have any more to say on the subject, but he *was* cold and he *was* bored so his temper wasn't far from the surface, no matter how cheerful he tried to be. The veneer had grown thin over days of following Toil from eatery to café, inn to flop house, smoke-den to alchemist parlour, and he was having to try hard to not snap at the young woman.

But she may have a point. If Toil's dragging us into something serious, how long do I stick around? I want to be a real soldier again about as much as I want to go into that bloody labyrinth. No flirtation or whatever in the deepest black there is between me and Toil is going to change that.

'Guess I've managed to adopt some mercenary habits,' Sitain said after a while.

'Eh?'

'Bloody gasping for a drink now.'

'Yeah, that bit you've got right. Reckon Anatin's going to have himself a problem soon, some of our boys aren't keen on being so dry.'

Sitain gave a little head tilt. 'Varain found himself some moonshine the first day we arrived,' she countered. 'Ulax reckons he's made a contact at the docks who can supply brandy and Llaith has word of a pleasure ship moored somewhere out on the west shore of the bay, where the nobles live. He says so long as it's out in the bay rather than docked, the authorities are willing to turn a blind eye. Need to be dressed like a nob to get in of course, but he's going to take a few empty hip flasks along once he finds himself a courtesan willing to introduce him to the right people.'

'Figures.'

'Better than having them beat the crap out of each other when they start to get twitchy.'

Lynx nodded. 'Aye, true.' He stiffened and eased back into the shadow of the building they were sheltering behind. 'Here she comes.'

Sitain followed suit, not waiting to catch sight of Toil before retreating. It was a simple enough task she'd assigned them, however dull it might be. Without alcohol even taverns here were restrained places, serving meals and a few of the milder narcotics to the masses. Trouble was unlikely to flare up inside those, while the smoke-houses and alchemist parlours had a cliental mostly reluctant to get out of their seats if the building was burning.

Given Toil was trying not to look like an agent of the Monarch or anyone else official, she wasn't watching her back even in the less salubrious areas, leaving that job to Lynx and Sitain. Thus far she'd got nowhere as she questioned owners and managers about Lastani Ufre, attracting only mystified looks from those overhearing the conversation. But it was a numbers game – they had no other cards to play in an unfamiliar city so had to hope Toil could sell herself as a decent bet.

Toil's muted footsteps tramped towards them across the packed dirt of the street. She appeared around the corner, hands stuffed in her pockets and a drover's hat leaving her face in shadow.

'Three more today,' she muttered as she passed them, not even looking in their direction. 'Badren Ovens next.'

She had passed before they could reply, but neither bothered to argue despite the cold. The pair waited a while for footsteps in the street beyond in case someone had followed Toil out, but all was quiet.

'Ovens,' Sitain commented, 'sounds nice and warm.'

'Don't remind me,' Lynx grumbled. 'If she doesn't bring us a loaf out afterwards at least I might shoot her.' He sighed and set off after Toil. 'This city might be dry as a . . . Dry as a place without booze anyway – but I like this idea of people gathering everywhere they make food.'

'I doubt Toil's much of a fan,' Sitain said. 'Makes her list of places to check twice as long. And that's even before we bother with opium dens and the like.'

'Sounds like this mage is a good and studious little girl. A smoke-house or alchemist parlour is one thing, but she'll steer clear of the more dubious houses.'

'Reckon we'll find the girl?'

'Dunno, but it's either this or we sit around listening to Deern recite the list of things he doesn't like about Jarrazir while Varain smokes whatever he can get his hands on. Or if you're desperate, I hear Himbel does a good lecture on genital hygiene and diseases. Been known to put some recruits off the life entirely, so Kas tells me.'

Sitain scowled. 'You promised me the mercenary's life would be all glamour and adventure.'

'Pretty sure I didn't.'

'I still blame you anyway.'

'Don't worry, I blame me too.'

Atieno descended the narrow staircase and emerged into the oven room. Whether intentionally or not the wide central room of the building resembled a great tree formed from ancient unglazed clay. A fat oak trunk of a chimney rose in the centre, its sides dotted with a few dozen charms of blackened glass that bore the devices of Veraimin and Catrac. Snaking out from that were six bloated roots that extended halfway to the walls before opening out to reveal the glow of coals within.

The air was heady with baking bread and the meaty aroma of stew, a nimble team of bare-limbed children attending the various oven mouths while patrons sat at the booths and tables skirting the outer wall. The mood was muted, news of the massacre at the Fountain adding to a sense of disquiet in all parts of the city. Atieno laboured over to the booth Lastani had adopted as her own and slid in opposite her. She flinched and looked up with panic in her eyes, but only Atieno noticed. He'd not heard anyone mention her by name yet and when they did, they'd be describing her as a local girl.

Lastani now had white-blond hair just down to her chin, one advantage of Jarrazir's prohibition being the plethora of alchemists selling all manner of potions, dyes and other chemicals. They couldn't easily change her eye colour, but a new jacket and pale hair made her look as northern as the name she'd adopted in public, Kovrul, to evade attention a while longer.

'Could you not bank the fires a bit?' Atieno asked, pretending to shiver, as one of the grinning urchins scampered over.

The oven room put him in mind of a benign sort of hell – dim with a heart of leaping flames and oppressive heat, populated by gleeful imps of a minor devil. The child, a boy of no more than ten, bobbed his head and exposed a few more of the gaps in his teeth.

'Fetch you a blanket too, grandad?'

'That'd be kind. Maybe a warming stew as well?'

'Day's stew it is.'

Once the boy was gone, Lastani hissed and closed her book. 'Veraimin's breath! Why do you encourage them?'

'You don't know?'

She sighed. 'I know why they started that with you; old stories about the south being a burning wastland, about black skin being—'

'We both know,' Atieno broke in gravely, 'but the stories told by fools about my homeland aren't their fault, and this is a white man's city in case you'd not noticed. The idle jokes of children are easy enough to endure.'

'So you play along and draw attention to us?'

'You'd prefer I rage and glower? Confirm all that some cretin told them about men with my colour skin? Each child has had a conversation with me over the last few days, each one found out for themselves I'm a man like any other.'

'Hardly that!'

He paused. 'Well, aren't you lucky that you can afford to think of yourself as better'n the rest. Men of my calling don't get that luxury, we're cursed as much as blessed.'

'I'm sorry, I didn't mean—'

'Most important,' he interrupted with a wave of the hand, 'they know us and like us. Customers who're liked and pay on time don't get informed on.'

He watched her chew his words over, reluctantly accepting he was right. Lastani was a highly intelligent young woman and a skilled mage, but her life had been a sheltered one. From her blushes and discomfort at pretending to be his young lover, she was inexperienced in a number of ways, but right now her inability to blend in was the one that concerned him.

143

Lastani possessed a blossoming beauty too that meant most men noticed her, a detail not helped by the fact she clearly didn't belong on these streets. When not nervous and wary of everyone around her, Lastani bore an aloof and scholarly air that made her even more conspicuous. Thus far a warrant for her arrest hadn't been announced, but it was common knowledge that a young woman had survived the opening of the Fountain. Soon the brown-jackets would be actively hunting her and as the population's fear deepened, folk would start to wonder about the strangers around them.

'You're right, my apologies,' Lastani said at last. 'I'm sorry. I'm not very good at this.'

Atieno smiled inwardly; 'this' being anything not considered proper for a nice girl from a good family. She'd not yet questioned that a wandering, dark-skinned mage would be anything but in his element when on the run amidst the lowest of her city's society.

Not to mention the fact no one's looking for me, he reminded himself, his gaze briefly drifting down to the silver ring on his left hand. *But a coward can't stick to the life he chooses and a fool is determined to. Somewhere between the two stands this old Vagrim.*

'Sitting out in the open reading three books at once isn't much of a start,' Atieno commented, dragging himself from his thoughts. He closed one and read the title embossed on the front. 'A commentary on Three Ancient Translations. You prefer the exciting ones, I see.'

'We must have overlooked something,' Lastani hissed, 'somewhere in the translations we used, the ones we did ourselves, we must have missed a crucial detail in the riddle. I'm going to find what it was, I've got to.'

'To what end?' Seeing her reaction to that Atieno softened his tone. 'You're torturing yourself. Even if you do find the mistake, it undoes nothing.'

'But I . . .'

'What's more,' Atieno continued, 'you may be looking for something that does not exist.'

'What would you have me do then?' she asked helplessly, the glint of tears in her eyes.

He spread his hands. 'Get out while you still can, how many more ways do you want me to say it? I wasn't going to abandon you then and I don't intend to now, but if you won't see sense maybe I should just walk away.'

'No, I have to defend our work, Mistr— *my teacher's* good name. They're saying all these deaths are her fault, but our work was sound and I can find no mention in any of the Duegar texts that any such defences existed.'

'Give that a go if you end up on trial,' he said. 'Until then, get out and live a few more years. Find yourself a boy to make some glorious regrets with, see the wonders of the east perhaps. If the Monarch's Inner Court wants a scapegoat, you'll serve well – and trust me, sooner or later the blame's going to start to fly.'

'No,' she insisted, 'I must write a defence. The scholars of the city will know of our work, they will understand reason.'

'They'll keep their mouths shut and their heads down. Some girl with no power or influence starts contradicting the official line while the City Regiment hunts her? They'll call that sedition and hang anyone who kicks up a fuss.'

Before Lastani could reply, a bowl of stew appeared on the table, steam curling around the edges of a slab of bread covering it. Atieno thanked the lad and set about his food as a young lutist made his way around the central oven, heading for a small raised bench across from the outside door. Soon the lad was singing a well-known lament, one an audience could normally be counted on joining in with, but today the room just watched him in captivated silence. Atieno barely noticed a woman in a drover's

145

hat enter the building as the lament built to its conclusion. It was only the cold air that crept in around her frost-kissed leather coat that caught his attention as she passed their table, but once he looked Atieno was quick to return to his meal.

The woman was armed, broad-limbed and beautiful but with a hard look about her that he doubted was just a result of the biting weather. He watched her out of the corner of his eye, warming her as she scanned the room. Something at the back of Atieno's mind prickled a warning and he gently reached out to close Lastani's remaining books, sliding them off the table and out of sight.

The girl frowned, but had at least learned to follow his lead in the last few days. She broke off a piece of his bread, letting her hair obscure her face as she leaned over the food.

'Owner?' the newcomer asked one of the serving children, catching a girl's arm.

'I'll fetch her, mistress,' she squeaked nervously.

'Tea as well,' she said.

Off to her right there was a man eating alone and with a tilt of the head at him, she was waved down into the chair opposite. She kept her coat on despite the sultry heat of the room, looking like a braggart gunfighter until she wrapped her fingers gratefully around a clay mug of tea that was brought over. On the far side of the room, the girl she'd spoken to ducked through a narrow door, re-emerging into the half-light of the oven room a moment later.

Behind her was a tall woman, taller than Atieno even, with the olive skin of southern Parthain and ruddy, plump cheeks, her hair hidden beneath the many folds of a headscarf. Sulais, the owner of the Badren Ovens and chief demon among this tribe of infernal imps. She strode over and inclined her head to the woman who'd asked for her, not quite a bow but as much respect as the woman could ever muster in her own domain.

146

'I am Sulais Badren. You asked for me?'

'I did, thank you.' The woman turned to her table companion. 'Could you give us a few minutes?'

'What? I . . .'

'Just go for a piss and leave us girls to our gossip,' the woman said firmly, her tone leaving little room for argument. The man spluttered a few moments longer then stopped as she fixed him with a hard look. Muttering he pushed himself up and headed towards the outhouse, leaving space for the owner to sit down with the stranger.

'Our temple dues are all paid,' Sulais started hesitantly, 'our licences are all in order and . . .'

The newcomer raised a hand. 'This isn't a shakedown. I'm just looking for someone.'

'Someone? I think you might have—'

'A woman, Lastani Ufre.'

'The mage?' Sulais frowned. 'You don't strike me as the City Regiment type.'

'I'm not. Just consider me an interested third party.'

'If I knew where she was, why would've I not told the authorities already?'

The stranger shrugged. 'She might not want to be found. If she is, she might find herself caught up in the games of others and that's never a fun place to be.'

'But *you* mean her no harm? Well I'm sure she'll be glad to get such assurances from a foreign relic hunter.'

'You ever known a relic hunter to care about what the local authorities want?' the woman said, pointedly not denying anything. 'Could be the girl can help me, make herself a worthwhile investment.'

'Investment for what?'

'She's got valuable knowledge in that head of hers. She might want to get paid for that knowledge or she might want

147

something in kind. Either way, getting arrested means her knowledge goes for free and I don't get an advantage in bidding for the contract when the Monarch sends a team downstairs. She's kept clear of friends and family so far, but she'll be scared, her funds will be limited and the city's mood is souring every day. She wants to talk to me and do some business, my name is Toil – she can leave a message for me at the Sothergen lodging house.'

Sulais nodded slowly. 'Any reward on offer?'

'Nope. I'm not looking to snatch her off the street,' Toil said, leaning forward, 'or make her disappear. If she tells me who passed on my message, they may get a generous tip next time I bring my custom their way. Which reminds me, have one of your kids fetch me a butter-loaf, largest you've got. There's a little boy I need to bribe.'

Atieno rose at that point and whispered, 'Stay here,' to Lastani before he started off for the rear of the building where the outhouse was located. From there, he remembered, he could skirt around the oven room and see which way the woman was heading.

I can't let her get too far ahead, not if I want to catch her in the street, he thought, glancing down at his heavy, stiff leg. *Should have brought your walking stick down from your room, you proud old fool.*

As he turned the corner he looked back as surreptitiously as he could and caught sight of a silver coin being tossed on to the table in payment, a gesture that spoke volumes given the price of bread. He drew back into the shadows of the corridor beyond and watched a few moments longer, trusting the woman wasn't looking for anyone matching his description.

The strange woman, Toil, rose and drained her tea while Sulais gestured for one of her staff. A butter-loaf was fetched fresh from the warming racks and wrapped in a clean cloth before being handed over. Toil tucked it under her arm and adjusted her hat before offering a small bow to Sulais.

'Thank you for your time, Mistress Badren,' she said with a hint of humour in her voice.

She didn't wait for a response, just turned and headed back out into the chill evening. Sulais was still sitting there, watching the closed door, as Atieno hurried out into the cold. He worked his way around the building as fast as he could, the rounded dome of the oven room a dark-tiled anomaly amid the snow-dusted roofs thereabouts.

The streets were near deserted as dusk fell, the suggestion of ghostly monsters enough to drive most indoors and the cold dissuading the rest. Walking was arduous, his lame leg feeling even more difficult in the cold, so once he'd reached the main door he thought he'd already lost sight of the woman. Luckily it turned out she'd headed down a long straight road that ran almost directly away from the front door. She was almost fifty yards ahead by the time he started off, but walking without haste so Atieno pushed on as fast as he dared.

The cold ground was slippery underfoot and just crossing the street was perilous to a limping man, but he pushed on with a long-practised shuffle. His stick was mostly there for balance when his muscles tired of the dead weight within, but Atieno figured he'd either quickly follow the woman to her next destination or be left behind. He could only walk quickly for a short period before his strength was drained. Anyone hurrying through the cold would soon leave him behind.

Atieno looked around the dark empty street as he limped forward, feeling vulnerable though he was the pursuer. He put his hand to his belt where there were three unobtrusive pouches riveted to the leather. Each one was a small quarter-sphere of steel with a short plate serving as a lid to keep the glass mage-beads inside safe, though they also were coated in wax to act as limited protection.

Most free mages who lived beyond the academic pursuits would have something similar, cherry-sized balls charged with magic to hurl when matters got desperate. It was rather more vital for a mage of tempest, however. Their magic exacted a toll on the wielder that no other sort imposed. The more reflexive and uncontrolled his magic, the greater the consequences.

He rounded a corner and found himself on a wide avenue – two ranks of bare pollarded plane trees lining the roadway. The evening was rapidly darkening, one small spot of light punctuating the night as red paper lanterns swung from a pillared dome above a roadside shrine to Catrac. There was no one kneeling at the shrine or anywhere else on the avenue, but still he felt eyes on him as he lurched after the woman, using what cover the line of tree trunks afforded. Atieno mumbled the words of a prayer as he went, but it was mostly habit nowadays, his faith turning to stone as the years went by.

Up ahead she turned right, almost cutting back in the direction she'd come, and Atieno slipped his hand over one bomb-pouch as a sixth sense kicked in. True enough, he turned into the side street only to be presented with a large man lounging against a wall, a mage-pistol in his hand, half-hidden by the folds of his coat.

'Evening,' the man called. His face was shaded by a tricorn hat and the high collar of his coat, but Atieno recognised the look all too well. He'd met a few Hanese mercenaries in his travels and none had been anything other than murderous thugs.

Atieno pulled the sphere from his pouch and held it up between finger and thumb.

'No need for that, just want a chat with you.'

'We've nothing to discuss,' Atieno replied. 'Now let me pass.'

'Now what sort of man would let you pursue a lone woman through the streets?'

'She hardly looks helpless and vulnerable.'

The mercenary laughed. 'Aye, true enough. Still, it'd be bad form o' me.'

'Better than risking a fight, though,' Atieno pointed out, raising the ball a little higher.

'Could be right there.' The mercenary tilted his head to one side. 'How about we put our cocks away then, talk more civilised?'

Atieno peered forward to get a better look at the man. Definitely Hanese and not some young buck out in the wider world in search of adventure.

'Veteran?' Atieno ventured.

'Aye.'

'And Hanese – hardly two details that scream "civilised chat".'

'Aye, well, you should hear what folk say about your lot back home,' growled the mercenary. 'Don't mean you should play your cards blind now, does it?'

'Your point is well made.'

'Good.' The man made a show of putting his gun back in its holster, going so far as to slip the cartridge out of the breech once he'd done so.

Atieno breathed out, tension having taken a grip of his chest, and replaced the ball. Too late did he sense someone behind him, advancing softly across the snowy ground. He had only half-turned before a wash of blackness swept over him and the world vanished around him.

Chapter 10

The barge slipped silently into darkness as it entered the great gloomy purgatory beneath Jarrazir's Bridge Palace. Sotorian Bade watched the shadows slip over him like a familiar cloak settling on his shoulders. It had been a day of low sun sparkling on the tattered sail of cloud overhead, but now the sky was laden and dark, a faint scattering of snow whipping across the bows.

The sounds of a city at ease had greeted dusk, muted behind closed doors and shutters, while wood smoke and the myriad scents of a thousand evening meals drifted on the breeze. The waters of the Ongir Canal were almost still, the ancient channel a taut ribbon stretched across the landscape but somehow separate from it. The forty-yard-wide blade of water looked like a border between this world and the next, a boundary the ravages of time and weather left untouched. Then they reached the palace and the great arched tunnel drew them in, crossing that border into the timeless place beyond.

But this is where I reign. The dark places beyond our world, the shadows other men fear.

The clatter of steel and scrape of stone echoed all around. Dancing orange flames threw shadows over the half-seen bustle of labourers. The western shore of the great Duegar canal was given over to docks and storage yards leased to the trading companies that plied this great stretch of water. Repairs and construction work continued in the weak light of oil lamps and greenish alchemical globes, the forges heaved and hissed and spat as smiths laboured in service of this great channel of trade.

The red tiled walls glistened as though wet, dark as blood under the stain of soot. In the gloom overhead the flags of Jarrazir's monarch and merchant consortiums were reduced to twitching spirits in the gloom as white bats flashed past. Ahead of the barge, the lowing grunts of the great-horns towing it took on a fearsome echo under the high vaulted roof. The beasts were as vast and formidable as they were placid. Incredible strength and their single huge horn were enough to dissuade any predator, but in the dark they reminded Bade of more lethal creatures.

'Boss,' said a soft voice at his side – Chotel, his long-time lieutenant, 'Bug's stirring.'

'Well I guess you better go and put her back to sleep then.' Bade grinned at the dark-skinned man. 'Civilisation's no place for her, is it?'

'You got to admit it'd be funny, though.'

Bade barked a laugh and turned back to the long tunnel. He was a tall man in late middle age, more than a little grey in his beard, but as lean and fit as a man twenty years younger. He stood proud and straight-backed, the pale green of his eyes gleaming dangerously under the low brim of his hat.

'That it would be, friend, but Kastelian wouldn't approve.'

A whip-thin man leaning on the bow rail looked over, hearing his name. Unhealthily pale even for a northerner, he had thinning fair hair and teeth as prominent as his chin wasn't. *That's what inbreeding gets you,* Bade thought to himself, inspecting the man as he headed over. *Or is that an ancient and noble pedigree? I always forget.*

'Whatever it is, I don't approve,' Kastelian said.

'Told you, Chotel.'

'I'll get the smoke,' Chotel said, leaving. He was one of the few Bug would allow near her and still he needed to be quick with his wits and on his feet. More than a couple of Bade's regular crew were missing a finger after being careless around Bug.

'Remind your men,' Kastelian added with a graver tone, 'we're not to be noticed by anyone.'

'So the ladies can do as they like, eh?'

'The ladies too,' Kastelian said. '*Especially* some of the ladies.'

'Aye, right.' Bade glanced at Kastelian. 'Don't you worry, I was clear. We get to play later, they'll keep in check.' He nodded towards the faintly lambent arc of cloud ahead as the lagoon at the far end of the tunnel came into view. 'Sort of thing makes a man's reputation, they're not so dumb as to mess with that.'

'Still working on your legacy, my friend?' Kastelian snorted.

He had been Bade's contact for several years, the small studs on his collar the only indication of the Militant Order he held rank in. Even then it was an opaque link – to actually find a record of Exalted Kastelian you'd have to look in the closed files of the Torquen temple vaults, not a place even the regular Knights-Charnel were permitted to go.

'Just following the orders of my own ego,' Bade countered. 'If those orders mean I get a crack at the Labyrinth of Jarrazir, I'll not complain.'

Bade was under no illusions about Kastelian's role. He was a liaison whose orders could be taken as gospel, even if he'd be disavowed if any scandal resulted. The Knights-Charnel didn't want any actual links to come back on them and the collar studs were a private code within the Torquen, but that shadowy branch of the Knights-Charnel was all about control. If you were taking their money, they expected complete obedience and the great god Insar help anyone who tested their tolerance. Bade had heard all the rumours of what the Torquen did to heretics and enemy spies alike – after years in their employ he did not question even the more fanciful ones.

154

'Well your ego and I both so order,' Kastelian said. 'Get all your crates to the house and wait for me to return.'

Bade looked behind him to where two thin people loitered, looking uncomfortable in regular clothes and thick woollen hats. 'What about those two? Deepest black, could you ask 'em to look more conspicuous?'

The pair were a man and a woman, both in their thirties with freshly shaved heads under their hats. They were mages and scholars too, chosen both for their expertise and the fact they had children back at the Knights-Charnel Sanctuary they lived in, to guarantee obedience. From the scared-rabbit looks on their faces, they'd not seen much of the outside world and wouldn't be in any rush to escape anyway.

'Probably never worn anything but Sanctuary robes,' Kastelian commented. 'Get them carrying stuff and they'll not draw much attention. Keep your eye on them, though; we really don't want to explain losing those two.'

'I know. I've told Gull she's their handler for the duration, no need to worry there. You just concentrate on finding your contact. I'll be set up by nightfall and I don't want to wait.'

'Nightfall it is.'

*

Lynx stared at the insensate man lying at Sitain's feet.

'Useful little trick, that one,' he admitted. 'So long as he's not dead.'

'He's not bloody dead!' Sitain insisted as she crouched and put her fingers to the black man's throat. 'At least I . . . no, wait, there it is. Yeah, he's alive.'

'Good work.' Lynx nodded to the tree-lined street. 'Off you go then, chase down Toil. Tell her we've caught a fish.'

'Me? Why not you?'

'I'll keep watch over this one.'

'I can do that.'

'I outrank you.'

She gave him a level look. 'Really? You want to play that card?'

He grinned and tapped the breast of his coat, beneath which was the Stranger of Tempest card stitched to his tunic. 'Damn right I do.'

'Well you know where you can shove that card, eh?'

'Pity's sake, Sitain,' Lynx growled, shaking his head. 'You're faster'n me, just go bloody chase Toil down before she reaches the next tavern.'

She scowled, but eventually stood and set off at a trot. Whether it was Lynx's words or the truth about their ranks, he couldn't tell, but in the cold he didn't much care. Dragging the stranger into a relatively sheltered corner, Lynx found himself a low windowsill to perch on and wait. The man on the ground was certainly a surprise, his tied-back hair and prominent cheekbones making Lynx think he was from the Harbello Dohn peninsula.

Given we were looking for a young local girl, Lynx thought to himself, *either we've got some apologies to make or Toil's been holding out on some details. A man past fifty from the far south couldn't be much more different if we'd been trying.*

For want of anything better to do he started going through the man's pockets – gingerly at first in case Sitain hadn't put the man out as fully as he thought. The man wasn't armed, but those waxy balls he'd brandished looked like magic of some sort. They were packed in metal pouches of precise shape and fit, the sort of care a man only took with something liable to explode.

The man had no gun, only a small knife tucked into his belt, and a small purse that Lynx hefted appraisingly before replacing. In his various pockets there were no official papers or anything, but a myriad selection of miscellaneous belongings – string, a pencil, a bonetooth comb, a small tarnished pill case, matches and striker, fishing line and snares, and a bandage on top of a box of securely packed glass vials he decided not to investigate too thoroughly.

Lynx looked down at himself, at the various pouches and pockets of his own clothing. Anyone going through those would find a similar selection – this was a man used to living and travelling in his coat.

Looks like we could have a few things in common, friend, Lynx thought, looking down at the man as he started to hear footsteps in the distance. *Let's hope not holding a grudge is one of them.*

'He say anything?' Toil asked as she arrived, her face closed and taut, all business.

'Not much. Seemed reasonable enough, not some thug coming to kill you. Recognised you're a woman who can take care of herself, but didn't bring a gun – just these.' He held up one of the waxy balls for Toil to inspect.

She peered at it briefly in the poor light before grunting. 'Mage, huh?'

'Really?'

'Most likely, or friends with one. Best we take those off him once we get him back.' She looked around and scowled at the dark buildings. 'Shame we're in a city, would be good to toss one and see what flavour of mage we're dealing with.'

'Not a night mage,' Sitain supplied. 'Not if I could put him down.'

'True. The girl's an ice mage supposedly, might be he's the same. Either way, let's not treat him badly, eh? A mage who's survived to his age without getting snatched by the Orders must be tough and resourceful. Let's not give him any more reason to start a fight.'

She bent down and pulled one of the man's arms over her shoulder, indicating for Lynx to do the same.

'Come on, let's get him to the lodgings. Find him a bed to sleep this off. Sitain, you head back to the ovens – sit on the place for a while. If she's there she might bolt, follow any young woman who leaves with her belongings. I'll send someone to relieve you as soon as we've got him stashed.'

Sitain scowled but ducked her head in acknowledgement and disappeared off as Lynx heaved the surprisingly heavy man up with Toil. With the dark-skinned man between them, they headed back through the dark deserted streets towards the merchant district.

The icy wind had Lynx's cheeks stinging by the time they reached the lodging house and stumbled through the courtyard gate. Ignoring the watchful eye of the old man stationed in an annex of the stables and the stuttered bark of his mangy mongrel, they crossed over to the main entrance and heaved the door open. A gust of warm smoky air greeted them as they heaved their burden into the common room and shut the door behind them, panting slightly at the effort as they shed their coats and let the warmth of inside fill their limbs. Only once that was done did either of them take a proper look around.

'Oh, for . . .' Toil's curse tailed off before it was even spoken as about two-score faces stared warily back at her. Much of the room's clutter had been cleared away, making space for six or seven tables spread around the room. At each of those sat a knot of people, not all of whom were members of the Mercenary Deck. They did, however, all have cards in their hands.

'Toil!' Anatin called from the head of the largest table. He had a cigar jammed in one corner of his mouth, distorting both the sparker burn on one cheek and the broad grin smeared across his face. 'Come join us, we've made some new friends!'

Lynx looked around the tables. There were as many Jarrazir

citizens playing as mercenaries, he realised. Most of the strangers were young men, dressed like well-off merchant sons, a few craftsmen perhaps, and three in the expensive lace-edged clothes of nobility.

'What in Ulfer's teats are *you* doing here, Aben?' Toil demanded, spotting the big man of the Envoy's Lighthouse Guard.

'Got an evening off,' Aben mumbled, awkwardly scraping his wild curls back out of his face as Toil glared at him. 'They invited me for a quick game or two.'

'What do you reckon your commanding officer's likely to say about that, eh?'

He shrugged and looked away like a scolded teenager, but Payl was at his table and she waved a finger in Toil's direction.

'That puffed-up prick of a captain's not going to hear, right, Toil?' Payl's cheeks were flushed pink. Anywhere else Lynx would have thought her drunk, but her voice betrayed a cold sober anger. 'Don't go there, Toil, don't be that woman.'

'I ain't going to tell him,' Toil growled, 'but I don't need to hear complaints from that direction. Aben, Himbel, come help us. We've made a friend of our own, but he took a tumble.'

'Well this isn't going to end well,' Lynx sighed, as much to himself as anyone else. 'Gambling needs a licence in Jarrazir, right?'

While Aben picked the unconscious man up in his arms and Himbel went to fetch his doctor's bag, Anatin waved Lynx's question away. His gestures were overly expansive and dramatic. The man might not have been drunk, but it wasn't just good cheer or the joy of the game running through his veins.

'It'll be fine, we're all friends here and everyone's enjoying 'emselves, right? Friendly hand o' cards, nothing ta licence, eh, lads?'

A desultory smattering of cheers, grunts and nondescript replies came from around the room, but the spell seemed to be broken and almost instantly the conversation in the room resumed. Lynx saw one curious youth keep looking with an almost insolent disregard, but after a few moments Teshen gave him a shove and stared him down until he too went back to his cards.

With Aben happy to carry the man, Toil led them to the stairs, whereupon Himbel directed her to his own room where there was a spare bunk. Still chilled from the weather, Lynx fetched a burning log from the main room to light the small fire. As he did so, Toil started to unbuckle the stranger's belt to check every pocket in turn. She paused as she spotted a small silver ring on his finger then continued her frisking.

'Mage's belt?' Aben asked as she handed it to him along with the man's knife.

'Yeah. Which makes sense, not obvious why he'd be friends with our fugitive mage otherwise.'

'Now what?'

Toil finished checking the man and straightened. 'Now we check we've done no permanent damage. With luck he'll be up in a few hours, we can have a chat, then he goes back where he came from.'

'Which was?'

'Badren Ovens.' Toil cocked her head at him. 'Best you head over there actually, I left Sitain watching the place but she's been outside all evening. Borrow a coat and relieve her, okay? If you see a young woman leave, follow her but keep your distance. She's a mage and you really don't want to spook her.'

Aben raised an eyebrow at Lynx, given they were of a size, who nodded. 'Left it by the door,' Lynx said. 'Help yourself.'

Once he was gone, Toil allowed Himbel to fuss over his new patient a while, but once the man looked satisfied she nudged his elbow.

'Can you give us a moment?'

Himbel took a deep breath, the sly look on his face telling Lynx he was about to make a crass comment, but the look he received made him think twice.

'Sure,' he mumbled, heading for the door. 'He should be out for a couple of hours. Breathing's shallow but regular, shout if that changes.'

Once Toil and Lynx were left alone she lifted the stranger's hand and pointed to his ring. 'Look familiar?'

Lynx glanced down at the one he wore himself. 'Just a ring.'

'Sure about that? Pretty particular design that, three diamond shapes, black, grey and white.'

'Pretty cheap too,' Lynx countered. 'No gems to cost a fortune, just a small bit o' decoration that any traveller could afford.'

'Funny, though, how he's dressed in shades of grey too,' Toil said. 'But sure, a coincidence, fine.'

'There's nothing—'

She cut him off with a raised hand. 'It's your business,' she said firmly. 'I of all people got to respect that. You could have asked me a whole bunch of questions these past few weeks, but you mostly haven't and it's appreciated. All I'm saying is we need to win this man's confidence once he's awake. If you can do that better than me, just give me a nod and I'll say no more there.'

She looked him straight in the eye then, close enough to kiss and Lynx saw a slight, rare vulnerability in her eyes. 'But don't lie to my face. That I don't need.'

Lynx was transfixed for a moment, the scent of her perfume and closeness of her body enough to enfeeble him. 'Sure,' he croaked, 'no lies.'

'Thank you.'

Toil went quiet then, leaving a great gap of silence between them that Lynx felt like a pressure on his chest. An unfamiliar tangle of thoughts inside him choked his throat at first – that surge of desire he felt around Toil clashing with the dark knot of pain beneath the surface of his heart.

The broad strokes of his past were obvious enough to a woman like Toil, but the depth of the fissures inside him were something he was careful to hide. He had never told an outsider about the Vagrim brotherhood, certainly not someone he had felt something for. To do that was to admit more than he was capable of, to reveal the bandage around his damaged soul that was more precious to him than he could put into words.

'I could try,' Lynx muttered. 'Talk to him, see what I could do.'

The Vagrim were not like the Militant Orders. They had no structure or purpose other than to help their own and others who needed it. Most were like Lynx, men and woman scarred by the random cruelty of life and the more mundane sort of monster mankind threw up.

It was a philosophy that was too simple to be really considered one, just the stand they chose to take. In a random and violent world, you lived as best you could and didn't ignore what went on around you. It was the reason he'd signed with the Cards, back when he thought Toil was a kidnapped girl, the reason he'd done a lot of things over the years. When every day was a struggle, moulding your actions around the right thing to do made it all a little easier.

It seemed to Lynx as though Toil could see the emotions play out on his face, so intently was she watching him. It was all he could do not to turn away, find some unobserved corner and whatever Jarrazirans used to calm their thoughts, but there was a softening of her expression that only made him desire her more.

'Thank you,' she said softly. Unexpectedly she leaned forward and kissed him softly on the lips.

Lynx froze, as much in surprise as anything else, but when she pulled back it was just an inch or two. He stared into her eyes for a moment longer, then his wits returned and he kissed her. This time it was longer, but they were still half-frozen and standing over an unconscious man, so it went no further.

'That was unexpected,' Lynx said at last, his voice husky.

A small smile appeared on her lips. 'I don't like to be predictable,' Toil admitted, 'but sometimes the moment calls for action.'

'I uh . . . yeah. Can't complain there.'

'It wouldn't be very chivalrous if you did.'

Lynx managed a smile. 'Aye, that's me all over.'

'Really?' Toil raised an eyebrow and looked him up and down. 'I'll have to take your word about that.'

He laughed and took a breath. 'Yeah, I reckon you will. So – now what?'

She nodded to the man on the bed, but before she could say anything more there was a crash from the room below and a dozen voices cried out in anger. More crashes followed, tables or chairs being overturned, and the shouting intensified. She hesitated then her head sagged.

'Oh for the love of all that's shattered, your comrades are like children.' She shook her head and rose. 'Now, you watch over this one while I go and break some heads downstairs.'

She touched him once on the cheek, the tattooed one that read 'honour or death' in a language none round these parts could speak, Lynx included.

'Convince him of your honourable intentions, Lynx. I really want to make a friend of that mage.'

Chapter 11

Atieno woke flailing, moving from unconsciousness to blind panic in an instant. The room was dim, pungent with smoke and sweat. Slowly the details came into focus, wading through the molasses of his thoughts. A bed, a bunk – another opposite. A small fire at one end, a man in a chair sitting before it – settled down as though asleep, tricorn pulled low to hide his eyes.

He tried to ease himself up but black stars burst before his eyes like the hangovers of a relived youth. It was all Atieno could do not to heave his guts up.

'It'll pass soon,' said the figure, not looking up. 'Just lie back and breathe. A few minutes and you'll be on your feet.'

Atieno felt the spider-claw tingle in his fingertips as his magic surged to the surface, but he got a grip on himself a moment later.

'You,' he croaked, recognising the man at last. It was the Hanese veteran who'd distracted him in the street.

'Aye, me.'

'What do you want?' His hand went to his belt and discovered it was missing, his knife too. Atieno looked around and finally spotted the belt hung on a bedpost, the near corner of the other bunk.

'Take it back if you want it,' the man said, looking up at last but keeping his hands folded across his stomach. 'I just didn't want you to have it in reach the moment you woke up, in case you're as scratchy as me in the mornings.'

Atieno considered the belt a moment and the state of his head. 'I'll do for the moment.' Tempest magic wasn't as destructive as some, but its effects could be awful in their own way. He was far from helpless even if he had to be careful not to channel too much.

'Suit yourself. So, how about some introductions?'

'It seems you've got the advantage of me already,' Atieno said, gingerly easing himself up a little so he could prop his head at a more comfortable angle.

'We've got some tricks,' the Hanese admitted, 'but I'm told you've got one up those sleeves too, so I'm hoping we can all rein in and talk like civilised folk – despite the uncivilised start my side have managed.'

'My people pride themselves on their civilised ways,' Atieno said. 'I'll not let a Hanese show me up in those respects. Say your piece, sir.'

The stranger swept his tricorn from his head and leaned forward. Despite his words, Atieno could see little beyond the brutal exterior there. The battered face of a man who'd lived hard times, the jaw of a brawler, the eyes and nose that were pure So Han. The one thing that could be said about So Han was that they didn't care about a man's skin colour – but that meant little when you saw how they treated their white neighbours.

The Hanese just stared at him for a while, resting his chin on one fist. Atieno blinked at the man in confusion, but eventually the Hanese said, 'My name's Lynx, I'm thinking we might have one or two things in common.'

Atieno gave him a level look. 'If you say so.'

Lynx wore a plain grey jacket, unbuttoned to reveal a white cotton shirt underneath and bearing a playing card badge that Atieno recognised as the Stranger of Tempest. More significantly, now that he was leaning forwards, his

165

left hand was on full show. On his middle finger the man wore a silver ring that bore three diamond shapes, black, grey and white.

'You remind me of a man I once met,' Lynx continued after a while. 'Something about the eyes maybe. He was a good man, once faced down a priest and some soldiers who were about to execute a child.'

'Sounds like the right thing to do,' Atieno confirmed. 'Whoever the child grows up to be, some things are wrong.'

'Aye, that's what I thought – even if you have to take matters in your own hands after, some things are wrong.'

Atieno blinked, his thoughts moving slowly through the haze of confusion. *I suppose even a Hanese can be a follower of Vagrim – they are renowned for a stubborn, fearless streak so surely a few of them have morals too.*

That particular tale of Vagrim was one of the later ones in the book Atieno had read – the child he'd saved had grown up to be a savage warlord and brigand. When Vagrim had heard, he'd tracked the man down and confronted him with only two companions. The warlord had recognised him at once and embraced him – never even seeing the gun that killed him.

With a nod he reminded himself that he hadn't returned the introduction. 'My name is Atieno.'

'Once of Harbello Dohn?'

'Good guess.' Atieno raised an eyebrow. 'Or have you been that far south yourself?'

'Never made it that far, but enough to guess the difference between Ulethelain and Harbello.'

That was said with a smile Atieno quickly shared. It was a common confusion, certainly among the people of the north, for all that the southerners could never fathom how those two regions could ever be confused.

With an effort Atieno swung his body around so he could sit up on the side of the bed, albeit slightly hunched to keep his head short of the bunk above. His lame foot ached, a cold uncomfortable tingle that waxed and waned but was never absent. His muscles strained inside his boot as he tried to work them. The ankle and foot had set completely rigid over the years, every joint fused as his bones petrified, but the muscles around them still needed to have blood forced through them. That was all the harder when he could hardly move, but Atieno had found a few minutes of working at them eased the pressure.

A good reminder for an old man, he thought ruefully. *Change comes to us all, but the tempest is a lure that'll kill you if you let it.*

'What now?'

Lynx shrugged. 'We're looking for the girl.'

'What girl?'

The look he received was scornful, but Lynx's voice remained calm and patient. 'The mage, Lastani Ufre. You followed Toil out of the Badren Ovens when she started asking questions about Ufre.'

The vision of red-haired violence appeared in Atieno's memory. 'Maybe I just followed her, she's a beautiful woman.'

'That she is, but I'm guessing you're not the sort to press your suit in a deserted street.'

'Perhaps not, but you're still a few assumptions ahead of me,' Atieno countered.

'No doubt, but that don't matter. We're not going to keep you against your will, nor follow you out the door unless you want a hand.' Lynx cocked his head and looked at Atieno's stiff leg. 'Old injury?'

'Something like that,' Atieno said. 'So you'll just let me walk out right now?'

'If anyone's got other ideas, I'll be by your side. Can hardly wear this ring otherwise.'

167

'But you want something in return.'

'In a manner of speaking. If you do come across Ufre – by chance or whatever – we might be in a position to help her. The city's got a whole lot smaller for her now, the Monarch's lost patience and there's a price on her head.'

'What would you do for her, then?'

'She's got information we want, Ufre's the closest to an expert there is on the labyrinth. Making a friend of her would be worthwhile to someone who wants to lead an expedition underground, gives our relic hunters a big advantage over the competition.'

Atieno was quiet for a while as he thought about Lynx's words. 'Still quite a risk for a frightened young woman.'

'That it is,' Lynx agreed. 'Maybe think of it this way – if she's confident she can escape the city, she should be gone first thing in the morning. If not, she's going to get caught one day soon. It'd take a measure of faith that we'll not just hand her over, but that's the worst case if she comes with us. And does that lose her anything more than a day or two?'

'I understand. Your friend, Toil?'

'Aye.'

'She's a relic hunter?'

'Yup, I've seen that with my own eyes. She can read Duegar and navigate underground – seems just about as comfortable in the dark as others would in the sun. If Ufre wants, she can test that. The reading Duegar part anyway. Most folk who style themselves relic hunters do so because "murderous thieves" tends to offend. They're not the sort to actually learn things. Toil might not know anything like as much as Ufre, but she'll be able to demonstrate enough learning to set Ufre's mind at rest.'

'In that case, yes, I'll convey your message. If Toil is here now, I can ask her to tell me something that might serve – the glyph for "hello" or something along those lines.' Atieno paused. 'I see you've got a gun, but I doubt most of your company do – Jarrazir is pretty strict on that front.'

Lynx rose and nodded his understanding. He extended an arm to help Atieno up, which after a pause Atieno took. 'Point's made, only a fool picks a fight with two mages. There's someone watching the Ovens, but their orders are just to follow. The rest of us will be here waiting for an answer.'

*

From the diamond-paned windows of the Rainbow Council Chamber, the Monarch of Jarrazir surveyed her city with a strange mix of maternal pride and prickling concern. One hand resting on the swell of her belly, she luxuriated in the warm, tinted light that flooded in through the high windows. The sun was low at the horizon, casting its morning light across her southerly view of the city. Below her were the great jutting ribs that suspended the roof of the grand audience hall, the largest in the Bridge Palace. Stilanna preferred this one, however, and normally the feel of the sun on her face could soothe much, but today it eased little. She could sense the vibrations of anxiety rising up the city streets, could see the spilled blood in her mind and the haunted look in the eyes of her soldiers who'd survived the excursion inside.

A great curved bank of window stretched all around this side of the chamber, affording a view of half the city and bay – streaks of coloured glass across the top designed to follow the Skyriver's path. Through it she could see the frost glistening on the orange tiles of the merchant district and the waters of the bay glittering like a jewel. The Senate's long sweeping walls of pale stone stood out as a counterpoint to the brooding dark hump of the university, while scattered between the two were the verdigris-sheathed guild-houses like a meandering herd of giant beasts, and the dark den of the Deep Market.

From here it looks no different, Crown-Princess Stilanna mused, *as though the mysteries of the labyrinth remained dormant beneath us.*

'Crown-Princess, my humblest apologies,' cried a voice behind her as the door banged. 'I came as soon as I received your summons.'

Stilanna turned to greet the last of her private council. She had come late to this meeting to find most of her senior advisers already there – had come late principally because this man, Lesser-Prince Justeben Por, could not be relied upon to be in his own bed on any given morning.

Still he forces me to wait on him, as though we'd never grown up and I'd not been crowned Monarch.

'Lesser-Prince,' she replied with an inclination of the head as he bowed. 'I will instruct my messengers to be more assiduous about their task in future.'

'Or you could just stop screwing every girl you can get your grubby little paws on,' contributed the eldest council member sitting at the table. 'Perhaps then your household might have some clue where you spend your nights.'

'Lesser-Princess Aronei, my apologies to you also.' Por sniffed. 'I know every hour is precious to one of your advanced age.'

The silver braids of rank hung unevenly from one shoulder to the other, looking more like an uncomfortable growth than a magnificent echo of the gods' grand work, the Skyriver. The usual lazy smirk adorned Por's face. Needling Aronei was at least one of his favourite activities and Por was not a man to forego his pleasures whatever else was going on in the city.

'And your admonishment is doubly effective,' he continued as Aronei scowled. 'The disapproval on your face is enough to compel me to swear off all pleasures of the flesh.'

'If I believed that true I'd have spent a lot more time in the company of my idiot grand-niece,' Aronei declared.

She was a dumpy woman with long grey hair piled on top of her head and fixed in place with a dozen large, ornate pins, thin silver chains hanging across her chest to indicate her rank as head of one of the four royal families from which the Monarch was chosen. Her pale skin was almost as grey as a canal eel – something Stilanna's husband had been good enough to privately point out and now she couldn't get the image out of her head – and her thin lips pursed as though constantly sucking lemons.

'How is the fragrant Lady Rithol?' Por sighed expansively. 'You will remember me to her?'

'She has quite enough of a reminder of you,' Aronei countered, 'your wife remarked as much only last week. I believe she finds your resemblance to my *great* grand-niece less amusing than you do. Perhaps that's the reason why you're never to be found in your marital bed?'

Dear gods, are we so long in our peace the city's leaders bicker while they ignore a crisis? Stilanna pointedly cleared her throat and swallowed her anger. 'If the pair of you have finished your sniping, perhaps we can spend a few moments attending to urgent matters of state?'

She looked around the room before continuing. Her husband, Crown-Prince Tylom, sat at the opposite end of a long oval table, the gold braid of rank shining in the crisp clean light coming from above the table. The room was lit by Duegar stones: large milky-white ovals with the smooth, slightly dulled surface of sea-glass that shone with crisp white light.

Flanking Tylom were Colonel Pilter of the City Regiment, and Senate Voice Elax, both low-born and careful not to speak out of turn here. The last of the Lessar-Princes, Besh, was a burly man with ruddy cheeks and a voice like a startled donkey, while

171

the council was completed by Functionary Breks, the corpse-like senior figure of Jarrazir's civil service, and Commander Honeth of the Bridge Watch, the Monarch's personal regiment. Honeth looked like an ungainly, unsmiling thug in a black uniform, but aside from Tylom he was the only one in the room Stilanna could trust completely.

Once her bickering peers had mumbled apologies Stilanna took her own seat and gestured to the colonel. 'Colonel Pilter, an update on the labyrinth entrances if you please.'

'We have identified and secured seven entrances, Majesty. Of those, the one beneath the North Keep has been walled up and almost all the mage-spheres moved. There are no more incidents or deaths this morning, but a number of individuals have tried to enter. Only the threat of violence has kept them back.'

'Relic hunters or noble sons with more bravado than brains?'

'Both, Monarch,' Pilter said, casting a guilty glance towards Lesser-Prince Besh, whose son was among the labyrinth's victims, but the man's already grim expression didn't change.

Stilanna felt no such guilt in her words. None of the noble families were taking the threat seriously and their mansions were well away from the labyrinth entrances. 'All of you, let it be known across the city that any – *any* – man, woman or child attempting to bribe or browbeat their way into the labyrinth without my personal warrant will be shot. I don't care who their parents are, understand me? The Duegar ghosts or whatever they are have not yet ranged far from the entrances, I do not intend to provoke them to do so.'

'I shall instruct my house accordingly,' Lesser-Princess Aronei said. 'In the meantime, what do you propose to do? It is open after all these centuries; you must explore it before trying to close the entrances up, no? The threat of these ghosts is one thing, but everyone knows the myths about what's inside.'

'I am well aware,' Stilanna replied. 'Now the labyrinth has been opened once it can be done again; and its contents are a greater threat to the city than any ghosts. The lure of what may be inside means we must explore it or others will keep trying to. That may mean the more established Militant Orders using political pressure or the smaller and more crazed variety mounting night raids. We may have our differences, but I know none of you want to see madmen like the Sons of the Wind run riot on the streets.'

'Are the rumours of a competition true?'

'They are not,' Stilanna said firmly. 'Commander Honeth will be in charge of any expedition – but we need to assemble the very best scholars and experts to ensure the next effort does not end in disaster.'

'Experts?' Aronei's mouth twisted in distaste. 'You mean relic hunters?'

'Unless you know of anyone else adept at investigating Duegar ruins? Or perhaps you prefer we invite the Militant Orders in to take charge of the situation and trust that their troops will leave again afterwards, after first sharing with us whatever priceless artefacts they might have found?' Stilanna's tone was acidic, Aronei being the most prominant noble in the city to support the Orders.

'I . . .' Aronei had the sense not to finish her sentence and merely sat back, aware Stilanna's patience for debate had run out. 'What will you say publicly?' she said after a short while. 'The speculation and, ah, perceived inaction will only fuel fears.'

'I will make a formal announcement tomorrow,' the Monarch agreed. 'We have had representatives of the temples and Orders make enquiries already – they and the citizens need to know how I intend to respond. In the meantime the city will be prepared as unobtrusively as possible against the possibility that the Knights-Charnel or Knights-Artificer act in a more drastic fashion. The opening of the labyrinth may be a boon of the gods, but the whole of Urden must know it is under our sole control and the people must know we are indeed in control.'

'Surely the Militant Orders would not simply attack – not a gods-fearing city like Jarrazir,' Aronei protested.

'With the myths about God Fragments being hidden inside?' Lesser-Prince Besh replied with a glower that Stilanna guessed was more about his private grief than the public threat. 'Don't be certain you could predict what action one or all might take.'

Stilanna nodded. 'We need knowledge too – the city's foremost expert is dead, her writings incomplete and her surviving pupil missing. I require all noble families to inspect their private libraries and bring anything that might be of use, I know how we all hoard such things but the city will reward anything that helps our efforts. Just think of the stories you learned as a child – the Thousand Shards, the Tomb of Banesh, the Five High Kings. If the Militant Orders consider just one of those to be true, some among them will be willing to turn Jarrazir into a wasteland to secure such a prize.'

'Or ensure the other Orders do not,' Tylom added glumly.

'Indeed. Colonel Pilter – I want that pupil found. Every guild, civic body and noble house is to join the search. By the time I make my announcement I want her here, understood?'

The faces around the table told Stilanna she had finally succeeded in imparting the gravity of the situation to the others.

'Very well, I will see you all tomorrow.'

*

Sotorian Bade put his feet up on the long dining table and took a swig of coffee. All around him people moved with purpose, his team making final preparations. Thus far he had only had

174

to bark an order once – Chotel knew his business well and the extra troops brought in by Exalted Kastelian were all Torquen dragoons; disciplined, elite soldiers.

Bade's crew now numbered ten, a core six of whom had worked for Bade for years. Kastelian had procured twenty dragoons before they reached the city in that strange bartering way the Exalteds had among their own, then suborned the entire standing Torquen complement in Jarrazir, another ten in all. It added up to a packed townhouse by sunrise, bedrolls laid out in most of the rooms and carefully controlled traffic in and out so as to avoid official notice.

'How are we doing, Chotel?' Bade called out as the black man darted into view.

With a look of irritation the man stopped and turned to face his employer. 'Almost there. Kit packed, weapons ready and lamps prepped. The heavy stuff went straight down last night.'

'And Bug?'

'Awake and eager a while back so I dosed her again.'

'Time we took a wander downstairs then.'

Bade eased himself upright, drained his coffee and retrieved a smouldering cigar from the table. He gave a sharp click of the tongue and pointed at the two mages currently lurking near the window, watching the hard-faced crew at work.

'Heel.'

The mages were the only ones without guns. The barge that had brought Bade and his crew to Jarrazir had been fully laden with crates – a simple enough task to secrete mage-guns and ammunition in those, with a few token trade pieces to offer up to the city bondsmen. Bug had been a harder task and Bade's personal chest too – neither of which were small or would stand inspection by customs officials. But Kastelian had done his work and the Torquen's standing in Jarrazir had paved the way for their arrival.

With the mages in tow, Bade and Chotel headed to an un-assuming storeroom door just outside the pantry. The townhouse was a large one in a good area, but betrayed the faint signs of neglect that came from only occasional use. Its true value was a secret hidden from even most of the Order's intelligence branch.

With extensive renovations done decades before, purely on the off-chance of this day, the interior of the house had been changed to conceal the existence of a cellar here. Today, however, the floor of the storeroom was raised and a light shone from the room down below. A shaven-headed woman was in the process of ascending the wide stairway there, one of Bade's crew, but her grunt of acknowledgement went ignored in his eagerness to head down.

There he found three more of his regular crew, all carrying mage-guns and staring at a round block of stone in the centre of the room. Around the block, the floor fell away on three sides – shallow steps leading into unknown darkness below.

'This should be fun,' Bade commented, sharing a grin of anticipation with Chotel. 'Let's get started.' He raised his voice. 'Hey, Kastelian, where are you, ya pious bastard?'

From his belt he unhooked a small Duegar lantern, which looked like an egg-shaped chunk of black glass contained within a framework of brassy metal, itself contained within another frame. He twisted the metal disc that served as the lantern's base and activated its light as Chotel turned down the oil lamps.

From one of the mages there was a gasp. Bade rounded on him. 'Did I ask for your comment?'

'I . . . no, sir.'

'Damn right.'

He returned his attention to the stone column as Kastelian joined them, wearing a sleeveless fleece coat and no fewer than four pistols in holsters. The glyph that had been inscribed on the top of the stone column now shone with pale blue light and a lesser gleam of two small symbols now shone out from the smooth stone around it.

'Fire and ice,' Bade read aloud. 'Could've guessed that bit.'

'Number three,' Chotel added. 'Hardly poetic in their naming, are they?'

'Reminds me of Colec Harbour, that,' Bade remarked. 'All a bit functional, early-era stuff.' He glanced back at the steep stairway leading back up to ground level. 'Torril, you there?'

'Aye, boss,' called a voice. Torril's bearded face appearing a moment later. The man looked like a career soldier, but he was quick with a pen and had a remarkable memory so Bade used him as a notepad for his observations.

'Remind me about Colec Harbour later, okay? Same imaginative numbering and design.'

'Got it. Watch the walls then, eh?'

'Aye, the walls. Fetch out the notes on our old friend Hopper in case he was the one to build this. I want 'em ready when we come back from this first look.'

Kastelian rolled his eyes. 'Hopper?'

'Heh, just our little name for a Duegar architect. Might be it's just a style, but I prefer to think it's a particular adversary for us.'

Bade drew one of his mage-pistols and confirmed it held an icer.

'Right then,' he said to Chotel and the mages. 'Let's go wake up something nasty, eh?'

Chapter 12

It was mid-morning when Atieno returned to the Mercenary Deck's lodgings. The sky was a uniform bright grey, a persistent covering of cloud that promised no sight of rain, sun or Skyriver. The citizens of Jarrazir were up and about by the time Atieno returned with Lastani's reply, but there was precious little trace of the mercenaries.

A pair of easterners in kilts were practising archaic sword-forms in the courtyard, their blades a glittering whirl of death that mirrored each other's perfectly. Off to one side their jackets hung on posts, one bearing the Knight of Snow card, the other the 14 of the same suit. Atieno paused to watch them a moment, both possessing a grace and speed he could only envy.

'Toil's inside,' called the elder of the two as they paused, offering Atieno a short bow that the younger followed.

Feeling oddly formal, Atieno bobbed his head in reply and headed in, feeling their scrutiny until the door was closed behind him and he was faced with a near-empty common room. One table was occupied, however. Toil was sitting with a young woman who looked vaguely familiar and a greying, thin man with one hand and a sparker burn down his cheek. Toil's dark red hair spilled unchecked over her shoulders and she was finishing the last of her breakfast, but aside from that she looked ready to go out. That pleased Atieno, he wanted this to be over with.

'Mistress Toil,' he said, approaching.

'Master Atieno, good morning to you,' Toil said, swallowing the last crumb of food. 'May I present Anatin, benign ruler of this humble mercenary company?'

The greying man gave him a weak smile that had more to do with the redness of his eyes than much else, and extended a hand. 'More benign than this lot are humble anyway.'

Toil grinned. 'And Sitain you've already met, albeit briefly.'

Atieno frowned in thought for a moment then a flash of recollection came to him. This young woman's face, briefly glimpsed in the gloom of night – pale skin fading into darkness as the world went black around him.

'You're the one who put me out,' Atieno said stiffly. 'The mage.'

Sitain shifted in her seat. 'Yeah, sorry about that. No damage done, I hope?'

'It does not seem so,' he said, pausing a moment longer before awkwardly holding out his hand too. 'Let us try again at meeting.'

Sitain shyly took his hand. She didn't look like a mercenary to Atieno, for all that she wore fighting daggers on her jacket and had hair cut roughly short, but Toil was hardly typical of the breed either.

'Got any news for me?' Toil asked. 'Any reply?'

'She wants to meet you,' Atieno confirmed. 'She wants to look you in the eye before surrendering herself, talk to you alone.'

'Time's a-wasting,' Toil grumbled even as she swept up her hat. 'The longer she plays games, the more chance she's got of being arrested.'

'You blame her for being cautious?'

'Damn right,' Toil confirmed. 'I blame everyone who doesn't do exactly what I say and I go on blaming them until they've apologised for being wrong or dead.'

Anatin laughed. 'It's her easy-going nature that makes her a natural fit in the Cards,' he explained to Atieno. 'Probably also be the death of us all, but the gods are nothing but miserable bloody jokers, eh?'

Toil didn't comment, just drew her hair back in one deft movement and piled it up under her hat. With the brim pulled low she buttoned her coat to hide the pistol holster and waved towards the door.

'Lead on, my friend,' Toil said. 'On to glory, on to victory, on to whatever else that playwright said.'

'The dark fields of death,' Atieno replied after a pause for thought.

Toil shook her head and swept past him. 'Nah, don't take us there. Bloody stupid idea, what were you thinking? The dark will have to wait at least a day or two – be patient, my friend.'

'The dark? You mean the labyrinth? What makes you think I'm going with you there?'

'For glory and the other stuff,' Toil said, waving her hand dismissively as she headed outside.

'Once Lastani's safe, I'm done,' Atieno called after her. 'You can enjoy the labyrinth all you like; I'm not going down there for glory, victory or anything else.'

'How about money?' Anatin asked as the door banged shut behind Toil. 'You're a mage, right? Might be you'll be worth having with us.'

He paused. 'How much money?'

Anatin gave a careless shrug and fetched out a cigar from a battered silver case. 'It's her money,' he said. 'How does "lots" suit you?'

The mage thought for a moment. '"Lots" works for me.'

'Excellent. It's a deal.'

*

180

Lastani looked out of the narrow window at the ground below. There was a mass of storage sheds and decrepit single-storey buildings round the back of the Badren Ovens, tight little alleys leading back on themselves, mostly fully of rubbish. A dog scratched disconsolately at one such pile, but seemed to find nothing to interest its appetite and it began to move away as Lastani lowered her bag down as close to the ground as she could.

There were soldiers in the main room below. She didn't know how much time she had, but the books were too heavy to carry alone and too valuable to leave behind. Her fingers were already screaming at her as she tried to line the bag up, suspended from a short length of sheet that – now she was committed – was clearly far too short for the task at hand. At last Lastani managed to swing the bag right and she let go of the sheet. The bag thumped heavily on to a shed roof, slid a little way and held. Lastani gasped with relief then went to fetch a second.

She lowered that out of the window too, depositing it in a snowy pile of broken twigs to one side of the shed. That done, she pulled her cape on, slung a small bag with her remaining belongings over one shoulder and headed to the back stairs. It had been pure chance Lastani had seen the soldiers arrive. Her bags had been mostly packed already, but she'd not expected to have to flee quite like this. A rare prayer to Insar escaped her lips as she reached the narrow back stair and started down it. The god of Silence and the Cold Night was hardly a favourite of hers, despite her magic, but most toiling academics had said a prayer or two to Insar – also called the keeper of secrets – as they tried to unravel one mystery or another.

There was no overt sign of Insar's favour, but the stair was chilly, dark and empty as she reached the bottom to slip out of a side door. With a flush of relief Lastani headed out into the grey light of morning and crossed the street to turn the nearest corner, determined to get out of sight of the Ovens as quickly as possible. Her bags could wait half an hour, she doubted anyone would steal them in the meantime and it was better than skirting around to fetch them.

Ten yards down the street she stopped dead with a whimper of fear. From the shadows of an arched doorway, the barrel of a mage-gun swung down to point at her. Her fingers began to tingle, but then a second gun appeared and she stopped. One soldier she might be able to get the better of; handling two without getting shot would be tough. Though she was an ice mage and those guns were almost certainly loaded with icers, a shield was exhausting to maintain even if she got it up in time.

'Veraimin's blessing, what we got here now?'

A man stepped out of the shadows – not wearing the grey of the City Regiment to her surprise, but a quartered blue-and-white coat of House Gradelines, one of Jarrazir's oldest and most pre-eminent noble houses. There was little noble about the man himself, however; small piggy eyes and a bulbous nose complementing unshaven cheeks and stains on his jacket.

'Let me pass,' Lastani croaked after a moment of blind terror. 'I've done nothing wrong and I'm no vassal of your house.'

'Is that right?' He glanced off to the right where a tall man was advancing through the shadows of an overhanging roof. 'Well, that's good to hear. Still, looks like you scuttled out the Ovens quick enough once those soldiers went in.'

'I heard raised voices, I thought there was going to be trouble.'

'Sure. What's yer name, little miss?'

'Why do you want to know?' she demanded, despite the guns. 'You've no authority in the city.'

'Ah now, we've been deputised, so we have,' the man said with a broad grin. 'The whole city's to look for this rogue mage and you fit the bill pretty nice.' He took a step closer but kept a tight grip on his gun. 'So now, what's yer name?'

'I'm no mage,' Lastani insisted. 'Please, you've got the wrong person. Is it money you want? I've got some, but I don't want trouble. I've got to get home, my father's ill – he's expecting me back.'

'Let's get back to the money,' the guard said. 'How much do you have?'

'I . . . I don't know. Some.' She pulled her purse from her belt, taking her time in the hope a distraction would buy her time to use her magic, and tossed it at his feet. 'Here.'

'Keep an eye on her, Kreil,' the guard said, crouching slowly so he could pick it up without taking his sights off Lastani. 'She tries anything, shoot her.'

Lastani felt the tingle in her hands building, her magic screaming to be released, but she held back – hoping money was all the men wanted. It really was all she had, but while her magic was well schooled she was hardly a battle mage like they had back in the days of kings.

The guard hefted the purse then risked a peek inside. 'That'll do,' he said before looking up. 'Right, hands above your head now.'

'What? But I've . . .'

'Got no money and there's a reward out on this mage,' he finished for her. 'So if you're her, you're worth a lot of money to us. More'n I won at cards last night,' he added, nodding towards the purse. 'If you're not her, you're acting real suspicious and you've only got yourself to blame for being arrested. Now – hands right up, touch the sky and back the way you came.'

Lastani hesitated a moment then flinched as he raised the gun, aiming at her face. She gave a squeak of alarm and put her hands up in the air.

'Good girl, now turn around and walk slowly.'

Lastani blinked in surprise and didn't move. The guard growled but before he could do anything a voice came from further down the alley.

'Too early for a bit of chivalry is it, boys?'

Both men turned to see a smiling woman sauntering up the alley behind the taller guard. She had her hands spread wide to make it clear she was unarmed, wearing fingerless gloves and a red-stitched leather coat buttoned right up to a white silk scarf. Her hat was tilted to one side, shading her face, but dark red hair was visible down the back of her neck.

'Get lost, bitch.'

'Clearly it is,' the woman commented, answering her own question.

'You get one chance to walk away,' the first guard warned. 'Take it and fuck off.'

The woman paused and cocked her head. 'Don't you know who you're talking to?'

'Couldn't give a shit neither.'

'Well I suppose that makes two of us,' she acknowledged. 'More important, do you know who *she* is?'

'Aye.'

There was a pause, as though the woman was waiting for something, but when it didn't come she just sighed.

'That was your cue, love,' she muttered, tilting her head to one side to give Lastani a look. 'Never mind. Hey, who's that?' She pointed off to her right but neither guard moved.

'Think we're stupid?'

'A little bit, yeah.'

Lastani glanced over and gasped. Atieno of all people was standing there, half-hidden around the corner of a building. At her gasp the first guard did look and swore as he fumbled to turn and bring his gun to bear. This time Lastani was ready,

184

however, and a stream of cold magic shot out from her hands to envelop the man. Nothing as damaging as an icer, but the burst of cold was like a slap to the face all the same and the guard was enveloped by white fog.

That moment of distraction was all the woman needed. She raced forward, jinking left and right towards the other guard while he was still bewildered. She grabbed his gun and yanked it out of his hands, kicking him in the side of the knee for good measure. She followed that with a full-blooded slap across his face that rocked him backwards as a small cloud of yellowish dust was dislodged from her glove. The man gasped and reeled while Toil hurled the gun, butt first, at the other guard hidden in Lastani's fog.

By the sound it hit something and Lastani released the magic a moment later – just as the guard staggered sideways out of the mist. His hands frozen to the metal of his gun, the man was still trying to free himself as Toil made up the ground between them. A punch with the heel of her hand snapped the guard's head back and released another puff of yellow. He staggered a step more then buckled and fell.

Lastani looked back at the first guard to see him on his knees, already limp and toppling face first to the ground. The strange woman checked them both then yanked off her gloves and stowed them in a bag as she approached Lastani.

'Lastani Ufre, I presume?' the woman said with something akin to a purr. 'Or do I owe them an apology?' There was a flicker of delight in her eyes, the look of a woman who liked to prove herself against the odds at every opportunity.

'No, ah – yes, that's me. You're her? Toil?'

'The one and only.'

She looked down at the guards. 'And them?'

'Not dead, if that's what you're worried about,' Toil said. 'But out for a while yet. Come on.'

She grabbed the ankle of one and dragged him to an unobtrusive corner while Atieno did the same with the other. Then they collected the dropped guns and tossed them aside too.

'Let's go then.'

'Wait – my books!' Lastani almost wailed as Toil grabbed her arm and started to lead her away.

'Books? Where?'

Lastani pointed. 'Round the back of the Ovens. I dropped them out the window when I saw the soldiers.'

'Clever girl,' Toil said approvingly. 'Atieno – can you fetch them? You're not what they're looking for unless they were tipped off; no reason they'll question the owner too hard. I'm no academic, but a lone woman attracts more attention when that's what they're looking for.'

Atieno regarded her a moment then nodded. 'I'll meet you back at your lodging house.'

Toil beckoned to Lastani. 'Come on, we need to get clear. If we're quick we'll be back before Lynx has eaten all the breakfast.'

'Who's Lynx?'

'Just shift yourself.'

*

A pile of mushrooms wasn't the finest way to start the day, in Lynx's opinion. True there were a lot of them, true they'd been fried in butter and garlic, but after a heaped plate his stomach was still of the opinion that there was something missing.

'Cheer up,' Llaith said, nudging Lynx's shoulder as he sat beside him. 'It could be worse.'

'Is bacon too much to ask for?' he replied. 'Honestly, just a few rashers. What sort of a broken-down excuse for a town is this when bacon's not on the menu?'

'Oh it's available, but we're getting the discount rate so they're not wasting bacon on the likes of us.'

Lynx frowned. 'Who do I need to throw money at to change that?'

'The cook, I'm guessing.' Llaith paused, watching Lynx for a moment longer before laughing. 'Gods, you're really fixed on this, aren't you?'

'What makes you say that?'

'Because, my friend, you've not even asked how it could be worse – or noticed for yourself.'

'What? Why?'

Lynx cast around the room for a while. At least a third of the company were there breaking their fasts, most staring disconsolately at great mugs of spiced tea said to ward off winter colds, but one man caught his eye. He was a squat, balding mercenary with great galaxies of freckles across his chest and arms – interrupted by mismatched army tattoos and a Seven of Sun card tattoo on his right biceps.

'The hell's up with Brols?'

Currently Brols was inspecting the wall, one cheek twitching furiously as he muttered some sort of crazed incantation and made obscure gestures with his hands.

'The newest game – evidence if ever it was needed that Varain and Braqe should never *ever* be allowed to get bored in each other's company.'

Lynx looked a while longer at Brols then around at the others eating, then at his own plate.

'Oh, for . . .'

'Yup,' Llaith chuckled happily. 'Mushroom pot-luck every breakfast for us. The cook turned out to be happy to play along, now we just have to run a book on how long it takes for Anatin to lose his shit over it.'

Lynx pushed his plate away and shook his head. 'We've hardly been here long enough to get bored, have we?'

'You've never got between Varain and a drink.' Llaith shrugged. 'So – where's your mistress this morning?'

'Mistress? Oh, dunno. Why?'

'Just wondering,' he said with a wink. 'You just give us the word, Lynx, and we'll clear out for the night. Safir and I understand what it's like, the need for privacy. Could be tonight we'll be getting an invite to a booze-barge in the bay anyway. No need to say anything, just nod if you want us to make a special effort, mebbe take Layir too. The boy's too shy around women so it'd be good for him.'

Lynx looked away, as much to avoid the filthy leer on Llaith's face as embarrassment. He wasn't one for discussing his personal life, less so when he had no damn idea what was going on in it. Toil remained an enigma to him – the kisses yesterday aside, she'd been as elusive as a leaf on the wind for weeks. Whether that was by accident or design he couldn't say, but wouldn't rule either out.

'Shattered gods, sure – what Layir really needs is a boost to his confidence around the ladies,' Lynx reflected. 'Given how he made a damn good effort to screw every willing woman in Su Dregir, married or not, what the boy really needs is a new challenge in a city of proud noble families and regular duels.'

'Boy can handle himself in a duel.'

'And you want to explain that to the Envoy when it gets brought up at court?'

'Ain't you the teacher's pet all of a sudden?' Llaith snickered. 'By "Envoy" you mean Toil, right?'

'Fine, go do whatever the—' Lynx didn't finish his sentence as the door banged open and the woman herself entered, this time with a young woman close to half her age with short, white hair. 'Looks like she's got her girl then,' he mused.

'That's the mage?' Llaith whispered. 'Not a bad-looking thing.'

'Who could freeze your nuts off with a flick of her fingers,' Lynx reminded him.

'Ah,' Llaith said sagely. 'I've known girls like that.'

'This is Lynx,' Toil said as she reached them. 'The one with the dirty grin's Llaith, don't believe a word he says.'

'Nice to meet you, miss,' Llaith replied, rising and deftly kissing Lastani's hand while Lynx grunted a hello.

'Where's your friend?' Lynx asked. 'You get into any trouble?'

Toil nodded back towards the door. 'He'll be following soon. Might have some bags with him, though, fancy going to help him?'

'You serious or just want me to bugger off for a bit?'

'Serious. He's fetching her books. They're searching hard this morning. We ran into a couple of noble house guards who'd joined in the hunt.'

Lynx nodded and rose. 'Fancy a walk, Llaith?'

'And leave these two lovely ladies all alone? Not a chance.'

'Him I do want to just bugger off,' Toil said. 'The pair of you, go meet Atieno and get him back here as fast as you can. We've got work to do.'

Chapter 13

When the three men returned to the lodgings they discovered news had arrived while they were out. Aben, one of the Envoy's personal guards, had sent a message to Toil that there was to be an announcement the following day. In an attempt to calm the tensions and uncertainty in the city, the Monarch was to speak to the great and the good about the labyrinth and the Envoy was naturally invited.

Anatin and Toil sat at a table discussing the matter, various members of the Cards watching them like they were scorpions about to be pitted against each other. The company commander looked anxious, unhappy about something Toil had suggested. Anatin had a pack of cards in his one remaining hand, flipping the top card around to the bottom with a practised flick. The cards whispered like a blade being sharpened on leather, laden with promise. Two of his inner circle, Payl and the seer, Estal, sat close beside him and looked almost as cheerful.

With Atieno going to join Lastani, sat apart from the arguing mercenaries, Lynx found a seat with Kas who shifted to rest her elbow on his shoulder, making to whisper to him before a curse from Anatin cut her off.

'Dammit, woman, how's that a good idea?'

'I'm paying your fee, remember?' Toil said. 'You knew this is what I really hired you for, not some bloody escort duty.'

'You said you needed troops in reserve while you offered *your* services. We're not a relic hunter crew and I don't much fancy losing my other fucking hand to whatever it is they say is protecting the labyrinth.'

'I can't offer my services without a crew to back me up – otherwise I'm just some crazy bitch off the street wanting to get involved.'

'Funny, it looks to me like that's exactly what you are.'

Toil's knuckles tightened briefly. 'All I need,' she said in a low voice, 'is a few fighters I can trust to do what the fuck I tell them and all the rest are show. I won't be taken seriously without a crew at my command but most of the expedition will be Jarraziran.'

'So you assume! What if the Monarch thows all her regiments at this mystery shitbag maze to make sure she gets the prize before anyone else sneaks in? Or decides to use this large crew o' yours as fucking bait for these murderous Duegar ghosts we're hearing about? Reckon we can just change our minds then?'

'Leave me to sort that out.'

'Along with a whole lot o' other things you seem to reckon's none of our business.'

Toil slammed her hand on the table. 'I pay you, you follow orders. Isn't that how it works in your business? Have I spent all these years under some bloody misapprehension about what the word "mercenary" means?'

'And the first rule of the Mercenary Deck is to still be alive to get paid so I ain't fucking following you to play with horrors in the dark.'

Toil glared at him a while then took a long deep breath. 'I thought the first rule of the Cards was "don't get caught cheating"?'

Anatin blinked at her, thrown by the change in direction, but Lynx recognised an effort to diffuse the tension in the room. Clearly so did Payl, as the woman cleared her throat.

'That one's more of a philosophy,' Payl said. 'The first rule of the Cards is "don't ask Llaith about venereal disease".'

'Hey!' Llaith objected as there came a few cautious laughs. 'I thought it was "don't play knives with Teshen"?'

Payl made a dismissive gesture. 'Third or fourth at least. Well behind the gory details of your poor judgement.'

'Surely the first rule is "don't shoot your employer"?' Kas joined in. 'Which *someone* had to learn the hard way if memory serves.'

'Or "never believe anything Himbel says when he's drunk",' suggested Llaith.

'"Never scratch your balls with your gun," would be a good one,' Payl said, 'Saw a man do that once. Almost shit myself laughing.'

Before anyone else could join in Anatin stood up abruptly, his chair clattering to the ground behind him.

'Enough, the lot of you! Your point's made; you're all fucking heroes who laugh in the face of danger so you'll follow Toil wherever she leads you.' Without seeming to be aware of it he was massaging the stump of his left arm where he'd had a hand once, before he'd gone into Shadow's Deep. 'We'll play along,' he said to Toil. 'You'll have your relic hunter crew when required, but only those who're dumb enough to volunteer actually go with you – explaining any shortfall to the Monarch is your problem.'

He reached down and grabbed a card off the table, brandishing it for a moment before flicking it at Toil's face. She caught the card and calmly set it face up on the table. It was the Jester of Stars, the card worn by Ashis – one of the mercenaries who'd died in Shadows Deep.

'I understand,' Toil said. 'In the meantime, you're all in my employ still so . . . you.' She pointed at one of the mercenaries. 'It's Haphori right?'

'Yeah – ah, sir,' the man said.

'Right. Get to the Envoy's townhouse, find his guards; either Aben or Barra. If you meet the captain just tell him you've been sent for Teshen, he's needed back here and you're to replace him for the meantime, okay? Take this guy, Crast is it?'

'Aye, sir.'

'Good. You two tell Aben or Barra it's time to start moving and they should make supper plans.'

'Supper plans?' Anatin broke in. 'What in the name of Catrac's blood are you on about?'

'I want to see this announcement for myself,' she explained after pointing towards the door and sending Crast and Haphori on their way. 'The Envoy will get an invite, us not so much. So I need to have the Envoy's aides out of action for a day or so, make him scout around for someone who can serve as aide for him in a pinch.'

'And he'll choose you?'

'Any of you geniuses impressed your learning upon him? No? Well that's me shocked.'

'And then?'

'Then I find out who I need to charm to get an audience with the Monarch, mebbe a sight of the competion too since I'm not likely to be the only one who's heard about the laby-rinth outside of Jarrazir.' Toil craned her neck to look over the assembled faces and find Lastani.

'There you are. Before I can impress the Monarch I need to know all I can about the labyrinth. Inside knowledge and maybe even a guide to hand could tip the balance.' She looked around the assembled mercenaries. 'Until I've got myself positioned to be useful, you all just sit tight like good little children, hear me? That means no more making this place into a gambling den, understood? The last thing I need is you all getting arrested or some broken-headed grunt making free with a knife and messing everything up.'

'No wonder the Duegar died out if their foreplay was all such a fucking disappointment.'

Chotel nodded and turned to face Bade, the grin on his lieutenant's face almost invisible in the dark. 'So much for the fabled Labyrinth of Jarrazir, eh?'

'Aye.'

Kastelian sighed. 'You wanted this to be more exciting?'

'Well, I'll grant that no ghostly horrors emerging from the walls to butcher us is considered a good thing, but still . . . I've done shits with more magnificence.'

It really had been dull. The first set of steps led down to an oval chamber, where just a handful of glyphs glowed faintly from the bare rock, with a tunnel entrance to the rear. The chamber wasn't even big given the cavernous halls and mile-deep mines he'd seen in his career, nothing to impress at all.

Bade had kept well back and thrown two mage-beads – the simple glass balls every mage kept – into the room and brief flares of fire and ice erupted over their respective glyphs to appease the guardian. He'd spent a while inspecting and checking the rest of the room before ordering down the remaining supplies with his crew, but at last they'd set off towards the labyrinth proper.

The tunnel had proved to be a long gentle spiral descending twenty-odd yards further underground before running level for a quarter of a mile only to open out into another empty space as unimpressive as the last, with one modest exception. There were no glyphs, no signs that there was a danger there, but Bade hadn't lived this long being reckless with his own life so he spent a long time investigating before going any further. He used both Duegar lanterns and a white alchemical orb to check the space for any markings before finally approaching the stone door at the far end.

While it was blank, without handle or decoration, its surface was beautifully smooth – no general working of stone magery here but something rather more rare and elegant. With his lantern held close and his cheek almost pressed against the door, Bade inspected its surface until he found a slight irregularity. A smile appeared on his lips.

'Finally, a little titillation,' he muttered to himself as much as the rest.

'What is it?' Kastelian asked.

'A depression – pressure point I'd guess,' Bade replied. 'More importantly, it's looking familiar. I've seen this sort of door in a few ruins which means there might be fewer genuine surprises further down.'

He straightened and beckoned to the mages. 'Right, which one of you's which again?'

The mages looked at each other. 'I am Suthari,' the woman began hesitantly until Bade made a disgusted sound.

'I don't give a shit about your names, you're Spade and Fork to me. Just tools, understand?'

'Then I don't . . .'

'Your magic, you shaved monkey's nutsack!'

The bald woman shrank back at his shout as Kastelian chuckled beside them.

'He's fire, she's night – we thought those might be most useful.'

'Right then.' Bade beckoned to the woman. 'We'll try night first. If memory serves it don't matter a whole lot what magic is used, but best we know what tool we're using.'

The woman stepped forward, trying to smother her fear, and Bade jabbed a finger against the part of the door he'd found. Nothing happened, but Bade just gave a grunt and gestured for her to do the same.

'This place's been locked down for millennia,' he explained, 'probably need a spark o' magic to trigger the mechanism, some power to move it.'

Suthari nodded her head and closed her eyes. In the light it was hard to make out, but Bade's eyes detected the familiar shudder of darkness twist around her fingers as she pressed the depression. For a moment nothing happened then there was a whisper of smooth stone and the door began to rotate, sliding up to the left inside the rock face. It took another few moments before any change was visible, then all of a sudden a space was revealed and a gust of dry, musty air washed over them.

The mage gasped in shock. For a moment Bade thought the stale air was poisoned or something, then the light of his Duegar lantern picked out faint lines of stone running away into the distance. The night mage would of course be able to see far better than that with her magic flowing through her body.

He gave her elbow a nudge with the muzzle of his pistol. 'What can you see?' he whispered.

'I . . .' For a moment she continued to gape. 'It's huge, the rock is seamed with light – it's beautiful.' She made to step across the threshold but before she could Chotel darted forward and grabbed her by the scruff of her neck, yanking her back.

'Easy there,' Chotel hissed. 'It's a pissing labyrinth, remember?'

She blinked at him. 'What? But I can see perfectly well.'

'Yeah, ya damn fool,' he said, laughing, 'and that don't strike you as weird?'

'Why?'

'It's a labyrinth,' he explained as though to a child. 'Tunnels, passages, twists and turns. Not being able to see where you are and where you're going.'

'But it's just an open space.' she said, turned to look through the doorway again. 'The roof is high and sloping, I can see

196

flagstones for thirty yards straight ahead to where the roof comes to meet it, but it's at least a hundred yards of open ground to the left and right.'

'Which makes me suspicious, not least 'cos the buggers didn't cut flagstones often.'

Bade nodded. 'Burner?'

'If there's nothing there, why not? Nothing to damage and the flames spread nicely.'

He pulled his pistol again and checked there was another burner in the pipe. Picking the furthest point he could see in the light of his lantern, Bade fired. An orange streak of fire raced away into the darkness, exploding in yellow flames over the stone floor. As the flames mushroomed away they spread only a few yards on either side before they seemed to simply fall through the flagstones and vanish.

'False floor,' Bade breathed. 'Now we've got a game.'

'You're up, Spade,' Chotel said, prodding the male mage forward. 'Give the floor here a dusting of fire.'

'What?'

'Spread some fire around; trust me, we've done this before. The false parts aren't affected, the real ones get blackened up.'

The man opened his mouth to argue then shut it again and quickly knelt. As he tried to place his palm flat on the stones over the threshold his hand passed straight through. He snatched it back again as though it had been bitten and stared at his fingers.

'Hurt?'

'I, ah, no.'

'Then the man gave you a fucking order, Spade,' Bade growled. 'Start digging.'

With fingers splayed the man reached forward and a faint orange wisp began to drift from his fingers. In moments the light spread and billowed, a cloud of yellow flames washing over the flagstones in an impressive display of control. He stretched forward and touched his fingers to it, gripping his fellow mage for support as he leaned out the best part of a yard forward. The fire became snaking tendrils, hungry for fuel. It spread across the real stones like fat worms of light, charring the dust and dirt that lay atop, while the illusions simply swallowed the fire and remained untouched.

Chotel brought the alchemical globe up to stand right behind the mage, letting its white light illuminate the soot-dirtied path through the great chamber. It was four yards wide and extended ahead after the initial pitfall at the doorway, running towards the centre of the chamber. A second burst of flames revealed its course was straight before meeting a similar path that led left and right.

'Simple enough,' Chotel said after a while.

Bade nodded. 'Aye, once your visitors know the trick to see it, putting too much detail is just playing with yourself. Looks like our Duegar friend's more of a tease.'

'Or he's saving his games for elsewhere.'

'Of that I've no doubt. This is the upper floor, I've seen this mentioned in some of the texts I've read. They might be short on detail about what's at the heart, but several agree about this part. The real labyrinth comes next.'

'Luckily for us,' Kastelian said drily.

Bade shared a smile with his liaison as Chotel nodded and the rest looked mystified. 'Aye, now let's get moving. I want this door braced and the path marked in case our friend Spade gets his head ripped off by something playful.'

He carefully stepped forward on to the first real stone block, one hand holding Chotel's until he was sure it wasn't going to give way.

'Well, I ain't dead yet,' he commented as Chotel winced at the tempting of fate. 'Now, let's see how lucky we can be.'

He pulled out a brass-bound compass from his pocket and gave it a tap. 'North by north-east,' he said, looking up at the wall on the far side. 'That'll do. Kastelian, get your map out. Spade, heel.'

*

As the conversation between Toil and Lastani turned academic, the assembled crowd dwindled quickly. Atieno contributed little, contenting himself to sit at Lastani's side like a disapproving uncle, while for his own part, Lynx very quickly found himself fighting the urge to yawn and wonder about lunch.

After the kissing yesterday, he'd had a fleeting fantasy about sharing a long, lazy meal with Toil – honeyed pork, spiced eel and sticky rice parcels appearing prominently in his mind – but it seemed at least three of the gods seemed to be conspiring against him. Toil had eyes only for Lastani and the leather-bound books that Atieno had helped unpack from her bags.

Instead he contented himself with watching Toil as she spoke, the conversation ranging from discredited academics, the conflicting dogmas of the Revival period and exactly what Mistress Ishienne had thought she was doing in the first place. The main bone of contention seemed to be that last detail, but Lynx's one contribution had been a growl of the stomach loud enough to blunt both women's irritation.

'Veraimin's shroud!' Toil groaned. 'Can someone fetch Lynx some food before he goes feral? Come on, let's take a break. We've got a lot more ground to cover before tomorrow.'

'Gods, really?' Sitain said, almost looking startled that she'd spoken the words out loud. 'I mean, well, you've been at it for hours.'

'And if I'm to do what I intend, I'll need to convince the Monarch of my expertise,' Toil replied. 'I don't want to reveal my prince-in-the-hole if I don't have to.'

Sitain shrugged. 'So draw a map and tell her it's genuine. Not like she's got anything to compare it to, has she?'

Lastani snorted at the idea, but didn't speak. She'd spent the entire conversation looking pale and nervous – understandably so, for all that her expertise outweighed Toil's. The weight of days in hiding had clearly taken its toll and she had struggled to answer some questions as fatigue dulled her wits. None of that had been helped by Toil pointing out how Lastani would need to do better if trying to impress the Monarch.

'Anyone claiming to have a map'd be laughed out of the room,' Toil explained. 'But there are commentaries and references scattered across centuries, analyses on those descriptions of books now lost to decay or the Orders, and conjecture of wildly varying quality.'

In contrast to Lastani, Toil seemed brighter and more animated than ever. For all that she was a woman of action, Toil had an inner calmness much of the time, a poise and assurance that were part of what made her so fascinating to Lynx. But now he saw another side; the woman of learning who was intent on reading Lastani's books during the process of interrogating the owner. For Lynx, a book was a quiet luxury – a moment of peace that took his soul outside of the jagged, cracked shell he'd built around it, but clearly Toil saw them differently.

There was a pinkness to her cheeks that was decidedly attractive, Lynx realised; a flush of excitement and hunger more akin to lust than academic curiosity. The rush of the unknown drove her right then – the deepest black waiting to be conquered that no amount of lazy luncheon would be able to compete with.

It's like a drug to her, he realised, *let's hope it's not one that ends up consuming her. Fuck, let's hope it doesn't kill everyone around her too. I bet she'll be wanting me to volunteer for relic hunter duty and saying no to her worries me almost as much as going into the black again. Almost.*

'So what, then?' Sitain said, looking put out by the reaction. 'Do you even know what's at the heart of the labyrinth? I mean actually *know* rather than just the old stories everyone's heard?'

'No one knows,' Toil replied, 'not for certain. All the tales about the Arm of Catrac or the great cache were likely just invented by—'

'Ah,' Lastani broke in, 'that may not be correct, actually.'

'What?'

'The great cache – that might in fact be true.'

Toil blinked, her mouth working without any sound coming out until her mind could catch up. 'How?'

'You're referring to the heresy works?' Lastani said with a quirk of a smile on her lips at long last. 'Mistress Ishienne believes . . .' She faltered for a moment, her smile vanishing. 'Believed that Noxeil's claims might have some foundation given references she found to a man of the same name making up part of the original Brethren of the Shards delegation at Jang-Her.'

'Jang-what?' Sitain broke in. 'Have I missed part of this plan?'

'You never knew it in the first place,' Toil said. 'Jang-Her – the great conclave of the Militant Orders that broke the old kingdom of Urden into the Riven Kingdom. Where they made all their secret deals, bartered artefacts and Duegar texts. All hundreds of years ago now. The point is that a man called Noxeil supposedly claimed the last centuries of the Duegar saw a religion spring up, venerating the gods they'd lost, and gathering a great cache of God Fragments. They hid this at the heart of a labyrinth, hoping to resurrect one of the gods, but last I heard no one believed it.'

'Unless he was at Jang-Her,' Lastani broke in, 'where the concentration of God Fragments had a strange effect on at least a dozen attendees. There are some translations of Duegar texts that came from a time when humans possibly lived alongside the remnants, but most of what we have came from that one meeting. From those men and woman who heard voices and hallucinated a time of grand magics, upheaval and cataclysmic warfare. Between them they possessed insights into the Duegar language that seemed impossible, but overlapped with the others in such a way their veracity was unassailable.'

Sitain frowned. 'So this Noxeil was one of those?'

'We believe so, he just didn't exhibit the same affliction the others did – his gifts took longer to manifest.'

'But if he *was* there,' Toil finished, 'it turns this entirely on its head.'

'Exactly, although the mystery of the labyrinth remains. No one knows why it was built – or *when* for sure. Perhaps it is a vault for God Fragments that became the centre of an entire religion, perhaps it's older but was co-opted to another use. Mistress Ishienne's theory was that it originally had a specific religious purpose, some sort of test of faith to discover divine wisdom at its heart. However, some Duegar writers called it a tomb of the last great queen of the Duegar, others a vault of secrets.'

'The place of seeds,' Toil intoned as though remembering some distant lesson. 'The taproot of the Duegar, the stone of light – more bloody names than you'd think entirely necessary. They were a dramatic and self-important lot, those Duegar writers.'

'But let me guess,' Lynx broke in, 'not so good on the details of what nastiness waits for anyone who actually enters the labyrinth?'

'Yeah, funny that – almost like they didn't want us to rob it. Up until now, that didn't matter so much, the puzzle of the Fountain had everyone stumped for thousands of years.'

'Up until last week,' Lynx said with a sinking feeling. 'And now it's open and trouble's just waiting to pour out.'

'Only if the Militant Orders get inside first,' Toil said with feeling. 'Whatever is down there, it might overturn the balance of power across the continent, so let's beat them to it and tip that balance in our favour, eh?'

'Sure, sounds easy.'

Chapter 14

Progress around the upper level of the labyrinth was slow but steady under Bade's lead. He stood out front with the fire mage, using a long wooden staff to tap and prod each paving stone he reached before he trusted his weight to them. The mage was there to confirm each coming stretch was real. Though the effort was soon visible in his manner, he had the sense not to complain or hesitate as Bade ordered him on. Only once did they have a delay, one of the yard-long slabs proving real but counter-weighted so it tilted under the weight of Bade's staff. Anyone stepping on it would have pitched sideways into whatever lay below, before the stone slid neatly back into place.

The mage beside him trembled at the idea, but Bade only felt a frisson of delight as he watched the mechanism reset. There were few city-ruins with such deliberate defences, while this labyrinth had been designed with keeping people out entirely in mind. This was a rare challenge for the purist – not just another crumbling cavern system where maspids and the like hunted.

This place has been sealed for millennia, most likely, he reminded himself excitedly. *Warded against water intrusion and all the burrowing nasties that prefer the dark – a puzzle waiting patiently to try and kill whoever comes to test themselves against it. And now the game's begun; just me and this beautiful, lethal puzzle-box. Just this once I'm willing to say the anticipation's better than sex.*

Behind them came Chotel and the night mage, a contrasting set of expertise from each as they kept watch on everything beyond the next step. A pair of Bade's regular team followed them, marking the stones with white paint that would shine in the alchemical globe's light. At the trap-stone they put a large cross on the top. The Duegar lamps were the primary light, but Bade was well used to navigating by such dimness and the strange light they cast would illuminate any Duegar markings they came across.

With regular pauses to check the count of steps, consult the compass and mark on a map, Bade was already expecting to have arrived at his destination when the night mage gasped and pointed off to their right.

'Glyph?' he asked.

'Yes – a large one, with ornate decoration around the outside. A doorway below.'

'Good.'

Bade squinted off into the darkness. It took him a moment but eventually he spotted the faint play of glowing lines on the rock wall. He took his time as always, knowing haste was the first danger of the dark, but it wasn't long before they were all safely brought to the foot of another door, recessed slightly into the natural line of the rock wall. It was identical to the one they'd entered by, smooth with a slight depression, but still Bade spent a while inspecting it and the surrounding stone before doing anything more.

'What's that glyph say?' he demanded of the mages as he went about his checking. 'I don't recognise it.'

The night mage cleared her throat. 'It, ah, it appears to be some sort of composite word. The character for "Honoured", I believe, the other I do not recognise.'

'You?' Bade asked the other.

'I, no. Sorry, I don't think I've even seen it before. It's more complex than most Duegar script.'

'Mebbe a name then,' he decided with a shrug. 'We'll worry about that another day. Doesn't seem to be a warning, that's the main thing, and I reckon I know where we are.'

The night mage opened the door in the same way she had earlier, only this time the armed members of the group had their guns drawn and levelled. Unveiling the large globe lamp, its white light outlined a familiarly dull chamber and tunnel.

'Do we go in?' Chotel whispered to Bade after a few moments of nothing at all happening. 'Or come back when we're ready?'

'Spade and I go,' he replied. 'Might be we need to deal with another guardian spirit before we get the run of the room and I don't want gunfire in there yet.'

Bade reached into a pocket of his coat and brought out one of several steel boxes he carried. Opening that, he retrieved a small glass bead with the character for ice painted on the surface.

'Come on, Spade. Feel free to burn up anything that jumps out at you, just keep close to me, okay?'

They followed a shallow tunnel for two hundred paces by Bade's count, which eventually opened on to a tall cylindrical chamber with a zig-zag set of inclines rising out of the floor. The dozen shallow slopes led to a platform and a great stone door that stood open into the room. Before they reached that, however, Bade found what he was looking for around the lower part of the room – a pair of glyphs identical to the previous ones, halfway up the wall and glowing blue in the lamplight.

'Ready?'

The mage nodded and as Bade hurled his mage-bead at one of the glyphs, the mage set a stream of fire washing over the other. As the light of the magic faded, the competing magics neatly dividing the room in orange light and frost-kissed dark, the glyphs pulsed with light. Bade felt a flicker of relief, but kept his hand on his mage-pistol all the same as he ascended the slope with the mage in tow.

The door was a slab of mage-carved rock easily fifteen feet high and more than a foot thick, but it led nowhere as the doorway beyond had been walled up. Touching his fingers to his lips, Bade crept forward and inspected the obstacle. It was human-built, brick and mortar and hastily done from what he could tell. How thick was anyone's guess, but a test probe with his knife told him that the mortar was still slightly soft.

Patiently he worked one brick loose and slid it out. There were more behind of course, but it gave him an idea of what he was dealing with and, after waiting a short while to see if he could hear anything from the other side, they returned to the others.

'The intelligence is good, just as we were told,' Bade said at Chotel's inquisitive look. 'The entrance is open and the doorway's bricked up. You stay here with a couple of men and the big lamp, start the process of unpicking the wall, just be slow and silent. I'll send the supplies down so we're ready to move as soon as possible.'

'You're not going to explore the rest?'

Bade grinned. 'Work first,' he said, nodding at Kastelian. 'We can wait a day to play.'

*

A thump on his foot jerked Lynx awake. Before he could even focus he was reaching for his sword, but found nothing and after a few moments of blindly flapping, he looked up to see Toil. She had a small smile on her face and her leather coat on her back.

'Still a bit twitchy when you wake, eh?'

'Aye, looks like it,' he muttered. Lynx looked around and saw the back of Lastani heading through the door to the stairs. 'Giving her a break then?'

'The girl could do with a rest,' Toil confirmed, 'and I need to run an errand. Want to stretch your legs?'

He blinked at her for a moment then nodded and heaved himself up. 'Reckon I do, where are we going?'

'We're going dress shopping.' Toil beamed. 'You'll love it.'

'A dress? For you?'

'Of course for bloody me, who else?'

He shrugged. 'Dunno, just never seen you in a dress.'

'Here's your chance then.'

They headed out into the grey afternoon light and down the main avenue running south through the district. The streets were busy, people and horses packing the avenue, so they were forced to weave a path through slow-moving traffic until the green-sheathed roofs of guild-houses came into view. Surrounding each of those was a tight network of streets where the shops were mostly devoted to the trade of the guild-house. The Tailors' Guild was an imposing red-brick structure with fifty or more small flags flying above the pair of double doors that served as entrance to the great building. On the doors themselves was a brass crest, an eight-pointed star made of sewing needles.

'What're those?' Lynx asked, pointing at the flags.

'Guildsmen crests,' Toil said. 'Means they're accredited members and can charge more, sign of quality, see?' She pointed to one of the nearby shops where the great crest of the guild was reproduced above the door while a flag bearing the guild crest of that shop twitched in the afternoon breeze.

'But we're not going in there?'

She shook her head. 'Given I'm not looking for a soldier's uniform, no. Over there, that'll do.'

She led him across the street to an almost identical shop, but in the window of that one he saw a wooden headless mannequin wearing a green sleeveless dress. Lynx raised an eyebrow at the low-cut front as much as the bands of ribbon and crystal decoration, but Toil just snorted and shook her head as she reached for the door.

'Don't get any ideas, it ain't going to be that fancy.'

'Still, I'm liking the general thrust.'

Inside it smelled of expensive leather and dried flowers, scrubbed floors and cedar wood. They were met by a pair of hatchet-faced women who could have been sisters, both with their hair severely pinned back and wearing silk shawls over the sleeveless dresses that Lynx had realised was the fashion for civillian women of a certain status. One wore black, the other brown, but both sported the shop's crest worked into the decoration around their waist.

'May we help you, ah, madam?' asked one dubiously.

'I need a dress and I need it fast,' Toil snapped, marching inside like a duchess and turning her back on the pair as she scanned the boles of fabric lining the left-hand wall. 'Plain silk, high neck, in green and grey. To be completed by this evening.'

She shucked off her leather coat and tossed it to Lynx before sweeping back her dark red hair and giving the women an imperious look.

'Well?'

'I regret—'

Toil made an angry little sound and stepped forward, the shrewish tailor's platitudes tailing quickly off as the imposing mercenary loomed over her.

'No, no regrets.' She pulled a purse from her belt and hefted it to make the coins inside chink. 'I want quality work and I was told I could get it here. If you're not up to the challenge I will take my money elsewhere and refer the others accordingly.'

'Others?' said brown dress.

'Others,' Toil confirmed without bothering to explain further. 'Now, shouldn't you be taking measurements?'

The pair scuttled to work and Toil nodded approvingly. She removed her scarf and began to unbutton her tunic, flashing Lynx a mischievous smile before turning away. Underneath she wore only a thin linen shirt that showed the lines of her body to great effect, if Lynx was any judge.

'Don't worry, Lynx,' Toil called over her shoulder as she tossed him the tunic and submitted to measurement. 'I've not forgotten you and your friends.'

'Oh, great, the last suit you got me was such a success,' he replied gloomily.

'At least you got a few hours use out of yours,' Toil said, frowning. 'I never even put mine on!'

For the Skyriver Festival in Su Dregir, Toil had invited Lynx to the Archelect's ball and all festivities on that night were conducted in costume. Lynx had arrived at Toil's home dressed as the Knight of Blood only to discover two dead assassins inside. Sadly that had been only the start of the excitement. By the end of the night, even by Lynx's travel-worn standards his costume was less than pristine.

'So what do I get this time?'

'Nothing so dramatic, just a uniform. It occurred to me that having extras made for those of you assigned to guard duty would be prudent, so I had some made before we left just in case.'

'Not just for me then?'

'Me, Payl, Varain and Teshen too. I hadn't planned on using them quite like this, but that's the best laid plans for you.'

'Good luck getting Payl in after that public bust-up she had. This is for the announcement tomorrow, right?'

'It is. Payl's my problem, and frankly that face of yours may prove as much of one. However, if it's a case of forgoing his due dignity because of diminished numbers, I think the Envoy will agree in a pinch.'

Lynx was quiet a while, his thoughts following the path of Toil's plans to an unsavoury conclusion. 'And afterwards?'

'What about afterwards?'

'If you get your way,' he said in a tight voice. 'You'll be wanting me to volunteer?'

'Ah, that.' Toil nodded in understanding.

Lynx had found it hard to enter Shadows Deep even with a company of Knights-Charnel cavalry pursuing them. Even the thought of doing so again made his heart beat faster. His time in a So Han military prison camp was almost a decade behind him, but the misery and hardship of working in the mines there had left an indelible impression.

'Yes and no,' Toil said finally. 'I'll want you to volunteer, I won't ask you to. The choice is yours,' she added in a softer voice. 'You're good in a tight spot, but if you don't want to be there, no sense in dragging you.'

Lynx grunted, acknowledging her point. 'But you'll need Sitain,' he said at last.

'She's a big girl, doesn't need you watching over her all the time.'

'Aye,' he said dubiously.

Toil laughed. 'Shattered gods, you and the old man really are two peas in a diamond-shaped pod, aren't you?'

'Atieno?' Lynx was taken aback before realising she was just taking a friendly dig, not revealing that she knew anything more about the Vagrim. Even after months around the mercenaries, he sometimes still had to remind himself not to take everything said so seriously. 'Aye, I s'pose you could say that.'

He gave a wry smile, glad Toil's back was still turned. 'Some of us don't get wiser as we age, we just keep doing the same old thing.'

'Aye, might be you're the fool who's met the old fool he's going to turn into one day.' Toil glanced back. 'But Atieno's a handsome enough old fool, so things could be worse.'

'That's a relief, been trading on my looks for so long I wouldn't know what to do with myself.'

She nodded. 'Explains the state of your clothes at least. Jewellery too, mebbe.'

He glanced down at the silver ring on his middle finger, almost identical to the one Atieno wore.

'You could say that.'

'Want to tell me about it?'

'Not much,' he admitted. 'If you don't know, I'd prefer to keep it that way.'

'Aha, I like a man of mystery,' she said, making a clear effort to keep the conversation light.

'No great mystery, but folk read a whole lot into nothing sometimes.'

'Nothing likely to bite you in the arse?'

Lynx laughed at that. It might not be easy to follow the Vagrim path, but when it caused a problem you tended to know pretty damn quick. Saving Sitain had been one instance of that – he'd pulled a gun on a group of Charnelers without really expecting his new comrades to back him up.

'You don't need worry on that front,' he said as Toil shot him a quizzical look.

'Good,' she said after a moment. 'How are we doing, ladies, almost finished?'

'We've barely started, madam,' protested the one in the black dress. 'Your measurements are done, but there is cut and material to consider next.'

'Bah, I'm not planning on being the belle of the ball, just need to not look out of place as an aide. Your guild training should mean you can guess well enough, it's speed I'm interested in. I'll be back this evening for fitting.'

'Ahem, there is one further detail, madam.'

'What?'

'Your arms.' She plucked at Toil's sleeves with a fastidious disapproval. 'As you know, the custom of bare arms is an established tradition in Jarrazir.' She gestured to her colleague who let her shawl slip back and revealed the neat braiding around the shoulder of her dress which was as far as it went.

Toil pulled her own sleeve up. Her arms were corded with muscle and more than pleasing to Lynx's eye, but he wasn't blind to the fact she had a good variety of scars and blemishes, especially on her forearms. One long, jagged scar ran up the inside of her right arm while a smear of pinkish burned skin covered her left wrist.

As much anything, however, it was the haphazard direction of the scarring that was as noticeable as the largest injuries. Some Lynx could tell were knife cuts, other more irregular ones had to be the result of clambering around caverns and city-ruins.

'They might not help me blend in, true,' she admitted before brightening. 'However, you two seem like women of great resource. I've no doubt that by this evening you'll have come up with a solution.'

With that she stepped between the two and went to the neat desk off to the side. Emptying a dozen silver coins on to it she gestured for Lynx to pass her tunic and headed for the door.

'That should tide you over, we can discuss the rest later.'

Lynx lingered a moment longer, enjoying the stunned looks on the two women's faces. Finally they focused on him, whereupon he tipped his hat to them.

'See you at the fitting, ladies.'

Chapter 15

'I could kill you for this.'

Aben grinned. 'You can't buy authenticity, my friend.'

'Fucking can,' Barra groaned, 'it's called talent – acting, damn you!'

'Ah, it wouldn't be the same.'

'Go shove a burner up your arse, bastard. How fu— Oh, hells!'

The slim woman froze for a moment then turned and ran back to the privy, looking stricken. Aben's grin became wider. It was all he could do not to laugh out loud despite the fact he was going to suffer some sort of retribution. Barra would no doubt make him pay for weeks, but it had been a hugely entertaining sight to watch all of the Envoy's staff emerge from their rooms one by one, faces pale – embarrassment mingling with alarm as a great gust of stink accompanied them.

'Private!' snapped an angry voice from behind him. 'What's going on?'

Aben smothered the look of amusement on his face and turned to salute Captain Onerist as crisply as he could. 'Illness, sir.'

'Merciful Ulfer!' Onerist exclaimed as the smell reached him. He reeled back for a moment then pulled a handkerchief from one pocket to cover his mouth. 'What's happened to them?'

'Something they ate, sir, so I'm guessing. All the staff are down with it, they're, ah, not in a good way.'

'Something they ate?'

'Last night, sir – I was fortunate to be absent when the cook served the evening meal to the staff, and you, of course, ate with the Envoy.'

'Gods man, *all* of the staff? Is it as bad as the smell suggests?'

'Oh yes, sir, shitting like their lives depended on it,' Aben said with all the cheer of a man who'd supplied the laxative instead of swallowed it. 'Evacuating their bowels like rats off a sinking ship.'

Onerist paused, frowning. 'I'm not sure that's quite the correct analogy.'

'Don't know that word, sir,' Aben continued, trying not to enjoy himself too obviously, 'but it sounds right given what Corporal Paranil's saying about his backside.'

'Fetch them a doctor then, quick about it. Senator Ammen must have a staff attending him this afternoon – an Envoy of Su Dregir can't be seen at a foreign court with just two guards and no aides at all!'

'Begging your pardon, sir, but I've seen this before,' Aben replied, throwing in another salute for good measure as Onerist's ears were starting to turn red with fury. 'Out on campaign once, consignment of mutton some thieving shitestick of a merchant padded out with rat meat. Rotten it was, every man in the squad spent a day with the shits and couldn't move. A day at least, sir, any doctor'll tell you the same, I'd wager my beer rations on it. Nothing to be done but drink all the tea you can then watch it run out just as fast. These poor bastards ain't going nowhere.'

The captain went very quiet and for a moment Aben thought he was going to explode with fury, but when he eventually spoke it was in a quiet, worried voice. 'Private, we must have attendants, do you understand? The Envoy is calling for his private secretary right now, but later we will be in public! We are still waiting for final meetings with the Monarch's staff. The Envoy cannot arrive alone like some pauper.'

'Onerist!' roared a voice from elsewhere in the house, unmistakably the booming presence of the Envoy. 'Dammit, captain, where are you?'

Onerist closed his eyes briefly, wilting at the prospect of the Envoy's rage, but Aben just had to fight the urge to grin even more. Given he wasn't really a Lighthouse Guardsman and only playing the role, being bawled out didn't matter a jot to him. As a man used to besting most people he met in size and strength, he didn't intimidate easily. His greatest concern was laughing in the face of his betters, given they tended to dislike that.

'Come on, sir, let's give him the bad news together. Never good to do that alone, they tend to focus all their rage then, eh?'

Onerist made a choking sound, no doubt as confused by the sudden comradely manner as anything else, but he let himself be caught up in the big man's wake as Aben strode upstairs to where Senator Ammen stood, hands on hips and still bellowing as they came into view.

'Where in the living piss is everyone, man? You, private – what's going on?'

'Apologies, milord,' Aben replied, 'your staff's got the shits, if you'll pardon my language, sir.'

'What? Onerist, what's he talking about?' Ammen demanded. 'All of them? All at once?'

Onerist began to splutter more apologies and was well on his way to grovelling when Aben got bored and talked over the man instead.

'All of them, sir, rotten meat in last night's meal is my guess. I've seen it before, sits on the stomach badly overnight and as soon as you move in the morning, well, things start to move. Don't stop all day neither.'

'Every single member of my staff?' Ammen repeated, purpling with rage. 'Unacceptable, get them out of bed or the privy – I don't care where, they're no use to me there. And string that damn chef up before you do, no wait. Bring him here. I'll do it my damn self! I'm invited to the Monarch's court for a special function this afternoon; they're not allowed to be ill!'

'Fired the cook myself, sir,' Aben claimed cheerfully. 'Man didn't even put up a fight or argue his case. Knew he'd been caught the moment the first of 'em got up and left a trail to the privy. Wasn't sick himself neither, bastard knew what he was doing that's for sure. I gave 'im a kick in the nuts on behalf of my mates and told 'im if he came back he'd get worse. We'll not see the bugger again, even once he does prise 'is balls out o' his gut.'

'Private!' roared Onerist, finally recovering his senses. 'Guard your tone and hold that language in front of your betters! My apologies, Senator Ammen, the man will be reprimanded for forgetting his place.'

Ammen, no stranger to a military campaign, looked far from perturbed by Aben's tone. He was already lost in thought and waved his hand dismissively.

'As you choose, captain, but it can wait. This man is the only soldier we have left at present.'

'Still got the mercenaries, sir,' Aben added, unperturbed by imaginary punishments. 'Think I recall we brought a few spare uniforms too, in case you needed a larger honour guard anywhere.'

'Did we indeed?' Ammen said thoughtfully. 'The mercenaries, eh? You said my secretary would be ill all day? You're certain of this?'

'At least a day sir, spilling out everything they put in. It's ah . . . It's a mess back there already, if I'm honest. Reckon I'll need to see if any of those mercenaries is handy with a mop too, like a troupe o' monkeys have just been flinging the stuff about!'

217

'Thank you, that's quite enough, private,' Ammen said sharply. 'Go to the mercenaries, bring Commander Anatin and his lieutenant, that Toil woman, here directly. If there's anyone else in that gaggle of thieves with some manners, have them come too and find out where those spare uniforms are kept.'

'Right away, milord,' Aben said, saluting once more. 'Sure they'll be delighted to oblige you in any way you require.'

*

The city wall of Jarrazir cut a long arc through the landscape from the hills on the west all the way around to the craggy cliffs of Parthain's shore on the eastern flank. Three huge towers rose from a great ridge of earth backed against the wall of stone and brick. Coupled with smaller emplacements and the fort atop the hills, they presented as fearsome an approach as the two monstrous towers guarding the bay.

The city had long ago grown up to the very perimeter of this great wall, but the buildings were low in this newer part and the great blade of the Ongir Canal cut through both. From the western shore of the canal, Exalted Kastelian could see all the way to the wall. He had been there an hour, just one dragoon for company, though of course neither of them was in uniform. To any interested onlookers, of which there seemed to be none, the pair appeared to consist of a merchant of modest means and his bodyguard.

When boredom started to intrude, Kastelian pulled a cigar and a packet of matches from his pocket. He knelt and struck a match on one of the great blocks of granite that comprised the canal bank, the match's dirty yellow smoke billowing across the water as he lit his cigar and tossed the match away. He'd chosen this spot because it afforded him a clear view of all traffic on the canal, but there was also one more sight of note.

The North Keep rose between roofs on the far bank of the canal, half a mile away.

At this distance there was little to see, but the great portcullis-covered gate had remained closed the entire time. The keep was isolated from the rest of the wall with only one entrance and supplies enough to withstand a modest siege. With the deep armoury of bombardment spheres somewhere beneath it, he doubted the standing guard changed often. It was a massive structure, a blend of stone and brick that no doubt had layers of earth encased within to absorb the power of mage-spheres hitting it.

The outer wall was rounded with a squared-off back, seventy feet high with a wall protecting the great trebuchet stationed on the top. It was a formidable building, all the more so for the fact these defences were mostly a precaution. The trebuchet ensured that threats to the tower would come in the form of sneak attack – its range was so long and the power of the bombardment spheres so great, no army could march up to Jarrazir without being obliterated.

Yet that's exactly what we intend to do, Kastelian reminded himself. *It would be the perfect time to indulge my theory about a barge-mounted catapult, but we're already considered mavericks by the rest of the Knights-Charnel. No need to give them further reason to think so.*

Finally the sight he'd been waiting for came into view. A long barge, two-decked and flying the flag of the Knights-Charnel of the Long Dusk. It was an easy one to notice, not least because of the consternation it was already provoking among the citizenry here. The barge had waited a long time where the canal met the wall, the great-horns pulling it lowing gently as Jarraziran soldiers kept a close watch without being too threatening.

No doubt a message had been sent back to the palace and the number of armed men on board carefully noted, but this was an official delegation from the Knights-Charnel of the Long Dusk. They would have little to hide and the soldiers on the wall would be careful not to give offence to the powerful Militant Order.

'Fetch Bade,' Kastelian called to the dragoon behind him. 'Tell him we're going to a party.'

'Sir.'

The man scampered off and Kastelian puffed thoughtfully on his cigar as he watched the barge advance. As it came close he walked forward about ten yards to where a swing boom was standing idle and kicked it into movement. The barge's great-horn team was still twenty yards away and had plenty of time to slow as Kastelian signalled for the helmsman to heave to.

The helmsman rang a bell and the teamster waved back to show he'd heard before coaxing his four huge beasts to a halt. Even the smallest of the four was as tall as a carthorse and far broader, with a great curved horn that ran down the centre of its head. As the monstrous creatures ground to a stop Kastelian nodded to the teamster, a scarecrow-ragged figure who ignored him entirely, before ducking under the tow-rope and stepping down on to the barge's side-rail so he could announce himself to the nearest soldier.

'Take me to your leader,' Kastelian called as he moved nimbly forward to the central deck of the barge.

'Your name, sir?' replied the soldier in an immaculate dress uniform.

'Isn't for your hearing, trooper,' Kastelian said. 'But I'm an officer of the Torquen and I need to speak to the general.' He nodded towards a small flag that fluttered behind the large sun and spear device of the Knights-Charnel. The smaller flag depicted a pair of ravens, the personal crest of General Derjain Faril.

'You're out of uniform, sir,' the soldier correctly pointed out. Clearly he'd served in the general's retinue for a while and wasn't intimidated even by the elite Torquen branch. Kastelian had heard General Faril was a stickler for rules and as he looked around he realised all the soldiers were perfectly turned out, the white quarters of their uniforms pristine. Even officers of the Torquen were required to be correctly dressed in the presence of a lord or general.

'That I am, soldier, but I'm attached to the Pentaketh regiment. If the general don't like how I'm dressed . . . Well, that's my problem, eh?'

The soldier bowed his head in understanding. The Pentaketh were irregulars even within the Torquen; auxiliary specialists like Sotorian Bade and worse who couldn't fit within the rigid structure of the Order but were useful nonetheless.

'This way, sir.'

The soldier led him to the rear of the main deck where there were two armed soldiers guarding a door. Through that and a cramped antechamber where several clerks were hard at work, then into a low captain's room. The near half was taken up by a long dining table, complete with butler polishing the silver cutlery, while the far end had a wide desk and four armchairs arranged before it. Three officers stood to one side; a pair of captains and a commander. They parted without a word to reveal a small woman no bigger than a child: General Faril.

Kastelian bowed to the general. She was older than his mother with grey hair and thin spidery fingers, pale parchment skin, and eyes like the pitiless black of far underground where not even maspids dared go. Kastelian bowed low and stayed there, waiting for her to speak.

'Exalted?' the general said at last, having noticed the studs on his collar. It wasn't an official mark of rank, of course, but it was considered polite within the Order for officers of the Torquen to give an indication of their rank when meeting others.

'General Faril, good morning.'

Kastelian straightened and did his best not to flinch under Faril's scowl.

'Name?'

'Exalted Kastelian Ubris, Pentaketh regiment liaison.'

'Good, I've been expecting you. Report.'

He nodded. 'First of all, I ask that you wait here a while longer before continuing to the palace. I've summoned a few of my men, they should be along presently.'

'See to it,' she said to one of the captains, who scuttled out. 'Right, where are we?'

'In an excellent position – an informer has confirmed one of the labyrinth entrances has opened into the North Keep. Our specialist is preparing the ground so we can breach it at our leisure, should that prove necessary. He will then scout his way into the labyrinth proper – however, an opportunity presents itself.'

'Which is?'

'The Monarch is addressing the guild leaders and noble families today, announcing the city's response to the situation. I'm sure you'll be invited to attend forthwith. To act effectively they will be in particular need of specialists such as ours. I believe your influence could win us a presence on the city's official incursion, perhaps even to lead it. The choice would be yours as to whether we send a covert group ahead and delay the Monarch's troops, of course.'

'Your man's a renowned relic hunter, no? That's what the Lord-Exalted informed me.'

'Indeed, general. More than qualified to lead the incursion. Your oncoming troops will have been noticed and reported back by now. I'm sure the Monarch will not want to give you a reason to take offence.'

'All this will not stretch you too thin?'

'No, sir. My team is ready to move with an hour's notice even without Bade and his crew on hand.'

General Faril sniffed and looked Kastelian up and down.

'Very well, but get yourself into uniform. You'll not be part of my delegation looking like that.'

'Of course, sir.'

Chapter 16
(Now)

'Toil!'

Lynx started forward on instinct, only to have the butt of a gun thumped against his chest to drive him back. They really were under arrest now, there was no confusion about it this time and no one was getting out without being shot.

'Keep back,' the other soldier snapped, levelling his mage-gun.

Away down the corridor, Toil looked up and smiled slightly. She was under escort too, limping slightly and the right-hand side of her face looked swollen. Her silk dress was torn and stained, her feet bare – though she had been given a man's coat to drape around her shoulders. It was plain and dark but clearly made for someone with money. Puzzled, Lynx looked past Toil and spotted a large bearded man with a red scarf around his neck and white shirtsleeves showing.

Who's this one? Friend of Toil's I'd guess if he's given her his coat.

Aside from the stranger, Toil was accompanied by a pair of guards and an officer in the same black uniform, burly and balding with a magnificent dark moustache and muttonchops. As they came closer the strange man reached out and touched Toil on the shoulder. He said something to her and gestured off down another corridor, whereupon she nodded and slipped the coat off her shoulders. She returned it to him and gave his hand a squeeze before he set off and disappeared from view.

Despite the events of the day and the threat of flogging that gnawed at the back of Lynx's mind like a rat, for that one moment jealousy eclipsed all. He soon got a grip of himself, but it remained in the darkness of his head even as he forced himself to focus – a mouse as dark and determined as the rat, nibbling away.

He made to start forward again, but Payl hauled him back.

'You'll keep still if you know what's good for you,' warned a second guard, levelling his gun.

Lynx snarled and pointed at the large tattoo on his cheek. 'Do I fucking look like I know what's good for me?'

'Lynx!' Payl said, putting herself between them with one hand resting lightly on his shoulder. 'Reel it in, you hear me?'

He glared at her, for a moment the spark of anger inside him blotting out all rational thought, but at last he remembered to breathe and his wits came back to him.

'That's better,' she said firmly, increasing the pressure on his shoulder. 'Now step back and let's just wait to see what's going on, eh?'

'Fine,' he muttered, looking away.

They had been dumped in a small room with barred windows that wasn't quite a cell, not with chairs and a table, but without any of the finery of the last place they'd been confined to. From the table Teshen looked lazily up at Lynx, clearly less worried than Payl about his comrade getting a beating. Aben was with him but watching them all warily, Toil included.

'Evening, boys and girls,' Toil called with forced cheer as she entered.

The guards moved aside to let her and the officer through, but she stopped short of the chair Aben offered.

'We all having fun in here?'

'Loads,' Teshen said with a yawn. He stretched and got lazily up. 'It's been a madcap few hours of getting threatened, sitting down, standing up, sitting down again. If it wasn't for the witty repartee from our hosts I don't know how I'd have coped with all the fun.'

'Sorry to break up the party then, but there's work to be done.'

'What sort?'

Toil paused for a moment before replying. 'That rather depends on the Monarch,' she admitted, 'and what she wants.'

'*That*,' interjected the Bridge Watch officer, 'rather depends on how the Knights-Charnel react to your little stunt.'

Toil turned to look at the squat, moustachioed man. 'Ah yeah, this ray of furry-faced sunshine's called . . . um. No, I forgot it again.'

The man fumed quietly but was careful not to shout in reply to her needling. 'If you cannot even remember that, I doubt you'll prove much use to the Monarch.'

'How about I crack your skull and you try to remember my name?'

'Have at it,' he said, not backing off an inch. 'The Monarch does not need you wasting her time, best for all concerned if you take a swing at me and my men shoot you.'

'How about you both calm down?' Payl sighed. 'Gods, how much more am I going to have to say that by the end of the day? You, captain, what's your name then?'

'Cothkern,' the man said slowly.

'Ah, I was going for cock-something, so close,' Toil said.

'Enough, Toil!' Payl snapped. 'Captain Cothkern, may I ask what your orders are now?'

'To escort you and your comrades back to your lodgings. Apparently this one thinks she can be of more use out of her dress than in it – broadly the conclusion my men have come to.'

'That surprises me in a city of pederasts,' Toil growled. She turned her back on the man and Lynx saw her take a moment to focus on the matter at hand rather than starting another fight. 'We've got kit to pick up; the Monarch's got officers fetching our weapons to bring them here.'

'Here?'

'We're foreign mercenaries, she doesn't want us wandering the streets armed. I need to prove I can lead an expedition underground before I ask her to arm the Cards. Right now I just need a few people to volunteer for the scouting mission, not the whole Mercenary Deck.'

'I can think of someone who might not volunteer for relic hunting duty,' Lynx said pointedly. 'Other than me that is.'

'Her with the white hair?' Toil nodded. 'Tough shit for her then, I need an expert and she's not a Card so I didn't promise Anatin anything about her.'

'You gave her your word!' he said, dismayed.

'What a scamp I am then.' She caught the look on his face and scowled. 'Oh don't give me the kicked puppy routine, I'll persuade her.'

'And if you can't?'

'I'll just have to succeed, I'll use charm and everything.'

Teshen laughed. 'Been working well for you so far today.'

'I'll take a long run up at it.'

'And if she doesn't agree?' Lynx pressed, ignoring Cothkern as the man cleared his throat to interject.

'Then it's *my* problem,' Toil said, before offering up one of her best winning smiles. 'Do we need to have this argument now, honey, in front of the kids?'

As Teshen chuckled, Lynx tried to react angrily but found his temper melting away in the face of that smile. With a disgusted sound he turned away. 'Fine, let's go.'

Before anyone could take a step towards the door there was a roar in the corridor beyond. 'Where is she?' bellowed a voice, followed by the heavy stamp of feet.

'Oh goody,' Toil muttered just before Envoy Ammen rounded the corner – face purple with anger.

'There you are, you damned idiot woman! What in the name of the blessed gods do you think you're doing?' Ammen stormed up to her until his face was mere inches away from hers and the spittle flew as he continued to yell.

'I'll have you hanged the moment we set foot on Su Dregir soil, you hot-headed little whore! Have you any idea of the damage you've done to relations between our cities?'

Lynx found himself tensing, mostly getting ready to pull Toil back. Ammen was a large and well-built man, but somehow he didn't think Toil was the one at risk there. Her temper was fiery, she'd already proved that well enough today and he'd seen her fight – hard, dirty and without relent.

Of course, I could be wrong there, he thought to himself, *let's not test the theory.*

To Lynx's astonishment, Toil just stood and took the abuse, even ignoring Ammen prodding her in the chest. Out of the corner of his eye Lynx saw Aben edge forward, nothing too provocative but closing the distance between his boss and the man working himself into a lather. Captain Cothkern just smirked, apparently not intending to interrupt a foreign diplomat – especially one who was insulting a woman he didn't like himself.

Behind the Envoy Lynx saw the pale face of Captain Onerist, looking more confused than anything else. Clearly he'd been thrown by the whole thing and wasn't much for thinking under pressure. Instead of getting involved like he should be, the man was just watching and vacillating about what to do. Lynx couldn't help but suspect his superiors had passed a high-born weakling off on to escort duty where he wouldn't command troops under pressure. Given Toil's *other* mission, that seemed likely.

'What do you have to say for yourself, woman?' continued Ammen. 'Speak! Get that idiot tongue moving and explain yourself!'

In response Toil closed her eyes. Ammen paused moment-arily, clearly thrown by her action, and she gently reached up and wiped the spit from her face before looking back up at the Envoy.

'Best you take a step back now,' Toil said mildly. 'Before you get hurt.'

'Don't even think about threatening me, you low-born cunt!' Ammen raged. 'I've half a mind to—'

A whip-crack sound echoed around the room and Toil slapped him full across the face. Ammen was driven back as much by shock and insult as the force of her blow, but the rage quickly returned to boiling point on his face. Before he could respond Cothkern stepped forward and the Bridge Watch soldiers levelled their weapons at the pair.

'Enough,' Captain Cothkern said in an irritated voice. 'You two want to kill each other, you do it outside of the Monarch's palace. There'll be no brawling here, anyone tries otherwise and they get a warning shot in the knee. Understand?'

'To lay a finger on me is to assault the Republic of Su Dregir,' Ammen snarled.

'To the seven hells with the Republic of Su Dregir,' Cothkern said with a shrug. 'Never liked any o' your people anyway, even before an official delegation tried to commit murder in my Monarch's hall and insulted her name. Your Archelect isn't renowned for being sentimental, certainly for those who screw up in public, and he's keen on improving trade relations.'

'You make an excellent point,' Toil said with an unnecessarily polite nod of the head, apparently happy to afford the man all possible respect now she was in the presence of someone she disliked more. 'Perhaps you would now escort me and my comrades to our lodgings so I can begin to make amends?'

'No, wait!' interjected Onerist. 'They're official guards of the Envoy – they're coming with us.'

Toil grinned. 'Not so much,' she said. 'You're both free to come with us, but there's an evens chance you'll get nailed to the wall as soon as you open that fat mouth of yours, Envoy. I suggest you scuttle back to your own lodgings and pray to whichever god you favour that I forget your words to me before I see you next.'

'I'll do no such thing – you don't even know what you've done, do you?'

'What would that be then?'

'An army has been sighted from the city walls!' Ammen declared triumphantly. 'Getting ready to march on the city; a war is coming all because of your stupidity.'

Toil ignored the gasps from those around her and adopted a carefully nonchalant voice. 'The rest have arrived already? Well, that moves things up a little. Best we get a wriggle on.'

Lynx could see her knuckles whitening, down by her waist, and recognised the rage she was holding back. Toil wasn't a woman of restraint at the best of times from what he'd seen and certainly a man screaming in her face was normally provocation enough, but she'd lost control once today already. To slap a man like that was a socially acceptable response, but he knew she was itching to open the Envoy from groin to gullet.

'You're confined to your lodgings until I say otherwise – Captain, arrest her and bind her hands!'

Toil shook her head, forced amusement on her face as she gestured to the door. 'Come on, we've got some preparations to make before I can make good on my promises to the Monarch.'

'You'll—'

Captain Cothkern pulled his mage-pistol from a holster and brandished it in the Envoy's face as he made to grab Toil's arm. 'No more of that, sir. I've got my orders and they involve her. Your domestic issues don't interest me, but I'll shoot you if you try and impede me in the execution of my duties.'

Ammen was left speechless by that and the mercenaries simply walked around him, out into the corridor and back the way they'd come. Aben raised an eyebrow to Toil and she gave him a small shake of the head so he kept his place.

Cothkern leaned closer to Lynx as they went. 'Hanese, eh?'

'Yeah.'

'Right. So are all Su Dregir folk so fucking troublesome or is it just these two?'

Lynx cast his mind back to the time he'd spent there. 'Mebbe not *all* the ones I ever met, I guess,' he conceded. 'But then I'm only a Hanese ex-convict turned mercenary, so I always try to find the good in people I meet.'

'Aye, I hear that about you lot.'

'One of our many fine qualities.'

*

Five hundred miles away and fifteen years in the distant past, a group of four people broke through a great stone doorway and had their breath taken away. Even Sotorian Bade had nothing more to say, there at the end of their quest, though words had rarely failed him during the intervening time. It had taken three days and four lives, but finally success lay before them and Toil found the fatigue in her arms and legs fading away. The climb down here had been draining, but now it was all worth it.

Not to Master Oper, she reminded herself. The sight of him tumbling out of sight and into the black was one that replayed over and over in her mind.

231

The hurrying man hurries straight to his death. Oper had said that the night they camped outside the cave entrance, had made a point of stressing it to all his new recruits.

And he'd tried to keep to it, Toil realised. The man had been moving slowly and cautiously along a high ledge that looked over a vast, deep pit criss-crossed with bridges and stone projections. It wasn't his fault the section of rock had tumbled away underneath him, but Bade's dark mistress had taken him all the same.

I didn't even hear him hit anything. He just kept falling and screaming until he ran out of breath.

Toil shivered. It had been a better death than Fittil had managed. Bitten by some angular monstrosity that scuttled through the dark, he'd managed only two steps before his legs gave way underneath him. His face had gone scarlet, his chest had heaved like a bellows while his throat was as tight and white as a strangling ligature.

The other two had been less dramatic. One had tried to prise open a doorway and been struck on the head in the ensuring rockfall, the other had simply wandered off. They'd only noticed he was gone when they stopped for a rest, about to debate whether to return to their camp or not. The oppressive darkness had claimed him, Toil realised. It crowded her too, pushed and teased and prodded from all sides – testing her defences, seeking a way in. And last night they'd slept inside the ruin itself under weak lamplight, having followed ramps and rappelled rock faces so deep into the ground there was little value in returning for the night.

She tried to imagine how far down they were now. There was no clear way of working it out, no regularity to the levels that great square pit led to, but twenty of the houses she'd grown up in could have been stacked beside them on the descent. *And we still never found Oper's body.*

'This is it, boys and girls,' Bade said at last. 'You're a lucky charm, my girl.'

'Lucky?' Toil protested wearily. She was exhausted and filthy – four days in this Duegar ruin had taxed them all right to the limit. 'Wasn't luck that got us here.'

'I make no charges nor complaints,' Bade said, waving her words away. 'I thank the day that old bastard hauled you up on to his wagon. I'd even get on my knees and honour whichever of the gods sent you our way if my knees weren't getting a bit old for that sort of thing.' He paused. 'Assuming we get out alive, that is. Getting out is still the most important bit.'

Even that little aside couldn't diminish his obvious excitement. The wonder was clear and childlike on his face, even in the weak lamplight. For a man so assured and full of himself, it was a revealing contrast, and one that made it real to Toil. This was a Duegar tomb, undiscovered for thousands of years. A magical moment in the life of any relic hunter, she knew, and a fortune for them all, just waiting to be plundered.

And Toil had played a crucial role in finding it – following the undulating paths of this strange, functionless section of the ruin until the shape of it had taken root in her mind. Something had struck her as out of place and Bade had agreed, soon discovering the great panel that hid the stairs to the inner chambers.

Bade crouched and picked up a chunk of stone, tossing it over the floor of the tomb. A bright, hissing light seemed to fill the air – jagged slashes of lightning exploding across the main body of the tomb. They all flinched back and covered their eyes, the brief burst of magic leaving a stinging trail across Toil's vision.

'Banesh's broken balls,' she howled. 'Give us some warning next time!'

'I just saved your life, girly,' he chuckled. 'You should be puckering up, not pouting.'

'Bring your face over here and you'll get your reward,' Toil said, wiping her watering eyes.

'Plenty of time for that when we're rich as lords.'

'Don't hold your breath.'

He gave a throaty chuckle. 'Reckon I'll look a whole lot more handsome covered in jewels.'

'I doubt it.'

Toil crouched and inspected the floor as she'd been told, searching for tripwires or triggers before venturing forward.

'Anyway, I'll be just as rich so if you're after a thank you, I'll hire some poor girl to do it for me. Let her catch whatever lordly rash you keep scratching at.'

'Watch yourselves,' Bade said, tossing another stone. Nothing happened and he took a tentative step forward, tensing for a few moments, ready to spring back before finally relaxing.

'Come on, we won't have much time.'

'How long?'

'How should I know?' he laughed. 'Stay there if you want, but I ain't sharing.'

They scampered forward, Toil, Hoyst and Sovirel – an agile black man from somewhere south of So Han. Another relic hunter veteran, but no great friend of Bade's so far as Toil could tell.

There was a large stone sarcophagus against the far wall, intricately carved and flanked by massive stone sconces in the shape of coiling carapaced insects. Six pedestals formed a ring in the centre of the room, each bearing some sort of gem-encrusted golden headdress, beneath a glittering mural of the night sky emblazoned on the ceiling. Some sort of crystal served as a thousand stars scattered around the pale golden arc of the Skyriver, which met the horizon in other images on the walls. A temple complex and array of waterfalls, both shown at dusk and lit by hundreds of lanterns that gleamed like the stars.

There were fat projections of glass or crystal extending from the side walls, each of those bearing more Duegar artefacts, but Toil could not guess at the function of any. For a long time they all simply stood and stared, marvelling at the fabulous decoration in the chamber as much as the treasure.

The journey underground had been awe-inspiring in parts but exhausting and perilous – traversing ancient halls and caverns degraded by time and the elements. This room was different, though, this room was almost untouched and the fatigue melted away as they beheld for the first time a room from another age entirely. The Duegar race were long dead, thousands of years gone, but they had stood here too and seen the room almost as it was now. They had created something beautiful and locked it away, preserving some magical spark of their lost civilisation for Toil to remember all the rest of her days.

'Don't touch anything, not yet,' Bade warned them all as Hoyst reached for one of the headdresses.

'What, then?'

Bade tied string to each headdress with a deft touch, not moving any even a fraction of an inch, while the rest held their breath and watched. They didn't have much rope left, but a pocket's worth of string would be enough to reach all the way out of the tomb again. Leaving the remaining lamp with Sovirel, Bade gently knotted the six pieces together with a longer section and played the rest out until he was all the way outside at the extent of the string's length.

While he was doing that, Toil went to investigate the sarcophagus itself. It wasn't a solid piece of stone as she'd first thought; instead there were angled panels of smoked glass set into the sides while the top was one large sheet of clear glass. She peered down inside it, careful not to get too close, then gasped.

'Look!' She waved the others over, Sovirel raising the lamp high. 'What's that?'

There was no body inside. All that remained of the Duegar buried here after several thousand years was dust. What did remain were strangely proportioned sections of worked metal, ceremonial armour Toil assumed. Encrusted with gems and dull with age, the flashes of gold were clear, but what had caught Toil's attention were chunks of something like green jade, hung on chains of black metal and half buried in the dust.

'Not cut gems,' Sovirel breathed with the same mounting excitement Toil felt. 'Not that shape and size.'

'Shattered gods!' Hoyst broke in, finally realising what they were talking about. 'Are those God Fragments?'

'Here's hoping!' called Bade. Toil looked back and saw the man was at the very edge of the light, just an outline amid the black. 'Can sell 'em to the Orders, get money and men to excavate this place properly.'

'You'd trust the Orders with all this?'

'We don't have the hands to work this tomb properly. Hands off that sarcophagus, likely it's a decoy. I'd wager the biggest o' these gems that the first man to crack it ends up crispy.' He patted something at his waist, a black glass sphere the size of a man's fist encased in crossed metal bands. 'Or you can help yerselves. I'd be interested to see what happened.'

Toil opened her mouth to reply but then saw him twist one of the bands and the words died in her mouth. Nothing happened but she faltered still, sensing something terrible was coming.

'What are you doing?'

'Ah well, yeah – sorry 'bout this.'

Bade tipped his hat at her then yanked hard on the string, running a few paces back as he hauled on it. All six of the headdresses flew through the air and clattered down on to the stone floor, but Toil didn't see it. She threw herself down beside the sarcophagus even as the other two turned and the air burst into flames.

Someone screamed, the sound almost lost amid a great whump of fire erupting from each of the stone columns. The bright yellow flower of flame flashed out over her head, and in a second it had spread to fill the air as Toil cowered on the floor. Arms across her face, she felt the surge of heat wash over her and shrieked in terror as she heaved for breath. No air reached her lungs; her jacket and arm covering her mouth. The panic increased for one interminable heartbeat then another, the searing heat eclipsing everything else before vanishing as suddenly as it had come.

Toil flapped at her clothes, rolling madly as she tried to disentangle herself and put out any flames that might have caught. Somewhere there was a strangled cry and the mad thump of flailing limbs, but she could see nothing beyond the smeared memory trails in her eyes. The crackle of burning fat, the whisper of cloth aflame and faint whimpers of men continued for a dozen heartbeats before all fell silent. Then the darkness descended once more, a cool touch on her skin as the burner flames receded. When finally she managed to take a breath Toil heaved at the scorched, bitter air with relief then renewed panic.

The darkness was near total and even as the trails of light faded from Toil's eyes, the weak flames on the dead men's clothes faltered. Through her watering and pained eyes she could see nothing, not even the last embers on the clothes. Her fear started to bite as she turned and banged her knee on something, the sting of pain eclipsing even terror for a moment. Then she managed to right herself and reached out, feeling something solid under her hand. She could hear nothing more from the others, could see nothing and only smell the foul, sickly-sweet stink of burned flesh.

'Bade!' she screamed in panic. 'Bade, come back!'

There was no answer, not even the sound of footsteps echoing through the darkness. She knew she'd never hear him, the man walked almost silently – said it was the only reason he'd lived as long as he had. If you made much noise in the dark, it quietened you.

'Bade!' she moaned, too frightened to scream now. 'Don't leave me here.'

The darkness made no reply. Toil found herself drawing her arms and legs tight to her body, hugging herself close against the malevolent presence that now enclosed her.

He's gone, he's left us.

Her stomach lurched and went cold. *The others are dead, he's just left me. Oh, merciful gods, I'm all alone.*

The hours of climbing they had done to reach this place, the miles of streets underground, long walkways descending into the belly of the earth and thin lengths of rope leading them down. It had taxed them right to the limit under lamplight. And now here she was, in the pitch-black belly of the world and utterly alone.

Desperately, Toil waved her hands in front of her face but she could see nothing. The lamp was gone, Bade was gone. The rest were dead and she was blind at the bottom of an ancient ruin.

I'm all alone.

Silently in the dark, Toil began to weep.

Chapter 17

Under the city, in the cool bubble of light cast by the alchemical globe lamp, Sotorian Bade watched his men work for a long while before tapping one on the shoulder and beckoning. There was a makeshift rope system set up there, two men filling buckets with earth and rubble, a third behind lowering those to be emptied at the bottom of the chamber. The work was painstakingly slow, but almost silent to avoid betraying their presence to any guards on the other side of the wall.

Four Knights-Charnel dragoons stood guard behind, watching the relic hunters work and trying to conceal their own disquiet. Bade's crew had all been underground at least once before. Enough that they were used to it, but he could see on the faces of the dragoons that they weren't yet past the stories they'd heard all their lives. The pitch-black warrens of streets where monsters lurked, the mines that delved miles into the ground. They kept as close as they could to the white light of the lamp, its feeble cast undoubtedly a bastion of the human world in their eyes.

Best they get used to it now, Bade thought as Chotel downed tools and rose, brushing dirt from his clothes before following Bade down the stairway to the floor. *There'll be no time later. If they're still thrown by that when we enter the labyrinth, our lady of dark will take 'em fast enough.*

He led Chotel through the propped-open stone door and into the great Duegar-made cavern above the labyrinth before he spoke. The faint blue glow of the seams in the rock spread out around them and merged with the black beyond, Bade's small lantern barely giving any definition to the huge chamber they stood at the edge of.

'How long?'

Chotel scratched his cheek as he thought. The dirt was almost invisible on him in this light but Bade could smell its damp, earthy aroma in the stale air of the cavern.

'Depends what you call done,' he said at last. 'We're through the first brick wall, but this rubble is pretty deep. I can't tell how deep yet – only that we didn't need to be quiet at first, which is a fine joke given that now we know that we *do* need to work as quiet as we can.'

'Done is when we can get through. One at a time is fine.'

'Gonna be a tough fight if we're going single file. Something happened to make this more pressing?'

Bade grinned, his teeth suddenly bright in the darkness. 'You could say that. I ran into an old friend at the Monarch's announcement. Turns out she wasn't delighted to see me.'

'Who?'

'Woman called Toil. She's, ah, not a fan o' mine. Tried to kill me once before, mebbe five years ago.'

'Was I there?' Chotel asked. 'It's hard to keep track of all the times people try to show how much they love you.'

'Out Vether-un-Seil way, earthquake had uncovered that great hole in the ground.'

'Ah yeah. I always thought you started that bar fight?'

'In a fashion, I did,' Bade chuckled. 'Left her behind on a run years before – first intact tomb I found. Made my fortune and won me the everlasting friendship of the Order in the process.' He shook his head. 'Almost shit myself when I recognised her in that bar, thought she was a ghost or something. Turns out she's got decent rep as a relic hunter now, which ain't any great surprise if she climbed her way out o' that deepest black deathtrap.'

'And she holds a grudge? Funny that.'

'Yeah, some people, eh? Point is, the general's got the hump and made some pretty drastic demands to ease her wounded pride. No way the Monarch will agree to free rein in the labyrinth and companies of our troops guarding each entrance so that makes us more'n likely going our own way, but the schedule is pushed up. So we get this ready for Kastelian to breach if he needs to while we go on ahead.'

'Wouldn't want to be breaching this single file.'

'We came prepared,' Bade said with a shrug.

'Our night mage ain't gonna put a whole garrison out.'

'Ah well, I've got a few other toys in my chest. There's a plan forming, just need to know how the chips will fall.'

Chotel nodded. They'd worked together for a few years now and he knew Bade wasn't joking much when he said 'toys in my chest'. He was one of the most successful relic hunters in the business and hadn't sold everything he'd found; he kept as much back as he could, even from Chotel. There were several booby-trapped chests that came as part of Bade's luggage whenever they went on a job and Chotel was one of several in the crew with cause to owe their life to the contents.

'More men then, another globe lamp for when that one burns out.'

'I'll shift all our kit underground, make it so we can block up the cellar behind us if we need to cover our tracks. We've proved we can leave by one of the other entrances now.'

'All the others are guarded,' Chotel pointed out.

'It'd only be a last resort,' Bade clarified, 'but once this all kicks off we may need another exit. Kastelian's going to keep a squad in reserve near one of the other entrances – if his lovely friend the general can't take the whole city, they'll be waiting for activity at that one. If it looks like the guards are getting ready to drop grenades or anything, they'll surprise 'em in the rear and not in the way the men o' this city enjoy.'

'How long do I have?'

'Fast as you can. The signal could come any time.'

*

Toil opened the door to the lodging house and swore long and loud. Lynx craned his head to look over the woman's shoulder with Payl and Teshen and found himself blinking in disbelief. It was early in the evening with the sun just going down outside. The great arc of the Skyriver was starting to loom prominently in the darkening sky – a sign back in Su Dregir that the evening's drinking should be starting. Here in Jarrazir that would be illegal, of course, so the good men and women of Anatin's Mercenary Deck had found an alternative that was to their liking.

'When I said no more making this place a gambling den,' Toil roared, 'I didn't mean to turn it into a fucking brothel instead!'

From the table directly in front of her a figure swivelled round in his seat and eyed her unsteadily. For some reason Anatin had a red silk scarf draped over his head, while his tunic was unbuttoned to the waist as some plump local woman explored the skin inside.

'Ah my dear,' Anatin declared, brandishing a cigar expansively. 'In our defence, you didn't explicitly tell us not to either.'

Captain Cothkern stepped in and looked around. 'In the interests of not wasting my time by shooting or arresting anyone, I'll wait outside. You've got five minutes, understand?'

Toil nodded and the captain scowled once more at the mercenaries, shook his head and closed the door behind him.

The room was dim and full of people, at least half the mercenary company by Lynx's guess, along with perhaps twenty whores, both men and women. There had been a desultory attempt to smarten the place up and drapes of red and yellow covered half the walls, but most obvious was the amount of flesh on show and the haze of spiced smoke and perfume in the air. As they gaped, an instrument started up from one corner – a hypnotic wavering screech emanating from some sort of bulbous flute that was soon accompanied by a rapid skittering drum beat.

Lynx finally spotted the source of the smoke; a large clay bowl in one corner that had a ball of something sputtering and fizzing in the gloom. The smoke curled up in ever-shifting patterns as orange and green sparks burst out at random and cut ribbons through the air. Tending the bowl was a pale man in blue silk robes, a whole variety of glass-stoppered bottles laid out before him – clearly the alchemist providing the various drugs flowing through the mercenaries. He gave them both an expansive grin, his teeth flashing gold, but that faltered after one look from Toil.

The assassin marched forward, about to yell at Anatin before abruptly stopping. She looked around once and shook her head.

'You know what? I don't care, get it all out now while you still can.'

'Is that an invitation?' called someone. Lynx eventually saw Llaith leaning out from behind a great brass samovar.

'Sure,' Toil growled. 'Just don't whine if it gets cut off.'

Llaith grinned and winked at her. 'Does the dress unwrap like a midwinter present?'

'Just like your skin will, given a sharp enough knife,' Toil snapped as she pushed her way through a knot of dancing figures, one of whom was a burly, red-haired mercenary named Darm. He wore no shirt and his skin glistened with sweat as he swayed with drug-induced languidness with a woman, fondling her exposed breasts with a sexless ecstasy as she traced the patterns of his spider-web tattoo on his chest. If the group even noticed Toil shove her way past they made no sign and Lynx eased them out of the way so he could follow with the others.

Heading to the back rooms he passed a vacantly smiling Sitain wedged on a crowed sofa by the fire, sitting between a muscular young man with painted eyelids and Kas. The company scout gave Lynx an ambiguous look as he passed, before reaching for the man's glazed pipe. Sitain looked more than comfortable with Kas half-draped over her so he left them to it as Toil went in search of Lastani, finding her in the rear room at a table all of her own, currently covered in books and loose pages.

'Not partaking in the fun?'

Lastani scowled as she looked up, then blinked in astonishment at the sight of Toil. While she'd borrowed another coat for the journey back, she still wore a figure-hugging dress of silk even if it sported a variety of rips and stains.

'What happened?'

Toil laughed at that, wearily shaking her head. 'All too much.'

'The Monarch rejected your offer?' Lastani ventured hesitantly.

'Ah, well now, that's the thing.' Toil paused and looked down at herself. 'Look, I've not got a lot of time to spare and I need to get some proper clothes on.'

She beckoned and headed back out to the corridor. With a puzzled look at Lynx, Lastani followed and the two of them headed up to the room Toil had taken for herself towards the rear of the building.

'And where do you think you're going?' Toil asked with a raised eyebrow as Lynx entered last and closed the door behind him.

'To join the conversation,' Lynx said firmly. 'I can do that with my back turned.'

'What?' Lastani broke in as Lynx did just that, but the only reply was the click of a brooch pin and the whisper of unwrapping silk. 'Oh!' she exclaimed, flustered. 'You really did mean . . .'

'That I need proper clothes, aye,' Toil said, her voice taking on that velvety mocking quality Lynx knew only too well.

Even with his back turned, his thoughts remained firmly rooted and in a few moments a pink-cheeked Lastani appeared beside him, facing the cheap ink-painted scroll that had been hung as the room's only decoration.

'Don't have sisters then?' Toil called.

'I . . . no, I do not. Two brothers, both older.'

'I'd have liked a sister, I reckon. My mum too probably, bit too much of my dad in me – and my brother has rather taken after him too.'

Lynx paused at that, a memory stirring in the back of his mind. He'd been to Toil's home only once, but it was a visit etched into his memory. One detail of that had been the pair of portraits above her fireplace. A beautiful woman and a great lump of a man; her parents. He'd noticed her mother more, that same dangerous, alluring little smile as Toil had, but now his thoughts turned to her father. Hardly a handsome face, but noticeable all the same with a hard look about him.

Didn't she once say the man had been a mercenary captain? Huh – and of course a brother offers his coat to his sister, even one like Toil. Guess a man passes on all he has, even if it's a merc company.

'And your brother went into the family business?'

There was a small pause. 'Aren't you the keen-eyed little sparrowhawk all of a sudden?'

Lynx shrugged, not wanting to explain *why* he'd been musing on the sight. 'Are you decent yet, woman?' he asked gruffly.

'In body or spirit?' He heard her finish cleaning up, then a rustle of clothing and a small grunt. 'Oh for . . . You can turn round, I'm decent enough.'

When he did so, Toil still wasn't wearing a lot, just cotton underclothes but those were long, shapeless and plain so even Lastani didn't look uncomfortable as Toil hauled on her trousers.

'Now, the Monarch,' Toil began. 'I think I've persuaded her, with events rather forcing her hand.'

'What events?'

'You've not heard? Well some fool picked a fight with a Knights-Charnel right before the Monarch's announcement could take place. It's made things, ah, complicated.'

'What does that mean for you? For us?'

'It means the Monarch is under pressure to crack the labyrinth, one way or another. The Knight-Charnel want what's inside. Shattered gods – they want the whole thing if they can get it! Doesn't matter what it is really, but if there are God Fragments they won't stop until they control them. Letting Jarrazir possess divine relics would be bad enough, allowing a rival mage-cartridge industry to threaten their market . . . well, they'd rather level the city. Long story short, there's an army outside the walls.'

'The city's under siege?' Lastani gasped. 'Since this morning?'

Toil shrugged, looking slightly abashed. 'Events seem to move quickly when I stick my bloody great foot in.'

'This was all your doing? This is my home! This is where my family live! I've been trying to keep them safe, to keep them out of all this, and you go and put the whole city at risk?'

'Hey, not like it was deliberate, just some bad luck. Unlike some fucks I could mention who decided to open the damn thing in the first place without any thought to the consequences beyond academic interest. But sure, let's stand here and argue about blame.'

Lastani opened her mouth again to shout then checked herself and frowned. Looking pale, she sat abruptly down on a bed, staring blankly at Toil as she digested the news fully. Lynx reminded himself that she wasn't like him; she was a part of this city and had a family within it. Being on the run in her home city must have been hard enough, keeping clear even of family and friends for fear of what she might bring down on them.

Lynx was used to walking away – to cutting ties when things went to shit. More often than not he was the one burning his own bridges, but he'd always known that the road was where he belonged however long he stayed in one place.

And by the same thinking, Lastani had likely always known she belonged here. She was a child of Jarrazir and hadn't fled even when she became a fugitive. Lynx's home couldn't be threatened, his world couldn't be torn apart any more than it already had been and he'd made a form of peace with what remained. Lastani still had everything to lose.

'So what now?' she asked in a small voice.

'Now I crack the labyrinth before anything more than harsh words gets used, give the Monarch something to bargain with. That means a first foray as soon as I can organise it and a full expedition once I've proved I know what I'm doing.'

She nodded slowly. 'And you want me to go with you.'

'You guessed that bit, eh?' Toil said with a nod.

'I am as close to an expert as remains in the city. I may be no great scholar but I am intimately familiar with the works of Jarrazir's greatest on top of the fact there's a warrant out for my arrest and this is the best way to win a little favour from the Monarch. But I'm no relic hunter.'

Toil pulled on her tunic and buttoned it up. Before pulling on her long boots she sat down on the bed beside Lastani.

'Keeping folk alive is my job,' she said with surprising gentleness. 'I'm the one out front, but if I've got your brains to back me up that could prove the difference – for me and for this city.'

'I cannot tell you what lies in wait down there.'

'But you can read better'n me,' Toil pointed out, 'and you've got a greater breadth of knowledge. There will be traps to kill the unwary and puzzles to defeat the unworthy. You don't build a labyrinth to keep the entire world out, just the bits that aren't worthy of the prize. This'll require brains as well as brawn.'

'Very well,' Lastani said eventually. 'I will join you.'

She looked from Toil to Lynx with a spark of determination in her eyes. The young woman looked terribly small and frail to Lynx, but he said nothing. She was a mage and that meant she was tougher than most, plus she would have people he could trust to watch over her – Toil, Kas, Teshen, Safir. Atieno too, most likely. If the ageing Vagrim was anything like Lynx he'd not absolve himself of the responsibility he'd assumed when he saved her at the Fountain.

Toil nodded and pulled her boots on. 'Are you ready to meet your Monarch?'

'Not really.'

'I'm sure we can find something to steady your nerves downstairs, looks like they've got half an alchemist's shop down there.'

Lastani frowned. 'I'm not sure that would be a sensible idea.'

Lynx burst out laughing. 'You're pretty much joining Anatin's Mercenary Deck,' he declared. 'The refuge of bad choices, blind stubbornness and wilful ignorance. Stupid ideas'll just help you fit in round here.'

Chapter 18

Toil and Lastani left directly for the palace, escorted by Captain Cothkern with two of the Bridge Watch soldiers carrying a chest belonging to Toil. She left Lynx to round up whichever of the company's officers were still able to see straight, but first he headed to his room intending on changing out of his uniform at long last. To his dismay, Lynx found the door wedged shut by a chair or something. Whoever was in there, all he got was muffled curses and laughter when he hammered on the door.

Growling, Lynx resisted the urge to kick it in and merely shouted, 'Five minutes,' through the door before heading downstairs. In the common room he spent a while sorting through the crowd, trying to work out who was in any condition to come with them. His efforts weren't helped by the musicians putting renewed effort into their screeching and Lynx was putting serious consideration into shooting one by the time he hauled Kas up off the sofa she was lounging on.

Eyes glazed and mouth fixed in a drug-induced grin, Kas took a while to work out what was going on, but when she focused on Lynx's face she gave a happy little sigh and wrapped her smooth brown arms around his neck.

'Come to join in the fun?' Kas purred, pulling him closer.

As best he could, Lynx turned his head to speak to her without either shouting or ending up with their lips pressed together. He found his hands sliding all too easily around her waist and had to check himself as Kas stretched up.

'Time to work!' he called out.

'Get fucked,' she replied merrily, nodding back to the sofa where Sitain swayed as she watched them. 'Come enjoy yourself with us instead.' Her grip tightened. 'Or enjoy yourself somewhere else mebbe, if you've come to your senses?'

'Eh?'

'Toil,' Kas said, fingernails digging into the back of his neck briefly. 'That girl's gonna be the death of you.'

'Yeah, sooner rather than later too.'

The scowl on his face was enough to pierce the clouds in Kas's mind and she leaned back a little so she could focus on his face better. There was little doubt she was in no condition to do much exploring underground, but she'd been with the Cards long enough to still have her wits about her while drunk or high.

'What's happened?' she sighed. 'Fuck's that madwoman gone and done now?'

Lynx gave a wry smile. 'Where do I start? Our night's only just started, you in any state to think straight?'

'How long have I got?'

'Well the army putting Jarrazir under siege has only just reached the city, so a little while.'

'Did you just say fucking *siege*?' Kas yelled just as the music hit a lull. More than a few faces turned their way and Lynx realised their embrace was now the focal point of the room.

'Knights-Charnel!' he replied loudly.

'Of shitting course it's the Charnelers,' Kas growled. 'Who else?' She let go of him and sat back on the wooden back of the sofa.

'Shit, tonight was looking like all sorts of entertaining up till now.' Kas cast a mournful glance back at a man just behind her, no more than twenty years old and shirtless to show his lean physique and rings in his nipples.

'Sitain, how're you doing?' Lynx leaned down to look at her and blinked in surprise as she straightened up. 'Gods, where'd you get that?'

Normally Sitain left her hair to hang loose above her shoulders, but now it was pinned back by a handful of silver clasps. Around her neck was a brass necklace composed of eight chains, interwoven through each other and studded with coloured jewels or glass.

Sitain gave him an owlish look. 'Like it? I found it in a market today.'

'You know what that is?'

Lynx found his thoughts completely derailed by the sight of Sitain in that necklace. It was a traditional Hanese style, one given to daughters by their mother during the Festival of Songs. Often they were pieces handed down through the generations or shared within a family, a common sight on any So Han street. To see Sitain wearing one was like a punch to the stomach – her parentage for some reason all the more obvious by that small addition.

'Course I do, my ma had one. Never got a chance to give me my own.'

'Shit,' Lynx muttered, shaking his head as though he could clear out the memories crowding his mind. 'Yeah, right.'

His own mother was long dead, but when he pictured her it was wearing just such a necklace at the dinner table. The first girl he kissed, around the back of the livery yard while their parents headed to temple, had been wearing one. He tried not to think much about So Han and the life he'd left behind, but now the warmth of memory washed over him. The militaristic society was not ascetic or stale, however humourless their rulers were. He had plenty of good memories buried under the pain, plenty of gentle moments between the arduous training grounds and bombastic speeches at the temple.

'You okay?'

'What?' Lynx blinked. 'Oh, yeah. I'm fine. Come on, time to work.'

'Now?'

'Yeah, get your kit in case we're not back here any time soon. You too, Kas.'

The lithe scout took a few unsteady steps. Lynx reached out to help her but she slapped his hands away. 'Get off, I just need to walk this off. I'll be fine.'

'Sure?'

'Get the others,' she insisted, waving vaguely at the rest of the room.

Lynx took her at her word and did just that, interrupting Reft and Deern as gently as he could before kicking Llaith off a tall woman when he wouldn't stop doing whatever was making her eyelids flutter alarmingly. Teshen was at a side table playing some sort of forfeit game with knives and tiny vials of clear liquid – apparently intending on a little catching up of the others before doing anything else.

Anatin just giggled malevolently when Lynx tried to rouse him from his chair, prompting the thought that this had all been at his deliberate instigation to spite Toil, while Safir was nowhere to be found, and Payl was swigging from a bottle of something potent-smelling rather than helping.

'You too?' Lynx said, glancing at Teshen.

'Toil don't need us yet,' Payl replied. 'I'll come when the Cards are needed but fuck her and her scouting group. I've got better things to do than find out how safe it is down there.' Without waiting for him to reply Payl hauled her lover Fashail up out of his seat and off towards their bed with such a look of determination Lynx didn't try to stop them.

Deciding Payl was at least halfway right Lynx returned to his room to discover the door unbarred and Safir mostly naked inside. He was out of his bunk and trying to light a pair of small cheroots while Estal, the company seer, lay under the blankets of his bed. The white-haired woman smiled up at Lynx, almost purring with contentment, the large jagged scar on her head looking more dramatic in the weak light of the single lamp.

Lynx stared at her for a moment as Safir passed Estal one cheroot and she began to puff away at it.

'You okay there, Lynx?' Estal asked through a cloud of smoke.

'Eh? Oh, yeah.' Lynx turned himself to the matter at hand and started to unbutton his tunic.

'Hey, whoa there,' Estal laughed, 'I ain't that sort o' girl!'

'Who says it's for your benefit?' Safir said with a wink.

'Is that why you boys are so happy sharing a room together? I should have known Llaith's flexible morals would rub off on the lad.'

'No one's rubbing off on anyone,' Lynx said firmly before raising an eyebrow at Estal, sprawled back across Safir's bed. 'At least, no more'n they have already. I'm just here to change, you two might need to as well.'

At that Estal frowned and glanced at Safir as Lynx started pulling off his boots. She sat up, keeping the blanket draped over her chest while reaching with her free hand towards her jacket. From a large pocket on the jacket's breast she pulled her diviner's deck. Her company badge, the Diviner of Stars, was stitched over that pocket, a larger picture than most with more detail than you'd find on a usual playing card.

It portrayed a black woman sitting at a table, cards spread on its surface in front of her. One eye was all black, the other all white. Her right hand was raised, showing a card with the three stars of her suit, her left steadied a war-axe standing upright beside her, while around her neck was a moon-and-Skyriver pendent.

Estal began to shuffle the cards and Lynx found himself slowing as he changed clothes, watching her movements as though she'd started to hypnotise him. Under her breath he heard her mutter, not quite a mantra nor a song, but something that sounded like an invocation to a god he didn't know. He'd never seen her do a reading, wasn't sure if he even believed in any of it, but something about her otherworldly manner commanded him to silence.

Breaking off from her muttering, Estal put one card face down in front of her, then a spread of five in an arc above it, lastly one upturned above those. That was the moon card, Lynx knew, and while its value was only a Five of Tempest, in Estal's deck every card had a unique image in the centre. This one bore a five-petal flower growing amid a wasteland.

'Hope dominates,' Estal muttered, turning the arc cards next, starting with the topmost. 'Bones, the many-coloured man, the blank die, clockwork heart, hound.' She reached the bottom one, nearest her, and tapped it twice before turning it: the Princess of Blood.

'The great lover,' Estal pronounced, looking askance up at Lynx with a blank, trance-like expression.

'Him?' Safir scoffed. 'A bit well padded for that, isn't he?'

'Behave,' Estal said in a distant tone, more like her usual self but still caught up in the reading.

'What's the verdict then?' Lynx asked, caught between feeling a chill on his neck and an urge to laugh at the superstition.

'Hope rules the heavens,' she said hesitantly, 'but death remains a close companion. The many-coloured man and the die together show the choices and chances that abound, the hound embodies pursuit and seizing, the clockwork heart opposes it with patience.'

Lynx paused and looked over the cards spread out on the blanket. 'What the buggery's that all supposed to mean?'

'Take your chances when they come,' Estal said before flashing him a smile, 'just don't come whining to me if those chances end up getting you killed.'

'Unless of course you're just the hound to our Princess of Blood,' Safir added.

'Oh thanks. Not even the main attraction at my own reading? Sounds about bloody right.'

Lynx finished changing his clothes without a word, trying not to look at the Princess of Blood card. The picture was of a woman's head, red hair half-obscuring her face but her piercing eyes both visible through that tattered curtain and her full red lips curved in a smile. Behind her stood two figures, one male and one female, both naked and facing away from her.

'Coming?' he said once he was done, his long grey coat draped over one arm and his sword belted on to his waist.

'For what?'

'Toil's offered her services to the Monarch, she'll need extra hands to scout the labyrinth entrance out.'

'Didn't think you'd be so keen to go back underground,' Safir said, settling down on the bed beside Estal. 'I'd been joking about the princess's hound, you know.'

'I know, and I ain't. Mebbe there'll be enough to do above ground now the Charnelers have brought an army to the gates. She'll need the most skilled Cards as she scouts, though, then the rest ready to follow on a full expedition.'

Safir nodded. There were plenty of decent soldiers in the company of course, they were professional mercenaries after all, but some had skills beyond the usual set. As a classically trained duellist, Safir was one of those – born into a noble family of a warrior culture where the martial arts were taught to all sons and daughters. The giant, Reft, was another, cat-quiet

Kas a third; her bow nearly silent compared to mage-guns and five times faster.

'I'm going nowhere right now,' Safir said eventually, 'and frankly I'm not going to be much use for anything upright. She's scouting out the Fountain entrance?'

'Just gone back to the palace now to get ready for it.'

'Give me an hour then and I'll meet you there with anyone willing to sober up. Before that, whatever trouble she's got herself into is her own problem, find someone else to help.'

'Payl's of the same mind as you,' Lynx said, nodding towards the bed. 'Anatin's out of his gourd of course and I can't even tell if Reft knew I was there.'

'You'll manage,' Safir declared, lazily reaching an arm over Estal and pulling her close. 'Shut the door on your way out.'

*

'Where are the rest?' Toil demanded when they joined her in the palace, standing over a large map that covered most of a long table.

'Balls-deep in a pile o' alchemist potions.' Kas grinned, walking in none too steadily herself. 'Or just balls-deep and pretty unrepentant about it.'

'On their way to sobering up?'

Lynx grimaced and glanced back at the few who'd come with him. 'Think the alchemist has packed up and gone home,' he conceded, 'but anyone chasing the whores out is gonna get lynched right now. Safir is going to round up volunteers for scouting and meet us at the Fountain. The rest need a few hours. Some are still armed and they're the ones in the worst state.'

'What an encouraging state of affairs,' said a man opposite Toil darkly, a bulky, balding officer of the Bridge Watch. 'I suppose that so long as you have enough to scout the labyrinth, though, I don't much care.'

'I like them already,' contributed a handsome nobleman. His eyes narrowed as he saw Kas and a glittering smile appeared on his face. 'Merciful passions of Catrac, are all of your company such radiant beauties?'

Kas beamed. 'Nope,' she said, managing an exaggerated sashay up beside him and offering her hand. 'I'm as good as it gets.'

'I have no doubt, lady,' the man murmured, bowing to kiss the back of her stained leather glove. The dozen silver braids that hung in an arc from one shoulder to the other swung forward to almost loop around her hand as he did so, the size making Lynx think they were some sign of rank. 'I have the honour to be Lesser-Prince Justabel Por, and you are . . . ?'

'No lady, that's for bloody sure.' Kas grinned. 'I'm Kas – he's Lynx, the handsome one is Atieno. The white girl who looks like she's about to be sick is Sitain. There's a good chance she will be too, so keep those fine boots clear.'

'I shall remain steadfastly at your side, Lady Kas.'

'If you're quite finished, Lesser-Prince Por?' the soldier in black said gruffly.

'Nowhere near finished,' Por murmured in Kas's ear, 'but duty calls nonetheless.'

'Good. Ladies, gentlemen,' the soldier continued, sounding like he was reserving judgement on both descriptions there. 'I am Commander Honeth, I will be supervising your efforts and relaying any necessary details to the Monarch.'

'And I will be joining you,' Por added, 'as is my duty and my right as a lesser-prince of the city. Indeed it will be my pleasure, but I think perhaps I should summon more of my household guards if Lady Toil's company are otherwise indisposed.'

'I don't need most of them if the commander here is bringing a regiment of his troops along for the main expedition,' Toil replied. 'And anyway, I brought mine because they're mercenary scum who know how to stay alive at all costs – an instinct that'll be more useful in the labyrinth than fancy uniforms.'

'There will be some additions to your scout crew,' Honeth said firmly. 'All of whom will be as good as anyone in your company, however fancy their uniforms might be. How many do you intend to take?'

'First foray? Half a dozen will do – just to go in and take a look. We make sure we can stop the guardian spirit then get an idea of what we're dealing with. I only need a few mages and a handful of others to look after them.' She nodded over towards a closed doorway. 'Mages tend not to be the most athletic lot, even Lastani.'

Seeing Lynx frown, Toil said, 'She's off explaining herself to the Monarch right now. Might be she's got some skills, but she's an academic and likely to panic if things go nasty. Better there's someone like you beside her; if it comes to trouble, you can toss her over your shoulder and run.'

'Is that likely?'

She shrugged. 'Depends what sort of surprises are waiting for us. At least we've got a clear run, no competition to dodge.' Toil paused. 'That's right, isn't it, commander?'

'Correct, no one else has been given permission to enter the labyrinth and all the entrances we've found have been guarded.'

'*Found?*'

The man inclined his head. 'From what we can tell, at least one is lost beneath the city, a second buried under the house that collapsed as it opened. No one has reported a problem with their foundations or a doorway opening up in their cellar, though, and the Monarch's edict regarding entering remains in force.'

'Because relic hunters are such a law-abiding bunch?' Toil sighed. 'Can you at least confirm Sotorian Bade left the city with the rest of the Charnelers?'

'The general and her entourage all went straight to the barge she arrived in and it did not stop until they were well clear of the city walls.'

'But did they all get back on it in the first place? Gods, man, Bade wasn't in a Charneler uniform! He could've slipped away in the confusion.'

'Confusion caused by your actions,' Honeth reminded her coldly.

Toil pointed down at the map in front of her. 'These are all the entrances you know of?'

'Correct. Each marked with a number, bar the Fountain itself and two others; the doorway that's been blocked up under the North Keep Armoury and another in the cellar of the temple to Insar. Those bear these markings. The numbers tell us there's at least one unaccounted for.'

He passed over a piece of paper which Toil frowned at before setting down. 'Pass me that journal, will you?'

A battered, soft-leather journal bound in twine was handed over and Toil spent a minute flicking through pages. 'Ah yes.' She turned it around to show Honeth. 'Look, it matches one of yours here.'

'What does it say?'

'I'm pretty sure it's a family name – or something like that. Mebbe best described as a coat of arms, I've seen it on a few holdings down south.'

'So what does that mean?'

'My guess is this entrance was reserved for one Duegar family, or guild or whatever it referred to. Like a Monarch's private entrance to a grand temple.'

Toil copied the marks down on the map beside each of the entrances they corresponded to, the one she'd recognised going next to the North Keep, the northernmost of all the entrances.

'They're in a line,' Lynx pointed out, tracing down through the unnumbered entrances. Toil nodded and drew a faint line over the streets to connect the three – it wasn't quite straight, but they all knew how inaccurate city plans were likely to be.

That left five marks on the map; Honeth quickly put a number or rough symbol beside each they had identified at Toil's request, and an X at the one buried beneath a building. The woman spent a while looking down at the remaining marked points, head tilted to one side and tapping her finger on the first of those. She traced a line across to number two, but there was no three yet discovered and there she stopped. After a while Toil turned the map on its head and paused. There was a look of frustration on her face when she looked up.

'This seem familiar to anyone else?'

They all crowded around the table, but no one spoke.

'Can you fetch Lastani back in, commander?'

'She's answering questions in private court,' Honeth said reproachfully.

'She's here to be my Duegar scholar,' Toil snapped back. 'So let's put her to damn use, eh? I'll go ask for her myself if you'd prefer?'

'You've interrupted the private court enough for one day, I think. Do it again and the Crown-Prince will likely shoot you dead.'

'Then be a dear and fetch her. I know I've seen this before, or something like it anyway.'

He was gone only a minute or two, the door opening on to a luxuriously appointed corridor similar to the one they'd stormed down earlier. Lynx had found himself turned around entirely as soon as he entered the palace via the north gate that seemed to be for the exclusive use of the Bridge Watch regiment. He could at least tell that the degree of finery increased dramatically in the part surrounding the private court and the great hall beyond it where Toil had caused a scene.

Lastani returned looking a little pale but relieved when she saw the mercenaries waiting for her.

Not quite a welcome sight mebbe, Lynx thought to himself, *but I can guess the reaction she's had from all the officers and nobles in the palace. They'll be wearing faces like she's something the cat's just dragged in, I've seen that often enough.*

'Lastani,' Toil said, jabbing a finger at the map where she'd drawn one line between the first and second exits, and another between the fourth and fifth. 'There should be another point or two on this map that connects these lines and the shape reminds me of something.'

The young scholar peered at the map for a long while, her hand tracing vague lines in the air. Then she shook her head and turned the map on its side so that the highest point of the hills to the west of the city was at the bottom. She made a few passes through the air again as though performing some silent incantation before nodding.

'There,' she pronounced, pointing at an area of the city.

'What? I don't see it.'

Plucking the pencil from Toil's fingers Lastani marked a part of the map in the east of the city with a cross and looked again at Toil.

'Let's just pretend this isn't a valuable fucking opportunity for me to learn, okay?' came the reply.

Lastani swallowed and nodded her head. 'Of course.' With a sweeping motion she drew a curve from the second point, around through the new one and looped it back around to the fourth. 'It's the character for "the divine",' she explained.

261

Toil slapped her palm down on the tabletop hard enough to make Lastani jump. 'Dammit, I knew I'd seen the thing before. The Temple of the Divine, right under a carving of a tree.'

'That would be consistent with Duegar mythology,' Lastani confirmed before finally taking a proper look at what she was drawing on. 'Oh spirits high and deep, those are the entrances to the labyrinth!'

'All forming a huge word,' Toil confirmed, 'when you're standing on the high ground overlooking the city. That's no coincidence. But of course half the uses of the word in Duegar histories won't have seen the light of day outside of Militant Order fortresses for centuries.'

She looked up at Commander Honeth. 'There's a job for you however, commander,' Toil said, prodding the mark Lastani had made. 'Here's where you should be looking for the last entrance.'

'How certain can you be?' The commander scowled down at the map. 'It's a loop drawn freehand on an inaccurate map.'

'The character is probably more precise than your map,' Lastani replied. 'The peak of the loop must not be higher than the top, nor lower than the end, and must retain a natural symmetry. It gives you a dozen streets to scour, I admit, but that's better than nothing, if there's even a chance it can be used to reach the armoury entrance?'

'Lynx – go with him, you can report back to us once it's found. Kas, you too – looks like you still need to walk the day off.'

'If the alternative is drawing lessons from the ancient Duegar,' Kas said, 'then I'll take the walk. Do I get my bow back?'

'All of your company's weaponry has been brought to the palace,' Honeth confirmed. 'Obviously we don't want the city to see mage-guns being handed out at one of the major stores in the city, half the sailors and merchant guards might start asking for the same, but the regiments are aware that mercenary companies have been retained. You can collect what you need at the Watch gate.' He stepped closer to the map to look at the streets in the area that had been marked. 'It will take time to check this many buildings.'

'Take the Cards too, or whichever of them can still stand. Tell them you're looking for contraband alcohol, that'll get a good turnout.'

He gave her a scornful look. 'To enter private dwellings and search cellars? Perhaps not. You two can tag along behind, but leave the work to my troops.'

Lynx shrugged. 'If you think people are likely to be over-sensitive and object to a Hanese mercenary forcing his way into their house . . . then sure thing, lead on, commander.'

Chapter 19

Lynx watched a company of Bridge Watch form up behind Honeth in the silvery twilight with a faint sense of disquiet. This wasn't his city and the Bridge Watch were principally a bodyguard regiment for the Monarch, but something about the black uniforms made him uneasy – cold silver braids and clasps on the officers, dull steel on the soldiers.

They're too smart and neat, Lynx realised. *They don't look like real soldiers. Probably they're just made to be presentable around their rulers, but they remind me of the Sword Brethren all the same.*

The Sword Brethren had been a fringe society within the So Han army for generations, but with the brutal upwelling of tribal fervour during Lynx's youth, they'd grown in prominence. The Brethren had always been savagely contemptuous of foreigners and when the Shonrin had clawed his way to power were the first to embrace his message of superiority and conquest. They'd become his enforcers and his spies as much as his preachers – the driving force behind the tide of arrogance that had swept the whole nation along with it.

We commandos were the army's elite, but those bastards had almost as much blood on their hands and they rarely went near the fighting.

With dark thoughts filling his head, Lynx lowered his gaze so he didn't meet the proud, dismissive looks the soldiers gave him and Kas. It'd never been hard for him to start a fight and with the city as tense as it had been in years, everyone was on a hair-trigger. He kept quiet and let Kas do the talking instead, the scout having mostly shaken off the effects of whatever drugs she'd taken.

Before long they were out on the city streets making good time for the area Lastani had indicated on the map. The locals kept well clear as they marched smartly down the street, Lynx and Kas loitering at the rear of the column. Lynx saw fear in the eyes of those he passed, news of the Charneler army having clearly filtered out through the city. It would have been years since they'd faced a genuine threat at their gates – he couldn't remember the last battle to be fought here, but certainly not since before he'd become a mercenary.

'Here,' Commander Honeth announced as they turned off a long avenue of shop fronts and on to a street of townhouses. Iron railings ran down each side of the street, penning a yard or two of ground in front of broad, double-fronted houses that declared a certain mercantile wealth.

'This street to across the Riverway, running up three blocks. This is the central area, we'll spread beyond it if we find nothing.'

He sent his troops off in pairs to cover the ground as fast as possible. From where Lynx stood he guessed there were close to a hundred properties on this street alone.

'How about us, commander?'

The man turned, looking irritated. 'You're mercenaries,' he sniffed. 'You've no jurisdiction here.'

'Just want to be useful,' Kas pointed out.

'You're hired guns,' Honeth reiterated, 'and I'll not have you forcing your way into homes unless we're fighting from street to street. You are here on sufferance, remember that and keep out of our way.'

Kas raised her hands placatingly. 'As you wish. Come on, Lynx.'

She took his arm and led him further on down the avenue as the Bridge Watch started about their task – splitting up to approach each street from different directions. More than a few faces started to appear at windows as the black uniforms spread out, the anxious looks extending to Lynx and Kas as the mercenaries both carried weapons.

'Let's see if anyone's acting squirrelly,' Kas whispered, pulling Lynx on so they got ahead of the Bridge Watch. 'Just in case things are for the worst. If the Charnelers are here, they'll have lookouts or guards, no?'

'And then what do we do?'

She grinned. 'Report it to the proper authorities of course. What do you think we are, Lynx? Soldiers?'

They made slow progress down the next street while behind them the soldiers went about their search, and had nearly come to the busy thoroughfare of the Riverway before anything unusual happened. Lynx felt Kas's hand on his arm tighten slightly and he turned to follow where she was looking.

A man was sitting on the steps leading up to one house distinguishable from the rest solely because it was in a slightly shabbier condition. The man himself had pale skin and dirty blond hair cut neat and short. He wore a bulky leather coat with a cloth spread across his knees and was idly puffing on a fat pipe as he watched the black uniforms further down the street.

'Good Charneler face, wouldn't you say?'

Lynx shrugged. 'Thought we all looked the same to you?'

'Oh I'll remember that crack,' she replied darkly. 'Now shut up and answer me. You ever been far north? Never been to Order heartlands myself, but whenever I've got shit from some bastard in a uniform, they were some blond thug just like him.'

'Every bastard in a uniform gets on my case,' Lynx pointed out, 'but yeah, he's northlands somewhere.'

Belatedly the man noticed them staring and his head jerked around. Lynx saw a brisk, professional look take in all the details of them; their mercenary clothes, the tattoo on his face, the gun behind his back and Kas's sheathed bow.

'Evening,' the man said a fraction of a moment too fast. 'What's going on up there?'

Lynx glanced back. 'Bridge Watch,' he said baldly. 'Inspectin' houses.'

'For what?'

'Dunno.'

The man's eyes narrowed. 'What're you two doing down here? Don't look much like you belong round these parts.'

'We were thinking the same thing,' Kas replied. 'You're no house servant.'

The man smiled disarmingly. 'Afraid that's all I am these days.'

'Sure about that?'

'Yeah. Fuck's it to you?'

Kas glanced at Lynx, a small smile on her face. 'I love it when I'm right,' she muttered before raising her voice. 'What's it to me? Let's just say we're taking an interest too.'

'Well I'm the houseman here and it's my job to make sure trash wandering the streets keep clear. If you know what's good for you, you'll shift before I call those soldiers.'

'Be my guest, call 'em.'

The man ignored her suggestion. 'What do you want?'

'Just looking around.'

'Don't give me that shit. Neither of you two belong in an area like this.'

'Now that's just rude.'

The man opened the door behind him and made to head through until Lynx drew his pistol and levelled it at the man.

'Are you mad?' the houseman said, stopping dead.

'Aye, probably,' Lynx growled. 'Now how about you come back out here.'

The man twitched, just glancing slightly behind into the dim hallway. Lynx saw shadows moving on the wall – could make nothing more out but clearly they weren't alone. 'Why?' the man said at last. 'I've done nothing to you.'

'You were rude to the lady,' Lynx said. One thing he'd learned over the years was that bullshit statements and ridiculous reactions carried more weight from behind the gun. You didn't need to make sense when the other person was worried about being shot. 'Now come out here and apologise to her.'

'Fine – Shattered gods! Look, miss, I'm sorry,' the man said quickly. 'Didn't mean no harm.'

Kas yanked her bow clear and pulled a couple of arrows. Lynx had seen her fire a handful in quick succession like that, keeping the spares in her draw hand. 'How about you ask your friends to come out and join us?'

'There's no one in there,' the man said, hands raised with his fingers splayed.

'We can see 'em,' she said, drawing the bowstring back.

'Okay, okay!' He looked back and with exaggerated motions made to open the door fully.

When he paused Lynx knew what was coming next, but it still passed in a blur. The man dropped, Lynx fired a fraction of a second before someone behind the door did the same. The white streaks of ice-bolts flashed past each other, jagged bursts of light illuminating the frontage as an arrow thrummed through the air and slammed into the shooter.

A second arrow followed a heartbeat later, then Lynx and Kas were backing off. They were exposed out in the street – even the commando in Lynx, trained to attack with shocking, devastating speed, knew it was foolish to run into the unknown like that. Another icer split the night and the pair turned tail for the nearest cover as shouts came from down the street and the townhouse door slammed shut.

By the time Lynx and Kas found a low wall across the street and hunkered down behind it, there were shouts coming from the house too – the lamps inside were being doused and curtains hauled across windows.

'Think we found 'em!' Kas whispered. 'Now what?'

'Now what? This was your bloody idea, wasn't it?'

'We're here 'cos Toil wanted us to come and she's *your* friend!'

'You're blaming me for this?' Lynx pulled his long gun from the sheath on his back and checked it was loaded. 'What happened to waiting for the proper authorities?'

'I blame you for a lot o' things,' Kas hissed. 'Now put an earther through that front door!'

'I don't carry 'em,' Lynx said. 'And anyway, it could punch a hole right through the house at this range.'

'So?'

'Ulfer's horn, you're as bad as Anatin! This is a city, people live here!'

'For how much longer if those are Charnelers with an entrance to the labyrinth?'

'I still don't carry earthers.'

Kas squinted up at the windows, bow half-drawn. 'Shit, those toy soldiers won't either. Means we're not getting inside any time soon.'

'One siege wasn't enough for you, eh?'

'Shut up and tell me you remembered to bring a grenade or something.'

'Oh yeah, because I'm a bloody trigger-happy lunatic. And no, I ain't firing a burner at it neither, not going to set off a firestorm in the city.'

Another shot tore through the night, a white lance hammering down to shatter the brickwork by Lynx's foot. The pair flinched from the flying shards of brick.

'Shit, upper windows!'

Lynx raised his gun and fired almost blindly – letting the power of the ice-bolt be its own dissuasion – and in the next moment Kas was up beside him and drawing a bead on the windows across the street.

Only one was open so she fired on it, hoping to catch someone in the darkness. The arrow vanished inside silently, no scream following.

'Sparker?' Kas asked as she readied a second arrow.

'Yeah.' Lynx fumbled at his cartridge box, finding a spark-bolt by feel, and loaded it. 'Door or window?'

'Window.'

He fired and the jagged stream of light erupted up to the third-floor window. Glass shattered, claws of lightning tearing at the frame while staccato light illuminated the room inside and voices shrieked in pain from somewhere out of sight.

'That's better!' crowed Kas, scanning the other windows for another target. Before she could pick one the Bridge Watch arrived, a trio of soldiers with their guns wavering between the mercenaries and the house they were firing at.

'Hold your fire!' roared Honeth, pounding his way down the street like a raging bullock. 'Hold fire, damn you!'

'They started it!' Kas called, bow still drawn. 'Thought there were no guns in this city?'

The knot of soldiers quickly swelled as more arrived, a handful coming around the corner from the Riverway and looking just as uncertain as the others. Honeth reached Lynx and Kas, glaring furiously at them before realising Kas was right – no household in a middle-class area would possess a mage-gun. Only the nobility got away with bending the rules like that.

'That door?' he demanded, pointing.

'They were shooting from the window too.'

Honeth turned and pointed at the nearest Bridge Watch troops. 'With me. The rest of you, watch the windows!'

He advanced on the door at a crouch, a mage-pistol in each hand, and pressed himself against the door-jamb. One soldier took a position on the other side and the other crouched at the base of the steps while Honeth hammered on the door.

'Open up in the name of the Monarch!' he roared, loud enough to echo all the way down the street. 'Lower your guns!'

There was no response so he banged again. 'Answer me now or we break it down!'

Again there was no reply so Honeth gestured to one of the soldiers. The man nodded and took a step back, braced himself on the handrail of the steps, then launched forward to stamp his boot into the door.

It burst open under the impact. From behind his wall Lynx caught a fleeting glimpse of a hallway empty but for a small table set behind the door, a box on top of it. Some sixth sense made him duck his head as the table and box went flying.

In the next moment the house exploded.

*

Bade turned just in time to see the man vanish – swallowed by the floor without a sound or the tiniest disturbance. He heard the brief scream a second later, distant and muted.

'Guess that answers that question,' Chotel muttered.

Bade flashed the man a grin. The dead man wasn't one of theirs, but one of two dragoons running down the narrow path of the upper chamber. 'Didn't you explain rule one of relic hunting to 'em?'

'I thought you did?' Chotel said in mock surprise.

'Dammit, must've forgotten. Ah, well, looks like they've learned the hard way.'

The second dragoon stumbled to a halt, looking wildly around at the blank flagstones of the upper chamber. There was nothing to see – the illusion was pristine and unbroken, without even dirt to break its crisp lines. Eventually his gaze returned to the two men watching him and that shocked him back into movement, trotting forward with his oil lamp held high.

'Where's Exalted Kastelian?' the man gasped.

'What's happened?'

'Bridge Watch came to the house. We blew it.'

'Sure you brought it down?' Bade asked sharply.

'I heard it go as I was running here. We rigged the door with a whole box of grenades,' he confirmed. 'It'll take them days to dig it out.'

Bade nodded and turned back the way he'd come. 'No time to lose, then. Let's hope you're right about being ready, Chotel.'

Chotel offered him an obscene gesture in reply. They hurried the short distance back to the second labyrinth entrance where most of Bade's crew were camped with their kit on the narrow path of the upper chamber, four dragoons standing guard at the open doorway itself. They couldn't risk keeping anyone inside the entrance chamber now the wall was too thin to mask any noise so the remaining dragoons had been sent on to a broad platform before a massive stone doorway they'd found, where the mages were currently working on opening it.

'Timetable just got moved up,' Bade called once he was close enough not to shout. 'Get to the door and be ready to move. Sonna, you're in charge until I come.'

A tall woman with a long mage-gun in her arms nodded. By coincidence she was a local of Jarrazir, or at least a village down the coast, but the tattoos, fetishes and jewellery she sported showed how far the sharp-shooter had travelled – both before and after joining Bade's crew.

Bade headed inside to the main chamber below the keep, slowing his footsteps to be as quiet as possible. Just inside the inner door was Bug's crate where Ulestim waited, away from the wall they'd been patiently digging out. Bade waved the man forward and the three headed into the main chamber where the alchemical globe was still going, its light fading. Fortunately, they wouldn't need it for much longer, not now the townhouse entrance was no longer a secret.

Bade ascended the slopes until he was right at the door and Ulestim handed over a limp cloth pipe with a tapered brass nozzle. Ulestim was a tall man with tanned skin and round spectacles on his neatly bearded face. His clothes were non-descript but for a belt picked out in whorls of green and red that held a rapier on one hip and a pistol on the other.

Bade connected the pipe to an oblong metal object that had a grille covering much of its back half and two broad handle-like pieces sticking out at the middle. With most of the dirt and rubble blocking the doorway to the deep armoury removed, only a thin wall of bricks remained. They had already constructed a rough frame of sticks and cloth around the doorway to hide the globe's light in case there were gaps in the mortar so Bade simply sat on the floor and pulled the folds of cloth around him until he was working in near-total dark. Using a knife he slowly worked away at the mortar between bricks until there was a hole to push the nozzle of the pipe through, whereupon he pulled a wet rag from a small pail off to the side and tied it around his nose and mouth.

Ulestim pressed at two parts on the metal object that was connected to the pipe and a dull glow appeared within the main seam running down the centre. The pipe jerked like a snake waking from hibernation. Quickly it filled out and the machine silently started its work.

Bade watched it happen, enraptured. He'd not found this item himself – fortunately enough as it transpired. Another relic hunter had and had died not long afterwards, the object being passed between collectors until one worked out how to use it. Most likely it had been intended simply for eradicating vermin, but now the vermin were soldiers. He'd never had a chance to use the thing before, a sleep- or death-inducing gas that was lighter than air being not immediately useful, but finally he would see how effective it was.

If it isn't, we do this the old-fashioned way.

It was difficult to gauge how long it needed, but given the gas would rise and escape through any vent or window above they had to let it run as long as possible. After five nerve-tightening minutes Bade reached out and tapped Ulestim on the shoulder. The man nodded and shut off the machine again, stepping back before removing the rag about his mouth just in case.

'That should do it,' Chotel whispered from behind them. 'Now Bug?'

Bade nodded and Chotel crept back to fetch the remaining dragoons to help them carry Bug's crate up to the doorway, Kastelian following along behind. Waiting as long as he could for the gas to have taken effect and then dissipate, Bade worked the first brick free and peered through with his gun ready. He could see nothing inside – the gas also smothered any flames it encountered – so rather than assume there was someone waiting in the pitch black he started removing more bricks.

Ulestim helped him until there was a hole roughly the size of the crate's end. They slid the crate up to the hole and prised open the face until they could lift a piece clean away, leaving the crate open to the room beyond the doorway. Bade sat on top while Chotel braced it behind. Bug had been drugged and cooped up for days now. She'd not be in the best mood.

Best she finds something to kill and eat before I give her a scratch behind the ears, Bade thought as he peered through the small gap above the crate, his Duegar lamp held to one side. There was a soft scrape of claws on the bottom of the crate then nothing until he spied faint movement in the blackness beyond.

It was hard to make out, even though he knew what to look for, but the progress of a dark, sleek shape was just about visible across the room beyond. Eventually, Bade made out two shapes on the floor of the room, past a wooden mechanism like a dumb waiter and a triple row of steel lock-boxes covering the far wall. Neither was moving and the elusive shape of Bug paused only momentarily at them, her hunger overruled by the instinct to search out any threats first.

Bug crept to the stairs with small, precise movements where there was a touch more light and Bade could make out the familiar lines of grey carapace and black blade-like limbs. The size of a large dog, Bug had a blunt eyeless head with a wide slit mouth, shark's smile half hidden behind the double pair of mandibles that twitched up and down, tasting the air. Her fat lobster-like tail curled up high as she ascended the stone stairs, ready to explode into movement, but she continued with the slow stalk until she was out of Bade's sight.

'That's some runt,' Bade whispered to himself as much as anyone, but Chotel coughed a small laugh beside him.

'It'd have been a real pain to get a full-size maspid into the city, though.'

'Also tricky to train up from a grub I reckon.'

'How long do you give her?'

Bade shrugged. 'Time to find someone, rip their face off and eat what's underneath until she's not so hungry.'

'So a few minutes more?'

'Aye, probably best.' Bade took another long look at the room beyond then eased himself back to the ground. With Chotel's help he lifted the crate quietly away before enlarging the gap so a man could walk through without ducking. On top of the crate he put a small clay pot and removed the lid. Inside was a sticky substance that he dipped one finger into and dabbed some of the pungent secretion on his throat, Chotel doing likewise and indicating to those behind that they should also.

That done they moved on through, guns drawn, until they'd reached the lock-boxes. Under the light of Bade's Duegar lamp it was hard to make out much, but he could see that most of the locks had been removed and the boxes were empty. Most, but not all. There were two remaining – each big enough to contain one bombardment sphere that would nestle neatly in the wooden frame of the dumb waiter. A second smaller rack of boxes on the other side was also empty but for two mage-spheres about double the size of a standard grenade, intended for firing in groups to scatter in the air and cause maximum damage.

Still enough for our purposes given we brought a few boxes of grenades too, Bade thought as he inspected the dumb waiter mechanism. It was simple but sturdy, held by thick chains that were all freshly oiled and each strong enough to hold ten times the weight of a sphere with ease. The frame itself had blocks lined with leather padding that could be removed so a sphere the size of a large pumpkin could be fitted, then the blocks restored to protect it on all sides.

He nodded towards the stairs. There had been no shooting so it was unlikely anyone was left alive. Bug might be hungry but the runt was still a maspid, undersized or not. She was too intelligent to just stop and eat without investigating the remaining rooms first. Only daylight would keep her away and it was well past dusk by Bade's estimate.

He led a nervous quintet of dragoons up, keeping his gun drawn just in case Bug had decided to go feral and was waiting to ambush him. The secretion he collected from her and stored in the jar should tell Bug they were part of her pack, but maspids were clever. They could make choices of their own and he'd seen her kill one crew member she didn't like, despite the scent.

The first room was empty, the second a bunkroom. The soldiers inside had fallen where they stood or simply never got up, two broad puncture wounds showing Bug had indeed passed this way before moving on. The men on the top bunks she'd left or not noticed from waist-height, but they were already dead when Bade checked, knife at the ready.

They moved on and found more signs of slaughter, more bodies in a windowless mess-room and the kitchen beyond. A brick chimney rose through the mess-room, a protected path for the mage-spheres to reach to the roof. Above that was a garrison room with more dead and a heavy outside door reinforced with long bars of steel and bolts top and bottom.

Bade lowered the three long bars that served as additional protection, in case someone twigged what they were up to, then carried on. To get through it now any attacker would have to rip the entire frame out of the six-foot-deep stonework it was set into – going directly through the wall with earthers would probably be easier.

Up again and into several small guardrooms with narrow windows affording fields of fire in all directions. More dead there, and above in the watch commander's office. They found Bug in the guard rooms above that, keeping to the enclosed space and feasting on one of the corpses. The runt maspid twitched and tensed at their arrival, but Bade clicked his tongue at the creature until she relaxed a shade. They couldn't communicate properly, not as easily as a master and his dog even for all of Bug's greater intelligence, but the creature could sense what he wanted well enough.

Bug responded with a short burst of clicks and returned to her meal while Bade and Kastelian headed up to the roof. There they found more bodies; a pair of uniformed soldiers who'd been almost torn apart by Bug.

'Must've still been moving,' Bade whispered, pointing to the bodies. 'These ones she put down hard.'

'Lucky for us they didn't get a shot off.'

Bade gestured at the thick wall that ran around the entire platform to protect the trebuchet from gunshot. 'Probably still got a dose of the gas; this keeps it enclosed.'

There were slits around the edge for sighting, but most of the entire top platform was composed of a massive trebuchet on a pair of sliding rails that in turn sat atop a great turntable. Fat-toothed gears ran all the way around the outside of that, a great block of gearwheels set to one side with a handle protruding far enough for four men to grip.

Which in all likelihood, it'd take to move this monster, Bade realised, looking up at the great arm of the trebuchet – black against the dull glow of the Skyriver.

'The keep's clear,' Kastelian announced as another of his men ascended to join them and signalled to the Exalted. 'Time to rig it up.'

'Aye.'

They headed down again, leaving Bug to her feast and ushering the rest away until there was only Chotel and Bade left in the lowest room. One of the dragoons had provided them with the commander's key and they carefully unlocked the first of the sphere cases. Inside was a dull steel ball, made without finish or great care. Bade had seen them crafted once, back in a Charneler sanctuary. It was terrifying watching the glass ball be coated variously in wax and sawdust, then twine, before molten iron was poured over in stages. The slightest mistake and everyone within fifty yards wouldn't even notice they were dead.

Unlike a grenade, there was no flaw in the coating, nowhere for a pin to pierce the glass. The iron was a rough covering because it needed no more refinement than that. Some said that they could be dropped on to a stone floor without detonating, but Bade doubted anyone had tested the theory. When they were thrown by a trebuchet, they were light enough to be hurled half a mile and the impact would be all the detonator necessary.

Quickly they assembled a wooden frame and placed the sphere underneath with five boxes of grenades the dragoons had ferried up. Atop the frame they placed three primed grenades while a candle was set underneath one side of that, just beneath a thin rope that held the platform level. Before the candle was lit, Bade sent Chotel away to make sure everyone was well clear before fetching a sated Bug. The maspid followed him easily enough and sensed by Bade's manner than she needed to move carefully in the lower room, skirting her master before heading down into the depths.

Bade waited a short while, hoping for no gunshots as the dragoons saw Bug, but none came and a low whistle from Chotel confirmed that the maspid had gone through. She would catch the scent of Senna, the member of Bade's crew Bug liked more than the rest, once she was through the chamber and follow that across the upper chamber of the labyrinth.

Hopefully she's got enough sense to find the path, Bade thought to himself as he retrieved his matches from a pocket. *Reckon she'll be useful in the days to come.*

One last check of the frame and he lit the candle, checked it was burning correctly then scampered away.

The rope's thick, he reminded himself as he hurried down the zig-zagged slopes beyond the door, *you've got time.*

Still, Bade didn't slow up until he'd reached the upper chamber and saw the dragoons heading off down the path. He followed them a short way until he was well away from the door, whereupon he knelt and waited. Chotel joined him and lay flat, prompting Bade to copy him, and side by side they lay as the seconds ticked by.

'Really burning your bridges today, aren't you?' Chotel whispered. Bade laughed and soon the two men were giggling like children together, half-tensed against the explosion to come.

'Think there's a problem?' Chotel added after a while longer.

Bade opened his mouth to reply and then there was a distant cracking sound that was immediately swallowed by a long, deep boom that roared like an approaching firedrake, full of wrath. The sound shook the roof and walls and path beneath them, filled the air above with its deep rumble until Bade thought his ears would burst.

A great gust of air and dust spat from the stone doorway ahead, scattering shards of stone and dirt like rain across the upper chamber. It whipped at their clothes as the two men lay face down, hands clasped over their ears. Finally, ears ringing and limbs trembling, Bade looked up and blinked at the darkness beyond. He could see little difference with so much solid rock between them, but could only imagine the devastation wrought up on the surface.

'Nope.' He coughed, banging a fist against his lieutenant's shoulder. 'Reckon there's no problem.'

Chapter 20

Blurred light and distant sound. Pain and numbness, crushing weight and emptiness. A body he could no longer feel began to thrum with fearful energy – a flutter that rose from deep inside his chest to describe a shape, a form. The curve of ribs, a deep chest and thick limbs all traced in the dancing jangle of fear. It spread, became fingers and eyes and hair and finally the picture was done – a man traced in lines of panic.

With a jolt and a gasp, Lynx opened his eyes. A thin wail escaped his lips as the darkness pressed down on his chest – hot and sharp like tiny teeth. Flailing, he managed to haul himself around and dislodge some of the bricks on top of him, twisting where he lay to shake them off and relieve the pressure. He tried to make out where he was but the air was full of dust. The sky was dark above him, the Skyriver a distant dull haze while smears of orange flame shuddered at the periphery of his vision.

'You dead?' called a voice before breaking off into a pained cough.

Lynx shook his head, trying to dislodge the confusion filling his mind and the snarl of fear in his stomach. He struggled his way up to a sitting position and drew in a deep breath, letting the cold air wash over his face.

No stone, no walls or dead air. No chains, no hunger.

He repeated the words to himself several times, a mantra to quell the familiar feelings of panic threatening to swamp him.

'Not dead,' he said as the bursting stars finally faded from his eyes. He looked down at his hands, dirty and scratched, and wiped them uselessly on his trousers before looking over at Kas. 'You?'

She looked as bad as he felt, covered in dust and woozily touching her fingers to a cut on her cheek. There was plaster and brick fragments in her hair, a trickle of blood running down from the top of her head.

'Not sure,' Kas said as she inspected the blood on her fingers. She lifted her head and looked across the street. 'So – that's what an exploding building looks like.'

'Another thing to cross off your list, eh?'

Kas gave a pained laugh. 'Would've preferred watching it from a bit further away, though. Screaming hells that hurt.'

'Yeah. Shit – Honeth!'

Lynx pushed himself up to look over what remained of the wall they'd sheltered behind. There was a scene of devastation on the street, torn fragments of cloth fluttering amid the wreckage of several houses and smashed bricks everywhere. Dazed figures in once-black uniforms picked their way through what remained, but Lynx could tell at a glance they wouldn't find the commander or those with him alive.

'Don't know about you,' Kas groaned, standing and patting the broken stub of brick beside Lynx, 'but I'm experiencing some disturbingly warm and fuzzy feelings towards this wall.'

Lynx nodded slowly. It had taken the brunt of the blast and while the wall had collapsed on them in the process, he could forgive the consequences of its sacrifice.

'Hands up!' roared a voice as a figure loomed into view.

Lynx almost fell over in surprise, staring stupidly at the mage-gun muzzle that appeared directly in front of his face.

'Huh?'

'Put your hands up!' the man yelled, voice quavering, gun swaying slightly across Lynx's vision.

Finally Lynx managed to drag his eyes away from the muzzle and looked up at the man. A Bridge Watch soldier, soot and sweat staining his cheeks, clearly shocked by what had happened and ready to shoot anyone in his way.

'Okay,' Lynx croaked.

Trying not to stumble and startle the man he put his hands up, seeing Kas do the same out of the corner of his eye.

'We're on your side,' Kas added after a moment.

'What?'

'We came with you to search these houses,' she said slowly. 'With Commander Honeth.'

'Oh.'

The information seemed to confuse the man and for a while he didn't say anything more. Lynx kept his mouth shut. He was in no rush to be moving too fast anyway. Eventually the soldier's eyes narrowed and for a moment Lynx was sure he was going to die right there, but all he did was take a proper look at Lynx then Kas and lower his gun.

'Right, yeah, you came with us.' He looked back at the shattered house. 'The commander.'

Lynx took that as a question. 'He kicked the door in,' he said gently. 'He was right there when it blew.'

'You don't know that,' the soldier snapped.

'Yeah we do,' Kas said, slowly rising and putting a hand on the man's arm. 'I'm sorry, but we saw it happen. We'd be dead too if we'd not been taking cover.'

Lynx grabbed her arm. 'The grenades, they were right behind the door – they meant to blow it now! They're taking the armoury right now!'

'Oh shit.'

By fits and starts the pair staggered forward, leaning on each other for support. Lynx found a whole variety of new pains awaken across his body as he started to walk, trying to pick his way through the scattered debris and rubble until he found a man wearing sergeant stripes and looking more composed than the rest.

'Sergeant!'

The man glared at him, gaze darting to the gun on Lynx's back, but then settling on the badge Lynx wore. 'The mercenaries,' he growled, relaxing a shade. 'Did you do this?'

'It was rigged to blow,' Kas said with a shake of the head as Lynx blurted out, 'You've got to warn the armoury!'

'Which armoury?'

'The North Keep. Send some men to warn them.'

'What in Insar's name are you talking about?'

'It's in danger!'

'What? How?'

'Whoever just blew that house up,' Lynx said, trying to fight the urge to shout at the man, 'is going for the armoury – they have to be.'

'Whoever blew that up is dead, friend.'

He shook his head. 'They're not, they're alive and in the labyrinth. They blew it so we couldn't follow them. The entrance is buried under that pile of rubble.'

He pointed to where the townhouse had been entirely demolished and spread liberally across the street, the two neighbouring houses half-collapsed on to the pile of rubble between them.

'In the labyrinth?' the sergeant echoed. 'But that's . . .'

'Insane – unless you're a Charneler relic hunter who's fixing to head through the labyrinth and blow up the North Keep, opening Jarrazir up to direct assault.'

'Merciful Veraimin!' Finally the man realised the danger and grabbed at the two nearest soldiers. 'You two – can you run?'

'Yes, sergeant!'

'Good – fast as you can to the North Keep, shout up to the windows if they won't let you in, just make sure they listen to you – there might be Charnelers digging right underneath them.'

'Digging?'

'Not digging, there's an entrance to the labyrinth that opens into the lower levels of the keep,' Lynx broke in. 'They've got grenades and will try to blow it up!'

'So bloody run!' the sergeant added for emphasis, shoving the startled pair into movement.

Lynx watched them head down the street and be swallowed by the darkness before turning to Kas. 'Back to the palace?'

'If you like,' she said, rubbing her head. 'Think I need a lie-down first.'

'Don't think there'll be much of that going round.'

'Exactly,' Kas said with feeling. 'Once Toil hears about this she's gonna move as fast as she can. Reckon I need some rack time before any more excitement.'

'Leaving me to tell Toil.'

She patted him on the shoulder. 'Them's the breaks.'

'Shit.'

The sergeant had already forgotten them and moved on, yelling at his troops to get digging for the injured, so they simply walked away by fits and starts in the direction of the palace. The street had filled with people, some staring in horror, others coming to help dig. They passed a bewildered pair of City Regiment soldiers standing at the end of the street, watching the sudden swell of humanity milling about in alarm. The sound of the explosion, Lynx realised, had to have carried for miles – half the city would be wondering if the Knights-Charnel had attacked the walls.

If that keep goes, he realised, *they will do. That'll be the north face of the city open to assault.*

285

They reached the grand Eastern Avenue that cut across the city to find it full of people. Lynx had to display the written dispensation for their weapons three times before they could turn off and head to the lodging house. But just as they did so, a cataclysmic roar tore through the air. Lynx stumbled as the ground itself shook under his feet. They both flinched in shock as people nearby screamed and pointed. Turning north, Lynx saw a great cloud of orange-lit smoke rise up in the sky and streaks of light soar through the darkness before smashing into buildings like the rage of elementals.

'Oh, pissing gods,' Kas moaned.

Above the houses they could see the copper-sheathed roof of some grand hall come alive with light as it reflected the blaze of explosion. In the next moment it seemed to implode – crumpling in on itself as debris slammed into the peak of the roof. The building shattered under the impact, the near-side wall twisting and folding inward before dragging almost the entire roof with it.

They stood and stared with half the local residents, watching the sky flicker red and orange like the ground had opened up over the seven fiery hells. Children wailed, men and women wept, shrieks that could have been man or beast echoed around the street, but Lynx found himself just staring with horror and lost in another time.

Few battles were fought in a city – whether by deliberate choice or tacit understanding of the madness it entailed – but Lynx had seen it happen twice before and his stomach turned to acid just at the thought. The first had been terrible, an abomination, but swift for all its brutality. The So Han army had made an example of a neighbour early on in the war – a warning to all those who opposed it. They had swept over the city in a dawn raid and crushed unprepared, inadequate defences. By midday the battle was over, but such were the weapons carried by both sides, the city had been shattered.

And still that had not proved the worst time. No, that had been years later when he had signed up as a mercenary in some border dispute that quickly got out of hand. Exactly how it had happened had never been clear to Lynx, except small atrocities committed over generations had festered in the hearts of each side. The war had been short, Lynx's side outmatched by their foe, and culminated in an assault on the principality's capital – an old and pretty city that straddled a Duegar canal in the north-west. The battle had raged for three days and by the end there was simply nothing left. Just a great stream of refugees fleeing in all directions, bodies and rubble. Half the city had died as burners and earthers tore the buildings apart, grenades and small mage-spheres thrown without regard at all parts of the city.

Lynx had run with the rest and been lucky to survive, but he heard later that when victory was declared, the enemy general stood on a hill to survey his victory. He stood there for an hour and watched the wreckage burn, then retired to his tent. The army turned around and went home the next morning, the general stayed and while his bodyguard kept marauders at bay, he would not leave. On the third day he was found dead at his desk, unable to live with what he'd done.

A voice cut through the clouds of the past, distantly at first but increasingly insistent.

'Lynx, Lynx!'

He blinked and looked around. 'Huh? What?'

Kas grabbed him by the shoulder and physically turned him to face away from the glow of flames. 'Hey, wake up! We need to go.'

'Go?'

'The palace?' she reminded him, hesitating a moment then adding, 'Toil?'

'Oh. Yeah.' He shook his head and pinched the bridge of his nose. 'Right, the palace, sure.'

The pair went as fast as they could, but in the end had to wait a long time before anyone would admit them. The Bridge Watch swarmed the area with guns at the ready, a maddened nest of ants ready to attack the first thing that presented itself. Lynx and Kas kept calm and ignored the obvious, unspoken threat as they stood their ground and asked for a message to be sent. The lieutenant they spoke to was a young man struggling to maintain his calm in the face of chaos. Matters were only made worse when Lynx was the one to tell him that Commander Honeth wouldn't be able to approve their entry to the palace, nor come to take charge.

Eventually a message was sent and the pair kept out of the way while they waited. The soldiers on duty kept a close eye, seemingly unable to believe that they could be there for any legitimate reason. The guards were so on edge that when a familiar voice started roaring curses from inside the palace, Lynx would have sworn he was a hair's breadth from getting shot as the men watching them jumped.

'What in the name of Banesh's rage is going on out here?' Toil bellowed, storming up the corridor with a large Bridge Watch sergeant on her heel. 'You! Why the flaming crap-stain are you detaining my men when we're on the Monarch's business? Didn't you see them leave an hour ago?'

The lieutenant gulped nervously as Toil marched right up to him and jabbed a finger in the man's chest. 'I . . . No. I was not on duty an hour ago, miss.'

'Where the shit is Honeth?'

'Dead,' Lynx said. 'Charnelers blew the house once we found them, must've wanted to seal the entrance so we couldn't follow 'em down.'

At that Toil grabbed the lieutenant by his tunic and slammed him against the nearest wall. 'And I had to bloody well come and get that news myself? What's wrong with you, man? Think

I've got nothing better to do right now? Think I'm not pretty gods-burned busy at the moment?'

The lieutenant goggled, gaping like a fish for a moment before he could work his mouth. 'No, sir! Sorry, sir.'

'Who's in charge of the watch now?'

He blinked. 'Ah, it'll be Major Olep, sir.'

'Where's he?'

'I don't know.'

'Have him found and informed about Honeth. He's just inherited a shit-storm. Lesser-Prince Por has taken two companies to shore up the wall defences, but he'll need more if the Charnelers attack. The Monarch's sent messengers to all the noble houses requiring their private troops – since those chinless shites'll drag their heels about it, Olep's going to have to go and conscript them himself, shooting the first braying fuckstick who says no.'

'I'll have him found, sir,' the lieutenant confirmed. There was a spark of resolve in his eyes now, reminding Lynx that surprise, confidence and yelling were enough to take charge in most situations.

'Good. You two, come with me. We need to tell the Monarch exactly what's gone on.'

She led them back down the way she'd come, the palace noticeably empty compared to earlier. Once they were out of sight of the guards Toil stopped abruptly and turned.

'Are you hurt?' she said in a considerably softer voice. 'You look like you were caught up in the explosion.'

'Fine,' Lynx said, 'just got my bell rung a bit.'

'I'm fine too,' Kas added acidly. 'In case you care.'

'I don't much,' Toil snapped.

'Yeah, we've all noticed that,' Kas said. 'Not the best for company morale that, if you ever are actually planning on using your Card rank in anger.'

Toil snarled and pulled a mage-pistol from her holster, aiming the gun directly between Kas's eyes.

'Don't fucking test me, Kas, not right now!'

Kas tilted her head to one side and inspected the gun in a studied manner, her lips tight with checked anger. After a moment she indicated down with her eyes. 'And don't you ever think I'm your lesser, Toil, not now or ever.'

Toil and Lynx both looked. Kas had a pistol of her own drawn that Lynx certainly hadn't seen appear, but there it was, at her waist and pointing at Toil's heart.

'Both of you, stow it!' Lynx snapped, breaking the silence that had fallen over the stand-off. 'We've got bigger problems right now – you've made your points so step the fuck back.'

'Right then,' Toil said stiffly. 'Yeah. Point made.'

Kas gave a short nod and holstered her gun. 'Good. Let's get to work.'

It didn't take long for Toil to do the same and after a tiny pause she turned and carried on towards the room where she'd left Lastani.

The young woman looked up fearfully when they entered, half a dozen books open on the table ahead of her. Off to one side Atieno and Sitain stood amid a dozen plain backpacks, each one stuffed full by the looks of it.

'What's happened?' Lastani asked before the others could. 'Have they really breached the wall?'

'Sabotage,' Lynx said. 'Charneler agents took out the North Keep.'

Before Lastani could say any more the door on the far side of the room opened and a man wearing a gold arc of braids across his chest entered, two Bridge Watch on his heels. His face was thunderous, just as it had been when Lynx had last seen him.

That'll be the Crown-Prince, Lynx recalled. *Means they're still taking her seriously if he's taking the time to talk to us*

'Toil, come now, your troops too.'

They all headed down another corridor, this one short and opulent with two great tulip-shaped chandeliers lighting the way. At the far end was a massive door covered in decorated silk, but as it opened towards him Lynx saw it was effectively two doors sandwiched around a solid steel plate. That meant he was unsurprised to find himself back in the throne room and following Toil's lead in kneeling to the Monarch of Jarrazir. There was a small gathering of people of various ages and sexes to one side. Most looked like palace officials, with one man wearing the same dozen or more silver braids around his collar that Lesser-Prince Por had sported.

'Get up, we don't have time for formality,' Crown-Princess Stilanna called. 'The wall is breached and you need to get moving— Wait, you – you're covered in dust, were you near the keep?'

She was looking at Kas, who nodded, wavering a moment before she sat on the floor instead of rising.

'Not the keep, we were looking for the remaining entrance to the labyrinth,' Kas said. 'The good news, of a fashion, is we forced their hand. Lastani directed us to the right area and Honeth started searching houses. Lynx and I just took a walk and spotted someone looking suspicious, not least because they tried to kill us.'

'So what happened? Where is Honeth now?'

'Dead, Your Majesty. He led the attack himself and they booby-trapped the house. It blew as he kicked the door in, never stood a chance.'

The Monarch pressed her fingers to her lips, gasping in shock at the death of one in her inner circle, but she waved away the concerned hands that reached for her and after just a few seconds, looked up again. Her cheeks were pale, but her voice remained steady.

'And you call this good news?' she said icily. 'You pushed them to blow up the keep causing scores of my people to die?'

'No, Your Majesty, not good news, but they were past negotiating and ready to move. The Charneler agents were likely all safely underground already, in the labyrinth and preparing to break into the North Keep from underneath. That's why it blew the way it did.'

'So my trusted adviser is dead and you forced a hasty reaction that will lead to many hundreds more dying?'

Toil took a step forward. 'They were doing it anyway, otherwise they wouldn't have been able to blow it so fast – you knew there was an entrance in the keep and had walled it up again in the event of people getting in. This way, they couldn't have had time to signal the army. The Charneler army won't be ready for a full assault. You'd want to have a day at least before moving an entire army straight to a direct attack.'

The Monarch leaned forward. 'I'm told that's exactly what they're readying to do right now, under cover of darkness.'

'But it'll be a mess and you'll be able to crush it – the last thing any soldier wants is to run across open ground without artillery support. You'll have defenders waiting with grenade throwers, burners and sparkers. That's a hellish long way to go under fire, especially when you're basically a disordered rabble.'

'Where are your infiltrators now? Did they escape?'

'They're in the labyrinth,' Toil said. 'We've got to make ready and go in after them before they get too much of a lead.'

'Assuming they do not plan any more sabotage. I will have your expedition troops assembled at once.'

'I need to lead an advance party first – the last thing we need is to tramp a hundred soldiers into a Duegar ruin before we know what's down there and right now you're going to need your soldiers up top.'

The Monarch leaned forward. 'Then I suggest you get moving, I intend to throw everything I can spare at this problem, right down to all of the pots and pans in my palace if necessary. I have two agents ready to accompany you now and more waiting with your mercenaries at the Fountain. Your only mission is the saboteurs, mind – hunt them down so they can cause no more damage.'

'Why do we not simply wait for Bade to resurface?' Lastani said. 'All the entrances are within the city, the two most northerly ones destroyed.'

'Assuming he doesn't just wait for the Charnelers to take the city?' Toil shrugged. 'If I was him, I'd have kept back one bombardment sphere as collateral – or use it to wipe out anyone waiting outside a particular entrance.'

'I can flood the labyrinth with troops once the attack is fought off,' the Crown-Princess said. 'We leave nothing to chance, though; I intend to stop the Knights-Charnel while you both hunt and kill Bade. If he knows the trick to warding off the guardian spirits Lastani has described, I assume you do too, Toil?'

'There'll be a simple method,' Toil confirmed. 'I've seen similar things elsewhere so with a mage or two on hand, yeah, I'm willing to bet my life there.'

'What more do you need?'

'Lastani, you're all set with your books? Good, my kit's ready – I've got two lamps and Sitain has a third.' She paused and pointed up at the bright trio of egg-shaped lamps above them. 'I could do with one of those, however.'

The Monarch looked startled at the suggestion. 'One of the palace treasures?'

'The more people I take, the more they'll need normal light. Ask Lynx here how much fun it is to run around in the black with only the dark-lamps. Folk get scratchy surrounded by darkness.'

Stilanna gave Lynx a look, but didn't bother asking. The value of the oval lamp was likely enormous, but she had others and if it helped save the city, she wasn't going to waste time debating.

'Very well, have it taken down.'

Toil turned to her companions. 'Right – now I just need a sober company of idiots willing to follow me down into the labyrinth.'

Kas gave a brief laugh. 'It might be best if they ain't sober for that, but we'll see what we can do.'

'Pick me a scout group, ten or so – have the rest assemble to follow with the Bridge Watch troops. I mean to heavily outnumber Bade when we find him.'

'Pots and pans, right,' Lynx agreed. 'Safir should be rounding up experienced hands to bring to the Fountain, I'll hurry them up and leave instructions for the rest.'

'So you're in?' Toil asked, her tone neutral. Lynx instinctively bristled but realised she wasn't needling him.

'Better'n sitting on my thumbs round here,' he said with forced levity.

'There's work above ground too.'

'Aye – a full assault on a city. I may have my issues with being underground, but I've seen a city fight too and that's no picnic. If I get to choose, I'll choose the deepest black alongside folk I know. Besides, Sitain'll probably shoot herself in the head if I'm not there to watch her. Just don't give me time to think too hard about it, eh?'

'Very good,' the Monarch said and stood. 'We have limited time to react. Lesser-Prince Por has taken the first reinforcements to the wall – the City Watch is being mobilised as we speak. Tylom, you will take charge of the troops being mobilised in the noble district. I want you to lead cavalry out at first light to harry the enemy. Their camp must be hastily organised – disrupt and distract them as best you can.'

The Crown-Prince bowed to his wife and swept out without a word, his bodyguard and a few courtiers following along in his wake.

'And the Red Scarves?' Toil enquired.

'Are of little immediate use,' the Monarch replied, 'being, as they are, currently disarmed and half of them billeted outside the city walls. Commander Deshar is making arrangements to recall them safely, but the Knights-Charnel are moving to encircle the city. It may have to be done by boat and that presents new challenges. The Senate Voice will ensure they're reunited with their weapons, but there are more pressing concerns. Take my seal and warrant,' she said, indicating for a courtier to come forward with a small leather purse. 'Your letters of recommendation are acknowledged and accepted,' the Monarch added pointedly. Clearly she didn't intend to mention even in this closed gathering where the letters came from, but the intent in her eyes was clear. 'Should you fail to honour the terms of your employment, know that there are measures in place to exact reparation.'

Toil didn't look surprised by the statement, though to Lynx it was a clear threat to inflict death and destruction on Su Dregir. 'Can't promise I'll succeed, just that I'll try and I'll be fighting your cause.'

'See that you do. Now go.'

Chapter 21

Toil stopped outside Envoy Ammen's townhouse and looked at her two new companions. A local man and woman, Elei and Suth – both wearing Bridge Watch uniforms, but with a hard way about them that spoke of a darker trade.

The dark-haired Elei was a compact, swarthy man with the bearing of a knife-fighter, while the fairer Suth was slim and only average height, but the more dangerous in Toil's opinion. She wore at least four mage-pistols under her greatcoat compared to Elei's one, while the look in her eye was one Toil recognised. That faintly distant, aloof air of one who saw sight-lines and angles as naturally as breathing – who carried multiple guns for rapid firing and hadn't shot themselves yet. Toil had met a few of the other sort too, but experience told her Suth knew what she was about.

'Best you two stay here.'

'Not our orders,' said the woman firmly. 'We're sticking with you.'

'I've got a loose end to tie up here,' Toil said. 'Su Dregir business, best you're not present.'

'Are you mad? We're chasing your man's fucking tail as it is! Anything else can wait.'

'Two minutes – it'll take that long for my crew to grab their shit and, in case I don't come back, this has to be done.'

The pair looked at each other. 'Two minutes, no more.'

The townhouse was mostly dark as Toil hurried in, just a light in one of the top windows where Ammen's clerks slept. She took that as a good sign. If they were still ill most likely they'd be asleep, it was late in the evening and normally they'd be at their supper.

It was dark and quiet in the hall, a faint glow coming from past the stairway but no sound. Most likely the hired staff had walked out already. No one wanted to be working for foreigners at a time like this, not least ones struck down with illness. Toil followed the light and found herself in the kitchens. At the table was Barra, out of uniform and slowly cleaning the pieces of her gun in the light of a single lamp. Beside her was a gently steaming teapot and a tiny cup. The slim woman eyed her employer with a lazy scowl and returned to finishing her task.

'Feeling better?'

'Bet you think you're funny, eh?'

Toil shrugged. 'I delegated that job to Aben.'

'Yeah, well, he did you proud. I still feel like crap, though.'

'Able to work?'

Barra sneered. 'Of pissing course, I ain't some mewling secretary.'

'Climb? Run?'

'Better'n most, even if I'm not at my own best.'

'Then fetch Aben and Paranil, we're going exploring.'

That brought Barra up short, hands frozen in the act of starting to slot the pieces of her mage-gun back together.

'Official sanction?'

'And escorts outside – Bade's beaten us down there so I do mean I need you able to run, once I've finished my business with the Envoy.'

Barra gave a curt nod and briskly slotted the remaining gun-parts together before setting it down and doing as ordered – trotting past Toil and up the stairs with barely a sound. Toil

297

followed her as far as the second floor where the Envoy's private rooms were and walked straight in.

'What is it?' the man called as he heard the door open, eyes widening when he spotted Toil. 'You've got some damn nerve, woman,' he growled.

Toil closed the door behind her and checked the room in a glance. Ammen was alone and his mage-pistol lay on his desk. Clearly the man realised the same thing and he darted forward to grab it, but before he could get there Toil had her own drawn.

'Now now,' she said as he froze in the act of reaching for the gun. 'That wouldn't be a very good idea. Back up, that's it, now sit.'

Eyes full of murder, Ammen did just that and Toil tossed the man's gun away before sheathing her own. Ammen frowned, clearly not expecting that.

'What do you want, whore?'

'Ah, senator,' Toil said, walking towards him. 'There's no need for such language. We were both sent here with orders, just not the same ones.'

She could see the calculations going on in his eyes. He was a big man and stronger even than she was, but also sitting down and with no guns to hand.

'You knew the labyrinth was going to be opened? How?'

'I have my sources.'

'And you came here just to offer your services? On the Archelect's behalf? Was my mission just a smokescreen?'

'Your mission was just as vital,' Toil said almost soothingly. 'As Jarrazir witnesses, the Knights-Charnel and all their fanatical little friends grow bolder every year. Su Dregir needs allies and the states of the Parthain shore are an important first step. We had thought there'd be more time to establish trade relations, but life's inconvenient that way.'

'What now?' he asked.

'Now we talk about justice.'

'Justice?'

'Su Dregir justice,' Toil clarified, 'and the dignity of its government offices. Offices that shouldn't be sullied by the actions of their incumbents.'

'*That*?' Ammen spat. 'They were nothing, mere commoners. They should've been grateful for my regard.'

'They were children,' Toil said.

'Low-born trash, less than nothing.'

He lunged as he spoke, so fast and unexpected he almost caught Toil off-guard. Ammen surged up from his seat, left hand reaching for Toil and right drawing his knife. She turned just in time, throwing herself to the side as he clawed at thin air.

With a step back to give herself space, Toil kicked forward and caught Ammen in the side of his knee. He stumbled sideways, dropping his knife, but managed to keep his feet and kept on coming. Toil pulled a knife and threw it, but in her haste it flashed past his face and disappeared behind him. Ammen gave a roar and dipped his shoulder as he ran, slamming into Toil's gut and lifting her off the ground with the force of a charging bull.

He carried her several yards into the wall behind, almost crushing a side table there. The impact rattled her teeth as she cracked her head against the plaster, but as he drew a fist back to punch her Toil found something under her hand and swung wildly. Aiming for his face she caught his fist instead and shards of porcelain exploded over them both.

Ammen fell back, grimacing at whatever bone she'd broken. Still, the man didn't let it stop him for long. She had time for one gasp of air as his fleshy face purpled with pain and rage, then he swung a haymaker with his good hand. It would have knocked Toil clean out if it had connected, but she twisted inside the blow and caught his arm coming around.

With a dip of the shoulder Toil pivoted and let Ammen's rage and bulk carry him all the way over her. He slammed heavily down on to the ground, emitting a sound of pain as he fell on his broken hand first. Overbalancing, Toil landed on top of him but managed to break her fall by dropping her knee into his ribs. Before Ammen could recover she twisted his arm around to manoeuvre him into a better position. She braced herself then released him and snaked one arm all the way around his throat to grab her other biceps.

The big man began to kick furiously but Toil was already squeezing. Her joints creaked and her muscles screamed as Ammen tried to fight back – to haul at her sleeve, to throw himself around and escape her grip. Hurt and dazed, the man was still much bigger and stronger than her, clawing wildly at her head with one ham-sized hand while Toil could only close her eyes and keep squeezing. The seconds ticked by so slowly Toil found spots appearing before her eyes. She put all her strength into the hold she had on him, hardly daring to loosen any muscles enough to let herself breathe, less he find a way to escape.

After what felt like an age he started to weaken, the pressure on his neck stopping the flow of blood. Once his strength started to fail Toil knew he would pass out soon and she redoubled her efforts. With one final twitch he fell limp and became a dead weight in her arms. Only then did Toil risk taking a long breath and it was a few seconds more before she could unpeel her arms from around him.

Smears of light and dark swam before her eyes. For a moment she could see nothing but bursting stars, but finally the room came back into focus. Above her was a face, peering down. For one panicked moment she thought it was Ammen somehow still upright, then her wits returned and Toil realised it was Aben. He was saying something but her mind was garbled and when he reached down she flinched and shook him off.

She sat with Ammen's head half-cradled in her lap for a while longer then took another long breath as she took hold of it once more. With the weight of his bulky body pulling down she twisted Ammen's head back and up in one sharp jerk. She felt his neck give under the pressure, limbs twitching at a dull snap, and let the corpse drop from fingers that trembled with exertion. Toil looked down at the vacant, distorted face of the former Envoy Eltris Ammen – a man whose barony of Su Dregir and seat in the city Senate meant there had been no public justice for a half-dozen or more young children.

No justice but me. It's better than you deserved.

She took Aben's hand and let the man haul her up as she panted and rediscovered her balance.

'Looks like the Envoy's fallen down the stairs,' Aben commented neutrally.

'Yeah.'

'Shame that, proud son of a noble house and all.'

Once he was sure Toil could stand properly, Aben grabbed Ammen's arm and started dragging him towards the stairs.

'No sitting around now, Toil,' he commented. 'Barra tells me we got work to do.'

*

Fires punctured the darkness, cries and wails split the smoke-choked air. An infernal light was cast over the devastation as Lesser-Prince Justabel Por ground to a halt and stared. Heedless of his troops, he could only gape at the destruction, at the crater where once there had been city streets. The keep was gone, ripped from the ground along with hundreds of tons of rock and soil. In its place was a smooth-sided hole – almost pristine after the explosion that had scoured this place. The surrounding streets were shattered – entire rows of houses smashed to kindling and brick shards, burning behind the dark veil of smoke and horror.

Por looked around, the strength draining from his limbs as he tried to get his bearings. There wasn't anything here even he, a native of the city, could recognise. He saw rubble and ruin, nothing more. An enormous, unfathomable hole in the ground ringed with fire and terrified, bloodied citizens. A city street had led him and the Bridge Watch companies here. He knew what he should have found, but only the faint broken lines of city wall away to his left and right gave him any confirmation at all.

As though in a dream Por approached the edge of the crater. Over sixty yards across, it was empty but for mud-stained soldiers scrambling along its slopes. Every stone and brick within had been hurled away with unimaginable force, striking anything that had withstood the initial blast with the force of a siege weapon.

'Lesser-Prince!' roared a voice in his ear. 'Sir!'

Por found his arm seized and used to turn him around. A squat woman in a black uniform continued to shout at him, gesturing in several directions, but her words weren't making it through. He stared at her in a daze while the babble flowed over him, but finally the panic and confusion on the faces of those behind her filtered in to his mind.

Almost on cue there came the first gunshots from behind him, the sharp crack of icers splitting the night. Por flinched but it broke the spell and he looked back to see City Regiment troops hurrying for the far edge of the crater where some of their own were already firing.

He could see little of what they were shooting at. Through the fitful illumination of the raging fires, he could make out a shifting mass but nothing more. Then pinpricks of light appeared, the white streaks of icers surging their way down and it all fell into focus.

'Bridge Watch,' Por yelled, 'defend the crater!'

He pulled his own mage-gun from his shoulder and checked it was loaded before hurrying forward, not waiting to see if the others were following. A sour, sick feeling filled his stomach and he had to fight to avoid vomiting as he ran. The Knights-Charnel were swarming forward against their broken defences. If they breached the line, the city would be lost.

Por floundered through the rubble and mud until he found a long hump of earth that offered some sort of protection. There he dropped down and levelled his gun, firing almost blindly into the shadows beyond where the city wall had once been. He couldn't tell if he hit anything but continued to fire as soldiers appeared on both sides of him. Soon the air was a brutal drumbeat of gunshots.

More soldiers – grey City Regiment and black Bridge Watch – streamed forward. There was no artillery here, not yet. Cart-mounted catapults were being sent from the palace, but right now they were on their own. Normally to attack a city was madness itself, even an idle nobleman such as he had learned as much.

But now our defences have been turned on us. Por shivered. The North Keep had been almost entirely emptied of mage-spheres so far as he remembered, so there had only been a few left. *What damage would there have been if the Monarch had not ordered that? Shattered gods, this whole section of the city would be gone!*

He shook his head and returned to the indistinct shapes moving towards them. His eyes had started to adjust and he could make out clumps of troops working their slow way forward. Taking a breath he closed one eye and fired again, watching the white thread dart away into the black to strike into one of the formless masses. As he reloaded he realised the horror was still sinking in on the faces of many. Soldiers in grey or black, civilians milling through the devastation too, the shock of what had happened here – of what it meant – dulling their response to the threat.

'Firing positions!' Por yelled at the top of his voice. 'All of you, forward! We're under attack!'

The horror receded in his mind, unexpectedly replaced with a more constant force in his life – the cold voice of his father. Por the elder had been a bastard, pure and simple, one who had shown little interest in even his eldest child. But one piece of advice had pierced the veil of the man's disdain and, perhaps only for rarity's sake, Por had always remembered it.

The lies we tell ourselves are the most powerful and it's the powerful who should understand them best. Only a fool believes the gods placed you above other men, that breeding counts and you deserve your high station. The truth, my heir, is that most people fool themselves so they need leaders who see clearly.

Embrace the lie and it becomes the way of the world, a beacon of certainty others rely upon. Never more so than in battle is that light needed most to cut through the fear and confusion.

They want to believe, Por told himself desperately. *When the world is at its worst, they need to believe the man with power and money is better than they are – simply because purpose is better than fear. Give them that purpose!*

He stood, trusting the gloom and distance to protect him as faces turned his way. 'Any man or woman with a gun, forward! Defend the city, defend Jarrazir! The Knights-Charnel have sent saboteurs to weaken us and now they attack – fight with me! Show them we have no such weakness!'

Part of him wanted to spit or choke on the words as they came out, but that part faltered when he saw the eyes turn his way. The hunched and fearful straightened, the wild-eyed stilled for long enough to hear his words.

More gunshots rang out and Por looked back over his shoulder at the advancing Knights-Charnel. He couldn't guess how far they were but one of his men hurled a grenade out into the black. Writhing tendrils of lightning burst out somewhere before the advancing soldiers – he caught sight of some figures in the staccato flashes. In that moment he realised they were closer than he had guessed, the advance troops holding fire to let the light of the second wave draw the defenders' fire.

'They are upon us!' Por yelled, drunk with terror but more than aware that his only chance of survival was to stiffen hearts here on this broken line. 'Stand with me, people of Jarrazir – stand and fight for your city!'

He dropped to one knee as a ragged cheer broke out behind to be swiftly enveloped by the whip-crack of gunfire. White trails flashed harmlessly past him as Por fumbled for a fire-cartridge. His mage-gun training was a dull memory, but one that had been beaten into him from a young age. Eventually his fingers recognised the glyph he'd been searching for and he loaded it, aiming blindly at a point about fifty yards distant.

He fired and orange light bloomed across the landscape. Men screamed and more fires rose up. Then something exploded, a grenade-pouch maybe, and one long section of the advancing Charnelers was revealed. Clumps of soldiers in the black and white livery reeled away from the explosion as the defenders used the light to their advantage. More grenades were thrown, Por watched them blossom terrible flowers of light in the dark garden of the night.

'Keep firing!' he yelled as he did just that, pausing once to check around him.

There was a thin stream of soldiers heading to the defence, running without regard through the shallow crater to throw themselves against the humped edge. Volleys of icers hammered into the rough ridge of earth that had been thrown up by the explosion, but almost as many were fired in response and the more terrible ammunition the Bridge Watch carried had to be taking its toll.

Still the advance wave of Knights-Charnel had not fired, either that or they were mostly dead as burners and sparkers were fired into the path of those troops the defenders could see. A regular flowering of spark-grenades continued to burst, even a handful of white ice-bombs and orange fire-grenades too. The darkness seemed to swallow them all, but what lay hidden would be terrible death and destruction.

'For Jarrazir!' Por continued to yell, brandishing his mage-gun madly above his head for those who could see him and might find heart in such foolishness. This time the enemy icers flashed close by, then the night was parted by a searing burst of light as the remnants of the first wave unleashed their burners and the defenders responded. Por flinched back, falling on to his backside as great curls of flame washed over the ridge of ground he'd been perched on.

Somewhere near him a man screamed, high and agonised. As Por blinked away the glare from his eyes he heard his own cry taken up from each of the pockets of defenders. He struggled to his feet, barely seeing the hands that reached to help him, and added his own voice to the clamour.

When he did rise the world seemed in flux – shifting and moving in ways he couldn't explain. A stretch of ground lifted ahead of him, stone rubble began to shift and knit together. Por looked around and saw brightly coloured figures emerging from the chaos of the city behind him, two, then four then six – the colours of the city's mage colleges visible in the flickering light as Jarrazir's most exalted minority arrived to defend their city.

His father had always said Por's was not a voice for giving orders, more one for singing tripe to maidens. But a singer's lungs were what he needed now and he strained them as hard as he could – howling the words up to the Skyriver above until they burned with the effort.

'For Jarrazir!'

Chapter 22

Lynx and his companions reached the Deep Market as fast as they could manage, but as they neared the Fountain he made out faces in the lamplight and realised others were already waiting. There was a strange dome-like canopy of stone over the Fountain itself; a carved stone block with detailed decorations that opened on one side to reveal steps down. In the shadows behind were soldiers in both black and grey uniforms, just ten in all spared the horror of the gun battle going on in the city.

Flanking the steps were curious metal snakes that he remembered from when Lastani had recounted her story, while looking down on it from the inside of the dome was the puzzle inscription that Lastani and her teacher had devoted their lives to. Lynx didn't see much to get excited about there – just a few hundred glowing curves of metal set into stone, ancient, discoloured and lichen-stained.

The ground in front of the steps had a roundish discoloration to it, a skein of cracks visible on the darkened surface of the stone there – the result of whatever Atieno had thrown at the guardian, he realised. Atieno had demurred from explaining, but Lynx knew he had glass balls in pouches at his waist – presumably charged with whatever magic he wielded. Less effective than mage-cartridges, the crude weapons would still pack a punch and wouldn't require a God Fragment to make, just a competent glass-blower.

A pile of canvas packs lay to one side, behind them a steel-bound ammunition case and long pole on which several dozen mage-guns had been strung. There were liveried servants waiting alongside the troops, but before any of the mercenaries were reunited with their weapons Toil came forward to cast her eye over those Cards following Lynx and Kas – Teshen, Safir, Layir, Estal, Deern, Brols, Shoal and Haphori.

'And the rest?'

'Out of their gourds still,' Lynx replied quietly, 'and of no bloody use to anyone. They're following, Foren will get them here in time, but you don't want 'em underground yet or anyone reporting back the state they're in.'

'Anatin was willing,' Kas said, still looking pale after the explosion but resolute all the same. 'Eager, you might say – he was waving a mage-pistol around with great enthusiasm, but it wasn't the most inspiring of sights.'

'No Reft?'

Lynx looked back and shrugged. 'Passed out on his bed, we tried to wake him but got nothing. Deern assures us he's not dead, just not moving any time soon.'

He gave Deern a level look, which the scrawny rat grinned at. His presence *was* a surprise, but anyone approaching sober was good enough right now.

'You can try waking Reft,' Deern replied, 'but I wouldn't advise it. Man's kinda single-minded on a night of revelry. If you take away "fall over" as an option by waking him up you've only got "fight" or "fuck" left to pick from.'

'Is there a problem?' called a man in a Bridge Watch uniform nearby.

'No,' Toil replied, 'here's my scout group – the rest will be following, but best not to wait.'

'These are all experienced relic hunters?'

'They'll serve well enough, Elei,' Toil said sharply. 'I'll be the one out front if anything goes wrong, remember.'

As the mercenaries collected the supplies and weapons already laid out for them, Toil addressed the small scouting party.

'Listen up. You're all taking my orders from now on – that means you two as well, Elei and Suth,' she said, pointing to the two Bridge Watch soldiers keeping close by. 'Rule one is that you do what I tell you – when I tell you – or you get shot in the face. If you think I'm joking about that, ask Barra or Aben.'

As she spoke, Toil brandished a solid walking staff, using the blunt ends to add emphasis to her words. 'Those of you who've not done this before, keep out of the way and don't do anything stupid like wandering off on your own. Most city-ruins are huge, confusing holes in the ground and as far as you're concerned this labyrinth is actually *trying* to kill you. Don't prod anything that looks unusual or interesting, don't put your fingers in anything, don't chat away or talk at all unless you're telling me something useful. Aben and me go first, mages and their handlers behind.'

'Handlers?' Atieno asked, a note of disapproval in his voice.

'Mebbe you can handle yourself, but you're not exactly spry,' Toil replied, 'and while we're underground all mages are as precious and stupid as children so far as I'm concerned. Suth, you've got Lastani there to keep alive, Lynx, you've got Sitain—' She held up a hand as Sitain started to protest. 'Sitain – rule one, remember? Layir, you stick with Atieno in case he needs a hand. We're the scouting party – we go down, make sure it's safe and we know where we're going, then I'll fetch down the rest.'

With that, Toil activated her Duegar lamp, made sure her coat was clear of her holstered mage-pistol, and started down the stairs. Lynx had barely reached the steps when he saw Toil stop and raise her lamp, running it along the side of the wall before approaching a smoothed section opposite the bottom step.

Duegar glyphs glowed faintly blue in the strange lamp's light. He couldn't read them but all it took was a glance back from Toil and Lastani pushed her way forward. Toil pulled a glass bead from a pouch at her waist and nodded to Lastani – tossing it forward at one glyph while Lastani flicked her fingers forward at the other.

Pale wisps of cold shot forward from her fingertips and slapped into the glyph while a brief flash of orange flame crackled over the other. A strange wavering border appeared between the two for an instant until the fire magic in the bead was exhausted and a white coating of frost stole over both.

The glyphs both briefly glowed blue then went dark. Exactly nothing else happened, but Toil appeared satisfied and headed on down into the darkness beyond.

'That's it?' Lynx wondered aloud.

'Yup,' Toil called back. 'The guard dog's sniffed our hand and thinks we belong – it's just here to keep the wildlife out.'

'Is that what we are?'

'To the Duegar?' She laughed. 'Vermin probably, they were a long way from nice even by our standards.'

Lynx followed when it was his turn and saw in the elusive blue light a plain, roundish room with absolutely nothing of interest save a pillar and dark tunnel leading off.

'Certainly living up to its wondrous reputation so far,' Kas whispered to Lynx, ignoring the look she got from Toil as the relic hunter did an inspection of every wall with her lamp.

'There'll be nothing to see here,' Lastani said, 'the Fountain riddle says that the true labyrinth lies beyond the upper hall.'

'If you go around trusting riddles,' Toil replied as she searched, 'you'll not live long enough to hear me say I told you so.' She paused and gave Lastani a cruel grin. 'I can say it in a few languages and sign it in Wisp too, so I really hate missing out on the chance.'

Despite her words, Toil found nothing on her sweep and moved on to the tunnel – while Lynx experienced a flush of relief that no spectral monster had apparated to tear them apart.

They moved quickly down the tunnel, the now-familiar bluish tint of rock glowing in the Duegar lamplight overlaid by the yellow light of more mundane lamps. Just like the first time Toil had led members of the Cards underground, the tunnel became a long slowly spiralling slope. They went two abreast and moved as quickly as Toil's caution allowed. There was nothing by way of decoration or detail, just slightly sloped steps that corkscrewed down before levelling out into a shallow straight path that ran for several hundred yards. After a long, cautious procession they arrived at an oval doorway filled by a slab of stone. There was barely enough space for them all in the space before the doorway, the tunnel widening a touch for the last five yards only.

'Got a key?' Deern asked helpfully as Toil inspected the door.

She ignored him and ran her fingers reverentially over the stone's surface.

'Here,' she said to Lastani, pointing to a section that looked no different to the rest. 'Just a little magic to activate the door.'

The young woman nodded and crouched down, caressing the stone herself before settling two fingers on one part. There she stayed, perfectly still for a moment, while the light faintly illuminated fingers of frost creeping out across the stone surface. A few heartbeats later and there was a grate of stone as the circle of frost slid away left. A waft of stale air washed forward over them, peppery and sour to Lynx's nose, and perfect blackness was revealed behind it.

Lynx closed his eyes as his heart skipped an anxious beat, reminding himself of Shadows Deep just a handful of weeks earlier. The fear he'd felt at entering and the great scale of the tunnels and chambers he'd found himself in. He'd not developed a love of the dark – what they'd encountered down there had strangled any small chance of that. All the same, he knew the Duegar city-ruins were a far cry from the mines beneath To Lort prison.

The mine had been cramped and hot, stinking and airless. There you could feel the rock all around you, taste the dust in the air and sense the countless tons ready to collapse and smother you. In Shadows Deep, the caverns had been huge – on a greater scale than the halls of the Bridge Palace – and built to withstand the centuries by stone mages of unsurpassed skill.

When he had composed himself and opened his eyes, Lynx saw Toil raise her lantern to illuminate what lay beyond. She waved Sitain forward and the night mage crouched beside Lastani to peer into the black.

'I see a cavern, a paved floor – nothing more. Think I can just make out the far wall, it curves away, but no features.'

'The upper hall,' Lastani whispered excitedly. 'Somewhere there is the path down to the labyrinth. Whispers of Insar, I'm really here! After all these years!'

'We're all bloody here and some of us want to live to tell the tale. Where is the path exactly?'

'The Fountain inscription is no simple guide to follow,' she pointed out. 'But it does state that the path is to be found on a descent through the unseen dark.'

'What's that supposed to mean?' Sitain snapped.

'Sounds like it's hidden,' Toil said without the younger woman's irritation. 'I'd expect nothing less.'

'Hidden, certainly,' Lastani conceded, 'but this is only the upper hall, remember? One must simply think like a Duegar. The deepest black held no terror for them, the unseen black equally so.'

'Yeah well, stepping into *this* unknown black'll be scary enough – right up until you hit the ground.'

As though to emphasise her point Toil prodded at the stone slab directly beyond the threshold and hissed angrily when the butt of her staff passed right through it without a sound. She held it there a moment longer then probed around, forward, left and right. There was a hidden space there, a void about a yard long and wide. Toil crouched and passed her staff to Lastani, wrapped the rope of her lantern around one wrist then got down on her knees.

'Lynx, a little muscle here please?'

'Ballast more like,' muttered someone behind him as Lynx moved forward and took hold of her legs.

Toil eased her torso over the threshold. Her face was tight with anxiety and she took three short breaths before lowering her lamp then her face into the floor. She emerged a moment later, panting as though she'd been underwater, but Lynx could tell it was just nervous energy.

'Shattered gods!' was all she said before dipping back down again, her head, shoulders and chest all simply sinking into the cut stone slab that was some magical illusion.

She stayed that way for a few heartbeats, looking one way then the other judging by the movements, before she re-emerged and pulled herself back to her knees.

'Well,' Toil gasped, catching her breath for a moment. 'It ain't fucking that way, that's for sure.'

'You're certain.'

'Not unless the Duegar could drop a hundred feet or more. I could see a column supporting the path just beyond this, leading a long way down but it's sheer-sided. Guess we go on in, there's a walkway – just a yard or two wide, but it's better'n nothing. I think it widens further in, might be more there.'

'The upper hall's big. Really big,' Sitain pointed out. 'Surely the entrance is further down? Remember Shadows Deep? They weren't afraid of really big archways and the like – we've got to be looking for something a bit grander than a hole in the floor, don't we?'

'Shadows Deep was a city,' Lastani pointed out, 'this is a labyrinth with multiple entrances – each either a varied test of faith or some sort of competition. Either way, all the entrances leading to the one magnificent door would be somewhat pointless, no?'

'She's right – it's all illusion up here.' Toil stood and put the cord of her lantern back over her head. 'We're looking for a path into the unseen nearby. For the sake of all that's sacred or even just half-decent in a good light, try not to fall over the edge in the process. It's a *long* way down.'

Lynx heard Kas clear her throat and glanced back at the faces behind them. Teshen had been with Toil, Lynx, Sitain and Kas in Shadows Deep. No doubt Barra and Aben had done this before, Paranil too probably, if he was one of Toil's comrades, though the man still looked terrified. As for the others, even the agents of the Monarch, Suth and Elei, looked antsy at what was coming next.

'What is it, Kas?'

'Company tradition,' she explained. 'Prayers before combat.'

'Prayers?' Toil and Lynx asked in the same breath. 'What about Shadows Deep?'

Kas shrugged. 'Safir usually does it, but we left him with the rest before we got there.'

'Safir?' Lynx echoed. 'But he—'

'Is the one who does it,' Kas broke in sharply. 'And right now, I for one would like to stick with tradition, okay?'

Her tone of voice made it clear she didn't want any argument there, and given Kas wasn't prone to whimsy when on the job, Lynx backed off.

'Fine,' Toil said a moment later, clearly exasperated. 'Just be quick about it.'

Safir stepped forward and shouldered his gun before folding his hands piously at his waist. 'Take a knee then, the lot of you.'

Lynx hesitated while most of the rest obeyed. He exchanged a look with Sitain who shrugged. The pair followed suit as Safir closed his eyes and bowed his head.

'Hear us, our gods,' Safir intoned, 'in this our hour of need. Shattered though your mortal forms are, your spirits remain in this world to guide us, to sustain us and protect us from the indignities of fellow man and the machinations of spirits and demons.

'In which case,' Safir added after a pause, 'you've done a piss-poor job, you feckless, broken shitweasels. My praise is reserved for the one act of your brother, Banesh, when he shattered your mortal forms and kicked you the fuck out of this world.'

Lynx looked up as Toil made a choking sound. Lastani could only gape as shock overrode any protests she might have had, Suth frowning beside her. Kas offered Lynx a wink as Safir continued, eyes closed and a look of calm focus on his face.

'Veraimin, lord of light and heat,' Safir declared, 'impetuous and wilful child of power. Unending is the list of your misdeeds, but every drought I ever saw had your spirit of gleeful idiocy dancing across the scorched fields. Insar, gutless lord of cold and secrets – yet again your smug cockstain servants the Knights-Charnel are trying to kill us.

'Catrac, lord of passion and endeavour, you who gifted mankind with its witless avarice . . . Well, you know what you did, so fuck you most of all. Ulfer, brainless thug of the earth and seasons – I blame you for wasps in particular and what was with the fever I got just after winter? Did I really have to shit myself in the middle of the tavern common room or was that your idea of funny?

'And lastly Banesh, jester of change and chance, whose act shattered the gods and cast the fragments across the continent. Was the ocean too small a target to dump them all in and save us from the burning nightmare of mage-cartridges? And well done breaking yourself in the process, you misfiring cretin.'

There was a long moment of quiet, during which someone sniggered and Lastani emitted some sort of outraged squeak that likely only dogs could hear properly.

'So we pray,' Safir intoned finally, using the formal refrain of temple service.

'So we pray,' replied those of the Cards.

Lynx looked over the faces of the mercenaries. It seemed Kas had been right to suggest a prayer at least. The tension was gone from their faces as they eased their way back to their feet and readied their guns.

'Well now,' Toil said slowly, 'if Brother Safir's finished with his blessing, shall we be off?'

Safir bowed his head. 'We're in your hands, Lady Toil.'

Chapter 23

Toil led her scouting group out into the upper chamber with painstaking care. Behind her, the rest were mostly quiet, with Sitain and Lastani the only ones making any real sound at all. It didn't take Lastani long to pick out the shape of the path ahead, her ice-magic casting a neat line of frost down each side of the path where it met the illusion. Toil was quietly impressed at the young woman's precision and skill, but she kept it to herself as she moved down the now-slightly – treacherous walkway. With her staff she checked the path on either side, making long sweeps down into the unknown black to try and find hidden steps leading down.

On the other side, Aben copied Toil's movements with a mage-gun while Sitain and Lynx kept close behind them – one looking out for Bade's crew and the other ready to shoot if they were spotted. In the great black space of the upper chamber Toil's Duegar lantern illuminated almost nothing, but it was an absence she was used to by now and had to restrain herself from moving ahead of Aben. While the man had been on several expeditions with Toil, he wasn't as comfortable underground and took greater care over every step. Even more so now, when Sotorian Bade might be walking this same hall with a troop of Charnelers.

Out of nowhere the stink of burned flesh appeared in Toil's mind. She mentally cursed but knew it was inevitable whenever the smug, self-satisfied smile of Sotorian Bade came into her thoughts. It had been the same in the palace great hall. Despite the riot of perfume there and the scents of food, one look had been all it took for that to turn to charred meat in her nose. But this time would be different. This time she was hunting him – and this time she was no fearful ingénue lost in the dark.

That knowledge made no difference, however. She still couldn't help remembering her first time, her first taste of the deepest black in all its horror. How long she'd stayed in that tomb, Toil still couldn't say. Perhaps only minutes, just long enough for Bade to have crept away – guided by what she now knew was a Duegar lantern. Long enough for him to get well clear of a girl who could only blunder slowly through the darkness – after that, the minutes or hours had barely mattered. She remembered little of it bar the smell of burned corpses, had no sense of time under that constricting blanket of darkness, but back then it had seemed like an age.

Eventually the tears had run out, the juddering of her heart slowed to a steady beat and her moans quietened. The darkness was all around her, but it made no move to take her and eventually her wits returned. There was only so long that a sane person could sit and gibber. After however long it was, Toil came through the other side of that valley of fear. Still afraid, still tired and alone, but also still the daughter of her parents. In that moment she almost felt their presence beside her.

Her mother, iron-willed and calm; her father, effusive and explosive. Brought up by two such people, inheritor of all they were, Toil took a long breath and reached out to put her hand against the edge of the tomb.

I am here now. I will not just curl up and die.

Her mother's soft voice came to her from the darkness. *'Succeed or fail – never accept either until you have tried. Never tell yourself you cannot, never presume that you will not – most of all, never let others choose for you.'*

She remembered her father, the scars he bore and the looks some men gave him. A huge presence in all ways, a whirlwind of strength and energy when he returned home. A smile rarely far from his lips, a roar never far from his throat, but it was when he was still that Toil learned to listen hardest to him.

'Look death right in the eye – don't let the bastard blink. Some men spit in death's eye, some men curse him. But death's a rabid dog; you fix him with a look and run him through without waiting. One day the dog will be too fast for you and pull you down, save your tears for then. Until that day you stand tall, child of mine.'

Shakily, cautiously, Toil rose and stood tall. She could almost feel the great ursine warmth of her father beside her, the small smooth touch of her mother's hand in hers.

'Not today,' she whispered to the darkness and in her mind it retreated a shade.

Toil took a step forward, hand reaching out for the tomb's edge. She found it and ran her fingers along, shuffling her feet forward until she found something that felt like dead flesh.

Sovirel had carried a walking staff, she recalled – the perfect thing for a blind girl to feel her way. As the panic faded, a view of the tomb seemed to unfurl in her mind. She'd always had a good memory, now was the time to see just how good that was. Finding the bodies she fumbled her way over them, trying to ignore the warm sticky patches of scorched skin until her foot touched the dropped stick.

Moving slowly, Toil found the broken lamp without cutting herself, then felt at Sovirel's belt for the mage-pistol he carried. It took her a long while, but at last she had the gun strapped to her waist and counted five cartridges in the pouch it bore. Five would have to be enough.

Most likely I'll only ever need one, Toil realised. *Either I kill whatever I shoot at, or I'll never have time for a second shot. But maybe I'll see Bade in the distance. Maybe the gods will grant me that.*

Toil paused. 'If any of you are listening to prayers, though,' she said aloud, 'I'd prefer to get out of here. Killing Bade can wait for another day.'

There was no reply to her prayer and Toil didn't wait for one. Casting around with her stick and using the tomb as a reference point, she headed towards the door. She took the wrong line at first and found herself nearing the side wall, where the lesser artefacts were kept.

And here's me looking death right in the eye, Toil thought with a crazed smile.

With the stick she shoved one off the shelf and hurriedly ducked, but nothing happened. Relieved, she felt over what remained there. Three items of varying size and shape, she could guess at none of them so she fitted the two she could into her pack and continued around the wall towards the door. It was a long slow journey there and down the tunnel beyond it, one brief burst of light as she threw a shard of stone down that before the darkness reasserted itself. She almost succumbed to fear and dismay when she discovered Bade had pulled up the rope, but again Toil felt her parents beside her, keeping her unbowed.

There were steps projecting out from the wall, she remembered that much. A good third had broken when they got inside, the stone slab hiding the stairway crashing all the way to the bottom, but a good climber might be able to use what pieces or crevices remained on the wall. She would try, there was nothing else to do. If she fell, she would die, but if she did nothing she would be just as dead.

Toil tucked the staff into her pack as best she could and started up the broken stubs of steps, eyes wide open as she faced the darkness down.

*

'Some days, a man's just got to admit he's been buggered good and hard.'

The comment drew a nod from Chotel and a frown from Kastelian, but Bade ignored both as he continued to stare at his missing feet.

'Aye, first point to Hopper,' chirped Torril, the bearded man beside Bade who currently appeared to have no legs at all. 'But you know what I always say underground?'

'Whatever doesn't kill us leaves us horribly maimed and disfigured?'

The bearded veteran shrugged. 'Well, yeah, but also – first point's better'n first blood.'

'When have you ever said that?'

'I'm saying it now.'

Bade looked away. They were standing in the upper chamber of the labyrinth while the majority of the soldiers transported their supplies back from the grand doorway. Bade was too busy feeling stupid to help even if he'd been so inclined, but the longer he stood there the more his frustration subsided.

He tapped his unseen feet on the step supporting him. 'First point to Hopper,' he repeated. 'Lesson learned, eh, boys?'

'Could have been worse,' Chotel agreed, 'and we're now on track again.'

They had wasted a lot of time on the large square platform enclosed by pillars around the grand doorway – first checking for traps and then the mages, scholars and relic hunters trying to open the stone doors. Set into a cube of stone fifteen feet high, each door had four round handles. Each handle turned independently and bore four small symbols that could be lined up. They had worked hard and methodically only to conclude that the entire door was a dummy and the labyrinth designer was laughing at them from beyond the grave.

Now they were stood just outside the nearest labyrinth entrance, one that led up to an as yet unopened chamber. It had taken Bade just ten minutes to find the hidden steps once he was looking, located below the flagstone illusion on the inner side of the main path.

Without warning, a pair of dark, blade-like limbs flashed up from the floor around Torril's waist. The man gave a yelp and stumbled backward – he would have toppled off the unseen edge if Bade hadn't grabbed him and hauled him back. The limbs clacked down on the stone steps, once, twice, as a brief burst of inhuman chittering emanated up.

'What's Bug saying?' Kastelian asked.

Bade started off down the steps once the runt maspid had turned and disappeared again. 'Sounds like little Timen fell down the well and needs help,' he said over his shoulder.

'Eh?'

Chotel laughed and followed Bade. 'Bug ain't talkin' words, she ain't a person.'

'So what was that?'

'Catchin' our attention.'

With his mage-gun lowered to tap against the steps before he put his weight on them, Bade moved down the flight with practised care. Once he ducked his head beneath the illusion everything went black and he had to stop and blink hard to readjust. There was little to see even in the light of his Duegar lamp – just the suggestion of towering stone formations upon which the walkways had been constructed.

The stair he was on had been built up against the side of the main support, the sides of both going straight down with only the slightest of curves. It reminded him of giant trees he'd seen in the rainforests far to the south-west. Not terrain anyone chose to spend much time in other than the locals, he'd travelled fifty miles into one forest to find a Duegar temple that had been swallowed by foliage – an impressive feat given the temple spires were each seventy-odd yards high.

The steps led straight down into darkness, he could make out that much, but the lamp he carried was the smallest of the three he owned. There was a suggestion of depth and lines further below, but he knew in such low light his eyes could easily be playing tricks. All he was certain of was a central supporting column of rock around which the upper chamber ran – more than a hundred yards in diameter given the section of it they had travelled.

As they'd walked in the light above, Bade had checked the location of entrances on the map he'd brought, keeping his bearings. Not far from where they stood was the fake doorway to the main body of the labyrinth, an off shoot of the central column.

'Light-bolt,' he called back to Chotel behind. His lieutenant relayed the message and Bade waited for it to be passed all the way back before pulling a cartridge from his gun and replacing the sparker in the breach.

Once it was loaded he paused again, straining to see out into the darkness, but eventually he was satisfied he wasn't going to hit anything nearby if he aimed almost down the length of the walkway.

'Chotel, come down until your head's just above the floor level. When I fire, duck down. Might be you get a better look than me.'

'Got it, boss.'

Bade pulled the brim of his hat down as low as he could, screwed his eyes up tight and pulled the trigger. A crash hammered out around the upper chamber as a streak of white lanced across his vision, even through closed eyelids. Blinking furiously he watched the blurry line of white race through the darkness, arcing downwards. As Bug, somewhere further down the stair, screeched and chattered in protest, Chotel squatted beside Bade and immediately gasped in wonder.

The light-bolt continued to fall, finally striking further than he'd expected and casting its noon light across the unknown dark. It stayed there for just a few seconds, sputtering quietly in the darkness, but long enough for Bade to make sense of the view. He gasped too, lurching forward and forced to clutch Chotel's arm for balance as his mind boggled.

Below them was a gigantic near-cylindrical cavern as large as any he had seen before. The light-bolt could not illuminate much of it despite the intense brightness, but Bade's experienced eye estimated it was half a mile across and more deep. The shape suggested it had been carved by mages or at least enlarged and made regular – an astonishing amount of work. The narrow walkways swept down to form huge arches, a hundred yards tall and supported by a lattice of rock projections from the walls and central column. But that wasn't the astonishing part – that much old hands were used to seeing. The astonishing part was what the column stood on.

'I, ah . . .' Chotel whispered. 'That's . . .'

'Fucking amazing,' Bade finished.

He shook his head. He had no other words for it and for once the pair just stood and stared as the darkness returned and they were looking at nothing other than the image in their minds. No quip or joke escaped either. Both knew that in their long careers, they had seen nothing like that before.

'What?' hissed Torril. 'What is it?'

'It's, um. It's not exactly a labyrinth.'

'Eh? How do you mean?'

'Gods-in-shards, Torril,' Chotel moaned. 'You should've seen it. I . . . I never seen a ruin like that. I never seen anything like that.'

'Stop yanking my dick and tell me!'

Bade and his lieutenant looked at each other, a big stupid grin crossing the face of each. The mission be damned, cracking *this* really would carve their names into history.

'It's a puzzlebox,' Bade croaked. 'A cube by the looks of it, made up of smaller cubes.'

'A box? Are you shitting me?' Torril spluttered. 'We came all this way and started a gods-crapping war because of some bastard box?'

Chotel laughed. 'It's, ah, it's a *big* box, Torril. How many cubes down each side you make out? I saw five.'

'At least six, I think more.'

'Yeah, so maybe seven or eight.'

'Don't sound like Hopper,' Torril broke in.

'You're right,' Bade agreed. 'It'll be nine on each side, liked his numbers all neat that way. That's what, eighty-one cubes in all? Torril, each cube had to be fifty yards long!'

There was slight cough from above the ceiling as Torril digested the information.

'Okay, that's a pretty big box. So how do we get in?'

Bade looked down the stair he was on. They were typical Duegar steps, shallow and long. They had no rail or anything on the outer edge, just a sudden drop into the darkness, but there was a groove down the inside wall that could be gripped. The steps themselves were a good three yards wide, however, more than enough to make him feel secure descending.

'We follow this stair. Kastelian, send my crew down now – keep the soldiers up until we know what space we've got down there. Leave what we can't carry for the time being.'

'Done,' came Kastelian's slightly muffled voice from above. 'Good luck.'

'Aye, we could do with some.'

Bade set off down the stairway, lamp held high and mage-gun prodding at the steps as he went. Chotel followed silently behind, keeping a careful distance, while up ahead he could hear the skitter of Bug's spear-like feet on the smooth stone racing back to whatever awaited them at the bottom.

Chapter 24

As dawn began to reveal the churned horror overlaying Jarrazir's broken wall, a bearded man emerged from a street to survey what remained. The crater dominated everything, looking nothing less than a gods-inflicted punishment on sinful man. Commander Vigilance Deshar scratched his cheek and lifted his head to look beyond the city to the fields outside. Truth be told there was no difference between the two now. Furrowed and cratered mud, darkened smears of ground where blood tinted it, crumpled bodies and tattered cloth.

Makeshift barricades had been raised between the two broken ends of city wall – piecemeal, staggered obstacles that served more as shooting platforms and targets than any great defence. Behind those huddled knots of men and two small catapults. The fighting had waxed and waned throughout the early part of the night, one renewed burst an hour earlier, but now they waited. As Vigilance watched, several companies of grey-coated troops hurried forward to relieve the shocked and battered defenders. Bands of brown-jackets roamed the wasteland like jackals, hauling away the dead or carrying food and water to the stations.

'Next wave won't be much fun,' commented the woman beside Vigilance.

He turned and frowned at his cadaverous lieutenant, a woman of grey hairs and hollow, lined cheeks called Ulith.

'Compared to this playground?'

Her pale cheeks crinkled into a ghastly grin. 'It'll get worse.'

Vigilance nodded. It would, he knew. For all this scene of utter devastation, it would get worse. The ruin was at its worst beyond the line of the walls, where the defenders had desperately fired everything they had at the advancing Charnelers.

'How many dead do you think?'

'Can never tell on a battlefield.' Ulith gave a wave of dismissal. 'They always look worse'n they are,' she added, ''cept for the times they ain't and the ordnance hasn't left enough bits o' the dead to count.'

'But you don't try to exploit *that* unless you throw hundreds into the breach,' Vigilance said, 'and I doubt many came back out of that.'

'That they didn't. When's our turn then?'

Ulith didn't sound daunted by the prospect of defending this patch of mud, but then Vigilance had rarely known her to be surprised by anything, let alone worried.

'I've had no word. Might be they don't want to trust recently hired mercs to their vital defence.'

'More fool them then.' She tugged on the faded red scarf around her neck that Vigilance also wore. 'Our reputation should be enough, but if the Monarch wants her own men to die in our place, I ain't complaining.'

'After the next wave, it'll change,' Vigilance said. 'The Red Scarves will be mustered and armed by then. They'll find a use for our guns quick enough.'

'What if the city don't last that long?'

'Then we have our orders.'

He let the words hang in the air for a little while, lingering like smoke on the breeze before the inevitable explosion from Ulith.

'Shitting gods, from *her*?! I ain't letting your mad bitch sister drag us inta the deepest black. Since when does she give orders to the Red Scarves? She ain't you, she ain't your dad – she's nothing to us.'

Vigilance raised a hand. 'Easy now, she *is* my sister, and she's as much my father's child as I am. Toil needs only speak one word and she'll get command of a regiment.'

'You'd have a damn revolt on your hands!' Ulith spat. 'She'd get her throat cut by the next morning.'

Vigilance laughed, the sound drawing startled looks from the soldiers nearby. 'That would be her problem to deal with,' he said softly, 'but anyone trying to cut Toil's throat might not have everything their own way.'

'You can only hang a killer if you catch one.'

'That wasn't the problem I was anticipating.' He shrugged. 'It's almost worth doing. Toil's got my father's temperament; it might be good to remind the men how nasty the company discipline could be.'

Ulith opened her mouth to reply then thought better of it. 'You mentioned orders?'

Vigilance nodded. The woman might be a cold-hearted, fearless monster of a mercenary and one who'd only soured as the years passed, but she was no fool. Family was family.

'Establish our principal camp in Prophet's Square,' he said. 'Have food and ammunition stored there, encompass the neighbouring buildings and make preparations to seal off the streets if the city falls.'

'Box ourselves in?' Ulith queried. 'Why there?'

'Because my sister has an excellent sense of direction underground and will need to come up for air sometime.'

'There's an entrance to the labyrinth there?'

'There is. Any entrance that sits on ground we need to concede gets an earthshaker dropped down it first. The poetry of that might prove lost on Sotorian Bade, but it'll cheer my sister up.'

'Then what? If the Charnelers push into the city, it's lost whatever defence we mount. They'll burn it down around us if they have to.'

'There'll be no heroic last stand for the Red Scarves,' Vigilance confirmed, 'but if the city falls, best we have Toil with us. She's a girl for surprises and those might come in handy.'

*

'You know? This really isn't what I was expecting.'

Lynx glanced back at Deern, who stood in the middle of a knot of mercenaries. There wasn't much of his expression visible in the weak light of a single lamp, but Deern's bored tone told enough.

'What were you expecting?'

'More labyrinth, less . . .' Deern waved around at his companions, all keeping tight together on the narrow strip of paved ground that had been marked as safe. 'Less shuffling around,' he said at last. 'An' trying not to fall through the floor. Glad I passed on Shadows Deep if it was like this.'

'We're all glad you passed on Shadows Deep,' Sitain muttered from Lynx's side. 'The maspid packs were great fun compared to your moaning.'

'Ah, I've barely got started on moaning,' Deern said, 'it's all been helpful observations up till now.'

'In that case,' broke in one of the Monarch's agents, Suth, 'when you get really going on it, I'm going to shoot you in the face.'

To reaffirm her point the woman flicked open her long coat to reveal holstered mage-guns strapped to each thigh and a pair at her belly. Lynx guessed there were one or two on her lower back, too, looking at the line of her coat. Mage-cartridges could explode if they were within a hand-span of one being fired so all mage-guns were one-shot weapons.

331

'Deern,' called Toil from the front. 'If you want to lead the way, you're welcome to it. Until then, shut up and remember rule one.'

She stood on the wide path they'd found running along the centre of the great upper chamber. In the dark she could only see that it ran in both directions and an identifying marker stood above the stone doorway they'd entered through.

Crouching, she steadied herself and again put her head and lamp beneath the line of illusion. It was disconcerting to watch, her face and arm just disappearing from view, but this time there came an exclamation of success and she soon popped back up again.

'Found it,' Toil declared as Lastani edged forward, her excitement immediately obvious despite the darkness.

'Are you sure?'

Toil ignored her and moved a bit further along the path before prodding down with her staff. It sank a little way into the illusion then stopped with a crisp clack. Toil probed around the edge for a while, testing out the size of hidden stone, then pulled a pot from her pocket and dabbed her finger in. Lynx had seen the stuff before, back in Shadows Deep. Toil had used it to make her finger glow in the Duegar lamp's light – mimicking the luminescent fingers of the Wisps as she spoke to them in their sign language.

Now Toil used the concoction to mark the limits of the stone, thin smears two yards apart that glowed bluish-white in her lamp's black light. With the safe ground marked, Toil stepped down on to the hidden step and probed again each side, quickly finding another lower down. She made swift progress now she knew what she was looking for and before long ducked down so that only the pack on her back was visible as she surveyed the path ahead.

Aben gestured for Sitain to go after Toil. The young woman stared as though he'd suggested she jump off a cliff, but she said nothing and eventually followed, Lynx close on her heel. The steps were long and shallow, each a couple of yards square, but as Lynx went and the white light of the oil lamps was left behind, he felt a familiar lurch of fear in his belly.

Toil's black lamp illuminated little to his eyes. He knew Sitain would be perfectly happy, being a night-mage, but to Lynx the darkness seemed to swallow him up – all the worse for knowing there was a great yawning drop just a few feet away.

'What can you see?' hissed Toil, barely visible two steps further down.

'Sod all,' Lynx growled. 'Mebbe this wasn't such a good idea.'

'I think she meant me,' Sitain said.

'Yeah, I know, but talking's good.'

Lynx fought the urge to flee and instead pressed his shoulders against the stone wall behind him. There was some sort of handhold there, a long groove in the bare rock face, and he grabbed it gladly, but still the fear trembled in his belly.

'Keep talking if you need to,' Toil said, 'just so long as Sitain does too.'

Lynx couldn't tell if that was kindness or pragmatism, but chose not to ask, knowing how fractious he was in the dark. Any chance to pick a fight and he'd grab it down here, but there was also a voice at the back of his head reminding him that they didn't have time for that. He took a long deep breath instead and focused on what Sitain was saying.

'Sorry to disappoint, but I don't see a whole lot. The steps lead a long way down. The path we were on is the top of a bloody big bridge-type of thing, supported by some sort of web of stone. They all extend further than I can see. In the dark there's just a faint suggestion of lines further away but nothing I can make out.

'On the other side of the upper chamber there's a . . . a column maybe? The far wall's curved anyway, it's huge but looks like it's not just the far side of a great hall. Gods in pieces! If that's a column then . . .'

'Then we're in far bigger chamber than we thought,' Toil finished.

'Deep too,' Lynx added for no real reason other than to torture himself. 'Really bloody deep.'

'Don't worry; it'll be far smaller than the great rift in Shadows Deep.'

'Given what you bloody stirred up from the bottom of that rift,' Lynx said slowly, 'that's not as comforting as you might think.'

'I doubt there's anything alive down here,' Toil replied. 'With the canal and Parthain, if this wasn't sealed off from the outside, it'd be full of water by now.'

'Or we just can't see the water – or when we open up whatever this leads to, we release the pressure and a million tons of blackness rises up to drown us!'

'Lynx, take a breath,' Toil advised. 'The Duegar made things to last and this place is dry – you can taste it on the air. Now come on.'

Before she could turn to continue down the steps a sound rang out across the entire upper chamber. Distant and echoing, it seemed to roll forward like thunder and for a moment of pure mind-numbing panic, Lynx thought he'd been right after all. In his mind's eye he pictured a tidal wave of water sweeping over the path, dragging all of them in its wake down into the great depths far beneath.

'Oh gods,' Lynx moaned, sinking down to the floor, back pressed against the stone behind and arms tight around his body.

His heart started to hammer away in his chest, blood roaring in his ears like the crash of waves on rock. Bursts of light started to flutter before his eyes as the sound built and washed past them, becoming the resonant echoes of an impossibly large bell's toll. He felt it in his bones, shuddering through his marrow as the bitter taste of bile filled his throat. His head became a jagged mess of thorns snagging his thoughts and making every breath exquisitely painful.

'Sitain, check on the others,' he heard distantly as rough hands took hold of him and the sound began to fade.

Lynx closed his eyes and tried to breathe properly. A familiar cord of panic was pulled tight around his chest and he could only manage shallow pants, but the effort itself gave him a focus.

'Lynx,' Toil said as smooth fingers slipped over his cheeks. 'Can you hear me?'

He made a garbled sound, still with his eyes closed.

'Lynx, we're safe,' Toil continued gently.

Lynx didn't answer her. The words made it as far as his ears, but 'safe' meant nothing to him right now. There was only the stink of sweat and stone dust, mud and blood. The clink of chains, the groan of wood and the clash of tools on rock. He pressed himself harder against the smoothed stone wall behind him, finding comfort in the fact it was nothing like a chipped-out tunnel.

Toil kept quiet for a while, cradling his face but saying nothing more as he fought the panic inside him. Her presence was a help all the same, as much of an anchor as the rock behind him. After a short time he heard a cough from somewhere nearby and light footsteps. He opened his eyes and squinted through the dark as someone crouched and whispered close to Lynx's face.

'Ah, Toil?' Kas said, glancing at Lynx before returning to business. 'Bit of a problem back here. The shitting door's just closed up behind us, we're shut in! What in the name of all that's shattered do we do now?'

'Oh hells, shut? Well, get those bloody mages working – get it open again!'

'They already tried, it ain't shifting.'

'We're shut in?' Lynx wheezed, dark humour and increasing fear clashing inside him. 'Oh screaming black hells.'

'Lynx, you just breathe, focus on that. This is no different to Shadows Deep, not really.'

'Not different? We're fucking locked in!'

'In a magical labyrinth with multiple entrances that some have suggested is a form of contest ground. That sound we heard. That wasn't something breaking – doubt it was a trap either. More likely it's a signal of some sort – maybe that the contest's begun. It wasn't triggered by us or Bade getting into the upper chamber but it must have been something. My money would be on Bade having just opened the labyrinth proper, he'll have needed magic to activate the door most likely and it sets off some sort of magical locking mechanism. But the Duegar wouldn't have built this to imprison their own, they didn't think that way. Locking everyone inside until someone survives to crack the secret of the place, however, that's more than just possible. So we're not in a tomb, it's just another big space underground we need to navigate, nothing like a mine. No shackles, no guards.'

'Just fucking relic hunters looking to kill us,' Lynx muttered, 'and some sort o' labyrinth full of all sorts of nasty surprises.' He scowled at her. 'Explain how this is better?'

'No maspids,' Toil said firmly, 'no gigantic magic-hungry monsters chasing us, no walking for days without sunlight. You can handle this, just like you did last time.'

'Barely managed it last time.'

'But you kept your grip all the same and that's what counts.'

Lynx raised his trembling hand. 'Not much grip left.'

Toil pulled his mage-gun from the sheath on his back and slapped it hard into his hand, closing his fingers around the forestock. She let go and leaned back. 'Grip looks good enough to me – now on your damn feet, soldier.'

Shakily, Lynx obeyed and allowed himself to be ushered back up the steps to where the rest of their party were waiting.

'Lastani, should we be worried?'

The young mage shook her head. 'It looks like our test of faith has begun,' she confirmed with a wan smile, failing to hide her anxiety. 'Mistress Ishienne speculated something like this.'

'Right,' Toil agreed. 'So the labyrinth is sealed until someone comes out the other side. Not the best news, what with most of our soldiers still outside, but this isn't a children's party and we're not helpless or clueless.'

'But we could be stuck down here for ever?' Deern blurted out.

Toil gave him a nasty grin. 'If you think that's the most dangerous thing about this place, you've not done this before.'

'No one's done this before,' he pointed out. 'Ain't that the point? No one in the whole o' bloody human history has opened it before this bint came along.'

'Who is he again?' Lastani asked, cocking her head at Toil.

'The company jester,' she explained. 'Either that or a malingering curse from the gods upon the rest, I'm not really sure which. I assume that they find him amusing in some way – either that or they like being reminded there are worse bastards than them alive today.'

'Oh you're funny fer a red-headed—' again Deern was cut off mid-sentence, but this time it was Teshen clouting him around the head.

'Enough, Deern,' the man growled. 'You can fall off this walkway pretty easily you know, ain't no Reft here to stop me. My head's still buzzin', doubt I could even feel bad about it if I tried.'

'If you're all finished now,' Kas snapped. 'Mebbe we can get back to work?'

Toil nodded. 'Listen to the woman,' she advised them all. 'Now – me and mine are going down this stairway to check out what's below. You brave fighting types stay up here until I find us a way into the labyrinth itself – just in case that sound has told our friend Bade he's got company down here. Last thing we need is some shite doubling back and firing burners down these steps after us.'

When there was no dissent, Toil jabbed a thumb down the hidden steps. 'Right then, Paranil, Barra, Aben – come on. Lastani, you too.'

'And me?' asked Elei, Lastani's designated handler.

'Yeah, and you. You've got the Monarch's light in your pack there, right? Good. The rest of you, keep still and cover those oil lamps so Sitain's eyes give you an advantage. Once we find the bottom I'll send Barra back up.'

She gave them all a brief, incongruous grin and started down the stairs. 'Cheer up the lot of you, this is the fun bit!'

Chapter 25

'And what in the hairy holiest o' holes was that noise?'

No one replied. Bade watched the varying emotions play out on his comrades' faces. Chotel was looking up, as though expecting the great rumble to herald the roof falling, while Ulestim watched the stairs, one hand on his pistol. Torril had shrunk nervously back against the great door's jamb while, off to one side, Bug stood quivering with alertness – the runt maspid's eyeless head angled up as well.

The mages, Spade and Fork, both quailed, but they'd been pissing themselves over Bug for hours now so that was little change, while Sebaim, Bade's gnarled tracker, was as unruffled as ever.

'Thoughts, Ulestim?' Bade asked, hoping the most learned man in the group might have an idea.

'Very few, I'm afraid,' the bespectacled man said in a distracted tone.

'Even a few will do, old Sebaim here's shitting himself,' Bade joked, 'so give it a try.'

'Not ordnance, I'd say,' Ulestim said, to nods from several others, 'and nothing we did made any such sound.'

'Rock falls don't sound like that either,' Bade added. 'One single sound it was, echoing but clear and crisp for all o' that.'

'Indeed, so it was the labyrinth itself perhaps, something triggered by you touching the door.'

Bade turned to the stone door. It was . . . Well, for a relic hunter it was a thing of beauty, but right now it was just in his way. Anywhere else and he'd have put an earther through it by now, but this wasn't your usual city-ruin.

'Or we got company down here,' Bade said slowly, 'and the fun and games have started.'

They had descended no more than fifty yards before finding themselves on a half-moon platform set against a large stone block, two banks of Duegar script running all around it, while set into the centre was the doorway. The recessed arch was surrounded by more script, carved with an emphasis on beauty by Bade's estimation, even by the elegant standards of the Duegar language. The mages and Ulestim agreed that they were simply invocations of blessings and prayers that followed the familiar form. It was the black metal door itself that bore the secrets of its entry.

On the door were three stone circles set into the metal and marked with Duegar numbers, eight on each. In the very centre was a smaller disc, composed of silvery metal that shone faintly in the light and had the glyph for 'gift' inscribed on it.

'Sebaim,' Bade said, realising he had to make a decision. 'Back up the steps while we work on opening this, fetch down the rest in orderly fashion. If we're not alone down here I don't want to find a regiment of Bridge Watch stumbling across them so get 'em out of sight.'

The tracker gave a small nod and padded back up the steps as stealthily as a cat. He was a compact, ageless man who'd looked weather-beaten and greying when Bade had first met him, twenty years earlier. Even now Sebaim could run all day and spot a threat on the horizon before anyone thirty years his junior. He had no vices, expensive tastes or family to spend his money on. Bade had a strong suspicion that when he stopped bringing Sebaim to rare sights like this labyrinth, the man would just be gone one morning.

'Boss?' Chotel said, nudging Bade's elbow.

He nodded hurriedly, realising he'd been staring up after Sebaim as the man slipped away. 'Got an idea?' Bade said.

'Spade does.'

'Out with it then, we ain't got all day.'

'The prayers,' said the fire mage hesitantly, 'they contain numbers.'

'Eh?' Bade quickly scanned the writing around the door. His Duegar wasn't as good as the others, he knew, but still it didn't take him long to identify the words that could correspond to the Duegar numerals on the stone circles. 'Seems a bit obvious, don't it?'

'It's only the front door,' Torril remarked. 'Easy to get in, harder to get out?'

'Aye, true. Use numbers to keep the wildlife out, but if Hopper's got a nasty surprise for us, he'd probably want us trapped in a box first.'

'It don't sound so reassuring when you say it like that,' Chotel said with a snort.

'I'll hug you later, princess.' Bade gestured to the steps. 'Let's not take any chances, though, the rest of you back up on to the stair in case there is some trickiness.'

'And you?'

He grinned. 'We're about to open the fucking Labyrinth of Jarrazir itself, I ain't hanging back from this! You all feel free to exercise caution, I'll edit it out o' the history books, don't you worry.'

With it put like that, none of the others made for the steps. From their faces, his enthusiasm was infectious – the pay was good, but Bade knew none of them did this job just for the money. Once the mage had pointed out the numbers, Bade quickly turned the stone circles until the correct numerals were at a marked point. The stone moved easily despite its age and in no time he rested a hand on the mage's shoulder.

'Off you go then, Spade – gift.'

'Magic?'

Bade nodded. 'Bigger than the doors before I'd guess, a burst to kick-start ancient mechanisms. They'll draw in more themselves after that, but they need to be woken up first and you'd have noticed if that was going already.'

The nervous mage ducked his head in acknowledgement and placed his palm over the shining disc in the centre of the door. A brief flicker of orange flame washed over his fingers then was sucked down into the metal. The disc began to glow faintly with inner light and Spade grunted, his arm twitching as the disc began to draw hungrily. He left it a little longer then broke the flow of magic, jerking his arm away and stepping back.

He rubbed his fingers and frowned at the disc as it continued to glow for a few moments longer. Eventually the light dimmed and Bade was about to ask what had gone wrong when the disc was suddenly edged in crisp white light.

'It's drawing magic like you said,' Spade commented, the nervousness momentarily falling away from his face as he looked up in wonder.

'What's that?' Bade said. He cocked his ear to the door then looked around. 'Anyone else hear that, some sort of humming sound?'

'It's the mechanism,' the mage replied. 'Sucking in the latent energy in the air around it.'

'We in danger?'

'No, it's gentle. There's a slight pull on my own magic, but nothing that will leave me drained. It's simply gathering whatever is in the ground here, it'll take a while to build any great reserve.'

'In the meantime, how do—' Bade cut off as the door abruptly slid open to reveal a small room just a few yards across.

Inside there was another stairway, this one rather more elegant than the plain steps they'd descended thus far. It was all still mage-carved stone, but now the steps were delicately scalloped, the rail a twisting braid supported by tree-shaped banisters.

Bade took a cautious step inside. Nothing surged up out of the darkness to kill him so he clapped the mage on the shoulder.

'Good work, Spade. Ready for the real fun?'

Bade didn't wait for a reply. With his Duegar lamp held high, he slowly advanced inside and on to the first step. Still nothing bad happened, but the light of the lamp illuminated the stairway ahead – a long, regular spiral walkway with a grooved floor for grip. He'd seen enough of those before to walk a little faster. It was typical Duegar construction, bar the fact the stonework was far more carefully done and there was a clear swirling pattern to the mineral within the rock that caught the lamp's strange light.

Each side of the slope bore the blue glowing swirl while the path was speckled with the mineral. The mage drifted along behind Bade and gaped at the slope. The man might not have been a relic hunter, but he was highly educated within the field of magic if nothing else and the Duegar were a fundamental subject there.

The spiral sloping tunnel continued through a half-dozen turns then opened out abruptly on to a large black space. Bade lingered at the bottom, wary of stepping straight out before he'd got some sense of the room he was in. Fortunately, the usual Duegar illumination continued beyond the slope; a haze of faint, dark blue seams in the rock that looked more natural and haphazard. It offered enough for an experienced relic hunter to make out where he was, however. With the others close behind, Bade checked around as far as he could lean out before committing a foot.

There was little to see, just a wide and very high room that had to be the interior of one of those cubes they'd seen earlier. It was entirely featureless other than two doorways, one in the right-hand wall and one on the left-hand, similar to the one they'd entered by. They were made of the same metal, wider and taller than normal doors with a half-circle arch at the top. Neither bore the stone circles, but each had the shining centre plate with the glyph for 'gift' inscribed. The only difference between these two were the inscribed symbols above each – more numerals.

He realised he couldn't linger so, seeing nothing at all on the smooth walls, ceiling and floor, Bade walked out into the room with his heart hammering. Still no fiery death engulfed him so he started to breathe once more and moved around the sloped tunnel to see what else there was.

'Two doors?' Chotel remarked as he followed Bade out of the tunnel. Behind him came Bug, the maspid skittering down and out past him with her usual deceptive grace. The first time they'd tempted Bug out of the catacombs she lived in had been a dark night and clearly Bug had been wary and unsure. The feel of turf under her spear-blade limbs was not something Bug enjoyed, but still she'd been fast enough to chase down a deer. Underground, Bade guessed she was faster still.

'Aye – no, wait, there's another,' Bade replied as he skirted around behind the slanted shaft of the tunnel they'd entered by. The room was a cube just as they'd guessed, containing only the doors and the shaft running diagonally from the centre of the floor to the top of the rear wall. Behind that featureless projection was another block of stone with a third doorway set into it.

'And numbers,' Torril pointed out, 'hey, look, above where we came in, too.'

Bade did just that and, as Torril described, there was the Dueger numeral for 1 carved into the stone above where they'd come out of the tunnel.

'The others?' Ulestim said. 'Thirty-three and seventeen. How about round the back?'

'Twenty-five,' Bade said. 'They mean anything to you?'

'Not much,' he said as he went to see for himself. 'Door looks the same. We should light a proper lamp and inspect the room before we do anything else.'

'Aye, Spade and Fork – you keep away from the doors and don't do any magic until the rest have caught us up, understand? If the "gift" is a trigger for the doorway, it might shut the other one behind us.'

Chotel pulled an oil lamp from his pack and lit it with a sulphurous match rather than risking any further spark of magic. With the wick turned up it cast an acceptable light around the cube after the hours they'd spent in near darkness, but it only revealed the room was indeed plain other than the doors.

'Douse the lamp,' Ulestim said after a while, 'there's nothing to see and we don't want to turn the air bad.'

'Don't think that's a problem,' Bade replied as Chotel turned the wick down. 'The air's musty, but we're breathing fine. Must not be as sealed as it looks, otherwise the air'd be bad already in this box.'

A voice called cautiously down the slope and Torril went to answer it, cheerily bellowing up Kastelian's name to give the soldiers a fright. There was a slight clatter that sounded like someone dropping their gun but nothing else so, other than giving Torril a baleful look, Bade just waited for the soldiers. Bug attempted to clamber up one sheer stone wall, maspids being able to exploit the most unlikely of footholds, but was defeated and resorted to stalking the unoccupied area to the rear of the room.

'Should we be in a closed box with Bug?' Chotel asked softly as Kastelian's dragoons clattered into the room.

Bade turned to watch the maspid. Clearly she wasn't entirely happy, but was used to the company of humans to some degree at least. He hadn't paced out the room, but it was a good forty yards in each direction. Not vast but, at the same time, not small enough to force them all together. Even with a fat tunnel shaft in the centre, there was plenty of space.

'We'll manage,' Bade decided. 'I lead her back up, she's running free in the upper chamber but there's no certainty she gets back out again.'

Chotel lowered his voice further, not wanting the dragoons to hear him. 'Still, she could go for one of us. Strange smells, startled by traps . . . she ain't a dog you can put on a leash.'

'Yeah, but she ain't going for either of us first, if she does snap,' Bade pointed out. 'Unlikely any o' the crew. If we need to put her down, we do it. My biggest worry will be some grunt firing wildly, but one less soldier ain't going to lose me sleep.'

Chotel accepted Bade's point and stepped back, not wanting to draw any more attention to the matter.

'So which door then?' he said in a normal voice.

'Dunno. Ulestim, what do you reckon?'

'If there's a key, I can't see it,' the tall man declared, looking frustrated. 'There's no way of knowing what those numbers meant to the Duegar.'

'So we pick one at random? Sounds safe.'

Ulestim shrugged. 'You're the one who saw this place from the outside, got a preferred direction?'

Bade paused, hands out in front of him as he looked at the spiral slope and tried to work out how he'd been positioned.

We turned a few times. The steps ran that way, straight down to the platform which was at an angle. The labyrinth was positioned there, we came to it from there.

He opened his eyes again. 'We're about halfway to the central column I'd guess, more towards the middle of the nearer side. But do we want to go in or straight down?'

'Down's no good,' Torril piped up, joining them. 'All the good stuff is at the bottom in Duegar cities, remember?'

'Surely going down's a good thing then?' Ulestim said.

'Aye, but a bit fucking obvious.'

'First step in a labyrinth isn't likely to be in the right direction,' Bade agreed. 'A double bluff works in the favour of idiots and anyone with the brains to construct all this probably wasn't on the side o' the stupid.'

'Thirty-three or seventeen then?'

Bade sighed. 'Shattered gods and little fishes, guesswork'll be the death of us.'

'Thirty-three,' Torril said. 'This is a cube, innit?'

None of the others spoke for a while as they exchanged looks, taking long enough that Torril started to look worried that he'd said something particularly stupid.

'I can see it,' Bade said eventually. 'Always thought Hopper had a sense of humour, could be it's one o' his little jokes even. Anyone got any other ideas?'

When no one spoke up Torril looked relieved and they all turned towards the doorway on the left-hand wall.

'Thirty-three it is. Fork – you're up this time.'

The woman timidly approached the door before pausing to glance back at them. 'Are you sure?'

''Course we are,' Bade snapped loudly, 'we're the fucking experts so stop arguing and open the bastard door!'

She reached out and placed her palm on the centre plate, closing her eyes and wincing as she let her magic surge out.

Chapter 26

Everyone held their breath. There was a moment of complete silence then the door swung open on its own and they all flinched. There was only dark in the chamber beyond, black enough that Toil could see nothing at all. For a horrible moment she imagined herself stepping through on to nothing and falling silently into the dark. Aside from Lastani and Sitain the rest hung well back, clustered around the mouth of the tunnel they'd walked down into this cube-shaped tomb. In the light of the Monarch's Duegar lamp, she could see that most were watching her with a strange grimace on their faces, clearly expecting something terrible to happen very soon.

Toil shook her head and beckoned Sitain forward.

'You're up, girly.'

Lastani, who had opened the door with a burst of magic, edged aside for Sitain who peered forward into the next chamber of the labyrinth. The night mage had described what she could see of the labyrinth below as they descended the stair, providing plenty of incentive for Toil and Lastani to get the above doors open in a matter of minutes. A massive cube-shaped room on the other side, empty but for three doorways, had been something of a disappointment, but Toil had taken it as a sign they really were in the labyrinth now and the game had properly begun.

'Well?' Toil demanded.

'It's dark,' Sitain replied after a few moments. 'Dark and empty.'

'Is that good?' someone behind asked. Lynx.

Toil turned to look at Lastani, who made a non-committal face. Toil shrugged. 'Of course it's good news, we're not dead, are we?'

'You ain't stepped through the door yet,' Lynx pointed out. 'I'm just saying.'

'Yeah, well, thought I gave you all instructions about saying too much.'

Toil hung the metal handle of her Duegar lamp from a notch on the end of her staff and held it out over the chamber threshold.

'It's empty,' Sitain confirmed. 'Just doorways— No, wait. There's something on the floor. A circle I think.'

Toil checked the floor was solid then took a breath and stepped through into the room. With her lamp held high she looked all around, pausing when she spotted something above the doorway she'd just entered through. 'There's another number here, a two,' she pointed out. 'That follows on nicely from the "one" above the tunnel we came out of. Mebbe we did choose the right door after all.'

'And the others?' Lastani followed her through, advancing a few steps further into the room.

There was one doorway on the far wall, a second on the right-hand wall and a trapdoor in the floor, identical to the other doors, bar its orientation, right down to the shining disc inscribed with a Duegar symbol. Just before the trapdoor there was indeed a circle – or rather, a ring of Duegar glyphs almost ten yards across. They were inscribed on small squares of stone raised up on the inner edge so each glyph was angled slightly outward.

'What is it? A test?'

'Paranil?' Toil called back, the man looking rather more assured in a long plain coat and tunic than he ever had in his Lighthouse Guard uniform. 'Thoughts?'

Paranil joined them ahead of the rest of the group. 'Fire,' he said.

'What? Where?' Sitain demanded, whirling in alarm.

'Written on the floor.'

'Ah. Oh.' Though there wasn't much light to see, by the set of her shoulders Toil was pretty certain Sitain was blushing.

'Don't worry, Sitain,' she said. 'Any mistake that doesn't kill you doesn't count and there're huge holes in every Duegar expert's knowledge.'

She approached the ring but stopped well short and held a hand out to make it clear she wanted the others to keep clear.

'What do you think, boss?' Aben asked, joining her.

Toil glanced back. 'Are we all through?'

He did a quick head count. 'Aye.'

'I think we might have made a mistake picking that door after all.'

'Shit, really? How do you know?'

'Looks like a firetrap to me, one they're not even trying to hide.'

'So mebbe it's another test?'

'Let's hope so.'

'You want to go back?'

'You can't!' Lastani broke in. 'I mean, you really shouldn't.'

'I know, I know.'

Aben blinked at her. 'Well I don't, why not?'

''Cos it's a test,' Lynx said from behind them. 'You make your choices and you take the consequences.'

Toil managed a small laugh at that and looked back at him. 'The labyrinth of your life, eh?'

He scowled at her. 'Oh, funny.'

350

'He's right,' Lastani insisted. 'It is a test – the riddle of the Fountain made that clear. The labyrinth is a test for the worthy. Deciding to backtrack could prove just as dangerous as a wrong choice.'

'That's comforting,' Aben said. 'Think I prefer Lynx's way of looking at it.'

'Either way, we press on.'

Toil held her lamp high and took a lap around the perimeter, looking for anything of note on the smooth, plain stone walls. Eventually she came back to where the rest were waiting.

'Three exits, just like that first room.' She pointed to the door directly opposite where they'd entered. 'Twenty-two above that one, sixteen on the right-hand wall.'

'And thirty-nine on the floor,' Lastani finished, skirting the circle as she returned from looking.

The chamber was the same proportions as the one they had just left – forty yards in each direction. Toil realised it didn't echo as much as she would have expected. With stone on all sides and nothing to absorb the sound, to her ears it didn't sound quite right, as though the Duegar had done something to the rock to dull the sound.

Or maybe to stop you hearing the screams from your competitors, a treacherous voice at the back of her head added.

'None of those mean anything special to me,' Toil said. 'Right now I want to work out if we can keep that door open as we choose.'

'It's a risk,' Lastani said.

'I know,' she admitted. 'But how much of one? You're our expert on the riddle. Do you think this puzzle-box is one that'll allow us to learn its rules or expect us to know them from the start?'

'I, ah, I don't know. You mean some sort of cultural context?'

'I guess so. Who was this puzzle designed for? Other Duegar, right? I've never seen or heard of anything like the labyrinth before. We don't have much to compare it to, but it could be they all knew what they were getting into before they opened it up. Maybe some sort of priesthood on the surface to warn them they'll die if they make a mistake, die if they try to open one door without shutting the first or something.'

Toil pinched the bridge of her nose, feeling her thoughts turning full circle upon themselves and never nearing any part that looked like a conclusion.

'What sort o' dumbshit don't want the option?' Deern broke in. 'That glyph says fire, woman. If this whole box fills up with fire, we need a way out.'

'You really think leaving yourself a way out will help if this place wants to kill you?' Lynx replied scornfully. 'You think it'll just let you have another try?'

Deern sneered. 'Poor convict Lynx. No matter how far you run or how much you eat, you'll always be that broken little prisoner, eh?'

Lynx made to storm forward, but Teshen grabbed him. 'Hey, stow it! You too, Deern!'

'I ain't startin' nothin',' Deern said, pistol drawn and levelled. 'But if fat-boy does, I'll finish it.'

'And I'll finish you,' Teshen snapped. 'Either o' you. One of you pulls a weapon without cause again while I'm stuck inside a stone box with you, I'll kill you before you even fucking see me coming.'

'Sure, sure,' Deern said, a small smile on his lips. With a deliberate movement he turned his mage-pistol aside and made the hammer safe. 'Mebbe you can keep hefty o' Tempest on a leash since Toil clearly won't.'

'Merciful gods,' Lastani gasped. 'I'm stuck in here with madmen. You're going to get us all killed!'

'No they're not,' Toil said firmly. She took a few steps forward and laid a hand on Lynx's shoulder as Teshen released him.

'Lynx, keep it together. I know you're scratchy in the dark, but we can't keep having this conversation. You're right, though. We're not going back and there's no point not playing the game sensibly. Either the first door needs to be shut or it doesn't matter – either way, leaving it open does us no good.'

Lynx grunted and reluctantly unpeeled his fingers from around his sword hilt. He went to shut the door, giving Deern the evil eye as he passed. The door itself took little effort to shut and with a soft grind of stone, it closed behind them.

'There's a panel on the back of this door too,' he reported, pointing at the shining disc with the glyph 'gift' inscribed.

'Maybe there is some going back after all,' Toil said, looking at Lastani. 'But we're not for the moment, so let's move on. Which door do you fancy?'

'What about the circle?' Sitain pointed out. 'We can't just ignore that, can we?'

'Another offering?'

From the back of the group, Atieno cleared his throat. The ageing mage stepped stiffly forward, a glass ball tinted faintly orange between finger and thumb. 'Perhaps another gift?' he suggested.

'Seems a bit big for that,' Toil pointed out. 'How many have you got?'

'Of fire? Two.'

'Go on then, might as well give it a try.'

They all stepped well back before Atieno tossed the glass ball into the centre of the ring. It broke as it landed and a gout of flame washed over the stone floor. It spread like a pail of spilled water before winking out again – starved of fuel once the modest spark of magic had been consumed. The glass balls were far less powerful than burners, having been created without a God Fragment to focus the magic, but the fire extended far enough for Toil to see something important.

'It stopped at the glyphs,' she exclaimed, pointing. 'Look, the flame went up to the edge but never crossed it.'

'How does that help us?' Lynx said.

'It's more information than we had before. Now we just need to work out what it means.'

She walked around the circle once more, checking all the glyphs were the same. That done, Toil reached out with one end of her staff and pushed it through the boundary. She felt no resistance and nothing happened, but a sixth sense made her set it down on the floor rather than pull it out again.

'Two choices,' she announced. 'We pick a door and try it. Or we all get in the circle and then one of us leaves it to pick a door.'

'Why?'

'Magic didn't get past the circle,' she explained, 'but pushing something in was no effort, so it's not a physical barrier. I think it's like a test of faith – you have to step inside before you go any further.'

'And then what happens? You step out and get burned, or only when you try a door?'

'Doesn't a little mystery add spice to your life, Lynx?'

'Reckon I've got enough to be going on with,' he replied grumpily.

Teshen stepped forward, clearly having reminded himself that he was the senior Card there alongside Safir, Toil's unusual appointment notwithstanding.

'Vote on it then, mages and relic hunters. What's your best bet?'

'Vote?' Toil said. 'I don't think so.'

'Vote,' Teshen said firmly. 'Let's see how everyone who matters thinks before we talk about whether this is a democracy.'

To add weight to his words, Safir took a small pace forward to stand beside Teshen. The easterner said nothing, but he didn't need to. Toil didn't bother trying to glare them down. She'd browbeaten lords and hard-bitten veterans in her time, but she knew Teshen was a stone-cold killer, trained and tempered in the Mage Islands if her guess was correct. It was rare she came up against someone like that and she wasn't going to risk wasting her breath or life starting a confrontation.

'You heard the Knight of Tempest,' she said, inclining her head very slightly to the man. 'Cast your votes. After that we can have a lively discussion about democracy in Anatin's Mercenary Deck.'

She heard Kas give a snort, but ignored her as she looked to the mages for comment.

'Circle,' Atieno said first. 'It's there for a reason.'

'One of us tries the door,' Sitain countered. 'Either it works or it doesn't. A mage is harder to kill with magic anyway, you've all seen that, and we don't know the circle isn't a trap either.'

'I would prefer to test every option,' Lastani said cautiously. 'The gift to enter the room was modest; to channel it into a weapon and kill the mage it came from is unlikely.'

'Paranil?' Toil asked. 'Aben, Barra?'

'I agree with Atieno,' Paranil said with a nervous cough. 'Perhaps it's a ruse, perhaps it's a lure, but there is *nothing* else in this room. I would expect some sort of indication if the circle was anything other than integral.'

'I'm with you, boss,' Aben added loyally, Barra just grunting in agreement.

'I'm for the circle,' Toil confirmed. 'Anyone – anyone other than Deern – got an opinion I might be interested in?'

No one spoke up.

'How about you, Teshen?'

The burly man grinned and swept back a lock of hair that had escaped his topknot. 'Not me, Princess, you're in command here.'

'Oh, you remembered that, eh?' she said and patted the badge sewn on to her jacket. 'Thought I'd lost this for a while there.'

'So which door?'

'Buggered if I know.'

*

General Derjain Faril of the Knights-Charnel of the Long Dusk stood on the top deck of her command barge and surveyed the camp around her with one lip caught under her front teeth. It was an old habit dating back to her childhood, one she hated but somehow could not shake when she was lost in thought.

'Casualties?'

'Ah, unclear at present, general. Limited, I'm led to believe.'

'Because they were after the supplies?'

'Yes, sir.'

Faril was quiet a long moment. The east flank of her camp still burned, and she could see that the supplies were gone from there. The pickets had been taken unawares. Sloppy, that. Someone would be punished, but right now she had more important things to deal with.

'How many horsemen?'

The captain hesitated, standing a little more stiffly to attention as though regulation order would improve matters. 'Reports are unclear also,' he said, 'or rather, wildly mixed. I would expect it to be between four and five hundred cavalry given what the survivors claimed.'

'Five hundred cavalry,' she repeated slowly. 'Under Crown-Prince Tylom's banner? I thought the man was supposed to be a weakling whose wife ruled him? No soldier.'

'That was the intelligence we received.'

'And yet he leads slash and burn raids on our lines like an experienced campaigner. Raids we cannot easily counter given our lack of horse.'

'Yes, sir.'

They had only just broken the city line an hour or so before. All had been going to plan; a precise, efficient drive into the city. The breach had been consolidated, the great artillery unable to strike targets on the corridor her regiments had marched down. The fight at the crater had been surprisingly fierce it was true, mostly for the determination of the city's response.

But her superior troops and numbers had taken their toll and the Jarraziran soldiers were in full retreat – fighting street to street but only buying time. They had withdrawn all the way to the palace, Faril had been informed, and she knew they wouldn't stop there. The only question had been how long they could delay, how slow they could make the fight. How much blood they were willing to shed.

How much are they willing to bear? she thought. *They must know our resolve; they must know we will endure horrors in the service of our god. Will they see the whole city burn to resist, or salvage what they can?*

'Bring the camp closer to the walls; make it harder for them to raid. Dig fixed positions there, there and there – force him into the heavy ground if he wants to attack further. I will write orders for the regiment colonels, have runners ready.'

'Yes, sir.'

'Dismissed.'

Left alone she turned to the fires of the city, a more satisfactory sight in the dull afternoon light. Somewhere beneath all that was a prize the likes of which no living Knight-Charnel had ever secured. She had not long since visited the Charnel Vault of Highkeep sanctuary. The air was different there, the

357

gods-touched members of the Order more animated than she had ever seen before – and Faril had been a member of the Key-Circle of the Vaults, highest council of the Knights-Charnel, for more than a decade.

If this is a cache as the writings say, it might change everything. It might change the face of the world for ever. We cannot fail.

*

'Everyone into the circle,' Toil said, having stepped gingerly over the threshold. 'Sitain, here at the front. Keep your eyes on the doors, the rest of you too, just in case we get a wink or something. Lastani, Atieno – be ready to do whatever you can in case this is a trap, okay?'

With a slightly comedic amount of huddling, the group all stepped inside the circle and kept close to each other. Once she'd confirmed they were all inside, Toil turned to Sitain.

'Anything?'

'Not that I saw.'

'Damn. Your eyes are probably most like a Duegar's.'

'So our conclusion is that there's nothing to see,' Lastani said. 'Pick a number, Toil.'

'Twenty-two, sixteen, thirty-nine, and the two behind us. What was the first room's? Paranil, tell me you wrote them down.'

'Of course. A one above where we entered, as there is a two above this door. Our choices in the first room were the four on our left as we entered, which was the one we took, a seven ahead and twelve down.'

Toil shook her head. 'Anyone seeing anything like a pattern?'

'Why did you pick four, just out of interest?'

'We're in a cube and a square has four sides, I couldn't think of much else that seemed to fit in any way and we don't have the luxury of thinking for days. I did wonder about the gods, though; how scholars used to say that our gods were once Duegar, that they *became* gods and at first there were only four of them.'

'Banesh was said to have come later, it's true, though we don't know when in their history the labyrinth was built,' Lastani said. 'If the Militant Orders had built this, you'd probably have been right, but I don't think the logic extends.'

'Yeah, I know, it was mostly the square thing because that's all I had.'

'Glad we're doing this all scientific-like,' Lynx muttered.

'Welcome to the exciting life of the relic hunter, my friend,' Toil replied. 'Now enough talk. We've got a choice to make.'

'Perhaps the numbers don't matter, perhaps it's simply direction,' Lastani said after a short while.

'But we don't know what direction we need to go in. There's nothing I remember from anywhere that would suggest a certain path, not even the patterns on the Fountain.'

Lastani shook her head. 'Nor I,' she admitted. 'But we need to pick one.'

'Fine. Twenty-two,' Toil decided. 'There are worse things than moving forward when you don't know what to do.'

'We're all gonna die,' moaned someone from the back.

'Shut it, all of you. Lastani, you ready?'

The young woman nodded. 'Everyone move away from me, it's about to get very cold in here.'

They all edged away as far as they could as Lastani held her palms out, like she was pushing her way through the circle. The temperature dropped almost immediately, the Duegar lamplight flaring white and blue on a bubble of cold magic surrounding her. Lastani stepped forward and the room exploded around her. Lynx howled and threw his hands up to cover his eyes from the blinding flash of orange light.

A wall of fire erupted around them, pouring out from the glyphs in one expanding pulse of power. It lasted only a moment but in the next there was a shriek from someone behind him. Lynx blinked and turned, seeing only a blur of movement at first until he made out the flailing shape ahead.

'Hold still!' shouted someone.

'Fuck – I'm on fire!' the flailing figure shrieked back. It was Haphori, a hirsute man from somewhere so far away even Safir just described it as 'bloody miles east'. He'd lived most of his life on the shore of Whitesea Sound, however, so he swore like a local.

Brols pounced on the man, using his body to smother any flames while Haphori howled in renewed pain at the man now lying on his burned arm.

'Sitain,' Teshen snapped, rubbing his head and wincing, 'shut him up or I will.'

The young mage picked her way past the rest and reached out to Haphori as he kicked Brols off him. The darker man saw Sitain advancing and wriggled backwards but was pinned down by his comrades long enough for her to grab his hand and dull the pain to a point where he stopped screaming.

Lastani, in the meantime, had walked towards the next door and pressed her hand against the gift disc. With her magic up as a barrier the flames hadn't harmed her and she looked unruffled by the torrent of flame. With a second, smaller, burst of magic she triggered the door – again throwing up a shield of magic, but all that happened was the door silently opening into the next room.

Once Haphori's arm was wrapped, Toil led the company through into the next room and ordered the door closed behind them again. This one was empty but for the doorways ahead, on the right-hand wall and in the floor, so she told the company to pause and eat while the scholarly members thought about the new set of numbers. The entrance had a 3 above it this time, the exits displaying 55 ahead, 42 down and 33 right.

'Thirty-three comes up again. There must be a message in that.'

Paranil nodded as he added the new set to his record. 'I believe so, though the pattern still eludes me. Perhaps the repetition is the key or a sign that one awaits us.'

'How about we look at it a different way?' Toil said, feeling suddenly very tired. She dug a small honey-cake out of her pack, jamming the sweet treat into her mouth before continuing in a slightly muffled manner. 'If we made a mistake in the first room, getting that fire-trap, that means we're should've taken what?'

'Ah, twelve or seven.'

'Right. Then twenty-two gets us to an empty room. What's the link?'

No one answered and Toil felt her head sink. She was well used to taking risks in a city-ruin, but she had instinct to rely on there. Sometimes a jump wasn't worth taking, sometimes her gut told her to just walk away and she'd learned to listen to it. Right now it was grumbling uneasily and not out of hunger. There was something amiss, something she'd not noticed perhaps.

Or maybe I'm just feeling like I've used up enough luck for the time being.

'Come on, anyone?'

Paranil looked around at the others before replying for them. 'We need another room.'

Toil sighed and licked the last of the honeyed crumbs from her fingers. 'One more door, go on then. Your turn, Sitain.'

Chapter 27

'Two dead? Deepest black, we're only just started down here!'

Chotel rubbed at the icer burn on his cheek and hissed. 'Two,' he repeated before pointing to a dragoon being helped to the far wall by one of his comrades. 'Another who's not gonna last the day.'

'And this'll be the easy bit,' Bade added. *At least none of my crew was killed. It might teach the dragoons to step a bit more carefully.*

'Let's just hope this door is the right one,' Kastelian said, joining them. 'We don't need many more traps.'

'Hopper's just warming us up. Teaching us the rules of his game. A few more chambers in and mistakes'll get properly punished, I reckon.'

Kastelian looked back across the room they'd just crossed. There were bulbous studs jutting from the side walls and ceiling, while a chaotic spread of tiles occupied a ten-yard stretch of the chamber up to the door on the right-hand wall. Each tile had the glyph for 'ice' carved into it and putting the slightest pressure on any part activated a burst of ice magic from one of the studs. The bursts hadn't had the power of a properly charged ice-bolt, but they were lethal enough. Two bodies on the floor attested to that, and several others carried injuries from glancing blows.

Bade and his crew had moved carefully, ahead of the dragoons, one by one and with few mistakes. But when a mistake was made, it was hard not to fall – hard not to trip others and trigger a barrage. One of the dead had seven or eight wounds in him, his chest torn apart and half-frozen by the ice magic. His body had proved a useful waypoint for the rest, however, covering several glyphs as it did.

'Is your man going ta make it?' Bade asked Kastelian.

'Do I look like a doctor to you?'

Bade lowered his voice. 'He can't hold us up an' he can't be carried for long.'

'I'm aware.'

'Might be you need to step in then, they won't like me doing it.'

Kastelian's face hardened. 'Don't tell me my job, Bade, I'm the ranking officer here, remember? You do what you're paid to do and leave command decisions to me, understand?'

He received a lop-sided smirk. 'Oh aye, sure. Whatever you say, sir. I'll get back to work. Just tell me which door you want me to open, sir.'

'Don't give me the dumb soldier routine,' Kastelian snapped, 'you've known me too long for that.'

'Thought I did, but now you're pulling rank?'

'Oh don't start getting precious on me. You're giving me advice about *my* command and you complain I remind you about rank?'

Chotel stepped between the two of them. 'The pair of you, shut it,' he growled, using his greater size to present a physical barrier. 'Cock-measuring is over for the day – ain't neither of you going to win on that front anyway.'

Bade forced a laugh. 'Don't gimme that shit, I've seen you naked more often than's good for my stomach. You ain't winning nothing.'

'Aye, but Torril's wife has something of the poet about her on the subject o' her man's tackle. Don't give that horny ferret any

363

excuse to pull it out and show the ladies here again. I dunno what Sonna would do but Gull gets an appraising look that worries me.'

'He's got a point,' Bade conceded. 'Gull does go all thoughtful and intense at the sight.'

'Damn right I have, now kiss and make up the pair o' you.'

'Don't be disgusting,' Kastelian said primly, just the hint of a smile on his face.

'Oh go on, pucker up!' Bade pleaded.

'Get the right door and I'll think about it,' he replied and turned away to avoid laughing in the presence of his dead troops.

'Nothing like a bit of motivation, eh?' Bade rubbed his hands together. 'So what are our options?'

'Down is marked twenty-five, twelve there, nine ahead,' Ulestim said. 'Didn't we have a twenty-five already?'

'Aye, first room. Torril?'

'What?'

'You write all the numbers down so far?'

'Did you ask me to?'

'Oh for buggery's sake. Well, I'm asking now.'

Torril bobbed his head. 'Writing 'em down now, boss. I can remember the rest anyway.'

'What's it say on this side of the one we came through?'

Ulestim gave a grunt. 'That's worried me a shade, it's a five.'

'Why does that worry you?'

'There was no four. The room before this one had a three on the inside.'

'Think we missed something?'

'I think we might have taken a wrong turn.'

Bade shook his head. 'Course we did. Didn't the ice magic punching through flesh give you a hint on that front?'

'Certainly, I'm just concerned as to whether the missed four is significant in any other way.'

'Like what?'

'I've, ah, yet to quite fathom that part of the problem.'

Bade exchanged a look with Chotel. 'Well, you inform us when you've got around to it. In the meantime, we're taking twenty-five.'

'Any reason?'

'We've seen it before, mebbe it's Hopper's lucky number.'

'Really?'

'Don't be a shit-brained fool, course not. We came in at the door marked five an' twenty-five is five fives, no? That's a good enough reason for me.'

'You think the key is it's a multiple?' Ulestim said, eyes widening as though on the point of revelation.

'I think it's an idea when I've got few others from you lot.' He pointed to the door and raised his voice. 'Hoy, Spade, number twenty-five if you'd be so good.'

*

'Of course! I've been a fool!'

Toil stopped her investigation of the empty room and stalked over to where Paranil was waving his notes in Lastani's face.

'You're going to have to narrow it down for me there,' Toil said.

'The number code!'

'What? You've cracked it? How?'

'They all relate to the door you entered through, or rather the number above the inside of it. They're multiples – or rather the ones that matter are.'

'Wait, no, that doesn't make sense.' Toil grabbed his paper off him and studied the numbers a moment. 'There,' she said, pointing at the second set. 'We had a two on the inside of that first door we took and the options were twenty-two or sixteen, both multiples.'

Paranil smirked. 'The number informs the choice, you still need to recognise the right one. You took the right one this time round by the way, clever girl.'

'Enough of the patronising; short version?'

'Divide both of those by two. The choice you ended up with was between eleven and eight, since there was an odd number on the floor. In the first room the numbers get divided by one and don't change; we chose four and it was wrong, so either seven or twelve was correct. In the third room, after factoring in the three, you had a choice between eleven again and, well, nothing – the others don't divide by three.'

'Screaming firedrakes! A shorter version please?'

'Right, yes. Sorry. The important numbers are one, eleven, two, seven, three and eleven. They're all primes. I just didn't spot it until we came back to a "three" room, despite having no trap and therefore hadn't chosen wrongly.'

'So here, we . . .' Toil looked up. 'Which one? Fifty-seven?'

He nodded. 'Divided by three, becomes nineteen, yet another prime. It could be a coincidence, but it isn't – the deviser of this labyrinth was a lover of mathematics.'

'Ready to stake your life on that?'

'I . . .'

Toil raised an eyebrow. 'Ready to stake *my* life on it?'

'Oh, without a doubt.'

'You're lucky I enjoy this so much then.'

'Enjoy?' remarked Lynx from somewhere behind them. 'How can you enjoy all this?'

She turned. ''Cos I'm a gentle spirit whose nature is to be brimming with inquisitive joy, can't you tell?'

'And there was me thinking you're a madwoman who likes the smell of impending death on the wind.'

Toil snorted. 'I think we've both been around enough impending death to know the smell isn't a pretty one. But this is what I do, what I'm good at – and right here we've the ultimate challenge for a relic hunter. If Bade gets the prize ahead of me, maybe I'll give it all up and raise a brood of squealing babies – but until then I'm going to enjoy doing what I do.'

Lynx didn't say anything and Toil realised a few of the other mercenaries, the male ones at least, were looking at her strangely. She looked around, puzzled, as a hush descended.

'What happened?'

'Don't mind them,' Estal called, 'you just said the magic word, "babies".'

'Magic? Why?'

'Half are now stricken with terror at the word, the other half are picturing you makin' 'em.'

Toil pulled her mage-pistol. 'And which one of 'em is going to make a crass comment about it? Deern? Safir?'

No one spoke and slowly the male mercenaries averted their gaze.

'Damn right. Now let's get back to work. Lastani, door fifty-seven if you please.'

The young mage jumped to her task and opened the door, Sitain again peering through first before reporting that it looked empty. As Paranil gave a squeak of triumph, Toil led the mercenaries through and into another stone chamber, almost identical to the one before.

'Paranil, numbers.'

She checked behind her and saw there was a 1 inscribed above the door, almost like the labyrinth designer was confirming their theory. Of the other four exits, there was only one prime and it led down so they wasted no time in following. Again the room was empty and Toil felt a jolt of hope. Finally they were making some quicker progress. She just had to hope Bade had found an obstacle to slow himself up.

'Numbers,' Toil called. 'Which way now?'

Paranil gave a cough. 'Ah, yes.'

'What's wrong?'

'Ahem – nothing, per se. There's a three above our entrance – as for the rest. Five hundred and sixty-one, four hundred and seventeen, two hundred and seventy-three. This may take some time.'

'Bugger.'

*

Lynx watched Toil's cohort at its sums while he tried to ignore the growl at the back of his mind. This room, like all the others, was too much like a cell for his liking. A series of windowless cells that might contain something lethal behind every door.

And still they don't seem too worried. I might have my issues with the dark, but none of that lot act as worried as I'd expect – as I'd hope from people leading us through a maze of magic traps. Toil might be the only one actually enjoying herself, but even that girl, Lastani, seems more interested in the academic challenge.

He turned to the others. Kas was putting a brave face on it and Teshen was a closed book to the world around him, but of the others Lynx couldn't see one who seemed at ease with what was going on. The Monarch's lamp casting white light around the room improved matters, but still the enclosed spaces were grating on their nerves.

'What do you reckon our chances are?' Sitain whispered in Lynx's ear.

'They seem to think they know what they're doing,' he said.

'That's not what I asked.'

'Aye, I know.' Lynx found his hands tightening into fists, nails digging into his palms, and made an effort to release the tension in them before replying. 'I don't know about our chances,' he admitted, 'but given all we saw in Shadows Deep, what odds would you have given for us getting through that?'

'Poor odds,' Sitain agreed. 'Dunno if that's a comfort or not.'

'Me neither. Oh, here we go.'

Up ahead, the sums had been done and all but one door eliminated as a possibility. Atieno took a turn to open the door on the right-hand wall so the others weren't doing all the work and Lynx watched Sitain slope forward again to look. Soon they were all filing through and the door closed behind them. While the next set of numbers was being investigated, Lynx went to join Safir and Layir. The two easterners each offered him an inclined head and a slight smile, their actions and mannerisms strangely similar given Layir's formative years had been far from their homeland.

'Are you also getting the impression that we're far from useful?' Safir said, glancing towards the latest discussion.

'Yeah, but that also means there's nothing trying to kill us at present.'

'I hoped for a little more excitement down here,' Layir declared. 'This is the fabled Labyrinth of Jarrazir, after all.'

'We're in a giant puzzle-box, thousands of years old and hundreds of feet below ground,' Lynx pointed out. 'What more were you looking for?'

Layir shrugged. 'Riches for preference – statuary even? Great histories of the Duegar race inscribed on a hundred stone tablets? The secrets of life? Bloody *something* at least.'

'The youth of today,' Safir said in a mock-apologetic tone. 'Ever demanding. We, my dear Layir, are here as escort and, if we're very lucky, pack mules for whatever Toil finds. This is probably the good bit of our adventure.'

'Down we go,' Toil called across the room to the company at large.

Lastani opened the doorway and led them down into another chamber. Before Lynx had reached the bottom he heard exclamations of surprise and alarm coming from those in the lead. He had his gun drawn in the next moment, but no sound of fighting followed and he and the others edged their way down to find no obvious danger other than an enraged Toil.

'Godspit and damn, Paranil! You gibbering fool, what have you done?'

The bespectacled man scrabbled through the handful of paper in his fist, gabbling something nonsensical until he found the page he was looking for. Lynx ignored him and advanced into the room, a growing sense of fear in his belly. There were two doors in this room, both on the wall ahead, and a strange multi-piece sculpture occupying much of the ground between.

'Catrac's shrivelled balls, we must've gone wrong,' Safir breathed beside him, looking all around for anything on the walls that might prove a threat.

'I made no mistake!' Paranil screeched. 'I swear it!'

'Well what the buggery is that then?' Aben roared, pointing at the strange sculpture. 'Every room's been empty except for the one where there was a damn trap to punish our mistake, so explain how *that* is a good sign?'

It consisted of two groups of twisting shards of stone rising out of the ground, separate from each other and each set obviously corresponding to one door. What Lynx couldn't tell was what the sets were meant to be, they appeared to be just a random tangle of stone protrusions – clearly carved by a mage, seven or eight bizarre stalagmites to each set, but none of them looked like they served a purpose.

'Look, my sums were correct,' Paranil announced, waving the paper in Toil's face until she grabbed it off him. 'This was the only option.'

'So were we wrong about the pattern, or has it changed on us?' she mused.

'There's no reason for it to remain consistent,' Lastani agreed, 'but wouldn't we have had some indication? The maker took pains to establish that system – perhaps it's still in force, just adding another element?'

Toil scowled at the stone formations. 'What in pity's name is this supposed to be?'

'Those are more numbers over the doors?' Lynx asked.

'Just the glyphs for one and two,' she confirmed.

'Both primes then?'

'Aha, well opinions differ on that,' Paranil broke in, 'um, but I would be cautious about using it as a basis, given what we have here.'

'And what *do* we have here?' Lynx approached the formations cautiously, trying to view every obstacle like an experienced relic hunter would. He skirted halfway around them before backtracking and pointing. 'Is it just me, or does that look a bit like an arm?'

'What?'

He nodded and continued walking, head cocked, until he stopped and moved a little closer. 'Atieno, take that oil lamp around over there would you?'

The man did so, turning the wick on the lamp up so it gave a half-decent light and more importantly cast some shadows.

'It's a statue,' Lynx breathed, a spark of excitement filling his belly. 'Shattered gods, that's clever! Atieno, put the light in the middle now.'

'Statue?' the mage asked as he did so.

'Cut up – separated so you have to look at it from the right angle to see all the pieces together.'

Lynx edged forward until he was almost right in front of the largest and outermost formation. But he wasn't looking at that one, it was the other set of stones across the room that had caught his eye from there.

'Look!'

Toil went to join him, almost shoving Lynx out of the way in her enthusiasm, and the pair stared open-mouthed at the further statue. The statue was taller than a human, as large as the Wisps they'd encountered in Shadows Deep, but broader. It had no face, they could make out little detail at all, but still Lynx felt a thrill. He remembered all too well Toil telling them that the Duegar had not left statues or images of themselves.

No one knew what they looked like, with the exception perhaps of some Militant Orders who possessed the earliest writings about the gods. It was a matter of violent debate as to whether the gods had once been Duegar, but certainly that race had once worshipped other beings in their earlier ages. Whatever the truth, this was a sight that few, if any, had ever been permitted.

By the shape of the stone, the scalloped lines and straight edge to the face, it was clear to Lynx that it was an outline statue of a Duegar – or something – in ornate armour. Most significantly, it seemed to be holding a hand up – just a blockish shape composed of several separate pieces, but one that appeared to have a glyph inscribed upon it from where Lynx stood.

'It's like the statue has a two inscribed on its hand,' Toil breathed.

Lynx looked over at the doorway. He could only just about make out the glyph, but it did seem to correspond perfectly. On the far side of the room Atieno backed up so he was next to the group Lynx was staring at, and squinted across at the composite statue nearer Lynx.

'The one on your side also has a two,' he commented. 'Our statue friends seem to agree on which door we should take.'

'Wait!' Layir broke in, stepping behind Atieno. 'You're looking at it wrong.'

'What? How?'

'Each statue is telling you what the other would say,' Layir said, face splitting into a huge grin. 'Don't you see? It's a children's riddle!'

'Ah!' Safir exclaimed, crossing to the opposite side. 'Of course. You went a whole afternoon in a huff because I wouldn't tell you the answer.'

'I was only five years old!' Layir laughed. He was about to say more when he caught sight of Toil's expression and hurriedly moved on. 'Safir called it the two doors problem, heard of it?'

Lynx heard a gasp as Toil caught on. 'The two guards! One lies, one tells the truth!'

'Exactly. From here, you look across and see which door the other guard would tell you to take.'

'And you therefore choose the other,' Paranil finished. 'It makes sense – the only question is whether the ancient Duegar knew the riddle too.'

'Once you find someone able to answer that, you let me know. In the meantime, has anyone got any better ideas? Any pattern in the numbers we've taken to suggest a path?'

Paranil went back to his notes with Atieno looking over his shoulder, the others inspecting the stone formations from every angle they could think of in case they'd missed something. It took a little while, but eventually they all admitted defeat and Toil finally looked satisfied.

'Lastani, door number one it is.'

Chapter 28

Sotorian Bade felt a rare flicker of fear in his heart and for a moment he couldn't move. Beside him a stone slab flicked up and slotted back into place with a dull thud. Of Gull, the woman who'd been standing beside him a moment before, there was no sign. Just a strangled cry of surprise as she'd dropped without warning and vanished.

'Shit!' Chotel yelled from behind them, racing forward. 'Gull!' He hammered at the stone slab with the butt of his mage-gun but it didn't yield. Others went to help him, but push as they might, they couldn't budge it and as Bade slowly turned to face them, the relic hunters gave up, panting.

'She just dropped,' Chotel gasped. 'Shitting gods, she went like there was nothing underneath her!'

'Reckon I noticed that bit,' Bade said slowly. 'Also, I'm more'n a little aware that I'm standing on a slab exactly bloody like hers.'

'Deepest black,' moaned one of the dragoons who'd also stepped on to a square, a few down from Bade.

A tall, blond lieutenant, the man looked around at the floor then took a jerky pace backwards on to the unpaved section of floor where the rest still were. Out of nowhere there was a flash of light and a jerky arc of lightning slashed through the air – hitting him full on. The man didn't have time to scream as he was brutally slapped to the ground, the magic carving a path down his body, and he fell in a boneless heap.

'Stay still, boss!' Chotel shouted as cries of panic went up from the rest. 'Don't move off that!'

Several dragoons ran to their comrade's side, but it was immediately clear he was dead – a blistered line torn through his uniform and skin, oozing blood. Bade had to watch chaos reign for a while, hardly daring to move while the rest panicked and brandished weapons against an unseen foe. Eventually Kastelian got control of his troops and the noise level dropped enough for Bade to speak. He kept his voice low, calm and controlled though inside he was nothing of the sort. If anything he didn't want to move too fast in case it triggered a similar response.

He cleared his throat loudly. 'Someone check the others,' Bade ordered, having to remind himself they would be looking to him to lead. 'Put a bit more weight on the slabs this time?'

They had descended through the trapdoor in the floor of an empty chamber to find themselves on a shallow slope that didn't lead nearly as far down as they expected. No more than halfway to the bottom it opened out on to the platform where Chotel stood. They'd tried to backtrack, realising they had made a mistake, but it hadn't worked. When the mage had tried to open another door back in the chamber, the gift disc had pulsed briefly with light before exploding into a shower of lightning-magic. The nearest two dragoons and Spade had been killed instantly, the labyrinth's punishment for going back on a choice. Looking down at the charred corpse, Bade now realised that wasn't limited to doors.

'This one's solid,' reported a short woman with a corporal's stripe on her arm. To demonstrate she hammered at it with her gun butt then stamped one foot on the surface. 'See.'

'Go on then,' Bade said, feeling sceptical. *Better you test it out than any o' mine.*

As soon as her full weight was on the slab, it seemed to vanish. Bade heard the snap of bone as she tried to catch herself on the edge, but it was as though something had dragged her down into the darkness below. Another dragoon dived forward, dropping the barrel of his gun into the space to stop the slab returning to position.

There was a crunch as the metal buckled under impact, but just as it looked as though he'd done it the lightning spat out again. Bade looked away as the man's eyes burst under the impact. He fell back, convulsing as the slab dropped again and the mage-gun fell from its owner's hands, following the corporal into the black.

'Ulestim,' Bade called out over the hubbub of panic. 'Why'm I still alive here?'

'I don't know!' the man wailed. 'There are no markings, no nothing!'

'Sonna, slap that gibbering high-born weasel for me.'

His sharpshooter did exactly that, her palm cracking like a pistol shot around the small room. Ulestim's head rocked backwards, but he shut up and after a few seconds, nodded. Rubbing his cheek he took a long breath.

'Back with us?' Bade asked. 'Right – look at what we've got. What can you tell me? Whatever you see, I'm in no mood for "I don't knows", understand?'

'Yes, sir. We, ah, you're on a grid of seven by seven, no markings – no space around it. Clearly we want to get to the door ahead of us, I can't see any others. If you take a step back, you die. If you stand on the wrong slab, you die.'

'So why am I still alive when Gull's dead? Is this fucking prime numbers again?'

'I don't . . . Wait. Yes.' Ulestim looked up and counted his way across to where the dragoon had fallen through. 'Gods, it is primes! She fell through because she stood on the first slab – he was safe because he was on the fifth, until he took a step back from it, anyway.'

Bade looked at his feet. 'So I'm on the second, Gull stood on the first.'

'Exactly! One doesn't count as a prime.'

'Prove it.'

'Eh?'

Bade grinned nastily. 'Number three's right here next to me, come keep your old friend company before you show him the path.'

'I . . .' the words died in Ulestim's throat and he nodded nervously.

So gingerly he almost had his eyes closed, Ulestim stepped on to the slab next to Bade's and – and nothing happened. After a moment he opened one eye and squinted at Bade.

'Aha, I was right!'

'Nothing like the courage of your convictions, eh? Where now?'

'Good question. It should be, ah . . .' Ulestim paused. 'I should map this out.'

'Have at it, we've all day.'

The disgraced nobleman lapsed into silence for a while, sketching a grid on a tatty sheaf of paper and quickly marking numbers on it. 'Oh,' he said after a few moments.

'What is it?'

'Which way do the numbers go? Once you reach the end of a row?'

'Does it matter?'

'Very much so,' Ulestim muttered, scowling at the paper. 'I will try both.'

He spent a little while doing so, before brightening slightly. 'It starts the same,' Ulestim announced. 'No matter which way it goes.'

He looked down at the slabs, then at his paper again, double-checking before he risked his life. Finally and with the same bravery he'd shown earlier, he took a pace diagonally to his right. Again, he didn't fall to his death so Bade moved on to the slab Ulestim had been occupying.

'There's a curved edge here,' called Chotel, who'd been inspecting the line of slabs before stepping on to any. He pointed at the right-hand-most slab where, now Bade looked, there was indeed a slight curve to the top edge.

Bade looked left and right, realising there was a similar curve on the furthest left-hand slab of the second row. 'So the path of numbers snakes up the board?'

'It appears that way,' Ulestim murmured, 'but let's not make any more assumptions, eh?'

'Sure. Ah, Ulestim? How many prime numbers do you know?'

The man coughed. 'Certainly enough to get us halfway across. After that, there's a little guesswork, I'm afraid.'

'Oh, good.'

'Indeed. Someone mark these as we go please? Nineteen.' He took another diagonal step and still failed to die so Bade followed him.

'Twenty-three comes next.' Ulestim peered around for a curved edge of stone and found it on his right. 'If I'm correct, it's another diagonal move. Almost seems too good to be true.'

'Maybe it isn't?'

'Thanks,' Ulestim said reproachfully. 'However, I'm too far from the end to jump. So.'

He took another step and remained alive so Bade again followed, Chotel keeping close behind. Up ahead he could make out the door on the far side a little better now. It was the only visible exit, but still Bade felt a flush of relief as he saw the glyph for seven above it. Ulestim might have been slow in recognising the pattern, but at least his theory was supported by what awaited them. It was small consolation, but right now Bade was willing to accept it gladly.

'Next?'

'That's where it gets tricky. I believe the next prime is thirty-one, but I can't reach it from here. I can't jump that far either, it's that one – two in from the left on the next row.'

Bade followed where he was pointing. They were close to the right-hand side where an almost-sheer side slope ran down the side of the puzzle-board section.

'What comes after it?'

'Assuming the curved lines are correct about the path – and frankly we're dead if they aren't – it has to be thirty-seven. Which is, ah, directly ahead. Just a jump over the slab in front.'

'Sure?'

Ulestim shook his head and jumped. The slabs were not large, about a yard across, so it wasn't much of one, but given overbalancing would mean death, he took every care.

'You're still not dead!' Bade marvelled, feeling his usual humour returning. 'I was betting against you there.'

'Glad to hear it, feel free to take a pace forward,' was the retort. 'Now, where in the deepest black do we go from here?'

Bade frowned, there was only one row left. 'Can't you jump the rest too?'

'I can, but this game doesn't like you cheating. Before I try that, I'm going to work out which one *will* be safe – just in case. This jump I had to make because there wasn't another option available, the next I may not.'

'Well, take your time,' Bade muttered as Ulestim returned to his paper. 'Not like we got anything better to do.'

Ulestim found his next slab after five minutes of scribbled sums then stepped over and on to the platform on the far side. Bade joined him a few moments later with a flush of relief and they started directing the others across. It took Bug a long while to be persuaded to follow and Bade was already resigned to watching his half-tame maspid die. In the end the sight of the far door being opened was enough to tempt her over and she clambered along the steeply sloping side, creeping slowly and at an angle that threatened to tip her on to the slabs at every step.

'Let's not do that ever again,' Bade suggested as they watched Bug raced through into the empty room beyond. 'Please?'

*

After their little statue test, Lynx had hoped they would pick the pace up through the labyrinth, but it appeared the Duegar had other ideas. First the prime numbers had steadily increased in value, beyond the point of Paranil's studies. It was not impossible to work out the correct answers, but it took time – more and more each time – and Lynx's patience was wearing thin.

He could feel his inner demons scratching away, those tiny claws of fear and panic in his mind slowly digging their way to the surface. From the looks he was getting from Toil and Kas, they knew it too. They were keeping an eye out, but there wouldn't be much they could do if it all got too much for him. Down here, dead weight was dead.

The Monarch's lamp was helping, Lynx had to admit. The cool white light of that smooth Duegar glass kept the darkness at bay, but every time their winding path took them down a level in the labyrinth, the more smothered Lynx felt.

And the more this feels like a prison, he couldn't help but think. Lynx looked over at Toil as she sat with Atieno, both hard at work. *Gods on high and spirits below, I think I'd prefer Shadows Deep!*

'Toil,' he called, 'you sure the air's good down here? Feels like it's getting stuffy. We've been in here a while now.'

'The air's fine,' she replied, glancing back. 'You're just getting bored.' The look on her face made it clear she knew boredom wasn't the problem, but he was grateful all the same for her not saying it. 'Walk about, stretch your legs. The movement will help.'

'You sure about the air?'

'Yup.'

'Why?'

'Because it's a big space,' Kas answered for her, 'and it must've been sealed for centuries at least before we came along, but we could breathe fine when we came in.'

'That's right,' Toil added, 'and if it goes bad, I got a toy to help with that. This place is unusual – often in a city-ruin there'll be pockets that get sealed and you'll be dead before you cross the room. I always think of it as being Bade's parting gift to me, though of course the bastard would've taken it if he'd known. Was hoping it'd help me beat him to the labyrinth heart, but no such luck, it seems.'

Kas nudged Lynx. 'She's got a talent, your girl, I'll give her that.'

'Eh?'

Kas grinned. 'Cells and underground caves not being your favourite places and all, she's outdone herself finding somewhere that combines the two!'

Lynx forced himself to laugh at that, knowing that in such a mood it would help, even if he needed a run-up.

'Aye, well, she's resourceful.'

'Ah, but drugging half the men in the company and leaving you all stripped in a cell was resourceful,' she said. 'Sparking a war and opening up a fabled ancient labyrinth, all just to keep a man she likes off-balance, well . . .' She whistled. 'That's really going the extra mile if you ask me.'

381

'Put it like that, I almost feel special.'

Lynx felt his mouth waver into a smile before he looked again at the stark, blank stone walls all around him and it sank again.

'Mebbe,' Kas said in a more serious tone. 'Or mebbe she just thinks that, as passing the time goes, mushroom pot-luck is a game for amateurs.'

'Toil!' Lastani shouted, over-loud in her excitement. 'Sorry, but we've got it.'

'You sure?'

'I . . . ' She glanced at Paranil, who nodded. 'Yes, we've eliminated the other two. That door there, that's the one we want.'

'Four hundred and thirty-three?' Toil nodded and pushed herself to her feet. 'You know, relic hunting is more fun when you're not spending hours dividing numbers.'

'You just hate that Paranil's now the expert rather than you,' Aben chuckled, hefting his pack.

Toil stuck her tongue out at him in a curiously girlish way. 'I like to think of that more as salt in the wound,' she said as she extended a hand to Atieno.

She pulled the ageing man to his feet, Atieno looking stiff and weary after the hours they'd now spent underground. They crossed into the next room and Lynx again tried to picture their path through the labyrinth. They had moved down six levels, that much he knew, but if his estimate was right, they were moving away from the centre of the puzzle-box. He didn't know if that was significant, but it was something to keep his mind occupied at least.

'A new game?' Toil commented as they moved into the latest cell, where a small stone tablet stood at the centre.

There were four exits there, more than usual, and as Paranil read aloud the number above each for the others to confirm,

Lynx realised even without seeing the tablet that Toil was right. The numbers weren't as high as they had been earlier, but from what limited amounts he'd picked up thus far, they were all primes. The door ahead had twenty-nine above it, the left-hand was an eleven, thirteen was inscribed on the floor and nineteen on the right.

'A key to the puzzle?' Lastani suggested as Paranil confirmed the number of their entrance was a one.

'A sequence. Does it mean anything to you? One, one, two, three, five,' Toil read from the tablet aloud.

'Not much,' she admitted. 'Paranil?'

The thin man beamed, revelling in his new role of brains at the heart of the crew. Lynx guessed that he was normally trailing along behind Toil and her more practical colleagues. Her Duegar knowledge was extensive by most standards so Paranil wouldn't be needed much of the time, he was intellectual backup in the same way as Aben was violent support, most likely.

But this labyrinth didn't have maspids or rival relic hunters, just magical traps she couldn't fool the same way she could those in Duegar tombs. They lived or they died on the years of study Paranil had put in, the teachers he'd had and his love of sciences.

'It's a sequence,' he explained, 'called the golden sequence. Each number is the sum of the two before it.'

'So the next in the sequence is eight? But we don't have an eight.'

'We do, however, have a Duegar in love with prime numbers. It's no great surprise the elegance of the golden sequence is similarly favoured.'

'And only one of these doors is both a prime and a part of the sequence,' Toil said slowly, waiting for Paranil to nod before continuing. 'Right, thirteen it is. Down we go.'

Lynx dragged himself through the open hatchway and down the shallow steps as they levelled out into another spiral slope. As with every other tunnel and cell entered so far, the Monarch's lamp was carefully covered by whichever agent was carrying it and Toil's Duegar lamp produced. Once Toil had checked there was nothing hidden in glowing patterns on the wall she let them move on. Before long there were more numbers to be worked through on whatever scraps of paper remained so Teshen produced a deck of cards and the mercenaries all sat.

The next cell proved no different to the usual pattern, almost suspiciously simple compared to recent rooms. But there was no indication that the pattern had changed and little they could do, so Sitain opened the door and they all peered fearfully through. Lynx felt a sinking feeling as, beside him, Sitain stiffened. A frown of confusion crossed her face and as she looked around the next room, she said nothing at all.

'What's wrong?' Toil asked.

'I don't know,' the night mage said. 'I can't see a damn thing.'

'Nothing?'

'Three or four yards forward mebbe,' she said, 'then nothing. *Really* nothing.'

Toil elbowed the others out of the way and raised her black lamp.

'Huh,' she said after a while.

With her staff she prodded forward at the darkness, meeting no resistance until she felt for the floor. Bringing the Monarch's lamp forward didn't help. When she held the lamp out in front of her, it just vanished entirely. At the sight of that, Lynx felt his inner demons renew their frantic clawing. He leaned against the wall, trying to stop his hands shaking, but realised no one was watching anyway. All eyes were on Toil as the woman hesitantly leaned forward and put her face through the veil of darkness, lamp held out before her.

'Yeah, we're screwed,' she reported back after a few moments, a manic gleam in her eye. 'Barra – you're up,' she added, turning to her lithe comrade. 'And someone get Lynx a stiff drink. Reckon he's really going to need it now.'

Chapter 29

'So when you said "really dark" you weren't kidding, eh?'

'Which o' the words confused you?'

Bade shrugged and put a hand on Sebaim's shoulder. The ageing scout had ventured just a yard or two into the black, but that had been enough. He was cool-headed in most situations, but right now, even Sebaim looked on the ruffled side.

'Floor runs out pretty fast,' Sebaim continued, taking a swallow of brandy from the flask that was always at his hip. 'Some sort o' stone spur out beyond that – and a beam or somethin' crosswise above. Cracked my damn head on it 'cos, like I said, even with a Duegar lamp you ain't seeing shit.'

'Any guesses?'

The man's face crinkled as he thought. 'Felt cooler,' he ventured. 'Just a touch, sound ran further. I reckon it's open, or part is. We're heading down so chances are it's there.'

'We're supposed to climb down to the next level?'

'I'd guess so. Mebbe the beams and spurs are everywhere, room to climb and a different sort o' test.'

'Traps too, mebbe.'

'Makes things a bit random, though,' Torril added, joining them right at the edge of the dark wall. 'This is a test, not a tomb. In a tomb you don't want the raider to see it coming 'cos you want to kill every fucker who comes in. But in this place, if there's no way of avoiding the trap, you're just testing a man's luck.'

'And what'd be the point of that?' Bade mused. 'It's comforting, but I remain a suspicious bastard. Time to play our trump card.'

'What's that?'

He grinned and gave a low whistle. Almost immediately there were cries of alarm as dragoons threw themselves out of the way.

'One of our number don't have eyes.'

*

Lynx sat on the floor, staring at the wall of darkness through the open doorway. A scuffed foot nearby startled him and he shuddered slightly before taking another swig of the whisky Atieno had been helpful enough to provide. Up ahead, Barra was somewhere in the darkness with Toil and Layir. All he could hear was muttered curses and the clack of Toil's staff on stone. Paranil seemed to be making notes on what they were reporting while beside him Aben slowly let a rope play out through his fingers.

It was all background noise to Lynx, drowned in the hot rushing sound that filled his ears. The warmth of whisky in his belly helped, but there was a metallic taste on his tongue and the jangle of nerves running through his mind was hardly dampened.

There was a yelp from up ahead and suddenly figures were darting forward. Lynx blinked and watched Aben lurch half into the dark, legs disappearing from view as he took the weight on his rope.

Lynx didn't move beyond a shiver. He was a bystander in his own body as everyone ran forward and hauled on the remaining rope behind Aben. The big man roared with the exertion but

Lynx didn't hear it. Everything was consumed by the darkness ahead, an indistinct sucking void that was drawing them all inexorably in. Lynx could feel himself moving slowly towards it, the world tilting beneath him as his courage ran downhill into the deepest black.

Stars burst before his eyes as something struck his cheek. A distant voice yelled his name in his ear, but Lynx could only blink at the encroaching darkness. When it met him it was a hammer-blow to the face and snapped his head backwards.

'Hey! Get up, you shitbag Hanese convict!' roared a voice from the blur ahead of him. 'Move it, help us!'

Lynx could feel the heat of their rage on his face, the spittle on his cheek. He stared blankly, the words filtering slowly through his brain but not fast enough for his assailant. A whip-crack slap across the face jolted him around. His vision went from black to purple to red then he could see again.

Lynx gasped as he saw the bustle of bodies through the doorway, a mad tangle of limbs and shouting – the back of Kas running to join them as a flush of anger filled his body. His hands tightened into fists, but sat there on the floor there was nothing to vent that rage on. As he lurched to his feet his wits seeped back into his mind.

He pushed his way forward and grabbed the end of the rope, adding his weight to those hauling back on it. With so many hands helping, the clamour died and Aben's voice could be heard from up front.

'Stop, hold there!'

The mercenaries did so and a moment later Toil staggered out of the dark, a small cut on her forehead to add to her current set of wounds and a manic gleam in her eye. The tension on the rope went slack all of a sudden and soon Barra and Layir were crawling towards them, half-supporting and half-hindering each other as they tried to stand.

'Down,' Barra panted. 'Definitely down.'

'What happened?' Aben yelled.

'Damn tilt-bar threw me!' She winced and pressed her hand to her side as she straightened, Layir taking much of her weight. 'Seemed solid 'cos my weight was holding it down as I probed. Lost my bloody gun in the process.'

'How far?'

Barra took two long breaths. 'Did I fall? Five, ten yards mebbe. Hard to tell in the pitch black. Think you saved my life there, Layir. My feet cracked against something hard, felt like pointed stone spurs below. You took the weight just in time.'

'What now?' the young duellist asked.

'Now I lead,' Toil said. 'Barra, you hang back, let Sitain do what she can for the pain.'

'It's not bad,' Barra insisted as Sitain stepped forward. 'Don't think anything's broken, just gonna be a mess o' bruises.'

Toil nodded and hefted her staff again. She untied the rope from around Barra's waist and attached it to her own, then crouched to look at Paranil's notes a moment. With a nod she set off into the black, calling the instructions aloud to herself as she went.

'Forward three paces, step ahead and right, duck down – crawl two steps.'

'Need a break?' Lynx asked Aben quietly.

'You sober?'

'Close enough.'

The man gave a cough of amusement. 'Close enough,' he repeated. 'Here you go then.' Aben handed the rope to Lynx who passed it around behind his hips to anchor it. Teshen took up the slack on Lynx's right and fed it through to him as Toil continued to talk, Paranil occasionally chiming in as she paused.

'The tilt-table should be there,' Barra barked out abruptly.

389

'I feel the back edge,' Toil confirmed. Her staff clacked around, feeling out her surroundings and soon she was moving again – this time much slower as she broke new ground. The path wasn't too complex; the myriad stone platforms, bars and slopes would have been simple to negotiate had she been able to see. However, the invisible pitfalls, twists and turns made it dangerous at every step – every surface being made of stone. Toil would know as well as any of them that even a small fall in the irregular stone maze could prove fatal.

After a while Toil was far enough away that it proved hard to hear her and Barra went back in, following the line of the rope until she could hear Toil clearly again and relay messages. It took them a good hour, but at last Barra reported that Toil had found the bottom, so far as she could tell in the dark. She anchored the rope and the mercenaries began to slowly follow – guided by Barra who had created a map of the obstacles in her mind by then.

It took almost another hour, but eventually it was Lynx's turn. He and Aben had taken it in turns to anchor the rope and when the time came he found himself more than a little reluctant to relinquish it to Aben.

'You don't want to be going last,' Aben said, gently unpeeling the rope from Lynx's hands.

'I get that pleasure,' Barra agreed. 'Now come on, Toil says the dark doesn't extend far once you're at the bottom.'

Lynx pulled his pack and gun-holster on to his back and meekly allowed Barra to usher him forward. Stepping into the blackness was like a punch to the gut, but she'd been expecting his reaction and didn't push him any further than the first step until he was ready. Instead the woman talked to him in a quiet, calm voice about nothing of consequence – just letting her voice soothe him the same way you'd calm a skittish horse.

Barra had a pleasant, young voice – a more cultured accent than Toil's, he now noticed, and a breezy assurance that proved easy to trust. She smelled of soap and sweat, the chalk dust on her hands a faint tickle at the back of his throat.

'Okay,' Lynx broke in, heart still pounding but his chest not so tight. 'I'm ready.'

'Good, I wouldn't want Toil to think I was monopolising your time,' she said with a girlish laugh. 'I'll go ahead and lead you on, as it were.'

Lynx ignored both comments, shuffling forward on command and suddenly incredibly aware of both the size of his feet and his unsteady balance. Under Barra's directions he made slow but steady progress, down, around, up and through the tangle of stone. It took just a few minutes before Lynx had lost track of their progress. He was so focused on keeping his balance and obeying instructions that he couldn't manage anything else.

After ten minutes he had developed a profound respect for Barra's brain on top of her athleticism – she led him without hesitation or mistake through the stone path. After longer than he had imagined he could bear in utter darkness, he was on the bottom and sank to his knees as his strength seemed to give out.

'Lynx?' he heard Toil say from the blackness. 'You okay?'

'Aye,' he said in a hoarse voice. 'Your girl's done good here.'

A hand touched his arm then, almost shyly, slipped into his and held it tight. Toil pulled him forward and took his other hand so they were facing each other. Lynx suddenly realised they were just inches apart in the dark and feeling as intimate as lovers. He took a long, slow breath and held it, not wanting to break the spell.

'We're almost there now,' Toil said after a longer pause than necessary, her voice as low as a bedfellow's whisper. 'Just come with me and you'll be through it.'

'Thanks.'

Toil slipped one hand free and pulled him close to her side as she turned, their hips brushing against each other's for a dozen steps until something seemed to give in the air around them. With a jolt Lynx realised they were clear and, while it was dark, they were surrounded by the familiar blue-veined rock glowing faintly in the light of a Duegar lamp.

He blinked and turned around, somehow forgetting to release Toil's hand straight away until he saw the faces of those watching.

'What's this now?' he wondered, slightly awed.

What he saw seemed to make no sense, just a jagged mass of lines and shadow that seemed to stretch indeterminately into the distance.

'It's a maze,' Kas said, shrugging. Her bow was in her hand, he saw, and all their mage-guns were drawn. 'What did you expect?'

Slowly the proportions began to take some shape around them. It was the same sort of chaotic tangle of stone slabs, blocks and projections as he'd just climbed through, but on a larger scale. How far it went Lynx couldn't tell, but they weren't in a forty-yard-square box now. Either they were on the bottom level of the labyrinth, or they were beneath it. Either way, they were open and exposed to whatever forces the Knights-Charnel had brought down there.

'Last test of the labyrinth,' Deern said with a nasty rattle of laughter. He patted his mage-gun. 'Kill all the other fuckers in here with you.'

*

Toil looked around at the forest of stone that surrounded them. Making out much detail was hard, but she had a decent enough idea of what she was looking at. This was the lower floor of the labyrinth and she was pretty sure she could see a stone wall off to her right. It was as dark as any city-ruin, however, that lack of moon or stars highlighting how deceptive it was to navigate only by a hand-held lamp. The silence was somehow all the more profound and without her even needing to give the order the others instinctively knew to only speak in whispers and keep the Monarch's lamp covered.

The ceiling was forty yards above their heads, the interior a madcap and lifeless landscape of mage-worked stone punctuated by blank, black columns just like the one they'd clambered down through. Even with their Duegar lamps causing the stone nearby to glow faintly, great slabs of shadow hung close all around them. Underfoot was a gritty layer of dust covering level stone that whispered with every step.

'Orders?' Aben said softly in her ear.

Toil looked back at the rest of the group. They were mostly huddled in the lee of a high thicket of weirdly twisting stone – shapes that hinted at tentacles as much as branches, but directly copied nothing that Toil had ever seen. There was space for people to work their way inside and find some sort of shelter. As Sitain was currently proving, it was also possible to climb on top and get a better view of what was around them.

'Final test,' she said, mostly to herself, 'and we're near the outer wall I'd guess.'

'So we're heading inward, to whatever's at the heart?'

'Through an open space – a degree of cover, but not so much as you'd want. This does look like a battle arena, doesn't it? So, like Deern said, anyone taking the prize has to make damned sure no one else is there to claim it.'

'But we don't know how many they are or who got here first.'

'And we're not all fighters,' Toil added grimly. She turned and approached the others, beckoning over Teshen and

Kas who'd strayed to the edge of the lantern-light. 'Listen up. Unless Lastani's got anything to add, we're heading towards the centre of this . . . whatever this is. We go in two teams and we expect a fight. Lynx, Kas, Sitain, Barra, Paranil, Haphori, Suth and Elei, you're with me – the rest, you're with Teshen. Take Sitain's lamp and let's try to keep a good twenty-yard gap, okay? Guns out and fingers off the triggers; bright light and noise will kill us if there's anyone near to notice.'

Everyone moved awkwardly into their assigned groups, Toil pulling Sitain and Teshen together in the middle to determine their course.

'I think that's the outer wall,' Toil said, pointing. 'Sitain?'

'Looks like it,' the night mage confirmed. She turned and pointed the other way. 'So . . . the middle is roughly that direction.'

'Terrain?'

'Mostly clear, but if we're keeping twenty yards apart we'll be getting separated by these stone bushes.'

'High ground?'

She shook her head. 'Nothing bigger than this.' She nodded towards the tangle they'd been keeping close to. 'Ten feet at most and not too hard to climb.'

'Can you see black spots on our path?'

'Yeah.'

'We want to skirt those. Last thing we need is someone lurking inside one, waiting for any noise to fire a burner at.'

'You're in the lead, Toil,' Teshen said, 'so if anything happens, we'll try to flank them.'

Toil nodded and waved her group forward without another word, keen to return to silence as soon as possible. They moved slowly, but far too noisily for her liking, especially Atieno dragging his lame foot. It was a disconcerting sensation for Toil – so many people beside her in the dark, and not purely reliant on her instincts. Sitain might be inexperienced, but, galling to Toil's pride or not, the young woman could see much further. It would be madness not to take her lead.

'Wait, what's that?' Lynx hissed, his words making the whole group stop dead. No one spoke for a long few moments until Lynx added, 'Is that a light?'

She followed where he was looking and realised he was right. It wasn't much, but there was some sort of glow in the distance. Underground and with all the obstacles here, it was hard to tell how far exactly, but by her guess this entire lowest chamber couldn't be much more than four hundred yards across.

'Come on then.'

'What about the black area?' Sitain said before anyone could move.

'Which one?'

'Almost dead ahead. About a room-length.'

Shit, hells and damn, that's not a decision I needed.

'Good place for an ambush,' Suth muttered. 'Three dragoons each with a burner stand at the outer edge and take one pace back. They fire on anyone they hear come close then back away.'

'Maybe we get lucky, maybe the light's something else.'

'Yeah, right,' Lynx said.

Toil paused to think for a while. *No, it'd waste too much time setting that up. Maybe Bade's got two Duegar lamps, but if there's a prize at the heart of this place why waste the time ferrying soldiers to outposts?*

'We can't announce ourselves, we've got to risk it.'

'Damn big risk.'

Toil found herself grinding her teeth in irritation. 'Anyone want to volunteer to sneak in and check?' she whispered sarcastically.

There was a pointed silence from behind her.

'Didn't think so.'

She continued on and the others followed her, embracing the risk of the lightless area wholeheartedly if it also gave them cover against whatever had a light shining on it. She gave a soft click of the tongue as she reached it, looking right towards the light of Sitain's lamp. An answering click told her that Aben had understood her message, whereupon they rounded the block of perfectly black ground and made for cover.

What in the name of . . . ?

Further ahead, perhaps fifty yards away, the stone was more visible – a lambent glow coming from somewhere within the random formations. It wasn't bright at all, midnight on an overcast night, but compared to the pitch black of underground it was *something,* some tiny order imposed on the tangle of darkness around them.

Toil hesitated. The dark rocks themselves appeared to be seamed with white, less than even the dull blue shine under a Duegar lamp, but she could make out the shape of nearer stone formations despite the light's source being hidden from view. Another type of stone she'd not seen before, or something else entirely?

'We keep going,' she whispered. 'Move closer and look for sentries. Might be we can catch them off guard.'

'And if we're spotted?'

'Then like our mascot said, kill anything that moves.'

Chapter 30

It was a long time before anyone could speak. Half the dragoons had fallen to their knees, some mouthing prayers, others merely gaping. Bade took another hesitant step forward and found himself grinding to a halt again, as though the dull glow ahead of him was a fire's heat he could barely stand to approach.

He tried to speak but it came out just as a croak. For a moment, Bade felt something touch his heart, something that stripped away all the cynicism and pragmatism of his life. What it exposed he couldn't say, but the aura around this stone clearing seemed to shine on some inner part of him he'd long forgotten.

'Pretty,' grunted someone beside him. 'What is it, then?'

Bade turned and stared at the man. 'What is it?' he echoed, astonished.

Sebaim shrugged. 'Some sort o' jewel, right?' The ageing scout looked far from impressed, while in the background several Knights-Charnel began to chant a prayer – stumbling over the words as they too felt what Bade was experiencing.

'It's . . .' Bade was lost for words and found himself flapping his hand in the direction of the light. 'How can you not tell?'

They had entered a ring of stone formations – a crazed mass of interlocking arches, obelisks and stylised trees a good thirty yards in diameter – and found the source of the weak light. At the very centre of a gently sloping hollow stood twenty or more short pedestals like the broken stubs of pillars. On each of those were five or six irregular shards of glowing crystal.

The largest was the size of his fist, most closer to a finger-joint, and all of them shone with a soft light that bore the faintest of tints. The nearest columns had a pinkish glint to their light, those behind were more yellow, while he could see two that bore crystals shining with a shifting, shadowy blue edge.

'Never seen glowing stones like that before,' Sebaim said, taking a few steps forward to squint at the nearest. 'Worth something, then?'

'Worth something?' Chotel gasped behind them. 'They're priceless!'

'That's the good one, right?'

'Sebaim, they're bloody God Fragments!'

'Oh. Definitely worth something.'

Bade advanced until he was almost close enough to reach out and pick one up. There were three pieces on the nearest pillar, irregular in shape but arranged in a way that could fit them together neatly.

'Pieces of the gods themselves,' Bade breathed, struck by renewed wonder. 'The biggest hoard I've ever seen, ever heard of! Do the Knights-Charnel even possess this many in their charnel vaults? Kastelian?'

'You think I've seen inside the vaults?' Kastelian croaked. 'Only the highest of Exalted would be permitted, and even then . . . Spirits below, this is a find for the ages!'

Bade reached out to touch one of the pieces. His fingers hovered over it, struggling to move those last few inches as a dull pressure began to build in his ears. Nothing painful, it felt almost like a low buzzing – the deep, distant sound of a giant hive of bees somewhere under his feet. He frowned at the shard as the noise shifted and changed to a faint rush of wind almost like voices, then the pressure on his hand lessened and he found himself able to pick the God Fragment up.

It was warm in his hand, his skin tingling like the fringe effect of a spark-bolt. The sound increased again, trembling up through the bones of his arm and making his hand shake. With a jerk Bade released it and dropped the fragment back on to the pedestal, blinking around at his companions as though just waking from a dream.

'So, God Fragments, eh? Interesting.'

Sebaim joined him at the pedestal and nudged one of the other shards with his finger. For a moment it pressed up against the other and they seemed to stick together, but then he prodded it again and the pieces fell apart.

'Aye, interesting,' Bade laughed. 'Never been one for the gods, eh, Sebaim?'

'Nope. Didn't think you was either.'

'I . . . I'm not. but, well . . .' He gestured at the pedestals. 'It's an incalculably valuable collection of actual holy relics – the shattered bodies of the gods themselves. Look, you see the different colours? This one's pinker than the others? This is a fragment of Catrac, god of passion and endeavour. Millions pray to him every day and you can just pick up a piece of his actual body right now.'

'Is that so? Well, it's an odd world. We got all of 'em here?'

Up ahead, within the array of pedestals, Kastelian laughed – sounding light-headed to the point of hysteria. 'All of them? I think so. Yellow for Veraimin, White for Insar, red for Catrac, green for Ulfer.'

'So the funny-lookin' ones are Banesh?'

Kastelian's laugh tailed off and he scowled at the pedestal Sebaim was pointing at. 'Banesh too,' he admitted at last before turning to Insar's fragments and pulling the pack off his back. 'Ditch any food you have left, wrap the pieces carefully.'

'Anyone else hear that funny noise?' asked one of Bade's crew, Sonna.

'We got company?'

'No, that sort o' buzzing.' The sharpshooter shook her head and scowled, looking uncomfortable.

'It's the fragments,' Kastelian explained. 'I've heard of it from those stationed in sanctuaries and vaults. The magic inside each and the tiny trace of divine presence that lingers still.'

'Just so long as I'm not going mad.'

'Come on,' Bade said, beckoning her forward. 'Let's find our way out o' here.'

The woman joined him, slipping her gun back on to her shoulder as Kastelian directed most of his troops to guard the perimeter. Bade led Sonna past the pedestals and through the rear break in the circle of tangled stone perimeter. They were close to the central column now, just yards short of the huge stone pillar that served as the main support for the labyrinth above.

To his intense relief, the light of his Duegar lamp picked out a change in the smooth blank walls of the central column. Not far from the stone circle there was an opening about ten yards across, a cut-away section that led to a circular room with Duegar glyphs inscribed on the walls.

A peaked dome roof of dark metal stood above it, supported by a dozen fat struts that ran into the ground at the edge of the room. The floor had a series of circles marked out in glowing blue light, but it was the centre of the room which drew his attention. On a spur of stone there stood a sphere made of shining silvery metal, just like those on the doors and again inscribed with the glyph for 'gift'.

'Looks like this is our way out,' Sonna commented.

Before Bade could reply the crash of a gunshot rolled out across the huge lower chamber, sounding not too far away.

The pair pulled their guns and edged back to the entrance of the room. This close they couldn't see much past the stone circle, but had a decent view of the ground on either side of it.

'Stay here, hold this room for us.'

'Got it.'

Come on, Toil, Bade thought as he headed back to the stone circle. *One more try at me, eh?*

*

'Who the fuck fired?'

'Shit, there's something out there!'

'What?'

'What's that?'

Fingers were pointed off into the darkness. Someone whimpered with fear, someone raised their gun and aimed before Teshen slammed a fist into their shoulder.

'Who fired?' he snarled, louder this time.

There was a moment of silence.

'Me,' admitted Brols. 'But I saw something, movement. It weren't human!'

'What then?'

The tattooed man grimaced. 'Dark, big like a mountain dog – but it weren't no hound.'

A cold sensation ran down Teshen's neck. *Oh hells, down here?* 'Thick grey body? Legs like spears?'

'It moved so damn fast I never got a good look, darted away like a spider.'

'Shit.' He craned his neck to look over their heads, trying to get a view all around. 'Which way?' Teshen asked, loading a sparker into his gun.

'Over there, went off that way,' Brols said, jabbing forward with the muzzle of his gun.

401

'Behind us? This just gets better and better.'

'Maspid?' Estal asked quietly.

'Sounds like it. Let's pick up the pace; Safir, you and Deern watch right, Estal, Layir and Brols behind. Shoal and Aben, you're left. Lastani, up front with me and Atieno. If it comes at us, throw up something to make it hesitate, Lastani. And pick your damn shots, these things hunt in packs so don't all you lot kill the first one five times over, okay?'

With Teshen leading the way and the others keen to match his pace, they wove a stuttering path through the strange stone formations towards the light. There came a skitter of movement behind them, but by the time Lastani had turned and summoned her ice magic, the noise had dissipated.

'Bear right,' Teshen whispered. 'Black patch ahead.'

He sensed half their heads turn towards the obsidian block of nothingness, everyone realising together that there could be a maspid waiting to ambush them there. Teshen walked with his head constantly moving, swinging left and right without much regard for where he was walking as he scanned the route ahead. Just as they drew level with the black patch Lastani stumbled and fell to one knee, uttering a brief cry of pain.

The group immediately crumpled in on itself, some members turning to see what was going on only to have others walk into them. As Teshen grabbed Lastani's arm and jerked her up before anyone could trip on her, he heard a clatter of feet on stone that he remembered all too well.

'Fuck!' he let Lastani drop back to the ground and swung his gun around, but it was too late. In a blur of movement and chaos something crashed into them. A man screamed, a gun went off and the single white flash of light illuminated a moment of death. The maspid had Brols impaled on its forelimbs – smaller than the ones they'd seen in Shadow's

Deep but still big enough to grab a man and drag him to the ground with ease.

Someone barged Teshen and threw his aim off just as he fired. The corkscrewing burst of lightning erupted from his gun and flashed off into the shadows behind. Sparks clawed at the maspid's carapace causing it to flinch and toss the gutted mercenary aside. With one sweep of a leg it hooked Layir's leg and pulled him off his feet. Safir fired and winged the creature, pulling his rapier in the next movement to slash at the limb snagging Layir.

From Teshen's left a figure loomed forward, Atieno. The mage wielded his heavy walking stick, despite the fact he carried a gun, and a shudder of twisting dark flashed forward. The magic swept around and over the maspid, the creature screeching and clicking madly at its touch. One coil caught an upraised forelimb and the chitin simply crumpled under its touch.

Another slashed across its eyeless head leaving ash-white scarring across the surface. Yet more flashed and glittered over its body. Blood burst out from its side as the maspid writhed and shuddered, back legs kicking savagely at the stone floor. The magic seemed to have torn something open in its belly and before anyone could even put an icer into its brain, the maspid fell still.

'Eyes open!' Teshen demanded as Atieno whimpered and sagged. 'There'll be more!'

The mercenaries contracted into a small knot, guns swinging back up again to face out. For a moment they were all perfectly still, panting with shock while Brols lay dead under their feet. No more maspids came, no more gunshots echoed out across the chamber. Teshen counted a dozen more heartbeats then made a decision.

'We move. Must've been a scout or something, but that noise'll attract anything or anyone here.'

He pushed his way past the kneeling Lastani and Aben who stood over her, gun levelled.

'Come on,' he hissed. 'Follow me.' Aben nodded and slid a hand under Lastani's armpit to lift her gently to her feet. Once she was up he gave a short whistle, presumably to signal Toil they were still alive and moving.

'Just what sort o' mage did you say you were, Atieno?' Teshen said as the tall man moved up alongside him, his limp all the more pronounced.

'I didn't.'

'Oh great, another stubborn prick. Keep that up and Anatin'll offer you a job.'

*

When the first gunshot went off, Lynx and the others stopped dead – guns raised. At the sudden flurry of fighting, he'd been about to run over when Toil clapped a restraining hand on his shoulder.

'Nothing we can do there, it'll be over by the time we find them.'

'And if it isn't,' added Kas, 'they'll likely shoot us themselves.'

'So let's make the most of it.' Toil unloaded her gun and replaced the ice-bolt with a burner. 'They've just waved a flag to announce their presence. Let's move quick and quiet, see if we can take Bade unawares.'

'That didn't sound like a gun battle,' Lynx said. 'Screaming usually comes after a gunshot.'

Kas nudged his arm with her bow, four arrows in her hand waiting to be nocked. 'Usually.'

'Aye, but there ain't many like you.'

'Aw, aren't you sweet? Now shift that hefty backside. We're not in burner range yet.'

Lynx nodded and they wasted no time in advancing as fast as they could. Up ahead the thickets of stone seemed to grow larger and denser – their edges highlighted by the faint glow in the air that seemed to have no direct source. Before too long they rounded one high formation that almost reached the ceiling and saw a longer curve of interlocking stone.

'Wait,' hissed Barra. 'I'm going up.'

'What?' Lynx asked, but Toil was already nodding.

'Wait till we fire if you can,' she said.

To Lynx's astonishment Barra slung her mage-gun over her head and started clambering like a monkey up the twisting parody of a tree they stood beside, despite her previous painful fall. The smooth stone sides proved no match for her agility and once Barra was a few yards off the ground Toil started off again.

'Hold,' Toil hissed after just half a minute. 'Look.'

Lynx took a moment to realise what he was looking at, but then he spotted the shapes of men huddled under the cover of a stone formation. They were too far to make out much detail, but clearly it wasn't Teshen's group. There were five he guessed, all looking off to Lynx's right where the commotion had taken place.

'Teshen will move wide,' Kas said. 'Skirt around fifty yards before advancing.'

'But still, they're ready for us,' Toil added grimly. 'They're only just within burner range here and we're exposed if we go any further.'

'Take the shot. If you miss, it'll still ruin their night vision,' Kas pointed out. 'Just give me a try first.'

Toil nodded so Kas stepped out a little, drew the bow full and paused, picking her target without having to worry about breeze. As she fired, Lynx saw only the briefest flash in the dark as the arrow sped off – silent compared to the detonations of a mage-gun. Toil was already aiming, gun held as high as she could to arc the burner shot without hitting the chamber ceiling. Lynx never heard the arrow strike, only caught the slight jerk as it struck one of the waiting soldiers, before Toil pulled the trigger.

A thunderclap tore the air as a fat stream of orange fire soared forward, dropping just short of the soldiers' hiding place but then it exploded into an expanding tide of flame. The others fired icers as the scene was lit up, but they didn't wait to see the result, the experienced among them dragging the others away. Mage-guns at night meant you announced your position to the enemy and unless you were firing earthers, your night-sight was gone for a while. Hanging around, half-blind, as you reloaded was often a fatal mistake.

They skirted back around a coiling mess of stone and hesitated, listening for noises other than the shrieks and crackling flames they'd left behind. Satisfied, Lynx led the way now – his commando training calling for swift movement before they could be outflanked.

From up above came the crackle of a sparker – Barra spotting someone just around the corner from them. There were shrieks from where it struck, but a cry elsewhere followed by the double-crack of icers elsewhere. White trails slashed through the dark up to her position and Barra gave a brief cry before they heard the sound of a body falling on to stone. Lynx broke into a run, Toil at his side. They rounded a spur to see two surviving Charnelers reloading.

Toil shot the first and the second fumbled his cartridge in his panic, dropping the thing on the floor. Sword drawn and gun forgotten, Lynx barrelled forward. The Charneler swung at Lynx with his empty gun, but he dodged it and chopped down at his head. A flash of movement made him spin around, two more Charnelers rounding a thick column of stone, but the Monarch's agent beat them both to the shot.

Suth strode forward with a pistol in each hand, firing in quick succession. One of the Charnelers fell, the other was winged, but Suth dropped her guns and pulled the second pair – her next shot killing the remaining soldier.

There was a breathless pause while she checked around and saw no further threats, then retrieved and reloaded her guns.

'Look, there,' Kas said, pointing. 'A break in the barrier.'

'Bottleneck, though,' Toil said. 'Let's skirt around, see if we can't find another way in.'

She nodded towards where the strange barrier curved away from them. It faded in the dark towards the immense bulk of the central column, looking like it penned in whatever was causing the dim light.

'We need to go all the way round,' Kas pointed out, 'otherwise we're crossing open ground.'

Toil agreed and they backtracked to steer a wide path around the curved stretch of stone. Just as they started to near the central column again they heard gunfire – the stuttered burst of groups exchanging shots this time. Toil didn't need to say anything to her companions; they upped their pace as one. If eyes were drawn elsewhere, they could move fast and they had to move faster if their comrades needed assistance. The added risks would just have to be ignored.

Toil led the way, scuttling like a crab from one obstacle to the next while the others covered her approach. From the darkness a gunshot rang out and a white trail sped past her shoulder to burst open a twisting spur of stone. Toil threw herself to one side as Lynx followed the trail back to its source and returned fire. The hammer-blow of more gunshots battered at his ears, icers punching forward through the night at whoever had fired on them.

He dropped behind a jutting slab and flicked the spent cartridge from his breech in one deft movement, loading another icer with a second. Lynx levelled the gun and tried to find a target in the dark, but couldn't see much. Staggered formations stood between the stone perimeter that stood higher than the rest, hiding any Charnelers from view. The dark outline of some sort of passageway entrance in the central column stood off to the left. As he watched, there was a flash of movement and an icer cut the night towards him. Lynx didn't have time to even flinch, but the shot went wide.

The man beside him gave a startled cough as he crashed backwards. Lynx turned to see Elei fall, black trails of blood spurting from his lips and a frost-rimed hole in his chest. Lynx gritted his teeth and sighted on the alcove's corner, firing blind into the dark before reaching for a burner.

'Sitain!' he called over his shoulder. 'Get forward.'

Not waiting for a reply, Lynx raised his gun again and fired the burner in the direction of the alcove. He knew it was going to fall short, but the flames still whipped around a nearer formation and a scream of pain came from the shadows beneath it. He didn't wait to reload as he ran forward, skirting behind Toil's position. The light of his burner shone briefly over the lower chamber – little enough to see by, but hurting the enemy's night vision for longer than he needed. Suth and Haphori followed him, Sitain hurrying behind them even as the fires died down.

'What is it?' Sitain yelled as she got closer to Lynx. She had a mage-pistol in her hands, but hadn't fired it yet to Lynx's relief. The young woman still couldn't hit shit at any distance, but wasn't stupid enough to try.

'If they fire burners, you better be ready,' Lynx replied. He stood and looked into the darkness ahead for a flicker of movement – firing another icer at the first twitch of shadow before ducking back down.

'Deepest black!'

He could see the naked fear on her face, but to be a mage in a gun battle gave her an advantage no one would expect.

'Cover!' Toil yelled, firing a sparker before advancing with Kas to the next obstacle. An icer snapped past Sitain's head, the flash of white making her yelp and drop. She crawled to where Toil had been, the darkness surrounding her now shifting and glittering as her night magic stirred.

Kas popped up ahead, sending an arrow into the darkness and hitting a Charneler just as they fired. A corkscrewing trail of white lashed at the ceiling above them, tearing dust and chunks of stone away. It pattered down like a tattered curtain between the fighting parties, punctured again and again by icers before dissipating.

Lynx stood to fire again, pulling the trigger just as he saw a burst of orange light. In the same moment Sitain screamed in fear, half-rising with her hands clawed. Lynx felt the fear sink cold in his belly as the burner streaked towards them. Just as it seemed too late a veil of shadow filled the air and the burner struck it full-on. Sitain's shrieks took on a greater intensity as a wall of fire erupted ahead of her fifteen yards wide, but somehow the night mage held it. Sitain staggered back under the impact, but before her concentration was broken the flames had been deflected up towards the ceiling and gone out, the magic that fuelled it spent.

That'll give 'em the shits, Lynx thought manically as he loaded another icer and scuttled forward to Sitain.

Ahead of him Toil broke off right, running at a crouch out of sight. Through the tangle of stone between them Lynx spotted the light of her spark-bolt a few seconds later. The lash of lightning whipped out to screams from those trying to flank them. Kas turned too, snap-firing shots past Toil – three arrows in the blink of an eye. Lynx heard another gunshot as he sought a target and offered a half-prayer that it was Toil's pistol going off.

'Suth, go right!' he yelled. 'We'll hold here!'

The gunfighter raced off without a word, pistol in each hand and coat flapping at her knees. Lynx loaded another burner and kept low, not wanting to waste his precious ammunition if the Charnelers had not held position. He glanced back and saw Haphori bent low over his gun, fumbling with just one good hand to reload.

'Haphori, here! Sitain, load for him.'

Lynx beckoned and unleashed his burner blind, using it as cover to change position. As he neared one stone formation it seemed to explode before him and Lynx was thrown to the ground, fragments of stone clattering over his already bruised body. Lynx hit the ground hard, distantly seeing the dark gouge of an earther's trail overhead as it tore through the stone.

He lay on his back, stunned, for a few heartbeats.

Banesh's chance, I'm not dead! Lynx realised slowly. He looked up at the stone sheltering him; half of it was smashed through. He struggled up to his knees and tried to keep as low as possible while Haphori returned fire. Sitain howled for him to get up while somewhere behind the fighting continued. Rapid crashes of gunfire indicated someone was still fighting on their right flank and keeping them alive.

He crawled to the next cover, icer darting through the air above as he went. Once safe, or *safer* anyway, Lynx flapped at his cartridge case with half-numb fingers before he could load his mage-gun again.

Not dead yet, he thought manically. *Let's hope Teshen's lot can say the same.*

410

Chapter 31

'Shift yourselves!'

Bade's words were unnecessary; the dragoons were already turning to run. Gunshots rang out on both sides, Sonna yelling from somewhere beyond the wall so two of Bade's crew, Dush and Koil, ran out the rear exit towards her. Through the opening, Bade saw the white flash of icers cut across their path and they skidded to a halt until Sonna had returned fire.

'Grab the rest!' Kastelian yelled to Bade from the other side. His remaining dragoons were still running out to reinforce the sentries. Kastelian grabbed the arms of two, pulling them back as the others disappeared out.

'Come on.'

With them in tow, Kastelain ran towards Bade. The Exalted was wild-eyed now. The clamour of battle filled the air around them but his eyes were still drawn to the God Fragments. Bade knew not to judge his friend for that. It wasn't just the awe of their presence Kastelian was feeling. He had his orders and the Lords-Sovereign would gladly sacrifice every dragoon there to secure this hoard – let alone Bade's irregular crew. The Pentaketh regiment was a fringe part of the Torquen so it could be deniable and disposable as much as to encompass troops too irregular to be part of any Militant Order.

But at the same time, those poor fuckers are more likely to sacrifice themselves, Bade realised. *Ask my lot the same and you'll get yer face shot off.*

'Quickly!' Kastelian snapped. 'Get the rest packed – not too many together, wrap them in clothing.'

'How exactly do you think we've been doing it up till now?' Torril grumbled, ignoring the furious look he received.

'What about those ones?' Chotel asked, pointing at Banesh's fragments.

'All of them!'

'I'll do it,' Bade said, hurrying over. There was a buzzing in his head from handling the fragments and that only worsened when he touched those of Banesh. The god of Chance and Change had been a quiet favourite of his – very quiet given his employers – but as colours swam before his eyes and the touch of the crystals seemed to burn his fingertips, Bade decided he wasn't enough of a gambler.

To the seven hells with you in future, Banesh, thought Bade as he scrabbled to finish. The chamber darkened as they went, tucking each piece away. Only when he'd nearly finished did Bade realise he could still see, that the darkness hadn't encroached far enough for sense to explain. The lambent light seemed to still hang somewhere in the air, the ghostly presence of the God Fragments lingering, though they were packed away.

With one piece left he found his hand wavering over it. Gunfire tore through the air still, but it was impossible to tell if Toil was about to fight her way through or already dead somewhere in the shadows. It was a thin shard, no more than an inch long, faint shifting shadows swimming through the blue-grey glowing crystal.

He left it where it was. Alone on its pedestal it seemed to gather the light to it and Bade realised he wanted Toil to live long enough to find it. To know exactly what she'd failed to reach.

'What about that one?' Kastelian called over as his two dragoons ran off laden with packs.

'Leave it – prize for second place!' Bade laughed.

'Is this about that woman?'

'What if it is? Bitch tried to gut me.'

The Exalted looked at Bade's expression and shook his head, realising his mind was set. 'It's Banesh's? Fine, just don't tell anyone. They make bad cartridges anyway.'

A great explosion tore through the air behind them and even Bade recoiled automatically – a cartridge belt exploding. Ahead of him the mage, Fork, shrank against one of the pedestals, overwhelmed by terror at the battle.

'Move!' Bade yelled, realising he'd need her to escape. 'Chotel!'

The big lieutenant swung three packs on to his back and grabbed the mage. An exploding cartridge case could swing the battle, and they were running out of time if it had been one of theirs.

Bade pulled out a pistol with his free hand and raced to the rear exit of the stone thicket where flames coated the nearby wall, casting an infernal light. He hesitated before running out, looking round at his remaining crew. With the four Knights-Charnel and one mage, they numbered eleven. Everyone but Fork had at least one pack containing God Fragments, but they didn't have far to run. The glyph-covered room had to be an escape route – Fork had confirmed his suggestion but they'd not been able to test it out without gathering the fragments.

It'll either be victory or one embarrassing death, Bade realised as he loaded a light-bolt into his pistol and fired it away into the dark, calling to his crew as he did so.

The searing white light tore through the dark and burst on a stone formation about thirty yards away. Bade's night vision was obliterated by the blade of light, but Dush had covered his face as soon as Bade's warning came. He only had a moment of blinking blind at the after-trails before a hand grabbed his elbow and directed him forward. They ran, Dush firing wildly as they went, and stumbled into the circular room of glowing glyphs.

'Do it!' Bade roared as more gunfire came from all around. 'Get it moving!'

Distantly he sensed flashes of light streaking past him and chunks of stone bursting overhead. He dropped to his knees, still unable to see much, but when Fork grabbed the shining sphere in the centre of the room it cast enough light for them all to be dazzled.

A great grind of stone rang out from the walls then the floor seemed to lurch around him. He heard someone fall and others stagger. Koil yelled and there was a scrabble of boots as a body was pulled across the floor. The lurching sensation came again and turned into a sharp twisting motion. He felt them jolt upwards and the glowing concentric circles on the floor blossomed with light.

The clatter of metal and gunfire seemed to merge in his disorientated ears. Bade turned, drunkenly trying to get his bearings, but before he could there was another twisting lurch upwards and this one didn't stop, the sphere shining brighter than ever as Bade fell on to his back. There was a sudden pressure on his shoulders as the movement pulled the whole chamber up, but that didn't stop Bade. He couldn't help himself – he opened his mouth and laughed long and loud as he pictured the fierce beauty of Toil, contorted into rage somewhere below.

'Enjoy being left behind in the dark, Toil!' he yelled over the sound of grinding stone and fading gunfire, not caring if she could hear him. 'You must be used to it by now!'

Lynx saw the flash and swirl of light up ahead. For a moment he wondered what new horror the labyrinth might have conjured now. Then he realised it was moving steadily up and vanishing from view.

Gods-dammit, are we too late? Have they escaped?

In the next moment a renewed burst of gunfire rang out. He leaned around a stone column as the jagged path of a sparker tore across his view. It illuminated a man in a Charneler uniform cowering behind another formation as sparks exploded all around him.

Screaming hells, they left a rearguard!

He raised his mage-gun again, the weapon by now radiating a familiar cold metallic scent. Lynx fired and watched the icer slam into his target's shoulder, throwing him to the side as it shattered flesh and bone.

'Come on,' he hissed to Sitain, not waiting for a reply. Lynx reloaded and stalked forward towards the rear of the stone circle. Sitain followed, mage-pistol in hand. They moved in short bursts while sporadic shots pierced the dark to their right, but Lynx ignored those for the time being. As they reached the break in the circle he paused and checked the alcove where he'd seen the blue light shining.

It was an empty space now – no trace of the Charnelers he'd been exchanging gunfire with. They really had vanished, some Duegar mechanism doubtlessly carrying them back to the surface. It was bigger than he'd realised, a circular room easily large enough to accommodate the squads left behind to cover their escape.

So what was worth abandoning your men for? Lynx didn't want to know the answer, not when it had just been whisked away from under their noses.

He risked a look around the corner. In the faint light he made out four Charneler uniforms, the black-and-white quartered tunics easy to spot. Quickly he pulled the icer from his gun's breech and replaced it with a sparker.

'Get ready,' he whispered to Sitain.

The young woman's eyes widened but she nodded and held her pistol with both hands. Lynx ducked back around the corner and took aim. The Charnelers were at the far side of the stone circle – the other side of some grand pedestals – but there was enough space to shoot between. He pulled the trigger and felt the sparker kick his shoulder hard. A stream of lightning raced out to engulf first one man then the next.

Out of nowhere a tall figure loomed around the corner, swinging a mage-gun up to shoot Lynx at point-blank range. Sitain yelped and fired wildly, missing both men by several feet but it was enough to make the Charneler recoil. For a moment he looked astonished that he was still alive – surprise turning to alarm as Lynx threw himself forward.

With his spent gun Lynx battered the man's weapon aside, but lost it in the process so he dipped his shoulder and charged. He hit the man square in the gut and drove forward, letting his bulk slam the man back and knock him off his feet. As the Charneler fell, Lynx hauled his sword from its scabbard with a roar and lunged.

He stabbed the man in the heart just as a stuttering burst of darkness swept across his eyes. Lynx wavered as his head swam and only the sword impaling the man kept him upright. Drunkenly he looked left and saw another Charneler, a woman with a dragoon sergeant's markings, falling to her knees.

The woman's eyes rolled up as Sitain stepped forward again, hand extended with a shuddering aura of night magic surrounding her splayed fingers. A mage-pistol dropped from the Charneler's fingers as she flopped forward, unconscious even before her head cracked against the stone floor.

As Sitain released her magic, Lynx scrabbled on the ground for his gun. After a few attempts he managed to drag it towards him and fumble the breech open. He loaded an icer and used the gun to push himself upright, desperate to not just sit still when there were enemies around. As he staggered towards the stone columns in the centre, though, the figures who burst into the stone circle on the other side were Cards – Safir and Deern.

Lynx gasped with relief and clutched at the pedestal until his head cleared enough to stand. As more of their company arrived, he realised the battle was over, the guns falling silent. He looked around at the pedestals, each one two feet in width and rising to just below chest height. Only one of the further pedestals had anything on it, however, a tiny piece of glowing crystal.

'Is this fucking it?' Deern exclaimed, cradling a wounded left arm. 'All that cocking around with numbers and bastard traps, and there's shit-all here?'

'They're gone,' Lynx said, leaning back against his pedestal. 'Back this way, some sort of magic carried 'em up.'

'They took everything?' Safir asked as Toil stormed in behind Lynx.

'Mostly I guess,' Lynx said, nodding at the one remaining piece.

Toil stormed up to it and looked at the shard of crystal, but made no attempt to pick it up.

'What is it?' Deern said through gritted teeth as he wound a strip of cloth around his bicep.

Toil didn't say anything, but even through his pain Deern paused and gave her a cautious look. The woman had gone very still, hands bunched into fists, and Lynx realised she was fighting to control her rage. He didn't need to see Toil's face to see how close to exploding she was and the other mercenaries sensed it too, each one edging back and keeping quiet.

More Cards filed in, several carrying wounds and burns. Safir's kilt was charred all the way down one side, his hands black from beating the flames out. Aben and Teshen looked unhurt, Atieno likewise but his face was thunderous and his limp more pronounced, while Estal had a flesh wound to her leg. Lynx felt a momentary lurch in his gut, but then Lastani crept through as well, her clothes dirty and torn but uninjured.

From behind Toil, Kas and Suth appeared – Kas clutching her side.

'Haphori?' Lynx asked. 'Thought he was right behind us?'

'Went back for Paranil,' Kas explained.

'Shoal? Brols?' he forced himself to ask, turning to the rest.

Teshen shook his head. 'Both dead. Layir, Aben,' the grim-faced man said after a grave moment, 'give me a hand. Let's not leave our own down here.'

As they returned the way they'd come, Haphori limped in, half-carrying Paranil who clutched his stomach and panted like a dog.

'Got a bad one here,' Haphori called, wincing as he spoke. 'Heard him crying out, must've caught a stray shot.'

That seemed to break the spell for Toil. She spun away from the crystal and went to kneel at Paranil's side.

'Dammit,' she said through gritted teeth, 'I told you to keep out the way!'

'Thought I did,' he moaned. 'Then it felt like someone punched me.'

Sitain had already joined them and was in the process of ripping open his tunic. Lynx didn't look; he'd seen enough gut-shots in his life. Even with her night magic to ease the pain, either Paranil would be very lucky or he'd be dead.

'So,' Deern began hesitantly, 'what *is* that thing?'

418

Atieno hobbled forward. 'Gods on high!' he breathed. He opened his hand and seemed to make a small gesture – the shard darted through the air to slap into his hand. 'It's a God Fragment – a piece of Banesh himself!'

'How do you know?'

Atieno gave him a tired smile. 'Oh, I know.'

'Shit and fire,' Deern hissed. 'You're a tempest mage?'

'For my sins, yes.'

'Remind me to never play cards with you, then! The magic of change, eh? Thought that was just a myth. Don't tell me, yer best friend's a dark mage?'

'Dark mages are no one's friends,' Atieno said with a scowl.

He raised the God Fragment to inspect it more closely then wrinkled his nose and closed his hand around it. The light in the air dimmed a touch.

'Hey now!' Deern yelled. 'If that's our only prize, why're you keeping it?'

Before anyone could start an argument, Suth stepped forward with a mage-pistol in each hand.

'I don't care who wants what,' the woman said in a dangerous voice. 'Any relics found are the property of the Monarch – and before any of you get any ideas, if I don't live to report back, your whole company's under death sentence. I'm your only chance now.'

'Elei's dead?'

She inclined her head, face betraying no emotion.

'Guess we better wrap you in kisses then,' Deern spat. 'You can use Lynx as a shield if you like.'

'It's not a prize,' Toil broke in loudly, stepping back while Sitain placed her hands over Paranil's wound. 'It's a parting fuck-you from Bade, just to tell us what he's escaped with. Atieno, you and Lastani go check that room out, see how they escaped. Suth – if it's a fragment of Banesh, it's best in

Atieno's hands, but feel free to follow him everywhere. Lynx and Kas, check the dead; we don't want to be low on ammo if we're heading up into a battle.'

Lynx nodded and went about his task, searching the soldiers he'd killed with a sparker first. As he went about the unsavoury task, Lastani walked into the centre of the stone circle and put her hands on her hips – the shock of battle fading now that she was presented with the heart of the labyrinth.

'Something wrong?' he asked, the look on her face less than impressed.

'I . . .' She gestured at the stone circle. 'I don't know, but I wasn't expecting this.'

'What, then? Probably looks more impressive with a whole load more God Fragments lying out here.'

'But the labyrinth is supposed to be old,' she said, '*really* old – I mean predating the fall, by some thinking.'

'What's your point?'

The young mage gave him a level look. 'Even assuming that was wrong, that the labyrinth really *was* built to protect a cache of fragments, why?'

'Eh?'

'What's the hold-up?' Toil called, leaving Paranil's side to approach them. 'Something wrong?'

'Does this not *all* strike you as wrong? Somewhat unimpressive?'

'Aye, well some ruins are like that. All dick and no balls.'

The analogy seemed to trip Lastani's thought process for a while, long enough for Lynx to catch up with her thinking.

'So,' he said hesitantly, 'you'd expect there to be more than just this? What if it was just a contest – an arena to find some lord's champion or something?'

'Because it's huge!' Lastani pointed out. 'Not the size of a city-ruin maybe, but big enough that it'd have taken decades of work – hundreds of stone mages alone. Too big for something so simple.'

She gestured around and Lynx realised she had a point. The stone circle was impressive in its own way, there was no doubt about that, but as the culmination of a gigantic stone puzzle-box? He had to admit, even he could have thought up something better.

'Mebbe there's no point showing off to whoever makes it here?' he ventured.

'Either the labyrinth was created to protect something,' Lastani said, 'or it was a contest ground, yes? If the former, why leave whatever you were protecting out in the open on stone pedestals? If the latter – you've just built a huge stone cube, why stop at some suitable grandeur for the victors?'

There was a moment of quiet, broken by a groan from Paranil. They all looked over to see Sitain sit back on her heels.

'I've done what I can to slow the bleeding,' she said, 'but Himbel's barely started to teach me. If you've got exploring to do, get going.'

Toil nodded. 'The room back there,' she said, beckoning for the others to follow her. Lynx finished pulling cartridge cases from the dead inside the circle and slung them all over his shoulder before following Toil's group, removing the ammunition as he went and emptying them all into his own case.

He scooped up two more of those he and Sitain had dealt with, suddenly remembering the woman might only be unconscious as he pulled hers off. He checked for a pulse and found one.

'Alive,' he pronounced. 'She'll be out for an hour or two, no?'

The young mage looked back with weary eyes. 'At least.'

'Sure the Monarch will have some questions for her. Keep an eye on her, okay?'

When Lynx caught up with Toil, she stood with Suth and the mages at the edge of the opening – holding her Duegar lamp high. The bluish seams in the rock were there as expected, but they twisted and coiled upwards in a deliberate way he'd not seen before. Leaning forward Lynx realised they stood at the base of an enormous shaft that stretched further than the lamp's light could reach – presumably all the way to the upper chamber.

'How do we get up, then?' he asked.

Lastani pointed to the floor. There was a single silver disc in the centre with the familiar 'gift' glyph inscribed on it. That was all Lynx could see in there – despite the dull blue glow to the rock it was too dark to make out much detail.

'Got your white light, Suth?' Toil asked.

The Monarch's agent nodded and pulled the shining oval lump from her backpack. Its white light bathed the bottom of the shaft brightly enough that they all had to look away, dazzled. When they could see again, Lynx realised there was something else there – something hidden by the darkness.

'What's that?' he breathed, pointing at another disc on the floor – this one made of a similar black metal to that which encased Toil's lamp. 'Those,' he corrected himself a moment later, realising there wasn't just one but seven discs, set in a ring around the silver one.

'Something else,' Toil whispered reverently. 'Lastani, can you read them?'

The woman walked forward, going around the circle as she stared at each. 'I think so. They're names – Duegar names of elementals.'

'Seven?'

She nodded. 'Stone elemental – troll, to the uninformed,' she said, pointing at one. 'Firedrake, thunderbird, shadowshard—'

'Falesh?' Lynx broke in, remembering the word.

'Correct. That's the leviathan, the earth elemental, and that one is the icebear. The other two I'm not sure – judging by the glyphs I'd say wind and light, but I've never heard of the elementals.'

'So do we choose one?'

Lynx glanced up at the darkness above – more distant with the white light unveiled but still there. 'Just get it right first time,' he muttered. 'This place doesn't encourage mistakes.'

They stood for a moment in silence, then Toil followed in Lastani's footsteps around the circle. Atieno took a step forward, across the threshold, and stopped with a surprised grunt.

'What is it?'

The mage looked up with an expression of wonder. 'I'm not sure,' he said hesitantly, raising his hand. It was the one he held the God Fragment in. Slowly he opened his fingers and the shard of crystal was revealed, hovering slightly above his skin.

'I felt it move,' he explained.

'Well, what now?'

Atieno shrugged. His palm was flat, the shard unrestrained but not moving.

'Toss it forward,' Toil suggested.

The mage of tempest did so and for a moment it looked like it would just clatter to the floor, but it stopped halfway and trembled in the air for a long moment. It slowly sank at an angle – coming to rest over one of the glyphs Lastani couldn't name, the one she thought represented a light elemental.

The shard halted in the centre of the metal disc and for a moment nothing happened. Then silently it began to glow with light. Lynx automatically backed off a few steps.

'I thought someone said this place was even older than the gods?' Atieno muttered.

'It is,' Lastani replied. 'Perhaps there is an affinity between them, either that or the magic in the fragment is enough to activate it.'

With a whisper of polished stone the floor turned and started to fall away on one side, chunks dropping down into the ground to form steps leading to a level below.

'Oh, Sotorian Bade,' Toil whispered, 'I think you're about to feel very silly indeed.'

Chapter 32

Toil retrieved the God Fragment from the disc to see if doing so affected anything. It didn't appear to so she handed the shard back to Atieno, who tucked it carefully away, and headed down.

The steps spiralled through a cylindrical shaft, walls decorated with interlocking sweeps of silvery metal. The familiar blue seams in the rock shone brighter than Lynx had ever seen before. Even in the white light of the Monarch's lamp, he could see the lines that blended into the normal organic flow with deliberate artistry. He could pick out stylised trees, animals, what appeared to be constellations and complex glyphs more ornate than the simple one-word symbols he'd seen elsewhere in the labyrinth.

'Any idea what this all means?'

'Not a clue,' Toil said absently. 'Right now, I don't care.'

'Why?'

''Cos there's light up ahead.' She hesitated and glanced back at him. 'Let's call the rest, we stick together down here.'

'What about Paranil?'

'Either he can be moved or he's already dying,' she said, grim-faced. 'He'll want to see what's down here whichever is the case.'

They quickly returned and recalled the others, Toil explaining that they weren't heading back to the surface quite yet. The prospect of not following Bade didn't seem to impress some, but when she revealed they'd found a hidden entrance, any objections melted like shadows from a flame. As she'd predicted, Paranil, fearing he was dying, insisted on accompanying them so Aben passed his weapons and pack to Lynx before picking the small man up.

'Hardly the first time I've had to carry the clumsy sod through some ruin,' he explained. His attempt to lighten the mood fell on distracted ears, Toil already leading the way back to the stair with Lastani and Suth eagerly at her heels.

Lynx kept close to them, preferring the white light Suth carried, while the rest followed under Sitain's lamp. The stair wound two full turns before opening on to another sloping tunnel seven or eight yards wide. Set at two-yard intervals down each side were alcoves containing spheres of milky glass the size of a man's head. They emitted a very faint glow, barely visible in the lamplight until Lastani reached up to one and brushed it with her fingers, whereupon it brightened considerably. A soft white light washed over them; swirling within that was a rainbow of other colours.

Toil barely looked back, striding ahead of the rest in her eagerness to see where the tunnel led. It arced left in a long shallow spiral that Lynx guessed took them all the way around the huge central column. The light-spheres grew steadily brighter as they went – reds, blues and greens slowly drifting over the pale stone corridor – until Lynx could see it coming to an end ahead and opening out on to a dimmer space.

At the end of the tunnel Toil ground to a halt, staring in wonder. The rest of the company shuffled up beside her and stopped too, at the threshold of where the tunnel opened into a cavern. Before them was an enormous vaulted dome a hundred yards across and almost as high, with eight great buttresses carved like stylised trees meeting at the top. In the very centre of the cavern stood a small island surrounded by a narrow moat of glimmering water – but it was the massive stone tree at the centre of the island that drew all eyes.

The huge trunk split into three thick main branches which each split several times more. The ends of the branches tilted down, putting Lynx in mind of an ancient willow tree, though it was bare of leaves. The stone of the tree itself was paler than the grey granite bedrock that the labyrinth had been made of – near white and seeming to shine by comparison. The trunk bore seams of white crystal that suggested the grain of a tree's bark, glittering as though the tree's core was dancing motes of starlight. It cast a pale radiance that the water seemed to gather and magnify while at the base of the wall all around were more light-spheres, fifty or more Lynx guessed, casting a weak speckled white across the floor.

The blue mineral decoration continued out from the tunnel like trails of ivy, reaching all around the room. Lynx could see constellations described in it on the dome itself high above, cut through by a huge representation of the Skyriver and all glowing in the dim space.

After a long moment, Toil recovered herself and headed inside, turning full circle to take in the proportions and decorations. Lost in wonder at the sight, she didn't seem to notice Lastani and Atieno passing her to go to the very edge of the moat and peer into the water. Lynx joined them. It was shallow, no more than a yard deep, and he found it hard to look down with the distracting bulk of the stone tree looming overhead. Closer now, he could see that it was the work of exceptionally talented stone mages echoing the form of a real tree, but maintaining an ethereal simplicity.

'What is it here for?' Lastani whispered reverently.

Atieno smiled and nudged her arm gently. 'You're supposed to be the expert here.'

'I . . . I never expected this.'

'The better question,' Lynx said, 'is why was this hidden?'

'When a cache of God Fragments were left in plain sight,' Atieno added.

'Can you see any writing?' Toil said, finally joining them.

Her face was flushed with excitement, the relic hunter's enthusiasm returning in force. Beside her was Aben, who set the grimacing Paranil down, supporting his head and shoulders so the man could see the tree better. Once on the floor the scholar's pain couldn't eclipse his delight and wonder at the cavern.

'Writing? Anyone?' Toil turned to look at the rest of the group who had spread around the walls, circling the moat as though preparing a siege on its secrets.

'Nothing here,' Safir called.

Lastani pointed at the tree's trunk. 'Look, worked into the design.'

For a moment Lynx saw nothing – then all of a sudden it clicked into place. Not a small disc this time, but the curve of the tree's branches had been subtly worked into the form of a glyph. Even in his ignorance he recognised it – just like all the doors they'd passed through.

'Gift,' he breathed. Lynx looked down. 'Can we cross the water?' he said dubiously.

It looked strange to his eyes, clear but not quite natural with its glimmering silvery quality. After a while he realised there were also tiny dots of colour scattered thinly through it, each one no more than a mote of dust but containing its own rainbow. The water was perfectly still, but contained some innate energy within it that seemed to create facets and ripples below the surface – reflecting, distorting and somehow even magnifying the dim light.

'Try it,' Deern suggested.

'You try.'

The scrawny man laughed. 'Toil's the one leading the way.'

All heads turned towards her. She didn't notice at first, so lost was she in the glyph design, but, when she realised, Toil scowled at the lot of them.

'Let me,' Paranil croaked.

'You sure?' Toil said after a pause. It wasn't lost on her that he was looking bad, the wound to his gut still leaking blood despite Sitain's efforts to staunch the flow.

'Yes.'

She eased him to the water's edge and moved his hand so it slipped into the water. Paranil gave a sharp gasp and his fingers splayed as though pained, but when Toil jerked his hand back out it was untouched. The water, however, splashed on to his sleeve and there was a bright light – a flash – and then the sleeve was burned clean through. The skin underneath was untouched, but the cloth started to disintegrate to nothing. The whole cuff had completely vanished by the time whatever was happening had stopped, leaving Paranil with a ragged sleeve but a pristine hand.

'It's okay,' he whispered. 'Sharp at first, like a frost, but not exactly painful.'

'Is it just me,' Lynx began, 'or is your hand cleaner than before?'

They all peered down.

'Gods, it is,' Toil said, 'look, even under his nails. The hand's perfectly clean.'

'A purification rite,' Lastani said in a voice of wonder. 'All Duegar rituals had them, but this must literally wash the skin clean too! Of cloth too, even.'

Deern laughed loudly off to the right. 'You heard the woman!' he announced loudly, dropping his gun. 'Get yer kit off, boys and girls. Time to show what yer holding, as Anatin's so fond o' saying.'

429

Toil watched the chuckling mercenary as he shed his clothes with surprising enthusiasm. Looking around, no one had followed Deern's lead, but curiously that didn't seem to dissuade him at all. They'd had little contact since their little talk on the ship, but she had to admit Deern had surprised her. Given most of the rest of the Cards had been buzzing on one narcotic or another, she'd assumed Deern would have taken the opportunity to avoid helping in any way. Instead he seemed to be relishing the challenge. She doubted it was out of any feelings of guilt, though, so for the time being Toil had to assume it was egotism driving Deern.

Turns out you're not a gutless piece of shit, Deern, she thought to herself as he hauled his shirt off to reveal a scarred, rangy torso. *Still a piece of shit who goes out of his way to be a bastard, but some might say I shouldn't criticise on that front.*

'What's wrong? You all shy?' Deern asked as he kicked off his boots. 'Or better at jumping than I am?'

He nodded to the moat, more than four yards wide.

Barra could have made it, Toil thought sadly before biting her tongue hard. *Dammit woman, no time for that! She's dead and there's fucking nothing you can do except make Bade pay.*

'We're waiting for you, Deern,' Toil said. 'To see if you die first.'

'Fair enough, just don't think I'll wait around for any o' you gibbering fools if there's something worth having.'

Once he was fully naked Deern stared defiantly around at his comrades before gingerly dipping a foot into the water.

'Shitting hells o' dark!' Deern exclaimed, juddering at whatever was being done to his foot. But after a moment he stopped and inspected it.

'Well?'

'Well, that were fucking weird,' he said, bunching his toes experimentally. 'More'n a bit tingly, that. I'll give equal odds between me passing out and getting the horn if I dip my balls in.'

Toil shuddered at the image in her mind. 'Please don't.'

'He, ah . . .' Lastani blushed furiously, but the academic in her won out. 'You should get entirely under – let it cleanse every part.'

Deern blew out his cheeks. 'Aye? Well let no man say I wasn't ever up for the rough stuff.'

With that he slipped into the water, first one leg and then the other. His eyes were wide and bulging by the time it reached his balls; not quite pain, Toil guessed, but some intense sensation engulfing his body. Deern gave a roar and shook his head like a dog, the muscles in his arms taut.

'Ulfer's hairy cock! This . . .'

Words failed him at that point, but clearly the sensation started to fade and with a manic grin he closed his eyes and ducked his whole body under the water. He rose like a man scalded, bellowing madly and limbs flailing, but soon even that subsided and he just stood there panting – too overwhelmed to even make another joke.

Eventually he caught his breath and looked around at the others. 'Spirits below, you lot ought to try this. It's a new one on me, but godspit and damnation, what a rush!'

That seemed to decide it for them all and even Lastani started pulling her clothes off in her eagerness to get to the tree. Modest propriety had never been a major factor in Toil's life so she'd been ready to shed them as soon as Deern failed to fulfil Himbel's wishes and die horribly.

It was a surprise to see Lastani strip, though. The discomfort was clear on her face, not least because she was standing between Atieno and Lynx – two large and imposing men who were similarly naked – but her determination overrode

431

everything. Soon Lastani stood clutching her shirt to herself to preserve a few more moments of modesty, while Deern leered on general principle.

Toil slipped into the water and gasped as every strand of hair and inch of skin seemed to blaze with life. Not painful but an intense tingle that wrapped itself around her and set her nerves aflame – driving the breath from her lungs. She saw Kas, waist-deep and eyes widening, give a short squeal of surprise. Their eyes met and they shared a slightly hysterical laugh before Toil ducked herself under and came up shrieking.

Her skin felt hot and cold at the same time, taut when she moved but the tension and lingering aches in her muscles had melted away. She kept her eyes straight ahead, careful not to look at Lynx as she felt her nipples harden in a most delicious way under the water's effect.

Just like Paranil's hand, though, she felt scrubbed clean and, as she inspected her body, Toil saw the cuts and bruises she'd picked up in the last day heal up into pink new flesh. Even her head felt clearer, the lingering dullness that had followed Crown-Prince Tylom hitting her was gone and, looking around, Toil saw she wasn't the only one to have healed.

'Aben,' she called, 'help me with Paranil.'

Together they stripped Paranil as carefully as they could then lifted him into the water. The small man screamed louder than any of them had, almost convulsing under the combined effect of the water and his wound. Slowly that subsided and before long he was ready to be fully ducked under – closing his mouth to let the water flow over his face like a newborn's first blessing.

That seemed to be all he could take and when Aben raised him up again a moment later, Paranil had gone limp. Aben placed him on the island side and checked his jugular, pausing a moment before nodding to Toil.

'Probably for the best with a wound like that,' Toil commented.

She leaned over the man to inspect his wound. It hadn't closed, but no more blood flowed out despite the removal of Sitain's rough dressing. Perhaps the water would heal even something life-threatening; right now she could only hope.

They all clambered out on the island side and looked up at the glittering stone tree, fifty or sixty yards high by Toil's estimation. It seemed bigger now they were on this side. After a while, Toil realised everyone was waiting for her – or rather, they were all standing around looking slightly self-conscious. Lastani was just staring at the stone by her feet, hugging herself, while Sitain looked perhaps even more uncomfortable.

As Toil looked around them she caught sight of Lynx, staring fixedly at the tree. The last time she'd seen him naked had been in a cell surrounded by a good few of the male Cards. He'd hardly looked at his best there and, she had to be honest, he probably didn't right now either.

Still, he's a solid lump of muscle, Toil reflected. *That belly doesn't look so bad when it's attached to a big frame. Shame this water doesn't heal scars too, though. Those bastards really made a mess of his back – doubt I've ever taken a beating to match the pain he must have felt.*

Her skin still felt the afterglow of whatever the water had done and the urge to press her body against his was almost overwhelming, but she fought it and eventually won out.

'Lastani,' she croaked. 'The glyph, if you please?'

The young woman gave a cough of surprise before she nodded and scurried forward.

'As before?' she said.

'Gift,' Toil confirmed with a nod.

Lastani reached out and pressed her palm against the stone tree trunk, closing her eyes. There was a flicker of cold on the air as her magic surged out and suddenly the dim light in the cavern intensified. Before Toil could say anything Lastani had taken a step back, mouth open with surprise – and then the water surrounding the island leaped up in the air.

The air turned silver with a blinding flash. Toil heard someone cry out, but her own throat was dry as she watched the water stream upwards to the branches of the tree – becoming long fronds of light trailing down like a willow's hanging branches. The shining water twisted into the shape of narrow leaves as it swirled up through the air; a hundred thousand shards of light turning and winking in the gloom of the cavern.

It was painful to behold after so much time in the dark, but Toil couldn't tear her eyes away. She turned around, looking almost straight up at the glinting trails of liquid hanging impossibly down towards her, some almost close enough to touch. Her hand stopped short of doing so, afraid to disturb something so fragile and beautiful.

Then the water fell back without warning, blazing silver light slapping down against the party's bare skin and driving everyone to the ground. The pain overwhelmed her. Toil barely cried out before she felt darkness engulf her mind.

Chapter 33

Lynx opened his eyes and immediately regretted it. Strange angular shapes loomed over him in the gloom, blurred and wavering as he tried to make sense of what he saw. His skin tingled, his muscles ached and his eyes had ghosting trails of light overlaying everything. How long he'd been unconscious was anyone's guess – it felt like he was emerging from a long night of fever-sleep where the hours had given him no rest.

Or like some bastard night mage just put me down again, Lynx thought with a growl of anger cutting through the confusion in his mind.

He groaned and tried to move, rolling on to his side to heave himself upright. As he reached out a hand, it met soft, yielding flesh. Lynx froze, then carefully withdrew his fingers from whoever's buttock it was.

'Good decision,' Sitain croaked softly.

Gods, did she put me down? Lynx wondered for a crazed moment, until he remembered the rush of glittering water, the fronds of light hanging from the stone tree.

He mumbled an apology and eased himself up, blinking at the strange flashes of light smeared across his vision. The line and shape of the figure ahead of him slowly came into focus and he quickly looked to one side as Sitain sat up, an arm self-consciously across her breasts.

'What happened?' he heard Kas groggily ask.

Deern's voice cut through the muzzy confusion like a rusty knife. 'Screw that – what the fuck's happened to my skin!'

Lynx frowned and tried to focus properly. His skin had a maddening itch to it, the nag of a half-healed wound, but he couldn't make out much with the bursts and smears of light that almost . . . He paused. Almost looked like willow leaves.

'Oh shit,' Lynx whispered as he took a closer look, blinking furiously. The mess of dull light in his eyes wasn't clearing, but as his wits returned he realised it was not as much of a mess as he'd first thought.

'What in all that's shattered is this?' Sitain said.

She looked up and their eyes met, then they looked each other up and down, no longer focusing on how they were both naked.

'We didn't just get drunk and find some light-mage to tattoo us, right?'

Lynx coughed a laugh and just stared, open-mouthed at her then himself. The markings on their skin were faint; fainter than he'd first thought, but distinct enough to make out as some sort of stylised willow-leaf pattern – and glowing to boot. Nothing very bright, but a dull shine seemed to have settled over their bodies as they lay unconscious. It covered much of Lynx's front, while Sitain had been lying on her side by the looks of her body.

He shifted his arm slightly to where it had been resting and realised the pattern now matched up – a gasp from Sitain told him she'd noticed the same.

'Gods, is this on my face?'

He prodded his cheeks, but Lynx couldn't feel anything different there. His skin prickled all over, even parts where he could see nothing of the lambent markings.

'Yeah,' Sitain confirmed, prodding his cheek. 'There, across the bottom of your tattoo and the bridge of your nose. It runs down your throat to your chest.'

'But not my back?'

She leaned to one side, her nose wrinkling a little as she looked down the mess of scarring running the length of his back. 'Nope.'

'Fuck's sake,' he said with a bitter laugh. 'Good to see the pretty bit of me was kept pristine.'

Lynx looked round at the others as he got unsteadily to his feet. They were all similarly marked, the leaf pattern almost identical but settling on each one in a unique way. The stone tree above them was bare again, the glimmering water of the moat returned as though nothing had ever happened. Only the marks on their bodies showed it was more than just a dream, but what exactly had happened was lost on Lynx.

'Lastani?' he called, approaching the young woman who stood clutching her head and leaning against the tree trunk. 'You okay?'

She gave him a wan smile. 'Just a little dazed and . . .' She tailed off, but a small smile appeared on her lips.

'What?'

'I don't know,' she admitted, 'but my body feels odd.'

'Mine too,' Lynx said, 'tingling all over like some sort o' bloody rash.'

'No, not that – I feel good, strong. Like I'm ready to run miles or lift great stones.' She looked past him to the other mages there. 'Sitain? Atieno? Do you feel different?'

Sitain nodded. 'Strong, yes. Full of energy. I reckon I could put you all out with a snap of my fingers if I needed to – feels like I've just drunk in half the world's supply of night magic.'

'Atieno?'

The ageing man took a few tentative steps towards them, looking more startled and worried than anything else, but he nodded slowly. 'I feel unusual,' he hazarded. 'Young, almost. My leg, it's—'

'Your bad leg got healed too?' Lynx said with a grin. 'That water's good stuff, eh? I still got my scars, but every bruise and cut's been washed away.'

'Not quite, but better than it has been in years.'

'Good news then. An old injury?'

The dark-skinned man gave him a wonder-struck look, tugging his long grey-black hair away from his face as he tried to frame his thoughts. 'No injury,' he said eventually. 'But that's the point – it's impossible. My limp, it's a consequence of my magic.'

'Tempest? Why?'

'It is the magic of change,' Atieno explained. 'To draw and use too much of it is to fill my body with that magic. Physical ailments and deformities are common among my kind – the more we use our magic, the more we change ourselves.'

Lynx frowned. 'What are you saying?'

'That I limped because the bones of my foot were turning to stone – not because of any injury I've suffered. But now . . .' He shook his head, the normally reserved mage now looking openly bewildered. 'Now it's noticeably improved, the magic here has reversed that. I feel strong, yes, but I also feel whole again!'

'Can any of you tell me what these tattoos are? What they mean?' Toil demanded, looking over her shoulder from where she knelt at Paranil's side. The injured man hadn't yet risen, or indeed woken so far as Lynx could tell.

'I've no idea,' Lastani said, glancing at Sitain and Atieno as she spoke. 'But it appears they are the prize of this labyrinth.'

'More valuable than God Fragments?'

'Older,' she said with more certainty. 'This place predates the fall, I'm almost certain. There *were* no God Fragments when this labyrinth was built, built to guide a chosen few to this chamber. And remember the glyph all the entrances formed on the map? The character for "the divine"?'

'Eh?' Deern broke in, swaggering forward and absentmind-edly rubbing at the glowing leaf marks on his inner thigh. 'You saying we've become gods?'

She shook her head, but slowly, dubiously. 'I'm not saying that, no, but if you could feel what I feel . . . I don't have the words, but the power here is immense. I don't know what's been done to us, but we're changed somehow, all of us. That glow on your skin is nothing compared to what I can feel, it's like a stone that's been left in the fire – some deep inner heat coming off us in waves.'

Lynx took a few steps, unsteady at first but swiftly becoming long and purposeful strides. His skin crawled and itched, yes, but Lastani's words rang true as he moved. There was an energy inside him, a warmth and strength that screamed to be used. Those few steps seemed to ease the tingle somewhat and made it less distracting, but his thick limbs remained brimming with restless power. Any last traces of fatigue were gone, tiredness itself a distant memory.

'What are we waiting for now?' he asked, pacing in a circle as others began to copy him or shifted their feet.

'We've no idea what's been done to us!' Lastani protested.

'I don't care,' he said simply. 'There's a fight going on and for once I'm itching for it. I can't stand idle down here while you make notes.'

'He's right,' Suth broke in. 'Whatever this is, we can find out once the city's safe. It might be this makes the difference if you mages are overflowing with power, but we won't know until we get back up there. Bade won't be wasting any time now he's got the prize. A prize anyway.'

'The man's a bastard still,' Toil pointed out, 'and he's booby-trapped one door with grenades already so we take as much care going up as we did coming down.'

'The armoury wasn't entirely emptied by us either,' Suth added, 'so he could have something bigger in one of those bags they were carrying, but a rat's first instinct is to run for safety and I've got friends likely dying on the surface.'

Clearly agreeing, Toil plunged back into the water with a grin of anticipation and waded back across towards her clothes. The rest eagerly followed in the next moment, a few whoops of enthusiasm accompanying them, while Aben carried his unconscious friend over. The touch of the water had no effect on any of them this time and Paranil was still limp when Aben set him down, but his wound had closed. Toil hauled herself from the water and sat on the side, pausing in the act of reaching for her shirt as a thought occurred to her.

'Overflowing with power,' she said hesitantly. 'Just how dangerous could you three be in a fight right now?'

'To everyone around us?' Atieno replied, moving with ease and naked delight on his face. 'Very, especially me. I don't have the precision Lastani has, my life's been mostly one of restraint – and I've never had this much power available to me. Sitain doesn't have the training to discriminate between friend and foe but at least she's likely to only put you all to sleep not turn your flesh to stone.'

'And with that God Fragment? They're used to focus power in making mage-gun cartridges, no? That's how something so small can be so destructive, right?'

'So a mage in battle,' Lastani said slowly, 'focusing their power through a God Fragment, should be terrible to behold.'

'For a minute or two at least,' Atieno said drily. 'Then some sharpshooter a few hundred yards away puts an icer through my head.'

'So don't wade in like a vengeful god,' Toil said. 'Worth considering, isn't it? There's an advantage if we use it right – I doubt the Knights-Charnel would even consider permitting a slave to use a relic so freely.'

Atieno scowled at the term, but they all knew that was how the Charnelers viewed his kind. He clambered out of the water and stood, looking down at himself as the silvery water seemed to wriggle and slide down his skin back to the moat below. In moments he was completely dry, the only strange sight on his brown skin being the gently glowing tattoos.

'Let's see, shall we?' Atieno said when he'd dressed and was satisfied his clothes weren't going to disintegrate off his body. He gingerly reached into the pocket where he'd stowed the God Fragment and held it up to the weak light. As soon as it touched his skin, the shard of smoked crystal blazed like a lamp's wick.

Lynx squinted through the sudden brightness, just able to make out the shape of the fragment as Atieno held it out at arm's length. It shone only for a few moments, however. Just as Lynx found his eyes begin to water the light faded and then all of a sudden the fragment crumbled to glittering dust and fell into the water below.

'What have you done?' Suth yelled, scrambling forward. She swiped her hand at the water but there was not even a trace of dust on the surface and she slapped the surface in anger.

'Our one damn prize from this whole journey,' she raged, 'and you've gone and destroyed it!'

'I did nothing; it just fell apart in my fingers!' Atieno protested. 'The magic inside it just seemed to fold in on itself – or was drawn down into the water.'

'Drawn down?' Lastani said sharply. 'Are you sure?'

He shook his head. 'That's how it felt, I'm sure of nothing.'

'Why?' Toil demanded. 'What does that mean to you?'

'Nothing as yet, I've yet to build a hypothesis.'

'But you've got an idea?'

'I've . . . I don't know what I have,' Lastani admitted. 'But the glyph for "the divine", the hidden tree – they put me in mind of old, half-remembered myths. Ones I've not read,' she added pointedly, 'but names that survived the purges. The heresy works, Noxeil and all those writings – the stone of light, the taproot of the Duegar.'

'Get to the point.'

'I don't have one, not yet. I need time to think.'

Toil stared at her for a long while. 'Do it while you get dressed,' she said at last. 'Whatever this all means, there's a battle going on in the city. Whether we've been touched by Duegar magic or some spirit o' the divine, if the Charnelers take the city anyone with fucking tattoos that glow won't see the outside of a sanctuary for the rest of their life.'

Before long, the entire group were dressed and following Toil back up to the larger cavern. They moved cautiously just in case there was a rearguard waiting, but in moments their concerns were forgotten. The deep darkness of the huge lower labyrinth was, Lynx realised, somehow less fearsome than before. The blackness less absolute, the shadows less threatening.

'Am I the only one who can see better?'

'No,' Toil said quietly beside him. 'This is different.'

One by one they agreed. Only Sitain seemed unmoved, but the mage had always had night vision that went far beyond anything natural.

'Sitain's eyes were touched by magic,' Lastani pointed out, her dyed white hair now looking ethereal in the gloom. 'It seems ours are now too.'

'I'm starting to like this game,' Toil said. 'Let's hope we live long enough to find out what else we can do. But first things first. You took a prisoner, Sitain? We probably shouldn't leave them in case the labyrinth seals up behind us then. That would be rude. We fetch them and burn our dead if they're close.

We won't catch Bade now but there's a fight to join and I've got questions for anyone taking Bade's orders.'

The Cards quickly went about their tasks, hauling the corpses they could find and dumping them outside the circular chamber once the insensate Charneler was secured. When they were reassembled Toil took one last glance up the dark chimney and nodded to Lastani.

'The disc now. Let's see where this chute takes us.'

The young mage nodded and touched her fingers to the central 'gift' disc at the top of the stairway they'd ascended. The stone blocks obediently slid back into place as she retreated out of the way again, but nothing more happened.

'Try the gift again,' Toil suggested. 'Bade escaped on some sort of platform and that's now at the top.'

Lastani repeated the action and this time retreated sharply as a blaze of bluish light came from somewhere high above in the shaft and the platform started to descend. While they were waiting, Teshen and Layir finished stripping their dead of personal effects before placing a burner under the folded hands of each.

The remaining mercenaries took cover as the platform dropped back down, guns at the ready, but, as expected, it was empty of Charnelers. Toil waved them inside where they formed a rough circle around the sphere in the centre, the prisoner at their feet. Teshen loaded a sparker into his gun and aimed it at the dead.

'We ready?' he asked, not wanting to set off a funeral pyre of several fire-bolts until he knew they were moving clear.

Lastani touched the sphere and a flash of light answered him, the floor giving a jolt before slowly starting to turn and lift upwards. Teshen grunted and adjusted his aim while the mercenaries beside him ducked down, but the platform started to pick up speed immediately and he only paused a second before firing through the dwindling gap. Lynx caught the bright orange flare and familiar whump of flames before it was lost behind a curved wall of stone and his thoughts turned upwards, towards the surface.

'Where are we coming out?'

'Somewhere Bade's been before,' Toil muttered. 'And the North Keep shows he knows how to set a bomb so keep your wits about you and follow my lead.'

Judging by the silence that followed, Lynx guessed the others found that as sobering a thought as he did. Magic-touched eyesight or not, he was still in a confined space with no way of controlling how quickly or quietly they reached their destination. One well-judged grenade and they were all dead, assuming Bade had left anyone behind to watch his back.

Let's just hope these mages are as overflowing with power as they say they are, he thought, but realised in the next moment he wasn't frightened of the prospect – at worst mildly apprehensive. The power running through his skin – his strange new tattoos – filled him with strength and confidence.

It was hard to tell, but if the mages were feeling as alive as he did they'd be ready to take on the entire Charneler army. By the way Sitain and Lastani prowled around the sphere, fingers flexing constantly, he reckoned they were itching to unleash that power too.

This could be quite a sight, Lynx told himself as he did another check on his cartridge case to count how many shots he had left. *Let's just hope we get to tell the grandkids about it.*

He paused and looked around at his companions; picturing children with playing card badges sewn on to their jackets and running around waving mage-pistols.

Shattered gods . . . Well, someone's grandkids anyway.

Chapter 34

Lynx tightened his grip on his gun as the platform slowed and came to a smooth stop. There was little to see, however, no opening anywhere on the wall – just long flowing lines of Duegar script formed within the rock that glowed in the light of their lamps. It was brighter to his eyes now and Lynx could see more detail, but he ignored that as he concentrated on a way out. It wasn't long before the walls seemed to start contracting around him, tightening like a cord around his chest.

'There,' Lastani said at last, pointing at one part that looked identical to the rest so far as Lynx was concerned.

'Can you reach?' Toil asked.

Lastani nodded and went to the section of wall. She placed her hand on a glyph, then traced a line with her other index finger along the curve of the glowing pattern. That continued until her arms were outstretched and she could only brush her fingernails against a second glyph, whereupon both pulsed with light.

'Get back, it could be rigged,' Toil ordered and the mercenaries briskly obeyed in the finest traditions of their profession. A crack appeared in the wall, a straight glowing seam that ran from the floor to ten or twelve feet up.

'Stop,' Toil said, but Lastani had already done so. She stepped to one side and Lynx saw the gap was less than an inch wide.

'You see a wire?' Teshen asked.

'No, but if there's one anywhere it'll be here I'm sure.'

Lynx looked at the shape of the wall. Two distinct curved sections were now visible, two edges of a doorway that opened outwards. He knelt and peered through the gap.

'There,' Lynx said after a while, seeing a dark shape breaking the straight lines of the outer edge. 'Lying on the floor, something knotted round it.'

The doors themselves were great slabs of stone at least a foot thick. Presumably at some point they would open enough to lift it off the ground, then, when it went further, the wire would break and drop the grenade down on to its pin. But an inch gap would direct most of the blast outside, most likely Bade would have rigged it to only blow once the doors were a foot or so wide.

He gave a grunt of surprise as someone placed a foot on his shoulder and put their full weight on him while they inspected the top.

'Can't see a second up here,' Toil reported. 'Seems sloppy, that.'

'He's got a city to fight his way out of,' Teshen pointed out. 'I'd save all the grenades I could for that.'

'True. Sitain, can you see anything up here?'

The young woman peered through, taking her time before replying. 'Nope, nothing.'

'Right then, just the one to deal with maybe.' She stepped down off Lynx and hauled him back up, giving him a patronising pat as he groaned and rubbed his shoulder. 'It's sitting on the floor. I can't see the pin from here.'

'How do we cut the wire so it doesn't lift as we open the door?'

'Atieno.' Toil beckoned the man over and gestured for him to crouch down with her. 'Can you see the wire holding it?'

'I . . . Yes, I believe so.'

'Can you cut it without messing with the grenade?'

The mage frowned then slipped his fingers into the crack as he pressed his face up close to get the best view he could. 'No.'

'Lastani, then. Bade'll have rigged it to lift then drop again when the wire fixed between the doors is broken. It falls on the pin and we all die.'

'Give me a sword,' Lastani said. One was handed over, then the mercenaries moved to the sides as Lastani crouched at the crack. Lynx felt a greasy crawling feeling on his skin as she cast a needle-tight stream of ice magic through the space, as far from the grenade as possible. The stone beneath it groaned and cracked under the sudden intense cold. She kept it up for ten seconds or more before breaking off and reaching out with the sword to bring it down with what little force was possible given the angle. It proved enough, though, the now-brittle wire needing little encouragement to snap.

'Done,' Lastani called. 'And we seem not to be dead.'

'Atieno take one side, Lastani the other – open it slowly.'

Toil stood defiantly in the middle, either sure of her assessment or confident any grenade would kill everyone in the room anyway. The curved stone slabs slid slowly open, revealing a square stone platform with pillars on both sides flanking an archway that led on to the familiar treacherous paving of the upper chamber.

Just as the doors passed halfway there was a snap of wire breaking and something dropped down towards them. Lynx felt a lurch in his stomach as a small dark shape appeared – watching in numb horror as the grenade swung towards Toil. Somehow the woman dodged to one side. He saw her eyes widen as the pin almost brushed her cheek as it passed, but then her hands moved in a blur and Toil snatched at the wire it was attached to. The grenade jolted upwards, arrested in its curve, but wasn't dislodged and in the next moment Teshen was there – slipping a hand under the bottom of the grenade to safely cradle it.

'Shit,' Toil panted, realising how close she'd come to detonating a grenade with her face. It had been tied so that the mushroom-shaped pin led the way as it swung, either colliding with whoever walked out or continuing up to strike the door lintel above. Either way, it would have killed them all.

'Shit,' Teshen agreed, extracting the pin and handing the pieces to Toil as he went to deactivate the one in front of the open door.

Lynx raised his gun, inspecting the platform and upper chamber beyond in case there were any Charnelers left behind. He could see no one, but kept his gun up until Toil had stepped out on to the platform and tested it for safety. Before too long she was satisfied with what she saw and went to the archway that led out.

'Paint,' she called back to the others. 'Bade's left us a path at least.'

'You trust it?' Lynx replied.

'Nope.'

Toil hefted her staff and gave it to Aben to check the path alongside Lastani. 'It seems solid, but keep testing the ground that's been painted.'

'What about you?'

'I'm checking the direction.'

She shucked her pack off her back and removed a folded map as Aben started to probe the slabs. Lynx tilted his head to see it better, realising it was the one of the city with the entrances to the labyrinth marked. She pulled her compass and glanced over at the upper chamber stretching away in both directions from where they stood.

'We go left.'

'How do you know?'

Toil grinned. 'I don't, but I'm guessing the Knights-Charnel are pretty determined when they want to be. Either the city's fallen or there's still fighting going on. Either way, we can try to follow Bade out and hope we're not in the heart of the enemy, or pick our own path.'

'What about the paint?'

'It's dry so it likely takes us to the keep, which he blew up, or their safehouse, which he blew up. Either way, you've got a lot of digging on your hands and he won't be there once you're out.'

'So you know where you're going?'

'Of course!' She squinted at the map and nodded. 'Yup, I definitely know where we're going – just not so much where we are right now. Sometimes you've got to guess, eh?'

*

The journey to the surface proved quick by comparison to their descent, the looming emptiness of the upper chamber less intimidating to Lynx now he could see through magic-enhanced eyes. After the maspid attack on Teshen's party back in the lower labyrinth, they kept a keen eye open for more of the creatures but the long unbroken reaches of the chamber continued to be empty. It was less than an hour before Toil had found one exit and used the glyph marked above it to navigate to the one she was looking for. Sitain joined her at the front of the small column as they trudged up a winding path towards a wide circular cave. Toil assured them that above their heads would be Prophet's Square, but she stopped short of entering the cave itself despite the fact there was the faintest light creeping down the stairway – a sign the labyrinth was open again. Lynx had been trying to ignore the possibility that they would get all the way through the labyrinth only to discover the doors still closed, but it appeared the ancient Duegar had been cleverer than that.

'What is it?' Lynx whispered.

'I'm listening,' she replied. 'We don't know who's up there, remember?'

'And we don't know if they've got orders to shoot anything that comes out of these entrances,' Suth added. 'Might not have been told to be overly discerning.'

'So, what? We just stand here?' Lynx tried not to shift his feet as the agitation clawed at him again, so close to the surface he could smell the faint smoke on the air. 'Wait, do you smell that?'

'Smoke?'

He shook his head. 'Something else? Piss?'

They all sniffed hard and Toil gave a laugh.

'That settles it then,' she announced. 'Only mercenaries'd be dumb enough to piss anywhere near one of these labyrinth entrances!'

'We like to think of it as keeping to the traditions of martial boldness from bygone ages,' Safir commented from further back.

'Aye, well, half of those ancient warriors got drunk before battle so mebbe you're right.' Toil took a step into the room. 'HEY!' she yelled, causing her companions to flinch at the echoing shout. 'Who's up there?'

There was a pause. Eventually a tentative voice called back down. 'Who's down there?'

'Someone who wants to come up.'

'Come on then.'

'Someone who doesn't want to get shot.'

'Come up slow then!'

'Who's up there, first?'

'Someone who's going to drop a fucking grenade down this hole soon if you don't stop yapping! Get your shitstain arses up

450

here and if you really fucking behave yerselves an' I like the look o' you, I won't shoot you. How's that for fucking assurances?'

Toil glanced back at the others. 'Varain?' she whispered.

Lynx shrugged. 'Sounds like his distinctive charm.'

'VARAIN?' Toil yelled up again.

There was another pause. 'Toil?'

She gave the others a relieved grin and set off. 'It's me!' she called. 'Give me a moment to stop the guardians here.'

She waved Lastani forward and pulled her last fire-charged glass ball, the pair of them casting fire and ice over the two glyphs on the wall. By the fading blue glow of their light, Toil checked around then set off for the open stairway, careful to have her hands up just in case as she neared the grainy light spilling down the steps. By unspoken agreement the others hung back a few paces. She realised this just as she started up the steps and cast them a half-amused glower before trotting up and greeting the Cards at the top.

Once clear it was safe, the rest quickly followed, blinking as they emerged into the grey of a predawn that was still brighter than underground. The plain stone steps led up into the centre of a large city square with apartment blocks atop arcades of shops on all sides. A stone statue lay fallen to one side – a figure Lynx didn't recognise that had been used to anchor a tent on the other side and a field canteen at the far end. Checking behind, Lynx saw the statue had once stood atop the stone block here, falling when one side dropped away to become steps when the labyrinth first opened.

The Cards were slow to wake despite Varain's yelling, the whole camp looking subdued, given their comrades were returning from an ancient wonder. Beyond them was a wide array of tents with a few flags scattered around – depicting an axe with a red scarf tied to its shaft. The buildings were dark, but presumably still occupied if the Red Scarves were camped in the square.

'You made it then?' Anatin said, pushing his way past sleepily rising mercenaries. 'Success?'

'Of a sort,' Toil replied.

'What the fuck's that?' Anatin demanded, blinking and pointing at her. 'What's that on your skin?'

'Long story. What's the situation here?'

'It's been busy for some,' he said, frowning in confusion. 'Us, not so much – though unlike you lot we didn't think of using the time to get new tattoos. When the labyrinth closed up behind you, the Monarch left a guard at the Fountain and sent us to the Red Scarves. Before we could be deployed to the fighting, the line collapsed and they were routed all the way down the canal.'

Toil cursed. 'The Charnelers have the city?'

'Not quite – Charnelers broke 'em in the afternoon,' Payl supplied, joining her commander. 'Messy rearguard work meant some major districts got chewed up in the process, but it was dusk by the time they passed the palace. Monarch didn't stay to defend that, had troops preparing the ground behind so they could make a stand at the Senate instead. Better ground for warding off attack, and she gambled they'd not be able to push through before nightfall.'

'Word is the Crown-Prince is harrying them hard. They pulled back on the main front once dark came because, well, you know what a confused shitstorm of fire and blood a night battle becomes.' Anatin grimaced at the idea as did several around him. 'They've dug in just out of catapult range and secured their lines, but we're separated from the Jarraziran troops so we've no idea what's left. Heard skirmishes all night, but your brother's made a deal with the Charnelers and we're all wrapped up tight. If I'd been in a position to object I might've not liked that, but . . .'

'Vigilance is doing as I've asked,' Toil clarified. 'I asked him to hold here, make sure we didn't come up in a Charneler camp.'

'Where is here again?' Lynx asked before anyone else could.

'Prophet's Square.' She nodded to the fallen statue. 'The prophet Otheq, for any scholars among you. We're in the north-east of the city, mebbe a mile from the palace. Far enough from the canal that I reckoned Bade wouldn't be aiming for this exit and the Charnelers wouldn't be so interested.'

Lynx eased his pack off his shoulders and wandered over to the disappointingly empty field kitchen. 'What's the plan now?'

'Now?' Anatin echoed. 'No rest for the wicked, eh?'

'Aye, kick the rest of these lazy shits out of their bedrolls. It's time for the Cards to earn their pay. And someone go fetch Vigilance.'

Reft pointed across the square. Heads turned and through the array of tents Lynx saw a party of Red Scarves was advancing towards them.

'Already on his way? Good, we don't want to waste any more time. Anatin, I want them ready to move out in five minutes.'

Lynx watched the group of Red Scarves march forward, the Cards only reluctantly making way as Toil's brother made a beeline for her. Clearly there hadn't been many friends made between the mercenary companies, but the Cards had more sense than to block his way and Vigilance walked like a man well aware of that. He was dressed ready for battle, a bulky jacket on his back, mage-gun over one shoulder and a dozen armed men and women on his heel. Beside him walked an older woman with a ghastly, skull-like face that made her look like some sort of demon in the weak light.

'Vigilance, old auntie Ul,' Toil said in greeting.

The Red Scarves' commander paused on the point of snapping a retort, looked at Toil's face then at the others around her too. *The tattoos,* Lynx realised.

'What the buggery happened to you lot?'

'It's a good question,' Toil said with a smile, 'but it's also a long story.'

'I don't care that much. Where are we?'

'Bade's grabbed a haul of God Fragments I think, we need to stop him getting them out of the city.'

He nodded and turned to the terrifying woman, apparently his lieutenant, then one of the others behind. 'Ulith, see to our nannies. Sathra, start getting the troops awake quietly.'

'Nannies?' Toil asked as the two broke off in different directions.

'A squad of Torquen dragoons and some officers, supposedly making sure I keep to the terms of my agreement. You've put me in not the finest position, little sister. I don't like breaking contracts, even if it ends up only being in pretence.'

'Reckon I can find something to distract our religious friends. Once I've got a proper sense of the situation we'll be moving.'

'The situation is that the city's been roughly romanced most o' the way down her canal!' Vigilance snapped. 'And a lot of it's down to you.'

'Yet if I'd said that, you'd just have called me arrogant.'

'Aye, you're that too. So you better give me a damn good reason why the Red Scarves broke their contract and sat on their arses here for a day and night while the bloody Charnelers tore the guts out of this city!'

'Had word of the Monarch?'

He threw up his hands. 'Fucked if I know. We've got a few squads of Torquen watching us and sentry posts outside the camp so getting intel isn't proving easy. I assume she's still alive and free but that's all I've got. The deal I made with the Charnelers means unless you've found something pretty gods-howling wonderful down there, there's a decent chance my captains will string you an' me up before they bugger off out of Jarrazir.'

'We found . . .' For a moment Toil seemed at a loss. 'Like I said, it's a long story. We found enough, the Monarch won't object about you breaking a contract unless she loses the city. Those Torquen troops . . .'

'Are getting a metal breakfast,' Vigilance finished angrily. 'Which I ain't happy about anyway, but at least they're Torquen scum and don't count as real people. We've been allowed to sit here all quiet and meek because they don't need the distraction while they take the city, but sooner or later today we'll end up co-opted or disarmed. The Monarch's troops won't last beyond midday from what I've seen. Either she surrenders or someone does it for her and puts her head on a plate to welcome their new fanatical overlords.'

'We've no time to lose, then,' Toil declared.

'So you *do* have a plan?'

'Don't I always?'

'Aye. I remember some of your plans when we were growing up, though,' Vigilance said darkly. 'More'n a few lacked any sort of sense.'

'Don't worry, I've learned from my mistakes.'

'What, then?'

She grinned. 'They'll be getting ready for a final push? Best time for an all-out attack, then. Get your men ready, it's time to cut the head off the snake.'

Chapter 35

There was little time for reunions for the Cards and little appetite for back-slapping and cheers. The past day and night had seen bloody and brutal conflict in Jarrazir. While they had been spared the worst of the fighting, the wholesale destruction that had torn through the ancient city like a rampaging elemental had lowered every spirit.

Only the strange new tattoos seemed to garner much more than gruff acknowledgement, and even then, in the growing predawn light, their faint sheen was barely perceptible. The design was obvious enough, especially once Deern cheerfully stripped to the waist to show it off, but the ethereal, magical quality seemed to have been left in the darkness.

Just as well, Lynx reminded himself, *given what Toil's planning. If we live through the day, we can bother with worrying what it all means.*

Even in the privacy of his own head, it sounded a hollow ideal, but Lynx could only grit his teeth and set about getting ready. He replenished his cartridge case and ate a scrap of gritty bread, shedding the pack he'd carried through the labyrinth so it didn't slow him down further.

A thin spread of cloud seemed to suspend the encroaching dawn, snaring its light and holding it ransomed in the heavens rather than permitting it to illuminate the broken streets below. The Skyriver had faded from a dull smear to almost invisible by the time the Cards slunk through the gloom to the western picket where the biggest barricade stood. Lynx had to fight the urge to just stand there with his arms stretched wide, staring up at the beautiful open sky and breathing in the clean fresh air of outside, as a weight lifted from his shoulders. Had he been on his own and somewhere else, he might have, but there was a hard day ahead of them all and it was no time for celebrating.

The barricade was a ragged affair, four yards high but flimsy all the same. Tables and chairs, carts, barrels and crates, even roof beams and a stone statue had been incorporated and strung together by a tangled mesh of wire. Few defences would stand up to an earther so few tried. This flimsy obstacle would be shot through in moments, but with a dozen cables looped through it all, it would at least remain an obstacle to invasion even if it offered little actual protection.

A small tunnel had been built into the design on the left-hand side, currently plugged by a large dining table. As Anatin led his Mercenary Deck to the barricade, they heard raised voices from the other side. The sentry sitting atop the barricade seemed unconcerned by what was being said, keeping his eyes on the street beyond and clearly only half-listening. At the arrival of the Cards, however, the man looked back and gave them a small nod.

'Officer's here,' he announced in a bored tone, 'you can come in if you want 'im.'

'Open the damn way then!' barked a man on the other side. 'You've as long as it takes me to load my gun.'

'Whoah!' Anatin said, hurrying forward as the mercenaries on the ground started to drag the obstacles out of the way. 'No need for shooting, certainly not this early.'

A Knights-Charnel officer with a puffy face and thin moustache appeared from behind the table. 'Have that sentry whipped for insubordination,' he snarled. 'Man's been refusing to admit us for five minutes. Unless you've forgotten your company's terms of surrender—' He broke off and looked around at the Cards. 'You're not Red Scarves? Why are you armed?'

Anatin gave him a friendly grin and pulled a pistol, pointing it at the man's face. 'Like I said, there's no need for shooting this early, so don't force my hand, eh? Call your men in. Any of 'em tries to run and you all end up dead, understand?'

The blood drained from the man's face, but as he was hauled forward he began to splutter in fury. 'You've signed the death warrant for every man and woman here, you know that?'

'We all got to go sometime.'

The man drew himself up to his full height. His uniform markings declared him an infantry captain, a narrow scar on his cheek worn like a medal in an army where commissions were bought more often than earned.

'When I do not escort Commander Deshar to the general, she will assume you've reneged on our agreement. You'll be wiped out. Drop your guns and get to your knees right now or every person here is as good as dead.'

'We'll go see her ourselves if you like, where is she?'

The captain paused. 'Gods on high, you're insane.'

'That's what my men say,' Anatin said amiably. 'Now, where?'

'Her command post.' The captain's lip curled. 'Enjoy finding it yourself, I'll not help you.'

'Thought as much, but I had to ask. Mebbe someone here will beat it out of you, mebbe not. I ain't going to bother.'

Three mercenaries started stripping the Charnelers of their weapons as the last of the captain's small command were pulled through the gate. There were only six in the end, not even a full squad, and the regular soldiers looked as resigned as their captain was furious. The man had the sense not to put up a fight or shout for help, though – the threat of having your throat slit tended to have that effect on a man. His loyalty to

458

his Order might be undimmed, but he saw the writing on the wall and complied meekly enough when his turn to be bound and gagged came.

'What have we got out here then?' Anatin commented, peering through the makeshift sally port with Payl and Toil, while Teshen and Kas scrambled up to join the sentry.

'Looks pretty quiet.'

'There's a regiment barracked in that building there, with the lights,' supplied the sentry. 'Pickets at every major cross-road. I saw a column move south not long ago, towards the university district.'

'Do we know where the general's stationed?'

'We've sent out some scouts. Only one's got back so far, but he said they're keeping to the canal avenues and her barge is inside the city.' The sentry sucked his teeth for a moment. 'Your friend came straight down this road,' he said after a while, pointing. 'Came from the right around that corner there, not the quickest route but likely they've only secured the main roads.'

Lynx glanced behind them and saw the Red Scarves were forming into their units. Other, smaller, groups had been dispatched on distraction missions and they would be slipping out through surrounding buildings right now. Speed was their only advantage – there were thousands of Charneler troops in the city and together the Cards and Scarves had no more than five hundred in total.

'The barracks is our target,' Toil reminded Anatin. 'We take that out and cut north, try to skirt behind the main body of troops as Vigilance's skirmishers create a distraction and the Red Scarves tie up the centre.'

'Sitain,' Lynx murmured, turning to the young woman beside him. 'How strong are you right now?'

She raised an eyebrow. 'Still buzzing after that water, why?'

'Could you put out a whole regiment?'

'What?' Sitain coughed. 'Shattered gods, how should I know?'

'If they're all in that building still,' Lynx clarified. 'All nice and close.'

'Ah, maybe?'

'Good enough. Anatin!'

The commander turned with a scowl. 'What now?'

'Let me and Sitain go ahead. She's full to bursting, all the mages are. Might be she can take out all the barracks there without us drawing too much attention to ourselves.'

'What?' Anatin opened his mouth to berate Lynx but, before he could, Toil laid a hand on his arm.

'If she can,' Toil said quietly, 'it's a huge advantage. Lastani – where are you? Could it be done?'

The other mage stepped forward. 'I . . . I don't know. I've never felt so strong, though, so maybe she has a chance.'

'All I needed to hear. Lynx, grab some coats off our friends there. Might give you cover enough. If anyone comes to challenge you, we start shooting, okay?'

Lynx ducked his head in acknowledgement and in moments two black-and-white greatcoats were passed over. He and Sitain put them on and slipped out into the deserted grey streets, glancing back once at the barricade before heading down the street to the building that had been pointed out.

The road was covered in debris – broken bricks and tiles along with the detritus of a fleeing population. They had a hundred yards to walk and, despite the chill morning air, Lynx's neck was tacky with sweat as they tried to act like part of a conquering army. The building was a large block five floors high with a smaller wing jutting off the side and a warehouse nestled in its lee. It seemed to be a consortium office of some sort, but the flags of its companies had been pulled down and a heap of goods had been pulled from the warehouse and set alight in the street.

They approached from the rear, holding back until a patrol had rounded the corner then hurrying to the stable gate while they assessed the problem. There was a face at one top window, but he was watching another approach. No doubt he saw Lynx and Sitain, but he'd have seen the delegation arrive at the barricade so would have no reason to be suspicious. Lynx could hear Sitain gasping short, nervous puffs of breath as she hugged her plundered coat close. They wouldn't stand up to close scrutiny, that much was obvious.

'How close do you need to be?'

'I don't know.'

'Is the wall going to be a problem?'

'I've never done this before, remember? Just hurry up – I can feel the magic seeping out of me.'

'What?'

She hissed in irritation, not at him Lynx realised, but at a lack of words to explain herself properly.

'Whatever happened underground, if felt like I was filled to bursting with magic. Like a wineskin.'

'So?'

'So I'm no trained mage. I can't keep it all in, the power's slowly draining out of me. Might be no human was ever meant to hold that magic, but every moment I don't concentrate on holding the seams together, more trickles out.'

'We probably should have planned this better, right?'

'Shut up and go.'

Lynx nodded and drew his sword, hiding it behind his back before he tried the ring latch of the stable gate. It turned and opened easily enough, revealing a small courtyard.

'Hey, who goes there?'

'Easy friend,' Lynx said, advancing towards the challenging voice. A man appeared from one of the stables, mage-gun in hand. 'Got some girls, I couldn't bring 'em in round the front, could I?'

461

'Girls?'

Lynx beckoned and pointed at Sitain, lurking in the gloom of the gate. 'Whores, Sergeant Ulain sent me out for 'em.'

On instinct the guard stepped forward to see Sitain better. 'What company is—'

Lynx lunged forward, closing the ground between them with one pace and driving his sword into the man's gut. The impact drove him back, and as Lynx yanked the gun out of his hands he almost ended up on top of the guard as he fell to the ground. He could smell the man's breath as he gasped his last – the stink of peppered meat washing across Lynx's face as he abandoned his sword and pulled his dagger. The man hardly moved, impaled by the sword and pinned by shock and agony, so it was a simple job to drive the dagger up into his brain and end his pain.

Lynx withdrew his weapons and quickly wiped the blades on the dead man's uniform. Sheathing both, he dragged the guard into one corner of the stable and waved Sitain forward. The young woman peered at him dumbly from the gate, face white, as Lynx hissed and beckoned – for a moment not realising why she was holding back. Then he looked down at the blood on his hands, the body at his feet and felt a pang of shame.

He'd killed the man without a second thought, it was an instinct etched into his bones and Lynx was under no illusions about himself, but Sitain . . . She'd seen her mercenary comrades kill before, but usually it was using a mage-gun or amid complete chaos. She might have even killed someone herself, by accident most likely given how poor a shot she was, but it would have been different. Here, Lynx had pounced on a man and stabbed him to death. He could see in Sitain's eyes that the awful truth of their chosen profession had never been clearer to her.

'Sitain!' Lynx said a fraction louder. 'Look at me, remember what we're here to do! They *all* die if you can't put them out before the rest reach us.'

That seemed to break the spell as Sitain flinched and swallowed hard, nodding. Eyes averted from the dark pool of smeared blood, she scampered forward and joined him in the shadows.

'Can you do this?'

'I . . . I'm going to have to try.'

Lynx caught her by the arm and saw the resolve in her eyes. She might not like it, but she was a stronger soul than she realised, and Lynx stepped back, satisfied.

She looked up at the large building. It was bigger than any of the inns the company had taken since she'd joined them – most likely there were more than a hundred soldiers camped there while they awaited orders. Clearly the Charnelers were confident that Toil's brother was as good as his word, happy to leave their flank largely undefended when there was no safe route around behind wherever the front line was.

Normally they'd be right to, Lynx reminded himself. *I doubt even Toil alone would have been able to persuade the Red Scarves to try something like this. They know the damage a breach of the line can cause once the burners start to fly, but they also know the casualties you'll take if you try anything more than a quick raid.*

He looked down at the back of his hand. The tattoo was clear on his skin there but not shining any longer. It just looked like a thin coating of pearly paint – hardly impressive, but perhaps enough to tip Vigilance over the edge. There was no doubting that they had found something in the labyrinth, something magical, and had three mages in their midst. Perhaps that would prove the key to success and, if not, it was the Cards out front. No doubt if they got obliterated Vigilance would shed a tear for his sister as he ordered his men to flee.

Just as well there was no time to explain what we found. The man might be less confident after hearing 'we've piss-all clue what this is, but it was all shiny earlier'.

'The main part of the building is there,' Sitain muttered to herself. 'So I need to . . .'

'Sure you can do this through a wall?'

'We better hope so, unless you want to try every room individually.'

'Good point.' Lynx stepped back. 'Any time you want then.'

She gave him a sharp look but didn't bother replying, just placed one hand against the wall and the other past the corner, directed towards the other part of the block. Eyes closed, Sitain bowed her head and took a few long breaths. In moments the air began to faintly shudder and distort around her, shadows turning in on themselves as the night magic surged out of her.

Lynx felt his breath catch as the shadows took on sharp edges, twisting and flittering like the wings of a butterfly. He'd seen this before not long after meeting Sitain – an elemental, night magic made incarnate. Shadowshard, that's what Lastani had called it.

The black shards seemed to radiate out from Sitain as the flow of magic increased, unfurling like wings from all parts of her torso and disappearing through the wall ahead. He felt a furious itch crawl across his skin, scratching once at his hand then catching himself. The sensation slipped like oil all over his body, but after that first moment it was strangely pleasant, not a maddening irritation.

As he looked. the tattoo on his hand suddenly glowed again with the cold shine of starlight. Quickly, Lynx pulled up his jacket to look at his stomach where the tattoos ran down it – those too were now bright again.

He opened his mouth to say something to Sitain before realising that, though half her body was now hidden by knapped fragments of darkness, she was also glowing. Her tattoos shone even through her shirt and were inscribed on the shadow shards of her magic, white lines traced clearly on the deepest black.

Then he felt her reach out, summoning her strength to drag yet more magic into her saturated body. This was no grand working, that much Lynx could tell, just a tidal wave of power about to be cast forward at the building and the soldiers inside it. His own tattoos seemed to jolt on his skin as Sitain reached higher, tugging him towards her and suddenly he felt . . . something flow out of his skin, as though he was a mage himself. Lynx gasped but could find no words for anything more. He simply stood there, astonished and enraptured as a power he'd never guessed at flowed through his body.

All of a sudden Lynx found himself able to feel Sitain's presence on his skin, like they were connected by a thousand spider-threads – the shape of her body, mind and thoughts. Nothing clear, but the strongest sense of 'her' as though they had grown up twins. Before he could do anything or make sense of it all, his body was ablaze with awareness of the others too. Lastani an icy sculpture in his mind, elegant and intricate, while Atieno was a roiling, shifting figure of smoke. Then those who weren't mages too – Toil's sharp edges and iron will, Teshen's cold heart and raptor focus, Safir's grace and the kernel of bitterness hidden deep inside . . .

He could feel them all, their minds crashing into his like the weight of some ancient shield wall, sweeping him up in their momentum and charging on towards Sitain. She embraced their power as it struck and added it to her own, blackness threatening to overwhelm Lynx's mind for an instant before it was all hurled away. The world seemed to be split in two – that wave of shadowy power bursting forth to engulf everything in its path even as Lynx was hurled backwards to his own body.

He staggered as though physically punched and found himself blinking and gasping for air. Ahead of him the night mage crashed to her knees. As for the building, there was no change, but Lynx could sense the power move like a fireball scorching the night. The power had been immense, so many more times more powerful than any magic he'd ever witnessed. He felt his hands shake at what it might mean – at how they'd been changed – but right now Sitain needed him again. He took a few unsteady steps, driven mostly by will, before recovering himself and sweeping Sitain up just before she flopped to the ground.

'Shattered gods,' she croaked, looking up at Lynx with unfocused eyes.

'Let's hope they didn't notice,' he said, only half-joking. 'Best they don't think they've got a rival on their hands.'

Her tattoos were still glowing and he could feel the ebbing magic tremble through her bones. It waxed briefly as his skin touched hers, but then continued to fade as the light of their skin dimmed.

Lynx headed back out of the gate, Sitain in his arms, and he saw the Cards closing fast – the shine of several tattoos clearly visible in the dawn light. Before he'd even reached them a volley of barely hushed voices rang out.

'What did she do?'

'Gods, did you feel it?'

'I'm bloody shining again, how do I make it do that?'

Lynx set Sitain down as they reached their comrades and held her steady until the young mage found her feet.

'Is it done?' Toil demanded over the voices of the others.

'Reckon so, aye,' Lynx said.

'You're sure?' Anatin asked.

'Didn't you see?'

'I saw nothing,' their commander said, jabbing a thumb at the tattooed mercenaries at his side. 'All of a sudden, this lot starting whimpering and moaning – then they started to bloody twinkle like pretty little forest fairies. What the hairy fuck's she done to you?'

'It wasn't her,' Toil answered for Lynx, 'and we don't have time to explain. Aben, go back and tell the Scarves what's happened. They'll be waiting for a fireball or something as a signal.'

'And the rest of us?'

'We move as fast as we can. Word is the Crown-Prince is still alive, harrying the Charnelers with his cavalry group. Most likely that's why the general moved her headquarters closer in, where Tylom can't threaten her. It also means if we stir the pot here, he might notice and hit the rear again.'

'So which way?'

'Suth?'

The scowling agent of the Monarch pointed, saying nothing.

'What's up her arse?' Lynx asked Toil.

Toil grinned wolfishly but it was Suth herself who answered. 'I just started to fucking glow like a Skyriver festival lantern when *she* did her thing. If that keeps happening, I'm either marked as some magic-touched freak the Charnelers will want to put in a sanctuary, or I have to resign my commission 'cos I'm stuck with you deranged idiots.'

'Now that's a worrying thought,' Atieno said.

Sitain laughed weakly. 'Join the shitting club,' she croaked. 'I'll get us all badges saying "I'm with those drunken madmen".'

'I think we're being impugned!' Safir declared with mock outrage. 'Permission to shoot them, commander?'

'Mebbe later,' Anatin said darkly. 'Meantimes, let's go and go fast. Suth, you're leading. Shoot anyone who gets in our way.'

Chapter 36

The Cards advanced a few more blocks, keeping as quiet and unobserved as possible. Somewhere behind them the Red Scarves were moving up – taking a more direct route to the canal that ran straight to the Bridge Palace. The Monarch had retreated from her palace, not wanting to see it obliterated and drawing the Charnelers deeper into the city. The Senate was as defensible as anywhere else in the city and forced the Charnelers to stretch their lines much further.

'Here,' Suth said, stopping at the corner of one street.

The dawn light illuminated their path and, though the sky was overcast, there was no hiding in the cover of shadows now. The stink of burned buildings was stronger here, carrying on the breeze across the city. Thin trails of smoke rose up into the sky, melting away before they reached the cloud cover. They stood like memorials to the dead, pyres arrayed across Lynx's view of the sky above the rooftops.

'This'll take us all the way?' Toil asked, peering around the corner.

'It's pretty much a straight run down this street and the ones beyond it.'

The nearby buildings were mostly intact, marked by a few stray shots but without the flame-scarring of burners or earther holes. It could almost be a normal street view but for the deserted road scattered with debris dropped by fleeing citizens.

Fortunately for the Cards, this was a poorer district with winding narrow streets and few vantage points. Against the background rumble of gunshots there came from somewhere closer the distinctive crack of icers over the rooftops, single shots rather than a skirmish.

'Hear that?' Safir said. 'Snipers.'

Toil nodded. 'They'll be watching the flanks of their supply line. Lastani, how strong are you feeling?'

'I'll not be outdone by Sitain,' the young woman replied with forced bravado. Her pale face betrayed her real feelings, but clearly she had them under control for the moment.

This is her home they've torn the guts out of, Lynx reminded himself. *Never underestimate what folk will do to stop someone destroying their home.*

'Good, we'll need the cover.'

Toil gestured to the air in front of them all and Lastani nodded. A shield of magic could hold back mage-shot sure enough – but it was a gamble whether they'd get the shield up in time. Normally no mage would be strong enough to maintain one for any length of time. If they could, mages would be co-opted into every army across the continent. After what Sitain had just done, though, and the link existing between them all, Lynx realised the Cards might now be unique.

'First we wait.'

'For what?'

'The signal.'

It didn't take long to come. The Cards had hunkered down as best they could in the street, not seeing troops of either side as they waited, then a boom rolled across the sky. Lynx looked back the way they'd come and realised it was probably the barracks even before the smoke began to rise.

Shit. Poor bastards, he thought as guilt stabbed at his gut. But how to persuade hardened mercenaries to leave a regiment of enemies alive at their backs, trusting in magic they'd never seen? He knew it was a faint hope even as his heart burned with shame. He chanced a look at Sitain but the young woman didn't seem to have connected the sound and he looked away, not wanting to be the bearer of those tidings.

The roar of fire followed soon after as orange flames and dirty black smoke rose high in the sky above the lesser pyres of the city – a vast obelisk amid a field of memorials. Enough of a signal to the entire city that the fighting had begun again. If the Monarch and Crown-Prince had any troops left, they'd know this was their last chance.

'Vigilance will be past the barracks, ready to ambush troops drawn by the fire,' Toil announced as she patted Suth on the shoulder and directed her forward. 'With luck it'll clear a path for us.'

'Here's hoping,' Anatin said as they filed out. The narrow street left little space for the Cards to spread out so the suits advanced in tight knots, guns raised. They saw no one as they followed the first section then came to a bend in the road where Suth hesitated.

'Tavern,' she whispered back. 'Thirty yards up.'

Lynx felt the tattoos on his skin renew their glow as Lastani drew on her reserves of magic. A haze appeared above them, a faint cloud of mist that caught the morning light. With her arm outstretched, fingers splayed, Lastani drove forward with the cloud ahead of her and the Cards trotted alongside. Around the corner they saw the tavern through the haze, three storeys of stone and timber that looked as dark as the rest of the district it towered over. They had barely gone a few paces when a gunshot rang out and a white streak arrowed into the shield of ice-magic Lastani had raised.

The Cards faltered, then a second shot rang out – this time the roar of a burner, but the flames also burst fruitlessly over the shield.

'Now, drop it!' Toil shouted over the crackle of fire.

The shield vanished and in the next instant Toil fired an earther into the upper floor of the tavern. The faint trails of their shots had betrayed the snipers' location and she hit it dead on – smashing clean through the wall and tearing the entire window frame out with it. Payl followed it up with a burner and fire exploded through the gap, sweeping the top floor and cutting off the brief scream they'd heard from inside.

'Faster,' Toil demanded as she reloaded. 'We've announced ourselves.'

The Cards jumped to obey. Rounding the burning tavern they came to an alley mouth. Suth glanced down it and jerked back as an icer flashed straight past her face. Before the others could do anything the Jarraziran soldier had dropped to one knee and pulled two guns from her collection. She fired in rapid succession while three Cards stepped past her for a better shot. The whipcrack of icers echoed down the tight alley and then all was still.

'Patrol,' Suth reported back, reloading as she went. 'Dead now.'

Ahead of them was a right turn so she upped the pace to the corner, pausing at the side to check around it again.

'We need to cross this square and bear left,' she called to Anatin. 'Couple of squads by the looks of it.'

'Sun takes the lead with Lastani,' he said. 'We advance until I call the halt, then cover Stars as they come. Blood and Snow to follow us, Tempest watches our rear.'

Not waiting for any acknowledgement, Anatin pulled his pistol with his one remaining hand and started forward. Payl, Karra and Varain moved ahead of him, guns ready. There was a shout from somewhere and they fired immediately, three crisp shots ringing out as Darm and Foren moved ahead. Once the last of Sun had gone, Estal led Stars out at a crouch, and then they were all following. More gunshots came. The bursts and echoes off the surrounding buildings had merged into one great jagged sound by the time Lynx turned the corner.

The flash of icers was everywhere, the jagged tongues of sparkers lashing a building on the far side. As they moved into the square, a burner roared out from their right and spilled flame across the ground. Two Cards were caught in the fire but Lynx didn't have time to see who as the whole of Tempest charged, firing. The lead suits jerked left, towards the open street leading off the square, but Blood and Tempest continued to hammer earthers and icers into the surrounding buildings.

'Move!' Teshen called.

Payl and Suth were already at the next street, firing on more Charnelers there, while Lynx reloaded frantically and continued to scan the shattered house fronts of the square. Teshen hurried forward to a blackened, writhing figure in the middle of the square, slamming the butt of his gun hard into their head. Lynx didn't know if it was one of theirs or not, but it was a mercy any soldier would offer if they could.

You lived your life fearing that – not the sparkers or earthers, but burning alive and every moment feeling like an age. The power of burners was undeniable and unavoidable, but Lynx wasn't the only soldier to feel sick every time he fired one.

'Reft!' yelled someone from up front.

The mercenaries of Blood hurried forward, adding their guns to the volley the lead troops were laying down. They edged forward every few seconds, a pace or two only but moving, constantly moving. Lynx saw Flinth shot through the head, but there was no time to pause. The Charnelers retreated under a steady hail of shots, the Cards' firepower and numbers overwhelming each small group they came across.

As the morning brightened, the sound of gunshots began to boom from somewhere south of them and they found their progress quickening. The number of patrols dwindled – some even fleeing from their path. They'd broken the flank lines, it appeared, and the Red Scarves were drawing most of the fire from the reserve troops in this part of the city. The bulk of the Charneler army was on the front line by the Senate buildings, too far to recall in time, but Lynx was well aware they had no idea what was being kept in reserve.

Press on, drive deep. The words kept running through his brain; at every pause and hesitation his old training screamed them. This was the commando way, the Hanese way. Heavily armed troops pushing hard and fast through enemy lines – wreaking mayhem and slaughter in those minutes when the enemy were unable to react.

The crack of icers started to fade from his awareness – the grey and ochre of the city became green and brown as he found his mind returning to the close, frantic battles of the Greensea a decade earlier. The unprepared armies of each city-state and principality. The dawn raids from the forests, sweeping inexorably and ruthlessly over camps and villages – killing everything in their path. Hand-to-hand fighting when they were too close to waste time reloading, axes and swords chopping a path through young men and women too stunned to fight back.

It all settled like a dark shadow over his mind, eclipsing everything but for the part that recoiled at that side of him returning.

But this is the part I need now, Lynx realised in one moment of quiet, when they paused at a demolished building and listened to the sounds of fighting somewhere to the south. *This is also me. Right now it's all I have.*

The Cards came to another square – larger this time, with a well and shrines occupying the centre. Around that were pitched tents and a ragged barricade so the mercenaries charged straight on. Earthers and sparkers smashed into the barricade and tore chunks from it. The surprised Charnelers were thrown back, some not even armed as the Cards pushed on through. They split left and right around the shrines, while Estal led her suit through the centre to clear it of defenders. Lynx saw Kas's deadly skills as he glanced across, three men shot down even as Lynx reloaded his own gun.

A flash of movement through a doorway caught his eye and Lynx turned, bringing his gun up. A glimpsed uniform was enough for him to pull the trigger and the Charneler was thrown back down the hallway. Nearby, Foren and Sitain were scavenging cartridge boxes from the dead, neither being much of a shot.

Lynx popped the breech of his gun open and yanked the spent cartridge out, hissing at the deep cold that stung his fingers. He loaded another icer but slung the gun on to his shoulder, drawing his pistol instead. The shorter range wouldn't matter here and he didn't want to freeze the barrel of his mage-gun in the middle of a fight. It could happen, firing too many icers in rapid succession could turn the metal brittle. Lynx had seen a man swap to a burner after a long fight at distance – the cold barrel hadn't been able to cope with sudden heat and it had exploded, killing him and everyone beside him too.

'Dragoons!' someone yelled from the far side, followed by streaks of flame overhead.

Icers hammered back across the square, tearing through a squad who'd run to support the defenders. Their bravery was their undoing as the others fled and they found themselves exposed, cut down in moments.

'Get their cases!' Anatin roared, knowing the dragoons would carry burners and grenades too.

All of a sudden the gunfire tailed off, the last of the Charnelers abandoning their positions. Lynx knew it wouldn't last, that it meant the next fight might be all the harder, but a pause for breath was necessary. He was almost out of cartridges and the rest would be the same. Not waiting for Sitain to distribute some he grabbed the nearest corpse and rifled through their cartridge case. Nine or ten icers went into his own, along with a couple from the next corpse before he handed them to the woman next to him. That was Braqe, the Jester of Tempest who despised Lynx for the actions of his people during the Hanese conquest. She grunted her thanks, enmity put aside for the fight.

'Sitain!' yelled a voice from the far side. 'I need you!'

The young mage blinked dumbly for a moment before realising it was Himbel, the company surgeon. She shrugged her plundered cases off her shoulders and scampered through the shattered mess of barricade as a wail of panicked pain cut the air.

'Catch your breath, get ready to move,' Teshen said, checking over his troops.

Lynx looked around. Other than Flinth, Tempest hadn't lost anyone, but he could see the bodies of several Cards lying still behind them. A burly, taciturn man called Sandath lay on his back, arms outstretched as though welcoming the icer that had torn open his chest. Another, Hald – a sandy-haired, grinning monkey of a man – lay crumpled in a ball further back, never to laugh again judging by the blood on his head.

'We're coming out on the canal,' Suth called, advancing towards the far end of the square. 'One last push and we're there.'

In the distance, the battle intensified, the snaps of icers and rolling booms of earthers followed by the thunder and shake of collapsing buildings. Lynx looked around once more, this time seeing more scars of battle on the once-beautiful city. There were faces at the windows too – scared, pale citizens peeking out only to shrink back as Lynx turned towards them.

The lower floors were most damaged, but nothing looked ready to fall so there was little to be done. A grenade had ripped away one corner of a building, some stone-built townhouse, while the packed earth and cultivated shrubbery was furrowed and torn – mostly by the Cards in their savage assault. Glass shards were scattered across the street, a dull glitter amid the dust and splinters.

'Burners!' called Aben, who'd gone to inspect the dead dragoons after first checking the street behind.

He checked inside one case then swung it by the strap and flung it back to the mercenaries. Lynx wasn't the only one to catch his breath at that, but Toil plucked the case from the air with ease and brought it down gently. She'd been wounded, he realised – jacket ripped open at the point of one shoulder and blood showing underneath, but not badly given she was still using the arm.

Teshen went to gather another case and handed out what few cartridges he could to each of the named cards of his suit, Llaith, Lynx and Braqe. Only two burners, but better than nothing when firepower was the only thing keeping them alive. Llaith was also injured, his jacket open and showing a bloody bandage covering a flesh wound in his side.

'Himbel, ready to go?' Anatin yelled, striding after Suth.

'Almost!'

Lynx followed Teshen round and saw it was Darm, wounded in his shoulder given the attentions he was receiving. He lay on his back, pawing feebly at Sitain as she pressed her hands to the wound – but he stopped screaming after her magic had done its work. His coat was slashed apart, exposing black spiderweb tattoos half-obscured by smeared blood.

'It's time,' Toil declared. 'You've done all you can. Either the locals help him or he waits until this fight is over, that's all there is.'

Himbel nodded, face grim but he'd seen enough battlefields to know that. You could patch up some injuries, give your friends a chance at least, but the fight waited for no one. Sitain looked more conflicted about abandoning Darm, but Himbel took her by the elbow and she was so drained already she didn't have the strength to resist.

The Cards all moved forward to the far side of the square. A short street no more than twenty yards long met another running across, tall expensive houses rising all around. Somewhere to the north there were explosions, presumably Vigilance's additional distractions. A small number of troops could make a lot of noise and confusion, slowing any response to the main threat. And given the main threat was the Red Scarves, who in turn were serving as distraction to let the Cards drive deep behind Charneler lines, it would likely confuse them enough to work.

Up to the point some fucker decides to tear the city apart with burners, Lynx reminded himself. *The Charnelers have done it before – lost patience when on the back foot, so they've destroyed everything in sight as they retreated.*

'That street runs parallel to the canal,' Suth said. 'The boulevard is just the other side. If we skirt right we'll be not too far from—'

'Or we go through,' Anatin pointed out, glancing at his sergeants while he spoke. 'People always forget the value of a straight line.'

'Through?'

'Aye – not civilised I grant you, but it's fucking war. Likely they'll be waiting for us at the side streets, but houses tend to back on to alleys and other houses. A few hefty kicks from our own man-mountain and most doors open. We can blow any that don't and break down walls in between.'

'Getting off the streets would be good,' Payl agreed. 'If there's a reserve force somewhere, we'll be badly outnumbered.'

'Reft,' Safir said, 'I believe this is your department.'

With one look around the corner, Reft crossed the street at a run. The far side was a row of near-identical townhouses, four storeys tall with ochre roof tiles and wide windows. Reft ran up three steps to the nearest and slammed a boot into the front door. It shuddered and there was a splintering sound, but it resisted the huge man's strength. A second kick burst the door open and Reft marched straight on to shouts of alarm from inside. A white-haired man was shoved aside as he rushed towards Reft, seemingly trying to push him back out the door.

'Health inspectors!' Deern called cheerfully, following close behind the big mercenary. 'Oh shut it, you old sod – the city's infested with Charnel-rats, ain't you noticed?'

Teshen led his suit down the side of the house and kicked in a heavy side gate. Lynx saw Varain do the same further down, the Cards spreading out so they wouldn't be bunched through one entrance. It was a narrow passage Teshen led Tempest into, but they came out into the rear yard a few seconds ahead of Reft. Vegetable plots and raised herb beds flanked a chicken coop, a paved path leading down the middle of the yard to a rear gate.

That came off its hinges easily enough and then they were in a dark central alley between houses. Lynx caught a glimpse of Lastani as he passed through to the yard that backed on to the other side. Her tattoos seemed to shine in the dull light of an overcast morning and his own tingled in response.

Teshen checked before heading through the gate on the far side. He slipped the bolts open but only peered through the gap, trying to get a sense of what they were emerging on to. Lynx found himself craning up to try and see past the man, but all he could make out was the exposed bone-white trunk of a tree that had shed its bark.

'How's it look?'

'Not bad,' Teshen whispered back, 'not great.'

'What's the plan anyway?'

'The general.'

'Aye, but kill or capture?'

Teshen gave him a blank look. 'Whatever we can manage.'

'Does it look like we'll manage either?'

'Think I'm going through this gate if we can't?'

'You ain't gone through yet,' Llaith pointed out, 'you're hiding behind it.'

'Shut up.'

In the distance, the sounds of battle took on a new intensity, rolling like a thunderstorm up from the south. Lynx paused to listen. It sounded more distant and punctuated – catapults hurling mage-spheres. The clatter of gunshots remained but that was the Red Scarves and the Charnelers, this sound was new and the Scarves didn't have that sort of artillery. It had to be the Jarraziran regiments renewing the fight.

'Sounds like the Monarch's seen our signal,' Lynx commented with a lightening heart.

'Just as well. If this lot get reinforcements we're screwed.'

That cut the conversation short and the handful of soldiers simply stood and waited a few more minutes until at last Lynx heard a muffled shout of 'Cards!' from one of the buildings off to their left. Teshen wasted no time in yanking open the gate and they trotted out towards the canal. The boulevards flanking it were open and largely deserted – a handful of uniformed soldiers escorting grey-liveried auxiliaries with laden carts. They didn't stop to fight – as soon as the Cards emerged en masse, both auxiliaries and soldiers abandoned the carts and ran like mice.

Lynx looked left and right. The boulevard was chewed up pretty badly, both banks bearing the wreckage of the previous day's fighting retreat with most of the buildings in one stretch completely destroyed. There was a fight happening half a mile away given the flames and movement he could see – that had to be the Red Scarves. What he couldn't see was a relief force being held in reserve anywhere nearby. There were knots of black-and-white Charnelers scattered up and down the canal, but those who'd spotted the Cards clearly weren't keen to fight.

'Where's the general?' Teshen demanded of the city at large as he prowled back and forth. The trees ran in a line down each side of the boulevard, punctuated by broken or burned stumps but affording a certain amount of cover from snipers.

'There!' called Kas from further down the boulevard. 'Far shore, there's a barge.'

Suth ran forward to the canal-side trees. 'Berthed at the amphitheatre,' she announced, suddenly animated.

Lynx was one of several who headed forward to get a better view. The barge was a large, low-slung affair with a crest of canvas running down the top which he guessed was a pair of small, folded masts. It bore typical Knights-Charnel markings, the spear-and-setting-sun repeated down its side, the hull was black with white hatches. It was a few hundred yards away, but hardly a hub of activity so far as Lynx could see.

'Shit, where is she?' Toil said.

'The amphitheatre,' Suth replied. 'She must be using it as a command post. But why isn't she moving out? Bade must have reached her by now – unless he's double-crossed her?'

Toil shook her head. 'He won't, the man cares more for his hide than any profit he'd make off those God Fragments. It must be the Crown-Prince – if he's raiding their camp, she can't easily escape without an escort.'

'Better to withdraw the whole army,' Anatin agreed, joining them. 'If they've got what they want, why bother taking the city? It's not like the Charnelers would be able to hold it easily.

If I was the Monarch, before I got forced out I'd blow the sea defences – leave any conqueror open to the rest of Parthain. If anything can bring the Parthain states together it'll be the threat of piecemeal conquest.'

Toil snorted. 'Why else do you think we're here?'

Lynx inspected the amphitheatre. It was a massive oval building that towered over those around it, two hundred yards long and six storeys high at the north end, sweeping down to only two at the south to embrace the afternoon sun. Each storey had great arched apertures around the outside, perfect vantage points for the general's guards.

'We're not getting in there,' he said, looking from the vantage points to the wide, open plaza around it. 'Not unless Lastani's as powerful as the gods.'

'We don't need to,' Suth said, flashing a brief, mirthless grin. There was a hunger for revenge on her face now, the chance to find her partner's killer. 'We just need to make it as far as there.'

Across the open ground at the north end was a square building with a sharp spire. At first glance it could have been some sort of shrine, but it lacked any of the details a shrine would possess.

'What is it?'

'The players' entrance – I'm guessing none of the Charnelers know about it, but that's how the players go in. They can't be allowed to see the labyrinth before the game starts.'

'Another damn labyrinth?' Deern moaned. 'What's with you people?'

Suth shrugged. 'Jarrazir's always been known for the labyrinth beneath it, so one Monarch a few hundred years back made one the people could actually enter. The amphitheatre floor can be cleared for other entertainments, but it was built for the games – played through a maze that's changed for each match.'

Lynx charted the route in his head. They would first need to cross the canal, the nearest bridge being two hundred yards north and guarded by a handful of Charnelers at each end. If they met any serious opposition they would be horribly exposed, it was probably only their numbers that had prevented the bridge guards from picking a fight as soon as they saw them.

'Move out,' Anatin barked to the company, clearly of the same mind. 'Spread groups, hold your shots until they fire. We don't want to draw any more attention than necessary and I'm betting those guards will run as soon as we close.'

'Yeah,' Lynx muttered darkly, 'what with them having an army nearby, they don't need to fight. Letting us run straight into trouble will be easy enough.'

'You got a better idea?'

'Depends,' Deern laughed. 'Is it too late to join the Knights-Charnel?'

'For you, I reckon so,' Anatin said gravely. 'I seem to remember a priest of Insar in some town on the shore of Whitesea.'

'Ah, yeah. Well I'm sure he saw the funny side eventually.'

'I really doubt that.' The mercenary commander gave a weary shake of the head. 'And you wonder why I don't let you have tattoo needles any more.'

'Enough chat,' Toil growled. 'Let's end this.'

'Aye, time to be heroes I suppose.'

Toil looked around at the arrayed faces of the company. 'Let's not go overboard,' she muttered as she set off.

Chapter 37

Staggered runs took them to the bridge, Blood and Stars taking one side of the boulevard, Tempest and Sun taking the other, while Safir's suit of Snow was rearguard. The guards on the bridge were alert to the danger, but weren't keen for a protracted fight. With two hundred yards of ground to cover, the Charnelers opened fire as soon as they had a clear shot, but the Cards continued their steady progress. At least one suit returned fire while the others advanced behind the patchy cover of abandoned market cabins and stalls.

The bridge was a high-sided stone affair – easily defended up to a point, but near useless beyond that, given it was built for carts to pass easily. A hundred yards out, Teshen led his suit at a crabbed sprint while the others kept the enemy's heads down. One sparker and they'd probably all be dead so they didn't wait to test the theory, having no such firepower themselves. It didn't take the Charnelers long to realise the danger and they retreated.

They were long gone by the time Teshen had secured the far bank and signalled for the rest to follow, though the gun battle had drawn more attention that anyone was comfortable with.

'Into the back streets,' Suth called as the main group caught up with Tempest. 'Leave them guessing which way we're coming at them.'

'Aye – give 'em a good reason to hold back and let us run at their guns,' Anatin agreed. 'That way then.'

The Cards ran in a disordered group down the nearest street, cutting left into a covered arcade of hastily abandoned carts and worktables. Anything of value had been plundered already so even Deern didn't linger long as they made their way to an alley and Suth checked the road ahead.

'We all going?' Teshen asked in a voice that made his opinion clear.

'Why not?' Anatin said.

The long-haired Knight shrugged. 'We're trying to take the general, a small group can do that just as well as all of us.'

'Volunteering, are you?'

'We need the mages,' Teshen pointed out, 'then just a few others good in close quarters. The rest spreads out, distracts the guards and buys us the space. Hells, might be Sitain can end this all herself?'

The young mage looked startled as she was brought into the debate, but didn't waste much time in shaking her head. Lynx could see the bags under her eyes, the weariness that hadn't been there before she'd quietened the barracks.

'Something that big? No chance.'

'But Lastani can shield you, while I watch the rear,' Atieno said confidently. 'It might give you enough time to take her or give your terms.'

'Let's do that then,' Anatin said. 'All you tattooed freaks come with me. Payl, Reft, Estal, take your suits and make some noise out that way. Estal, take the leftovers of Tempest, Reft you get Snow. Take a few potshots at the guards up around the amphitheatre walls. Don't get caught in a fight, but get 'em looking long enough for us to get in place.'

The three mercenaries nodded and beckoned to their respective suits, creeping back the way they'd come to skirt another way round. Up ahead, the streets all led to the open plaza that the amphitheatre looked out over.

There was only one safe path, a narrow alley which took the Cards to the large, odd building housing the players' tunnel. It was a block significantly larger than a normal house with an imposing gate on the nearer side, bulky enough to obscure the view from the amphitheatre's arches. Lynx followed the rest until they were stood right outside the gate, shoulders hunched against the anticipation of a gunshot, but none came. Suth was about to break the lock on the gate open when Atieno stepped forward and placed his hands over the metal instead. The tattoos on his dark skin pulsed briefly white, a tingle of the magic echoing through Lynx's own skin, and when Atieno removed his hands the iron had corroded, flakes of rust falling away under the breeze brushing past.

Suth's eyes widened, but she wasted little time in pulling the lock apart and easing the gate open. It was dark inside and smelled of smoke and sweat. The lower floor was a plain single chamber with four racks of wooden sticks, presumably required for the game played, and two clusters of benches. Stairs led up on the left and right, flags bearing team colours hung from each banister and the landing above. What light there was crept through narrow slatted windows on the upper level.

In the centre was a wooden staircase leading down – wide enough for four people to walk abreast, worn and old, without decoration. There were sconces for oil lamps lining the staircase, but they were all empty and the tunnel beyond was just a semi-circle of black that began before the steps had even finished.

Suth and Teshen each took a side stairway, stalking up almost silently before confirming the rooms up there were empty. That done, Sitain crept down the tunnel steps and peered into the darkness beyond a second gate at the foot of

485

the stair. She spent a few moments looking for guards in the tunnel, but quickly waved the rest forward and they shuffled into the pitch-black tunnel as Suth fumbled at her pack.

'Wasn't expecting to be glad I was still lugging this around,' she commented as the Monarch's lamp illuminated a chequerboard of white and red glazed tiles covering the tunnel.

'Just hold back with it,' Teshen ordered, nudging Sitain ahead so the two of them were clear of the rest.

The tunnel ran straight and clear, a damp smell the only obstacle as they slunk beneath the plaza and under the walls of the amphitheatre. At the far end was a half-open door. Sitain held up a hand to stop the rest of the Cards following, then crept inside with Teshen. Lynx heard nothing other than the slight scuff of a foot, but his tattoos tingled faintly before they were eventually beckoned forward.

Beyond the door was a very large, low room perhaps fifty yards by thirty. It was broken into three sections by fat brick pillars with dozens of smaller wooden posts between them, all supporting a wooden roof. At the base of one pillar were two Charnelers, presumably out cold. Lynx noticed both Toil and Deern giving them a calculating look before moving on.

In the centre of the room was a wooden platform with some sort of mechanism set to the side and a trapdoor above. A large lever stood next to it and Suth patted Anatin on the shoulder as she pointed at it, then the various narrow tunnels that led off the room in all directions.

'Three groups on platforms here, down there and there, a mage in each,' Suth whispered. 'Pull the lever and you'll ascend – fast, so don't let the jolt throw your aim off. There were no games scheduled this week, so the labyrinth walls will be down and the floor should be clear. We'll have to bet she's on the floor with her prize, ready to head through the canal gate and board once the army's moving up.'

Anatin nodded and divided his troops up. Before they headed off to their assigned platforms Toil caught their attention and turned full circle as she addressed them all in a hushed voice.

'Burners and sparkers in each group – mine goes up first. Take out any guardposts or soldiers in the stands to win some space to breathe, mages get ready to shield. Lastani, we're first so you'll be taking the brunt most likely. Whoever's nearest the general takes her captive unless you've no choice, understand?'

They all did and hurried to their assigned positions. Lynx joined Lastani, Anatin, Toil, Aben and Suth on the central platform. They drew and loaded their guns, taking their time to allow the others to get ready.

'What if the walls aren't down?' Lastani whispered as her tattoos started to glow steadily brighter.

'Then we're about to look bloody stupid,' Suth said, rolling her shoulders with one mage-pistol raised and her free hand poised over the release lever. 'But we shoot into the stands anyway, see who we can kill – after that, I'll have a bit of a think.'

Toil chuckled quietly at that and nodded. There was a strange mix of tension and anticipation on her face. She had a mission that brooked no failure or distraction butting up against a vendetta that robbed her of reason – a need for a cool head grating against her reckless, savage spirit. A leaf shape blossomed into light on Suth's cheek and Lynx felt his own tingle awake as the mages summoned their power.

'Ready?' Suth said after what felt like an age.

There was no reply, but they all instinctively bent their knees, ready for the ascent, and Suth took that as her cue. She pulled the lever and whipped her hand back just in time as the platform under their feet seemed to buck like a mule. Lynx felt the weight of the world on his shoulders as the trapdoor dropped open above them and the light of the sky slammed down with a clatter and a crash.

Up and out through the hole in a flash, Lynx felt his feet leave the platform as it shot up then jerked to a sudden stop. For a moment he could see nothing, just a blur of lines that made no sense, before the shape of the amphitheatre unfurled before him. Great banks of benches stretched almost all the way round, broken only by a squarish block of enclosed seating in the centre of the high north side. Against the wooden benches it was simple to pick out the knots of Charnelers there, but his attention was drawn to a half-dozen uniforms twenty yards ahead of him staring open-mouthed at the mercenaries.

His gun was already raised. Lynx simply tightened it against his shoulder and slipped his finger down to the trigger. The mage-gun seemed to fire as soon as he touched it and a jagged stream of lightning spat out towards them. The sparker caught the soldiers dead on and exploded in a shower of sparks. Bodies fell away, screams cut through the dull morning air, but Lynx was already reloading as more gunshots crashed out.

Distantly he heard the rush and clatter of the other two platforms erupting up through the floor of the amphitheatre – the roar of burners and crackle of sparkers blotting out warcries and whoops from the other Cards.

Beside him, Suth threw down two of her mage-pistols and drew two more. Off to his right Lynx saw a group of a dozen or more Charnelers, standing between a number of tables and a stacked pile of crates. Two guards were falling as Lynx took aim at a pair in the stand behind them. The burner screamed through the air and exploded – the two vanished from sight as benches were smashed aside.

He loaded an icer and followed Toil's lead as the woman surged towards what had to be the general's group. Suth shot two more guards, her aim unerring, while Toil unleashed a sparker at the fringes of the group and downed a handful as the rest reeled away. Those were without uniforms, Lynx noticed as he put an icer through the first Charneler officer to reach for his mage-pistol.

'Lastani!' Toil yelled as she raced to reload.

For a moment, Lynx felt his heart in his mouth. They were in the open and reloading as the Charnelers caught their breath and pulled their guns. Just as he watched a black man raise his mage-gun, a haze of white filled the air. Lynx shrank down as a volley of detonations smashed into it. His hands pulsed with light as Lastani staggered under the impact of more shots than Lynx could count. The pull on whatever magic was inside him grew to painful levels, but then it was over and Lastani steadied herself as Lynx slotted another cartridge into his gun breech.

'Enough!' Anatin roared as they continued on. 'Hold your fire!'

For a moment nothing happened but then the shield of magic fell away and revealed the stunned faces of their enemy, frozen in the act of firing. Mages weren't allowed anywhere near a battlefield, they were simply too precious when they could only deflect a few shots at best. They'd never seen anything like what Lastani had just done, but out of the corner of his eye Lynx spotted a roiled curtain of flickering grey and blue obscure another group of Cards. It was perhaps enough to confirm for the general that this wasn't just some crazed suicide mission and the woman at the centre of the Charnelers holstered her gun and called, 'Hold!'

'Raise your guns and you get burned, that I fucking promise!' Anatin roared as he advanced on them.

Lynx looked around the group. There were five officers still standing beside Bade's handful of relic hunters, but no mistaking the general. By far the smallest there, she had grey hair and a look of stern puzzlement on her face – unruffled by this sudden assault, let alone frightened.

Oh, this one's a true fanatic, Lynx realised, *a monster o' the worst kind.*

He felt his finger twitch at the realisation. It was a soldier just like this one who'd caused his downfall – not the same race or gender, let alone army, but he knew a monster when he saw one. The sort who'd not flinch to order rape and murder, who'd not even see how it could be wrong in service of their cause. Such fanatics were rabid dogs in Lynx's eyes, to be put down as quickly and efficiently as possible before they caused more hurt in the world.

'Fanatic by another name', he recalled someone calling him once. It was an uncomfortable comparison, but one he couldn't deny entirely. *But at least I only want to kill her. I won't actually do so unless I have to.*

'So you found your way out o' the black again?' called a tall greying man with a narrow beard Lynx remembered from the Monarch's great hall.

Bade, at last. Keep your head, Toil, Lynx willed.

'I always do,' Toil replied, pistol pointing directly at him. 'Just remember that. I'll never stop hunting you down.'

'Aye, well, if you're still chasing me, you ain't caught me yet and ain't that the story o' your life? Always a step behind, always second best.'

'Bade,' interrupted the general. 'Engage in your little banter on your own time. Are these godless wretches the ones you mentioned?'

'Aye. That 'un's called Toil,' he said, pointing. 'Relic hunter like misself. The rest are her crew so far's I know.'

'And that's how it'll stay I reckon,' Anatin said. 'More important is the fact we've got burners pointing at you and precious little inclination to hold off firing. So shut yer holes and listen up.'

The small woman took a considered pace forward.

'My name is General Derjain Faril. I am a High-Exalted of the Knights-Charnel of the Long Dusk and not some yokel to be cowed by dick-waving relic hunters, so save your threats. Speak your piece and be quick about it before I get bored and order my men to shoot on general principle.'

To his credit, or perhaps as a sign of his crazed sense of humour, Anatin grinned and bowed to her.

'Fair enough, miss,' he said with a laugh. 'Here it is then – we want the God Fragments and we want 'em now. As you've seen, we've got mages who can shield us from gunfire so if it comes to a fight, we might be outnumbered but you're not coming off best. Half o' you at least never bothered to reload by my count.'

Behind them, Lynx heard running feet and glanced back to check it was the rest of the Cards. The mercs clattered up behind and pulled in close together – spreading out wasn't going to be much use when they were surrounded by soldiers on every tier of the amphitheatre. They were close to the centre of the open ground, a long damn way from escape and only the various stacks of crates around the place offered any sort of cover.

'You want the God Fragments?' Faril laughed. With a slow, deliberate movement she drew her mage-pistol again but didn't go so far as to point it at Anatin. Instead she gestured idly with it, as though this was some council debate rather than a stand-off.

'Well, of course you can have these sacred remains of my gods, these holy relics of my religion and cornerstone of the Order I've dedicated my life to. Would you like me to wrap them in a bow too?'

'That'd be lovely, aye.'

'Allow me to make a counter-proposal,' Faril said. 'Drop your guns and, solely because I'm a busy woman, I'll allow you all to walk away unharmed.'

'Bade, tell her how likely that is,' Toil said.

'Oh, I think I can work that out from the look on your face, young lady,' Faril replied gravely. 'But while I'm not afraid to die, it would seem prudent to offer a way to avoid it.'

'There's one way you get to not die here. You hand over the God Fragments and get the fuck out of this city.'

'Now why would I leave? Even if I did hand them over, my orders are to secure the prize of Jarrazir's labyrinth at all costs. I can't leave without doing everything in my power to do so. In case you hadn't noticed, my army's got the upper hand in this fight and if I have to raze the entire city to secure these relics, I shall.'

'Two can play at that game,' Lynx called out, almost surprising himself at the interjection.

'Excuse me?'

He scowled as he tried to quell the growling anger in his belly and took a long breath before answering. Toil and Anatin both looked back at him with eyebrows raised, also surprised by Lynx's contribution, but his thoughts were on the one God Fragment they had seen.

'Scorched earth,' Lynx said, 'it's how monsters like you think, but two can play at that game.'

'If I must die to secure the prize, I'm comfortable with that.'

'Oh aye, I bet you are, but you wouldn't get the prize either.'

That got her attention, her gaze turning from cruelly stern to light-stealing rage in a flicker. All she said was, 'A bold claim,' in a neutral voice.

'See these tattoos?' Lynx said, raising his hands. 'Atieno, get over here.'

The tall mage pushed through the handful of Cards and stood beside Lynx as he indicated the tattoos on Atieno's skin as well.

'Very pretty.'

Lynx grinned, warming to his task. 'More'n that,' he said. 'They link us all – he can draw on our strength for his magic.'

'And?'

He pointed at the crates. 'The fragments are in there, right?' When he didn't get a response Lynx just nodded. 'Toss one over, I'll show you what I mean.'

'I've just said I won't give them to you.'

'And I've just said that we can both scorch the earth behind us – Atieno and our other mages can destroy your relics if they choose. While you might kill us all, your precious relics will be gone in the process – that I guarantee. Give me one and I'll prove it.'

'Preposterous. In case you hadn't noticed over in So Han, the Knights-Charnel know a little something about mages. I believe I'd know if such a thing was possible.'

'It ain't for *your* mages, it is for ours. You've seen 'em stop a volley already. Want to take the risk or test it out with one small one? Do you even use Banesh's fragments in your factories?'

She thought for a long while, biting down on her bottom lip as she did so. 'Very well. Fail and you all die, I'll brook no further delay.'

She turned towards the crates and Lynx inwardly breathed a huge sigh of relief. He'd not known what he'd have done if she'd called his bluff and claimed they were elsewhere. Chances were everyone's bluff would be called and they'd all die in a huge conflagration of fire and lightning, leaving behind some charred corpses all feeling a bit foolish.

The general pulled a battered pack from the crate and opened it, reverentially unwrapping the long white cloth to reveal the fragment within. This she inspected before replacing it and taking a second. That one she deemed suitable and she tossed the glowing chunk of smoked crystal over to Atieno.

In the same moment she nodded to her officers and, before anyone could react, they raised their mage-pistols, Bade's crew swiftly following. The mercenaries snapped their own up in response, and Lastani threw up a hazy shield between them, but no one fired. Everyone held their breath and glared like dogs at their now-indistinct enemy, hackles raised but all too aware what it meant to take the first bite.

After a long pregnant pause, Lastani released the shield and all eyes turned to Atieno as he held the God Fragment up between finger and thumb. It seemed to shine a little brighter in the winter light. Just as Lynx felt his guts start to turn to water, he felt a shiver run through his tattoos and the shattered piece of a god's body abruptly crumbled to dust and fell away. Atieno brushed the remains from his hands and gave Faril a sharp look.

'And that was without really trying,' he advised the woman.

The look on his face showed Toil wasn't the only person to feel they had a grudge there. Atieno was a mage who'd likely been looking over his shoulder his entire life because of people like Faril. He'd be as glad to kill her as Lynx would, and he'd have a better reason for it too.

'Your point is made,' she said in a more subdued tone. 'However, it means your death still. Do you honestly expect me to believe you'll do it? You're mercenaries, you care about your own skin above all.'

Toil took a step forward. 'I'm no mercenary,' she growled, 'so take a look at my face. Do you really think I lack resolve?'

'I think you're a calculating agent, one who'll prefer to try to win another day.'

'Deern,' Toil snapped, 'Teshen, step forward.'

The two men did so and Toil gestured towards them. 'If you don't believe me, how about this – do you really think this lot aren't shitbag crazy enough to do it, just to see the gods burn with them? Resolved or crazy, I don't care which you believe, but how many turns of the cards do you think you've got before the Jester appears?'

Faril matched Toil's gaze for a long while before glancing at the two men summoned forward. Finally, she gave a reluctant nod. 'I see your resolve,' she said at last. 'It is a familiar thing and I recognise it for what it is, just as I recognise one of your friends wears a Jester card on his chest. Very well, take the bags.'

'What?' exclaimed Bade and one of her officers at the same moment. Faril silenced the objections with a raised hand and looked around at the Cards as though marking the face of each.

'Take the bags and go,' she repeated. 'Bade, have your men unpack the crates. Let them take the fragments to the Monarch – I rather suspect she'll be more of a mind to negotiate with me.'

'Eh?'

She shot him a look that made even Bade's permanent smirk waver. 'You heard me.'

'Aye, sure.'

With a nod the relic hunter set his crew about the task. They pulled the various packs from each crate and dumped them all in a pile together between the opposing groups. It looked like there were a little over a dozen and Toil checked each one, replacing the shards as she confirmed there was something inside while Lynx found himself doing likely the same rough calculations she was. Once they were finished and Bade's men upturned the crates to show there were no more, Toil distributed the packs among the mercenaries and then hesitated.

'One more thing,' she said to the general.

'Oh?' There was a flicker of amusement on the woman's face now, clearly expecting some sort of insult to injury.

'I want Bade too. He and I got some unfinished business.'

'A final reckoning between you, is it? Perhaps we should form a circle and give you each a knife?'

'Nope, I don't care if it's a fair fight. The only reason I don't shoot him right now is that I've got a burner in the pipe and any gunshot will set all this lot off.'

'Sorry to disappoint,' Bade broke in, 'but I ain't going nowhere with you, Toil.'

'Who the fuck said you were getting a choice?' Toil roared. 'I'm talking to the mistress, not the dog.'

Bade shook his head with mock sadness and raised a bag that had been slung over his shoulder. 'I don't give a damn, woman, you'll keep your trap shut and listen a while longer.'

He held up the bag and half opened it to reveal the contents. Despite everything, the soldiers and mercenaries all took a small step back at the same moment.

There was a mage-sphere in the bag – the size of a melon and wrapped in frayed twine so none of the glass inside was visible. There were no markings on it, just roughly stripped-back oakum and flecks of yellow paint from an outer surface that had clearly been removed. Spheres were made to resist being dropped given the catastrophic results of accidents, but Lynx felt his guts turn to ice at the thought of this one falling.

'See, I thought this might be useful,' Bade went on with a vengeful grin. 'Just in case the army didn't reach the right point in the city by the time we escaped the labyrinth.'

'You took it from the North Keep,' Suth said, eyes full of murder. 'Their ammunition was marked yellow.'

'That I did – local lass, are you? Anyhow, there were still a few bombardment spheres in there so this little thing wasn't needed to breach the wall. Seemed silly to waste it.'

'Are you going somewhere with this, Bade?' Faril demanded, sounding about as impressed as she was intimidated.

'Aye – I'm walking away from this. If missy here or anyone else tries anything, it'll fall. Can't say I'm certain what happens after that, with the outer layer cut away, but in my experience there's shitbag crazy and there's suicidal. Some glassy-eyed merc might well try to survive a stand-off, but blowing yerself up is another matter so I'm walking away now. I've delivered the goods as ordered and whatever happens now is your fucking problem.'

'Are you quite finished?' Toil asked scornfully.

He gave her a nasty grin. 'Oh, I'm sorry, in a rush are we? I'm not surprised – the main body o' the army is disengaging from the fight under a flag of truce. That order went out an hour or more back, they should be tramping their merry way up the canal boulevards pretty soon. Feel free to hang around and let 'em shoot you on sight. Not like any of them will know about your mages, they'll just see some fucks who deserve to get shot, so let's see how it goes for you with a few hundred icers to chew on.'

'Still in love with the sound of your own voice, then, I see.' Toil raised her mage-pistol to point it directly at his face. 'And still full of shit too. You're a coward, Bade, you always were. Saving that scabby old hide of yours has always been your first concern so you're not blowing yourself up here.'

'Perhaps not,' General Faril broke in, turning to also point her pistol at the startled relic hunter. 'But I could always do it for him.'

Lynx looked around. The two groups all had their guns levelled – how many on the Charneler side actually had anything more than an icer he couldn't tell, but there were two Torquen uniforms among them at least, and Bade's own crew looked as villainous as Lynx's.

Not that it matters a whole lot, Lynx reminded himself, *given we've got more soldiers appearing on the stands all around.*

Now that he had a moment's pause to look, Lynx realised the whole scene was haloed by small fires burning in a dozen places around them. The wooden benches and tiers of the amphitheatre were easy fuel for the burners they'd fired. It would take a while to set the whole place going, but the longer the guards watched them rather than the fires, the more chance of an inferno there was.

'Hand the bag over,' Faril ordered.

Bade blinked at her a short while then did so, quickly backing off once the attention was back on the general. He glanced at his crew and the rest of them edged back a little way, guns still trained on the Cards but looking more like running than fighting now. Only when Faril ordered them to stop did Bade grind to a halt, face betraying his tension as he watched the confrontation between Faril and Toil.

'Changed your tune, haven't you?' Toil asked the general coolly.

Faril gave her a slight smile that was in that moment as disconcerting as Reft's. 'The fragments remain my principal concern and Bade has changed the options. Perhaps a mage-sphere can destroy them, perhaps it's something special to your tattooed mages. The look on your faces shows you're not certain yourselves and it's *my* soldiers who pick up the pieces once we're all dead. *My* Order that retrieves the God Fragments.

'If Banesh himself could only shatter the gods into fragments, it's not a bad bet that a standard mage-sphere won't make them crumble to dust.' She cocked her head at Atieno. 'It will mean you struggle to do the job yourself and save your mercenary hide at the same time. Look me in the eye and tell me I'm wrong.'

No one spoke. No one knew what to say so far as Lynx could tell. It wasn't quite an admission, but it opened the door to certainty enough for a crowbar to be inserted.

'Well that's disappointing,' Toil said eventually.

'It is, isn't it?'

Toil turned to look at the mercenaries behind her. Lynx saw her catch the eye of Atieno, Lastani and Sitain, nodding slightly as she spoke to the rest. 'Drop the bags,' Toil ordered. 'She's won this one.'

'Eh?' Deern demanded, lowering his gun and turning to stare, incredulous, at Toil. Lynx felt a sudden tingle on his skin, building with terrifying speed.

'You heard me,' she said as the bags started to thump down on to the wooden floor.

'Kas?' Toil called to the dark-skinned scout who still held her bow fully drawn, arrow pointing at the general. 'You too – do it!'

The tingle became a torrent of fire on Lynx's skin and swirls of light and colour erupted around them. Kas fired even as a veil of ice magic descended over them. Lynx caught sight of the arrow slamming into the general's chest – unaffected by the surging currents of power that knitted themselves into a skein of white.

There was one final glimpse of the shock on the general's face, the pain and surprise as she was hurled backwards under the impact. Then the shield solidified between them and Lynx had just a moment to crouch and cringe, to feel fear at what was to come. After that, the world blinked away in an explosion that eclipsed everything.

Chapter 38

Toil blinked and tried to move. Her whole body hurt; sharp pains mingling with a bone-deep ache. An orchestra of discomfort playing a hundred individual notes accompanied each movement as her wits slowly returned and she could begin to take stock. Each injury combined and magnified those around it to echo through her very bones – not merely the sum of their parts but some grand symphony elevated to shake the very rafters.

'Shit,' Toil croaked, pawing feebly as she tried to make some sense of where she was.

The explosion. The blinding light and the force of impact. Even the mage-shields hadn't been able to fully withstand it. They'd been hammered backwards, thrown from their feet and then . . . She looked around. There was wood everywhere. Broken pieces; planks and splinters. And it was gloomy – not dark, not night, but something not quite like day.

'Ulfer's horn,' groaned someone nearby. 'Am I dead?'

Slowly, Toil pulled a piece of wood from across her chest and shoved it to one side. Her hand was a mass of tiny cuts and her little finger burned with pain as she moved the wood. Toil frowned at it for a moment then, jerkily, lifted her other hand and tried to pull her dislocated finger back into place. The action made her scream at first, prompting a flurry of panicked movement all around her, but Toil could see little until she was done.

When it was in place, she lay back, panting until the pink spots faded from her vision. In their place came clarity and she finally realised where they were. A halo of torn wood seemed to hover above her, penning the sky overhead. They were in the lower chamber – the explosion had shattered the artificial floor beneath their feet. Toil looked left and right. There were Cards slowly rising from the rubble like the hideous risen dead – caked in dust, bloody and battered, scowling at a world that had tried to kill them yet again.

'Anyone got a gun?' Toil asked hoarsely.

Abruptly, Lynx rose from the mess of shattered wood a few yards away. 'Sod my gun. Ain't counted my legs yet.'

'Who's shitting idea was that?' Anatin said. The man whimpered as he tried to get to his feet with only one hand and an uneven pile of wreckage underneath. He slipped once, twice, then managed to steady himself and flapped at the empty holster at his waist. The Prince of Sun frowned, then kicked at the broken pieces, scanning around for a while until he bent and pulled a mage-pistol from the mess.

'Aha, that's better. Now I can shoot whichever shit-brained excuse for a heifer made the world blow up.' He scouted around, wobbling slightly and squinting at the faces nearby. 'Kas, where are ya? Here, girl, time to get shot in the face.'

'Put it away,' Toil said, grabbing Lynx and using him as support to get up herself. 'Or watch above, in case the Charnelers come looking.'

'Ain't they all dead yet?'

Toil shook her head and dragged Lynx to his feet, then went to help Lastani. 'Not the guards in the stands, the bomb wasn't that big. Doubt there's any bits of the general left up there amid the mess, though. I'll just have to pray that Bade was close enough to get the same but right now we're probably still outnumbered so no time for checking. You okay?' she asked the young woman.

Lastani blinked up at her with a blank expression, too dazed to reply, but Toil couldn't see any serious injuries so she didn't press the issue.

'Guess we got lucky,' Lynx muttered, looking at the wreckage around them. Almost the entire roof of the room had been staved in; part of one tunnel at the far end ripped open. 'I'm fine too, by the way.'

'Lucky?' bellowed Deern, lurching towards them with a mad look in his eye. 'You call *that* lucky?'

'Aye.'

'An earther,' Toil said, catching on a moment later. 'Gods yes. If he'd grabbed a fire-bomb, we'd all be cooking right now.' She looked up at the sides of the room. There were some scrappy ends to grab on to, but nothing that looked strong enough to pull her up and out of the hole. If it had been a fire-bomb there'd be no escape. As it was, the earther had destroyed the artificial floor and ripped open a chunk of ground beyond, but there was only a great cloud of dust hanging over them rather than the smoke of burning planks.

'Sound off,' Anatin called, still waving his gun around like a confused drunk. 'Who's left?'

More Cards struggled from the piles, Haphori, Safir, then Layir. Toil scouted around and found Aben lying prone not far behind her. She pulled him up and checked the man over. There was a wound to his head bleeding everywhere, but it didn't look fatal.

'Well?' she said to Anatin as there came unintelligible grunts from different directions.

'Sitain? Ah, there ya are. Lynx, pick her up, she ain't looking good.'

Anatin fished another mage-gun from the debris and tossed it to Teshen as the man sat up with his face hidden by his long hair. Teshen caught the gun seemingly without looking and swept his hair out of his face to give Anatin a baleful look. Then he stood, hauling Atieno with him. The mage looked as unsteady as Sitain, but Toil was happy to forgive him that.

'Looks like we all owe the mages a drink or two,' Toil commented. She grabbed a pack that hopefully contained some God Fragments. 'Get your shit, anything you can see, and head back the way we came.'

She pointed in the vague direction as the Cards turned uncomprehending expressions her way. 'The tunnel, clear the entrance.'

Finally, they looked back and some of them started to wade towards the half-covered tunnel entrance, its tile-strengthened walls mostly intact despite the explosion. Others started grabbing at the canvas packs that were scattered all around, apparently as intact as the mercenaries themselves.

'Shift yourselves,' Toil announced, finding a gun at last and realising with slight surprise that it was her own. She opened it and slotted a fire-bolt in. 'Burner in the pipe!' she called loudly, prompting startled looks.

Those guards won't be too far long, let's not stay like rats in a pit. The general didn't think God Fragments will burn and I reckon she'll know more about it than me. The Monarch can dig through the ashes in a few days.

'What's the plan, Toil?' Anatin asked.

'The finest traditions of the mercenary craft,' she said, feeling a manic grin cross her face.

'We're running away?'

Toil nodded. 'Followed swiftly by a good bit o' hiding too.'

'I like this plan.'

'How about this bit?' Toil aimed the gun down the far end of the shattered room and pulled the trigger. The burner hit the far side and exploded into flames, hurling fragments of burning wood high in the air.

'The fuck's this bit?' Anatin howled.

'Set the place on fire so no one follows,' she announced, sheathing her gun. 'Now get your shit and everyone into that tunnel!'

The flames spread quickly through what was now a huge firepit of sawdust and splintered wood. The Cards barely had time to grab their stunned comrades and all the bags they could see before the fire pursued them right to the tunnel mouth. Toil made sure she was last in, counting the heads once more to ensure only surviving Charnelers would burn. Half of them didn't have mage-guns and she guessed they were missing half the God Fragments too, but Toil didn't wait to search.

They scampered down the long tunnel, doing their best to ignore the sound of raging fire behind and glad the rush of wind in their faces showed it was drawing air in, not acting like a chimney for the smoke to escape. When they neared the far end Toil called a halt. They all sank to the ground, exhausted, while Toil arranged them to put Atieno and Sitain at one end, Lastani at the other.

'What now?' Lynx asked, settling the unconscious Aben down so his head was resting on one of the God Fragment bags. 'We just wait here?'

'We wait,' Toil confirmed. 'We sit and hide like quiet little mice unless it starts to fill with smoke. If anyone comes after us, the mages keep us alive while we use up whatever cartridges we've got left.'

'I don't think I can do much more,' Lastani said, her voice slurring with weariness and dyed white hair hanging limp over her face.

'Sit and rest for now. We've got an army out there with no leaders, the amphitheatre's probably on fire by now. They ain't getting the God Fragments in a hurry and no one in charge likely knows much about 'em. It might take a while to organise, but I reckon they'll withdraw and leave us to it.'

'Sit and wait,' Lynx said, nodding slightly drunkenly. 'Reckon I can do that.' He lay down beside Aben and stretched his legs out. 'Wake me if an army comes to kill us.' He paused. 'Mebbe don't, actually, not sure I'll want to know.'

*

The Cards sat in the dark of the tunnel for two hours or more. It was hard to gauge the time passing. They heard distant gunfire, shouts and the tramp of many feet, but didn't venture out to investigate. Toil kept awake and didn't say a thing as she saw others drift off – not even when the mages slumped and started to snore. Her hearing was sharp and she was confident of being able to wake them before a burner got fired down the tunnel, so until then she let them recover their strength.

When someone came, despite everything, Toil was so startled and jumpy she almost shot them on first sight. It was just a dark figure in the tunnel and the echo of boots, but then came a blessed sound – a voice even her exhausted, half-scrambled brain recognised. Her brother, Vigilance, advanced down the tunnel with a few of his lieutenants. After kicking the others awake Toil embraced her brother and happily allowed herself to be shepherded out into the grainy afternoon light.

Vigilance confirmed what she'd expected, that the Knights-Charnel had been harried out of the city in the confusion surrounding General Faril's death. Soon the mercenaries were reunited with the rest of the Cards and they were escorted as a group back to the palace while the amphitheatre continued to burn furiously. The city was a brutalised thing, whole streets shattered by earth and fire. Hiding in the shadows were frightened and bedraggled citizens shocked by the devastation and picking their way through the ruins.

Much of the fighting had taken place in the merchant district where they had lodged and those districts beyond it. Even from the palace Toil could see the damage done, the wreckage of a street battle. The great beasts of the city, the guild-houses and university, were holed and wounded amid the broken corpses of their lesser kin. And, among those, Toil saw bright robes of the dead, ordinary guildsmen in the uniforms of their trades alongside the mages of the city – selling their lives to defend it.

The palace itself was relatively untouched, one tower fallen and a lesser wing staved in down one side. Inside there was disorder and damage, but again it was minor. It seemed General Faril's control of her troops had extended to keeping them from looting, although Toil wondered if that would have continued after the battle was won. In the throne room, however, the white Duegar lamps were gone, recognised for what they were and plundered along with silver and gold ornaments. As Crown-Princess Stilanna formally received the tattooed group and all except Paranil, who was beaming from a stretcher, knelt to her, Suth pulled the one remaining white glass oval from her pack. Its light spread around the room and the Monarch gave a weary smile. The sight seemed to diminish the gloom in more ways than one.

'Not all plundered,' Stilanna said, gesturing to a servant to relieve Suth of the burden. 'Thank you, Suth.' She paused and looked again around at the faces. 'Elei?'

'No, Majesty,' Suth said, eyes downcast. 'Dead in your service.'

'As so many others.' She reached out and touched the arm of the Crown-Prince beside her, as though reminding herself that he was still there. Tylom was pale and still spattered in mud and blood, one arm in a sling. 'My husband tells me his life was saved more than once by those who gave their own for him. The sacrifices will not be forgotten.'

The Monarch took a deep breath and straightened. 'And yet, by most other measures we are victorious – thanks in great part to you, Mistress Toil. Your employer's faith in you was well founded.'

The packs they'd managed to recover were brought forward by more servants and unpacked on the floor in front of the throne. It was an incongruous sight; an untidy pile of plain canvas and white cloth before the great throne inlaid with jet and gold, then glinting shards of the gods themselves slowly appearing, to gasps from the watching court.

The servants were painstaking in their investigation of each pack, eight in all, and checked every fold of cloth before setting anything aside. The largest, a fist-sized chunk with jagged striations down one side that shone with a yellow light, was passed up to the Monarch. She cradled it in both hands and stared like a child, Tylom crouching down beside her despite the discomfort it brought.

'There are more,' Toil said, 'you just might have to wait for your amphitheatre to cool down a bit before you go collect them.'

The Monarch nodded slowly, reluctant to tear her gaze from the God Fragment. 'Yes, you do seem to have caused a fair amount of destruction in your wake,' she said with the hint of a smile, wonder eclipsing fatigue and shock. 'Perhaps we should not discuss a reward and I'll just hold back from billing you for a new amphitheatre?'

Toil gave a hollow laugh. 'Pretty sure I didn't cause most of the damage to the city,' she said, 'but I'll waive my usual fee as a gesture of goodwill.'

Crown-Princess Stilanna's face turned serious. 'Then good-will you have, for you and your employer. Might he have something to request of me?'

'No doubt a whole list of 'em,' Toil confirmed. 'With your permission, can we leave the details for another day when I'm not hurting and exhausted? It was mostly goodwill I was sent here to build. The Militant Orders are growing bolder, as you're now only too painfully aware, and divided we will fall. The Archelect proposes a League of Parthain – an alliance between states that have all too often been enemies. He hopes you will agree to meet him and discuss the foundation.'

'A League of Parthain?' The Monarch was quiet a long while before nodding. 'I will meet the Archelect. Goodwill wins you at least a discussion and the hope for more.'

'And the God Fragments,' Crown-Prince Tylom added, 'might serve to expand that – gifts for the other states to bring us all together?'

Stilanna looked startled one moment, then laughed the next. 'How very selfless of me that would be, to offer gifts no state would think of refusing and ensure we were all equal targets, should the Knights-Charnel ever come looking for the God Fragments again.'

'What about the labyrinth? What else is down there?' Tylom asked. 'Does it pose a threat to the city? Are there artefacts to be removed?'

Toil managed another weary smile. 'That's a question for the scholars, I think. I'll gladly guide a party back down. There are lamps to make your halls famous, but not much in the way of gold and jewels I'm afraid. I'm sure closing the Fountain is a lot easier than opening it so, once Lastani has recovered her strength, I think we'll manage it.'

'We shall have to be content with the treasure you recovered from your competitors, then. What about the saboteurs – Sotorian Bade and his crew? Did they die with General Faril?'

Toil shook her head. 'I wish I could say for sure. They were backing away but it was a big bloody explosion.' She paused.

'But Bade's the sort of rat who might survive. Right now we can only hope not. If anyone heard our conversation with the general the Charnelers aren't done with the Cards, not by a long shot. For the time being, however . . . with your leave, Monarch, I'm going to fall over very soon. I'd like it to be into a vat of wine.'

The Crown-Princess stood and nodded to them all. 'Such a thing of course is not permitted within the boundaries of Jarrazir, but I'm sure one damned foreigner or another has managed to pollute the city with its corrupting presence. If wine can be found, you're welcome to ensure as little as possible remains to drag our gods-fearing citizenry down the path of iniquity. In the spirit of goodwill, that is.'

She paused and gave the merest of bows to Toil, despite the fact she was a Monarch standing before her throne. There were no intakes of breath among the Jarrazirans watching, but Lynx saw a few note the gesture and all the seriousness it implied.

'You have my thanks, all of you – Mistress Lastani and Master Atieno too. For all that you were party to the start of all this, I have no stomach for retribution and the city has seen enough death. Should I have need of your services in the future, however, you will remember this generosity, I trust. Mistress Toil, we will speak again when you have rested. In the meantime I've got a city to rebuild.'

Epilogue

Lynx opened his eyes and smiled. A faint glimmer of dawn crept through the curtains, the smell of peppery sweat hung in the small room. Below the window was a disordered pile of clothing atop a travel chest, on the floor a jumble of discarded clothes and boots. In the far corner stood a chair, cartridge cases hanging from its back and the muzzles of mage-guns visible behind, propped against the wall.

He turned his head slightly. A holstered pistol hung on the bedpost, within easy reach, but when he stretched his arm out it was to luxuriate in the quiet comfort of early morning and slide it over smooth bare skin. A distant thump echoed at the back of his head and the edges of his vision were blurry, but he could not tell whether it was the after-effects of the explosion or something more self-inflicted. For the present Lynx didn't care. He was content just to listen to the soft sounds of breathing beside him, surrounded by the fug of unwashed clothes, sweat and sex.

Somewhere in the building he heard movement and faint snatches of song breaking the quiet. Lynx tried to make sense of it, but they'd been drinking until late so it remained a jumble in his mind. The events of the last few days began to play again in his mind, the frantic fighting and those damned explosions. The injuries he still carried, the protesting muscles and dozen scabbed-over cuts. Somehow, the fatigue and aching felt welcome, though, the lingering sense of hard-earned victory.

It's been three days and I bet I'll be pulling more damn splinters out of my backside, Lynx thought as the various pains announced themselves once more. *Still woozy after that explosion, reckon we all are. The drink's helped there, after a fashion. Always good when an appreciative population find a way ta thank their saviours.*

The singing grew loud, the unsteady footsteps echoing up the narrow wooden stairwell.

Someone's just back from celebrating. Lynx smiled. *That'll be their bonus spent, then – not that I've been saving like a miser, o' course.*

He glanced over at the chair where the cartridge cases hung. The Monarch had given a bonus to each of the Cards who'd ventured underground, after more God Fragments were unearthed from the smoking pit at the heart of the half-ruined amphitheatre. A leather-bound book sat on the chair, half covered by a stained shirt. *Tales of the Last Days*, it was called – one Lastani had recommended as a seminal collection of Duegar tales, or those that had escaped acquisitive eyes during the Revival anyway.

Unlike most books he'd owned, this one was in near-perfect condition, the green leather embossed with a spiral of ancient Duegar symbols. Lastani had told him the willow tree was sacred to the Duegar and he'd resolved to read every such book he found until he understood what their new tattoos meant for them all.

Lynx looked down at his naked body. The pale shapes of leaves were barely visible on the skin of his belly, legs and arms, and hardly more noticeable even on the darker-skinned Cards. The marks had faded quickly over that first day along with the power Atieno, Lastani and Sitain could employ, but a brief test had shown they would still glow when the mages used their magic. And that magic itself remained greater than before – not the vast amounts available in the hours after the labyrinth, but more than any other mage Atieno or Lastani had ever met.

And we're all a reservoir for more, Lynx reminded himself, *even if we're no nearer to working out what it all means.*

Without warning the door burst open and a dark figure in a long leather coat charged in. 'City watch!' the figure bellowed. 'Where's the contraband?'

Toil was up in an instant, moving from sleeping to action in the time it had taken Lynx to blink stupidly. The figure swung towards the bed and Toil twisted to avoid its onrush, grabbing one reaching arm and using it to add force to her knee. Connecting hard, Toil hauled the intruder around and slid one arm underneath theirs, drawing it up behind their back as she slammed them face first into the cheap plaster of the wall. The whole room seem to shake with the impact and the figure howled with pain.

'I win!' roared a voice from the doorway. 'Hand it over, ya squint-eyed turds!'

Lynx sat up, frozen in the act of drawing the mage-pistol, and frowned at the figure in the doorway. He couldn't focus very well, but there was something familiar about the voice.

'Aben?' he said groggily.

'What the fuck?' Toil roared.

She released the intruder and spun them around to look at their face. It was Himbel. The company surgeon gave her an unsteady grin, white teeth gleaming in the dim light, as he looked her up and down.

'Hey, look, you were right, she's nekked!' the surgeon declared, puckering up. 'Give us a kiss then.'

Toil gave a growl of irritation and hurled Himbel back towards the now-crowded doorway.

'Ah, boss,' Aben said, 'yer, ah, well . . .'

Toil's growl deepened. 'What is it with you fucks and walking in on me naked?' she demanded, whipping the sheet off the bed.

Lynx flinched, now exposed himself, and flapped wildly around.

'Oh put it away, big fella,' Llaith called from behind Aben. 'No one wants to see that.'

Lynx finally succeeded in yanking one of the pillows from the end of the bed to cover himself. Just as he did so, Toil hooked something white on the end of her toe and flicked it towards Lynx. He caught it and held the undergarment up.

'Mebbe a bit small,' he hazarded, putting it on the bed and fishing his braies off the floor. He had to flop like a landed fish to haul them on, but in a short time he was sat on the edge of the bed, not quite as on show as he had been.

'Fancy explaining, Aben?'

The big man's grin wavered. Lynx could see he was still drunk; perhaps not quite so bad as Himbel, though, and better acquainted with Toil's nasty side.

'I ah, well . . . we were talking, about you, and someone mentioned a bet. I . . .'

He turned to those behind him, letting go of the door handle in the process. That made him stagger under the weight of mercenaries pressing forward and they all spilled inside. Llaith almost ended up in Lynx's lap, Suth and Layir stumbled over Himbel, while Ylor, a blonde woman who wore the Seven of Snow, seemed to take the opportunity to drape herself over Aben.

'A bet?'

Suth coughed and straightened up with the theatrical care of someone drunker than they realised.

'It's all Llaith's fault,' the woman declared. 'Apparently he thinks I ain't drunk alcohol before. An' stupid too.'

'Not stupid!' Llaith protested. 'Just hoping you were a bit gullible and we could get some hazing in.'

Lynx blinked at the Jarraziran for a moment then realised she was wearing her new badge on her jacket – the Knight of Tempest. So it was official now, she'd been released from the

Monarch's service, or at least on indefinite leave. Teshen had been made Knight of Stars, the more senior of the sergeant positions and responsible for more mercenaries, while Suth got the misfits of Tempest.

There had been little choice for Suth or the Monarch really, the tattoos marked her as one of them and once word got out, they'd need each other to protect themselves. She was a tough and capable agent as well as a Bridge Watch soldier. No doubt all sides – Cards, Jarrazir and Su Dregir – would benefit by the new arrangement.

She wasn't the only new recruit either. Lastani now wore the Jester of Stars, being an ice mage and as bad a shot as Sitain, while Atieno had the Prince of Tempest on his jacket. The man had impressed Anatin but showed no interest in command, so he'd been given the same honorary position as Toil, which seemed to suit everyone.

True to Vagrim form, Atieno wasn't happy at finding himself tied to the Mercenary Deck, but he recognised there was little he could do about it for the time being. It was more of a wrench for Lastani, Lynx knew. Vagrim were wanderers by nature, but she was a city girl with a family to say goodbye to. The tattoos left her with no real choice in the end and with Toil's assurance that understanding them was a priority for the whole company, she'd signed up.

'Fortunately for us,' Llaith continued, 'Himbel's exactly stupid enough after a few drinks. My money was on you shootin' him, though.'

'I said you'd put him down before he got halfway in,' Suth added helpfully. 'Himbel reckoned you'd see the funny side and give him a kiss.'

At that Aben seemed to collapse into somewhat hysterical laughter, dropping Ylor in the process, and Llaith swaggered forward to haul the dazed Himbel up off the floor.

'Did I win?' the surgeon asked the room at large.

'Not even close, my friend,' Llaith said, laughing and patting the man on the head like a puppy. 'Just be glad you're too drunk to feel your balls right now.'

Lynx watched Toil's reaction. It was clear she was angry, but there was an endearing lack of malice to their idiocy that was thawing her. For himself, he'd woken up with a pleasingly sore head next to a beautiful woman. The only thing that could improve matters was breakfast and the Cards at play was something, to his surprise, he'd grown comfortable around.

'Letter!' Aben exclaimed. 'That's it – there was a letter!'

'What?'

He fumbled around his pockets, getting himself tangled up for a moment and almost ripping off the new badge on his jacket – the Seventeen of Blood – before extracting a folded, sealed missive from an inside pocket.

'That's why we came up,' Aben explained.

'Also we'd been discussing who was fastest in the company,' Llaith said, 'and no one fancied bursting in on Teshen to test him out. Himbel ain't *that* drunk.'

Toil grabbed the letter and inspected the seal. From where he sat Lynx couldn't see it, but by the look on Toil's face he guessed it was from the Archelect of Su Dregir.

'Out, the lot of you,' she ordered.

With a chorus of protests, they obeyed – Aben helping Himbel out by giving him a good shove. The man then gave Toil a nod, winked at Lynx, and shut the door behind him.

Toil opened the letter and scanned the message on it. After a few moments she nodded and tucked it away under a fold of clothing on the chair.

'Good news?'

She shrugged. 'Of a fashion.'

She let the sheet fall away from her and stood over him, entirely naked again.

'New orders,' she added in a husky voice as she bent to kiss Lynx.

'Somewhere nice?'

'For once, yes. The Mage Islands, ever been?'

Lynx pulled Toil down so she was straddling him and kissed her harder. 'Never,' he replied after a while. 'Meant to be nice, though.'

'Oh, it won't be for us,' Toil said. 'We're not going to make friends.'

'Reckon I speak for the whole company when I say I'm shocked by that,' Lynx said, grinning up at her. 'When do we ship out?'

'Not straight away,' Toil said. 'You've at least got time to get those braies off again.'

'How about breakfast?'

'Depends what you do once the braies are off.'

'I'm willing to rush.'

Toil raised an eyebrow at him. 'Not what a girl wants to hear, Lynx.'

'But there's bacon,' he protested. 'I heard the cook say so yesterday.'

'You realise that's not actually a good reason to rush?'

Lynx frowned. 'I don't follow.'

'No, you really don't,' she sighed. 'There'll be time for both, that I promise, but first we work up an appetite, understand?'

'Aye, as you command, princess.'

'That's better,' Toil purred. 'Now jump to it, soldier, that's an order.'

Acknowledgements

You might write a book all by yourself, but that's rarely part of the whole story. Without my wonderful wife, Fi, life would have less meaning and be far more difficult. This book wasn't an easy one to write, for a variety of real life reasons, but Fi and the rest of my family helped me see this through to the finish. Without their support I don't know how many books I would have left in me.

Thanks also to my brother and father for beta-reads, Juliet McKenna for advice on how Toil does what she does best, and Simon Kavanagh who went several rounds with me over some major details of the book. He might not have won every 'discussion', but this book is certainly all the better for his input.

Finally, the efforts of Marcus Gipps and Rachel Winterbottom made a huge difference, even more so than normal editing does, and I'm massively grateful for their input. There's no sense of foolishness quite like delivering a manuscript you've worked on for a year, only to have someone point out dozens of quite incredible, glaring mistakes you've missed entirely. I didn't sleep well for most of the time this book was being written and hopefully they've stopped you from seeing what that does to a fantasist of very little brain.

Turn the page for a preview of
Tom's exciting eBook-only novella
following on from *Princess of Blood*

The Man with One Name

Chapter 1
(Now)

'Reckon ya can't get much deader'n that.'

'Oh blackest hells.'

'Still reckon those are farmer's hands, Lynx? Or was it merchant's hands? I forget. Many merchants out your way got so many anger issues?' The old woman sniffed. 'Mebbe out *your* way, I guess.'

The skinny man at his feet clearly had no further interest in the conversation, or in breathing for that matter. A little further down the bar his friend gave a strangled squawk on his behalf.

'What the screaming shits . . . ? Jinks? Shattered gods, you killed him!'

The grey-haired woman cackled, voice as rough as the calluses on her hands. 'Ya think? Was it all the blood that gave it away?'

Lynx flinched at the laughter and stared at his closed fist. 'Didn't mean to.'

'Aye, luck o' the deepest black it was, that – but don't fret overmuch about it,' she said. 'I always reckoned Jinks there was soft in the head, you were just the one to prove it.'

The other man's lip curled as he backed away. Either he'd forgotten the mage-pistol at his hip or he didn't want to try his luck.

'You shut your trap, you old bitch.'

'Careful now,' she replied, 'old bitches can still bite.'

As though to make her point, she raised her tankard and took a swig before waving it in his direction. It was old and battered, but made of pewter and would mess up most faces. Though the wielder had limbs like an elderly sparrow, she'd already displayed a wiry strength. In a backwater farming village like this, when your strength failed you, life soon followed.

'Sulay,' Lynx said. 'A man's dead already, leave off.'

'You ain't the boss o' me.'

'The fella's twice your size and half your age.'

'You'll make no friends with that attitude, my Hanese acquaintance.'

'Last thing I need is lessons in not making friends, woman.'

She gave him a toothy grin. 'Ah, but you're a man who's always honing his craft.'

'Tell me something I don't know.'

'If you like – first off, Ashel there can't shoot for shit at the best o' times, I've seen him try. Also – he ain't as stupid as he looks, for all he might look like the shitting end of a toad. He takes a shot at me and, hit or miss, he's not long for this life o' suffering.'

''Cos your rug will get him?' Lynx said, glancing down.

'Yup.'

'It *is* a pretty scary rug.'

'Don't try to be funny, Lynx, it don't suit you.'

Ashel continued to back away towards the door, gaze switching from Lynx to the dirty-white heap at Sulay's feet as though unsure which was the more dangerous. He was an average man in most respects – shorter than his cooling friend, whose name Lynx hadn't caught as firmly as his jaw. He was on the slim side with pale skin and lank brown hair, his eyes narrow, his ears oddly small. Ashel managed to be mostly unremarkable bar the fact he carried a gun with less conviction than anyone Lynx had seen survive to claim the name of gunfighter.

'He'll kill you for this,' Ashel spat as he reached the door.

Sulay shook her head. 'For Jinks? Pah – you reckon anyone in this world ever felt so strongly about that dumb-as-a-stone wretch? I doubt the man's own ma cared much. Must've been better children to hand – mebbe neighbours or passing urchins, even.'

'Fuck you, Sulay!'

The sudden shout made the rug twitch and a deep growl rumbled across the room like thunder. Lynx looked down again. He honestly couldn't even see which end was making the noise – no part of it looked anything more than a shapeless heap of rough, thick cords. Ashel seemed more concerned, though, and he fell backwards through the tavern door. Lynx caught a glimpse of snowflakes falling, a thin frost on the ground beyond, before the door banged shut again.

Sulay gave a snort and turned to the bar, banging her tankard on the bartop. 'Dalis, stop cowering and fetch me another drink!'

'Reckon it's time we left.' Lynx made to drain his own beer, but hesitated and put it back down untouched.

'Listen to the man,' called Dalis from his back room. 'Bar's closed.'

The big barkeep had retreated there as soon as voices had been raised, anticipating gunfire. The other occupants of the room were like statues at their tables – only four people in total, all farmers in heavy coats despite the fire burning to the right of the bar.

'You takin' advice from strangers now?' Sulay asked.

'Ones who speak sense, aye. I don't want you round here when . . . When *he* comes.'

'Load of old women you all are,' Sulay declared, cheeks flushed pink. 'And I should know, what with being one myself. Least I ain't about to piss myself from anything but elderly lady problems.'

'Sulay,' Lynx said again.

'Aye fine.' She looked down at the dead man on the floor with an appraising expression. 'Might need this, though,' she said, groaning as she eased herself down on to one knee.

Lynx watched her unbuckle the man's gun-belt and pull it out from under him. He made no sound until she started patting his pockets, looking for his purse.

'Leave it,' he said firmly, one eye on the rug that had only just stopped growling.

'Oh right,' she said, squinting up at him. 'Yeah, yer morals. Damn useless things if you ask me. The pistol's okay, though?'

'We might need it, true enough,' Lynx said, only too aware of the paper-thin distinction he was making.

'And here's me with all this money I don't need?' Sulay grumbled, but she straightened up all the same.

'It's different.'

'If you say so, my stupidly named friend.'

She buckled the gun-belt around her waist and seemed to stand a little taller once she was done, the heel of her hand resting with familiar ease on the pistol grip.

'Well there we are then,' Sulay said, taking Lynx's abandoned tankard and draining it with one gulp. 'Heel, boys.'

The rug eased itself up, a straight back and the hump of a head that described the rough shape of a dog somewhere underneath. It was huge; its back almost on a level with Lynx's waist and made even more bulky by the long hanging cords of fur that hid its body from view. Sulay headed off towards the door, the massive dog padding alongside.

Lynx watched them go, the warmth of beer turning cold in his gut. The dead body at his feet stared accusingly up at him.

He'd only punched the man once – not that hard even. Jinks had been prodding him in the cheek, shoving one stinking finger into the tattooed flesh there. Telling him to back off had only worsened the situation as it turned out. Lynx hadn't put his full weight into that punch, but Jinks had fallen all the same. The side of his skull had just crumpled as it hit the corner of the short bar and then Jinks had been no more, a dead thing before he'd even stopped moving.

'I said "heel", Lynx!' Sulay called, half-through the open doorway. 'And leave all the talking up to me, understand?'

'What? No. What talking?'

'Exactly! That's why you leave it up to me.'

'Ah shit,' Lynx muttered. He stepped over the body and followed her out into the cold.

TOM LLOYD was born in 1979 in Berkshire. After a degree in International Relations he went straight into publishing where he still works. He never received the memo about suitable jobs for writers and consequently has never been a kitchenhand, hospital porter, pigeon hunter, or secret agent.

• • •

He lives in Oxford, isn't one of those authors who gives a damn about the history of the font used in his books and only believes in forms of exercise that allow him to hit something.

• • •

Visit him online at @tomlloydwriter or on facebook.

STRANGER OF TEMPEST

Tom Lloyd

Brand new heroic fantasy from the bestselling author of the TWILIGHT REIGN series

It's not easy being an honest man in a lawless world.

Lynx is a mercenary with a sense of honour; a dying breed in the Riven Kingdom. Failed by the nation he served and weary of the skirmishes that plague the continent's principalities, he walks the land in search of purpose. Bodyguard work keeps his belly full and his mage-gun loaded. It might never bring a man fame or wealth, but he's not forced to rely on others or kill without cause.

Little could compel Lynx to join a mercenary company, but he won't turn his back on a kidnapped girl. At least the job seems simple enough; the mercenaries less stupid and vicious than most he's met over the years.

So long as there are no surprises or hidden agendas along the way, it should work out just fine . . .

• • •

'Surely set to dominate the genre with an opulent, tangible world, captivating readers' imaginations' *Starburst Magazine*

'From the very first page, this first book in Tom Lloyd's new The God Fragments hurls you head-first into the action . . . the world that Lloyd wraps you in is just as gripping as his storytelling' *SFX*

'Tom Lloyd's *Stranger of Tempest* is a fantasy adventure in the modern style, comfortably mixing gritty realism with swords and sorcery. Imagine Steven Erikson's Malazan marines teaming up with Lara Croft for a mad dash across Joe Abercrombie's *Red Country* with an unplanned detour through the forgotten deeps of Moria and you'll be most of the way there'
Forbidden Planet International

THE STORMCALLER

Book One of The Twilight Reign

Tom Lloyd

In a land ruled by prophecy and the whims of Gods, a young man finds himself at the heart of a war he barely understands, wielding powers he may never be able to control.

Isak is a white-eye, feared and despised in equal measure. Trapped in a life of poverty, hated and abused by his father, Isak dreams of escape, but when his chance comes, it isn't to a place in the army as he'd expected. Instead, the Gods have marked him out as heir-elect to the brooding Lord Bahl, the Lord of the Fahlan.

Lord Bahl is also a white-eye, a genetic rarity that produces men stronger, more savage and more charismatic than their normal counterparts. Their magnetic charm and brute strength both inspires and oppresses others.

Now is the time for revenge, and the forging of empires. With mounting envy and malice, the men who would themselves be kings watch Isak, chosen by Gods as flawed as the humans who serve them, as he is shaped and moulded to fulfil the prophecies that are encircling him like scavenger birds.

• • •

'The world is beautifully realised, the battles suitably grim and the dragon, when it appears, is magnificent' *Guardian*

'Fantasy with a magnificence of conception, a sense of looming presences whose purposes are not ours to apprehend' *Time Out*

'Gallops along with scarcely a dull moment' *The Times*

'Lloyd creates a vivid world . . . he echoes writers such as Moorcock and Gemmell' *Interzone*

MOON'S ARTIFICE

Book One of Empire of a Hundred Houses

Tom Lloyd

Tom Lloyd kicks off a spectacular new fantasy series!

In a quiet corner of the Imperial City, Investigator Narin discovers the result of his first potentially lethal mistake. Minutes later he makes a second.

After an unremarkable career Narin finally has the chance of promotion to the hallowed ranks of the Lawbringers – guardians of the Emperor's laws and bastions for justice in a world of brutal expediency. Joining that honoured body would be the culmination of a lifelong dream, but it couldn't possibly have come at a worse time.

On the cusp of an industrial age that threatens the warrior caste's rule, the Empire of a Hundred Houses awaits civil war between noble factions. Centuries of conquest has made the empire a brittle and bloated monster; constrained by tradition and crying out for change. To save his own life and those of untold thousands Narin must understand the key to it all – Moon's Artifice, the poison that could destroy an empire.

• • •

'A hugely assured modern fantasy novel' *SFX*

ABOUT GOLLANCZ

Gollancz is the oldest SF publishing imprint in the world. Since being founded in 1927 Gollancz has continued to publish a focused selection of bestselling and award-winning authors. The front-list includes **Ben Aaronovitch**, **Joe Abercrombie**, **Charlaine Harris**, **Joanne Harris**, **Joe Hill**, **Alastair Reynolds**, **Patrick Rothfuss**, **Nalini Singh** and **Brandon Sanderson**.

As one of the largest Science Fiction and Fantasy imprints in the UK it is no surprise we have one of the most extensive backlists in the world. Find high-quality SF on Gateway written by such authors as **Philip K. Dick**, **Ursula Le Guin**, **Connie Willis**, **Sir Arthur C. Clarke**, **Pat Cadigan**, **Michael Moorcock** and **George R.R. Martin**.

We also have a strand of publishing in translation, which includes French, Polish and Russian authors. Gollancz is home to more award-winning authors than any other imprint, with names including **Aliette de Bodard**, **M. John Harrison**, **Paul McAuley**, **Sarah Pinborough**, **Pierre Pevel**, **Justina Robson** and many more.

The SF Gateway
More than 3,000 classic, rare and previously out-of-print SF novels at your fingertips.
www.sfgateway.com

The Gollancz Blog
Bringing you news from our worlds to yours. Stories, interviews, articles and exclusive extracts just for you!
www.gollancz.co.uk

GOLLANCZ
LONDON